Prais

The Fair Folk

"The fair folk here are often very fair indeed, but they are also scary, jealous of their rights, and willing to harshly use any mortal who gets on their wrong side . . . uncompromising . . . fast moving . . . funny, romantic, moving."

—*Locus*

"The tone ranges from almost farcical humor to much more serious matters, with both historical and contemporary settings . . . I find most short contemporary fantasy fiction to be rather slight, but not this time."

—*Chronicle*

"Intriguing . . . lighthearted . . . with a touch of romance and the subtle hint of something nastier."

—*SF Site*

The
Fair Folk

Edited by
Marvin Kaye

ACE BOOKS, NEW YORK

THE BERKLEY PUBLISHING GROUP
Published by the Penguin Group
Penguin Group (USA) Inc.
375 Hudson Street, New York, New York 10014, USA
Penguin Group (Canada), 90 Eglinton Avenue East, Suite 700, Toronto, Ontario M4P 2Y3, Canada
(a division of Pearson Penguin Canada Inc.)
Penguin Books Ltd., 80 Strand, London WC2R 0RL, England
Penguin Group Ireland, 25 St. Stephen's Green, Dublin 2, Ireland (a division of Penguin Books Ltd.)
Penguin Group (Australia), 250 Camberwell Road, Camberwell, Victoria 3124, Australia
(a division of Pearson Australia Group Pty. Ltd.)
Penguin Books India Pvt. Ltd., 11 Community Centre, Panchsheel Park, New Delhi—110 017, India
Penguin Group (NZ), 67 Apollo Drive, Rosedale, North Shore 0632, New Zealand
(a division of Pearson New Zealand Ltd.)
Penguin Books (South Africa) (Pty.) Ltd., 24 Sturdee Avenue, Rosebank, Johannesburg 2196,
South Africa

Penguin Books Ltd., Registered Offices: 80 Strand, London WC2R 0RL, England

This is a work of fiction. Names, characters, places, and incidents either are the product of the authors' imaginations or are used fictitiously, and any resemblance to actual persons, living or dead, business establishments, events, or locales is entirely coincidental. The publisher does not have any control over and does not assume any responsibility for author or third-party websites or their content.

THE FAIR FOLK

An Ace Book / published by arrangement with Bookspan

PRINTING HISTORY
Science Fiction Book Club hardcover edition / January 2005
Ace trade paperback edition / February 2007
Ace mass-market edition / January 2008

Compilation, Introduction, and Afterword copyright © 2005 by Marvin Kaye.
"UOUS" copyright © 2005 by Tanith Lee.
"Grace Notes" copyright © 2005 by Megan Lindholm.
"The Gypsies in the Wood" copyright © 2005 by Kim Newman.
"The Kelpie" copyright © 2005 by Patricia A. McKillip.
"An Embarrassment of Elves" copyright © 2005 by Craig Shaw Gardner.
"Except the Queen" copyright © 2005 by Jane Yolen and Midori Snyder.
Cover art by Jean Pierre Targete.
Cover design by Annette Fiore-DeFex.

ISBN: 978-0-441-01557-3

ACE
Ace Books are published by The Berkley Publishing Group,
a division of Penguin Group (USA) Inc.,
375 Hudson Street, New York, New York 10014.
ACE and the "A" design are trademarks belonging to Penguin Group (USA) Inc.

PRINTED IN THE UNITED STATES OF AMERICA

10 9 8 7 6 5 4 3 2 1

CONTENTS

Fairies Fearsome, Friendly and Funny

ONCE upon a time, in an enchanted realm claimed to be halfway between Heaven and Hell, there lived a race of immortals. Some people said they were fallen angels too naughty to reenter paradise, yet not wicked enough for damnation, and so their land is called The Middle Kingdom, and there they live to this day. Most of these folk are beautiful, some of them are tiny, and none of them ever grow old. They are well aware of the race of mortals; some display generosity to us, but others are decidedly dangerous. Some of these magic beings regard us as their playthings, but most want no traffic with us at all, and that is why we almost never meet elves.

Yes, they once were known as elves, and they greatly predate Christianity, from which the fallen angel idea derives. But there are other theories to account for their origin. In Scandinavia, for instance, according to Brian Froud and Alan Lee in their book, *Fairies*, when the giant Ymir died, maggots that fed on his corpse changed into two kinds of elves, gentle, blitheful light elves who inhabit the air and dark, malevolent ones who live within the earth and are obviously akin to George MacDonald's goblins in *The Princess and the Goblin* and the orcs of J. R. R. Tolkien's *The Lord of the Rings*. But in Iceland, the Huldre or fairy folk are said to be descended from Adam and Eve; when their mother denied their existence, her deception caused them to be changed into beautiful, but literally hollow, immortals. (Why innocent children would be punished for a parent's deceit puzzles me as much as similar questions irked Bertrand Russell; cf. his *Unpopular Essays*.)

In England, these elusive folk were thought to live in Elfland, ruled by King Oberon and Queen Mab. But during the time of the Tudor dynasty, the Anglo-Saxon word *ælf* fell into disuse, and with a little help from William Shakespeare's *A Midsummer Night's Dream* and Edmund Spenser's *The Faerie Queen*, they were renamed fairies.

Nietzschean scholar and translator Walter Kaufman stated that the slang usage of the word "gay" to denote homosexuality, though used as early as 1925, only entered common parlance in 1969 when the Gay Liberation Front came into being. Not so, however, for the pejorative meaning of "fairy." Etymologists trace this usage back at least to 1895. Blame it on the French; the word derives from the Old French terms *fae* and *faerie*: enchantment. The term is so identified with male homosexuality that, like "gay," its mythical denotation is virtually unemployable in contemporary literature with the possible exception of "fairy tales" for children (or adults), and if you disagree, go see James M. Barrie's *Peter Pan* and notice the tedious sniggers when Peter, to save Tinker Bell's life, pleads with the audience, "Do you believe in fairies? . . . If you believe, clap your hands!" (Anyone familiar with Barrie's life and writings will know he never intended such a meaning, even as a jest.)

That is why the collection you are now holding was not named *The Fairy Folk*, though "fair folk" is a legitimate appellation as well, as is "fey folk," though *fey* carries a darker shade of meaning. Its Anglo-Saxon root, *fæge*, denotes being fated, or doomed to die. Fey is not inappropriate nomenclature. In bygone days elves were always respected and feared for their capacity to inflict torment and worse. Nowadays, too often fairies are regarded as cutesy sprites with filmy wings and sparkly wands, an image largely, though not entirely, promulgated by Walt Disney. But thanks to the idiosyncratic elves of J. K. Rowling's Harry Potter books and Peter Jackson's award-winning adaptation of Tolkien's *The Lord of the Rings*, fey folk have regained some of their dignity.

You will not encounter any wee, adorable elves in these pages. Kim Newman's woodland fairies are quite formidable, as are Pat McKillip's entities. Tanith Lee's monarch may seem friendly at first, but that's just when a mortal needs to be extra cautious. True, Craig Shaw Gardner's amorous elves and Megan Lindholm's industrious brownie are basically comedic, but still, you don't want to get on a fairy's bad side—which is v-e-r-y easy to do. The only fairies in this book who show true affection and compassion for the human race are Jane Yolen and Midori Snyder's exiled sisters, but even they first have to learn things they never knew before about mortality.

The Middle Kingdom is so vast, of course, that it has scarcely been explored even in the hundreds and hundreds of fairy tales, films and paintings devoted to its mysteries. Some of its legends and inhabitants are glimpsed in the Afterword, "Some Facts(?) About Fairies," but the only true borders of Fairyland are etched within mankind's collective unconscious and our own individual imaginations.

—Marvin Kaye
New York City
June 2004

The
Fair Folk

UOUS

by Tanith Lee

Thanks to the distinguished British fantasist Tanith Lee, the style of my anthologies changed in the year 2000. Before then, they were mixtures of new and reprinted fiction, but then an e-mail from Tanith suggested a collection of six original tales of erotic vampirism, one of which she promised to write. The result was The Vampire Sextette, *which paved the way for* The Dragon Quintet, The Ghost Quartet *(in preparation), and* The Fair Folk. *Each of these books has one important thing in common: an excellent new story by Tanith, winner of the prestigious World Fantasy, Nebula, and August Derleth awards. Her novels and short story collections include* The Birthgrave, Companions on the Road, Dark Dance, Don't Bite the Sun, Drinking Sapphire Wine, East of Midnight, Red as Blood, The Storm Lord, *and many others. She and her writer-artist husband, John Kaiine, live on the southern seacoast of England.*

In The Fair Folk's *opening tale, "UOUS," a young woman asks the fairy folk for three wishes, never suspecting the startling twist that they have in mind for her.*

> I met a gallant in the wood;
> His cloak was green and red.
> The more we danced the more I would;
> Me like his book he read.

1

WE lived in the core of the forest for two years before anything really happened. And two is hardly a magical number, is it? Surely it should have been three . . .

Unmum bought the place, which was enormous, and she and the Boyfriend (Decrepit James) said they'd do it up. Because it was falling apart, the house. I mean literally. Slabs would detach from the ceilings and reallocate to the floors. Cracks ran busily up the walls, wanting to reach the ceilings before *all* the ceilings had fallen down. Moss and mould appeared more regularly than the mail. Rain and birds came through the roof, and mice, and nice big (disease carrying?) rats from the cellars. The wail: Ooh, there's a rat in the shower/bed/wardrobe/fridge was an everyday feature. Some of the windows were even broken. "Oh, soon get those sorted," opined Decrepit, expansively. But he didn't. He went as far as bringing in some of his "Men," and doing up a couple of rooms, and Unmum's and the Twa Ghastlies' bedrooms. (Mine, of course, could wait.) But anyway, all they did was slap new plaster on the old stuff, paint it, then put in carpets and so on. It was a bad face-lift and very soon the walls cracked again, bits of ceiling were dropping powder on rain-soaked areas of rug, and the odd rat was sitting on the TV sprucing its whiskers.

This, my home.

Well, no. Not mine. Never that.

*

DAD—my lovely father—died when I was fourteen. He killed himself, so much was obvious, at least to me. For it was never admitted by her, or her brats, and there was a very good reason for this. Because Dad did it so skilfully it had seemed to be an accident. And therefore she got the insurance money.

Her name was Irene—pronounced, I hasten to add, Ear Rainer. Ear Rainer—actually that's quite a fair comment on her altogether. She was tall and skinny, fake blonde and genuine bitch. She loved to talk at you, or anyone, that was, but me, about her own little self. The Twa, her daughters, were about the same, only a lot younger. *Their* real names were Andromeda and Ophelia. By the time I was sixteen, which was in the Fall Down House in the forest, Andromeda was eighteen, and Ophelia fifteen, so I suppose we could have been friends, but only if they had (all three of them) been totally different people.

I got taken out of school one week after Dad's death. And I never went back. This is reckoned to be impossible in our acute modern era, but it happened. As for And and Oaf (which is what I called them to myself, other than the encompassing Twa), they too left school.

However, once the financial storm settled so endearingly for Unmum and her brood, and we were all installed in the exciting adventure of the house, they, and Decrepit when there, lived the High Life. The girls had tutors—though these were all male, and picked because the Twa and/or Ear Rainer fancied them; nothing exactly educational got learned. The tutors were also always being sacked—or running away. Sometimes they just disappeared, usually after some particularly blistering row with Unmum. What happened to them? Made drunk on the endless fountains of vodka or Campari, and driven out into the wild wood, no doubt where they lost their way and perished horribly.

Yes, too. It was like that. The forest.

I forgot to say, the house also had four acres of land. That was, four acres of spiked briars, stinging nettles, huge, somehow leering trees, and poison ivy. There were quaint rat-pools too. I mean, not fish or frog ponds, but green scummy coins of water with rats taking a happy swim in them. The only birds I saw fly over the garden were tattered black crows or clattering magpies. At night there were bats and yowling owls. All these were *spawned* out of the forest, or out of our forest-influenced "gardens," as Unmum called them.

"Oh yeah," pontificated Decrepit, each hot, panting summer, poncing round the sunken fungusy top lawn in unsuitable shorts, "soon get this looking ace."

"Oh, James, I wish you would, honey-bun."

"Just let's wait for winter. That'll kill off a lot of these weeds. Then we can begin."

So they had another triple vodka and rolled off up to the sack to make—not love, surely?—mostly a lot of noise.

Meanwhile, the Twa would sprawl on the terrace (which Decrepit's Men had, amazingly, cleared), getting a tan and painting their nails the colours of earwax or salami.

And I? Summer, fall, winter, spring, I was always busy. "She's a real treasure," had said Decrepit during the first year, marvelling at this kid in frayed jeans and dirty T-shirt, with her itty duster, mop and bucket, or whatever. Or when he came across me baking bread, or a cake. Or when I put on a dress and served them all drinks and snacks. "She's a good girl," Unmum replied. "She knows she owes me everything now. And she's always ready to show me how grateful she is. Aren't you, Lois?"

That's my name, by the way. Or it was then.

What she truly meant, naturally, was that Dad left no proper will. So once he'd married Unmum, three years after *my* mother died, taken out massive insurance then got in financial shit and topped himself, his daughter, i.e., me, hadn't received a single sou.

He loved Ear Rainer. That was the awful part. He'd definitely loved her. I don't know if he loved the Twa. Maybe, for her sake.

He had seemed to love me too. At least, until everything fell in on him. I guess then he went mad. It happens.

But anyway, evidently, I had to be *very* grateful to Unmum, from that death-day on.

Meanwhile, to get back to the forest. I, and we all, of course, had now and then to go through it, to get to the town eight miles away. (The town was called Spawdock. I do not lie. It comprised endless pubs, restaurants, dress shops, supermarkets, arcades, cinemas and uncountable swirling meshes of streets.) It was where I went to do the family shopping. Where the others went to live it up some more. They used one of the two cars, what else. I'd take the bus. But the bus ran along the road that went through the forest. And to get to the road, you had to go down on foot into the forest first, and walk for one and a half miles.

Our poison-garden descended in broad nature-sculpted steps, and then there were some actual stone steps, crumbly, rocky and treacherous, between batches of evil formless statues caught in mid-lurch as if, when the darkness returned to them, they would start walking again. (You heard sounds like that sometimes, out in the garden at night—that was if you could hear anything for the owls, and Decrepit and Ear Rainer at it in the bedroom.)

Lastly you leapt carefully over an especially awkward narrow rat-pool, and went out a broken gate in a flinty wall.

Then you were properly in the woods.

I never know—even now—when is a wood a forest? When is a forest *not* woods? It was enormous, whatever it was. And old.

The estate agent had apparently informed Ear Rainer that parts of the forest went back before the Norman Conquest, which is that solitary date everyone knows, 1066.

In winter, if foul weather came, you could usually still, unfortunately, pass through the forest. The canopy of the cedars and pines and hemlocks managed to keep out such a lot of the rain or snow. But there were other trees—birches, rowans, hornbeams, oaks. In summer the forest was the most black of greens, pierced at unnerving intervals by uncanny splintered shafts of white-gold sun glare that, like spotlights in some trendy house, seemed always to be pinpointing something: an odd-shaped boulder, a dangerous purple toadstool, a cave in a bank that might be full of *anything*—an illegally loosed panther at the least.

Sometimes, even on cloudless *winter* days, the forest was crisscrossed by these shafts. It was like moving through visible laser beams. I always expected to set off some supernatural natural alarm.

It happened, too. Sudden claps of wings that sounded large as a dragon's—squalls and shrieks of unseen animal life—skitterings, tappings, slithers like those of a twelve-foot-long snake. And little bell-like notes, little crystal tinklings.

There were the smells, too. The forest had the usual odours of vegetal or animal growth—and death. But over these came the most extraordinary whiffs of food-like scents—roast chestnuts, sauté potatoes, beef slowly roasted, maple syrup and fudge. Or perfume. Glorious uncloying sweetness fluttering by through the air like an invisible honeysuckle bird. And too, sometimes a smell worse than that of any decaying fox carcass or rotted plant. Like—well, like bad *colours*. The colour of illness, or toothache. They made you, for a moment, sick, or a perfectly okay molar or bone would begin to ache. Twenty paces further along the track to the road, smell gone, the sickness or pain also faded away.

When you reached the road, the bus stop was in sight. The bus was generally on time. I tried never to have even five minutes to wait. Standing still, somehow there was more of a focus on you.

A sort of silence came then. Which had *sounds* in it, all tiny and caught up, like beads and threads in one gigantic spiderweb of green-black intense *nothing*.

People didn't talk much on the bus. Certainly nobody spoke to me, though plenty of them gave me an unliking look. I was one of those "new girls" from the "big house"—an incomer, unwelcome. They thought I was a stroppy, druggy tearaway too, because I always dressed so dirtily and badly and wore rubbish shoes, and why else would I? They knew our family was well-off. But I wasn't. I hadn't anything decent to wear, not even the dress I had to put on when I served Unmum her drinks.

Just now and then, though, I heard the bus passengers

speak about something to do with the forest; silly, rather upsetting things.

"It gets bigger every week, don't it?"

A woman said that, to her companion, softly, the very first time I was ever on that bus, age fourteen, in my unfashionable trainers with the split left sole.

And he said briskly, "Don't be daft." And she said, "Just my little joke." They seemed . . . scared?

Another time, a child pointed something out (I never saw what) yelling and bounding up on the seat—"Look! Look at *that*! *Look*—see *that*!" And was shovelled back down and slapped, so it all ended in tears.

Or there was that one night, the first winter, coming "home" on the later bus—having missed the earlier one because of a queue in Evermarts. The sun was sinking, dark was coming already brownly down in the woods, and I was shrinking inside although I was nearly fifteen by then, scared of walking that last one and a half miles alone up the track in the gathering dark. And then *I* saw, out among the trees, several tiny lights bobbing to and fro. They were like candles, but not so bright, yet brighter—hard to explain.

Lots of the other passengers stared out the windows, as I did. But then they all looked rigidly away. Some even fished out newspapers to read. And all at once the bus picked up speed. We reached my stop so fast (he took off fast, too, having dropped me) that by running I was able to get myself and the shopping to the house, just before the last of the light left the garden.

2

"Mum! Mum! There's a rat in the microwave!"

There was also a new tutor sitting in the vast kitchen.

Already he looked demoralized, and who could blame him? Well, Ear Rainer for one.

"Now, Dougal. We all have to pitch in here, you know. It's a sort of bivouac, until James can bring his men in, to tidy up. Are you any good with rats?"

Dougal, the tutor, pale, slender, with a mile of long auburn hair, and a college degree hidden no doubt in his bags on the stone floor, gaped in terror.

"*Me*, Mrs.—"

"Ear Rainer, *please*, Dougal. First names, or I'll feel *ancient*."

To Dougal very likely she was. He looked about twenty-three going on ten.

"I have," said Dougal, "a bit of a phobia about—rats—"

Just then And, ever-resourceful, threw a wet slimy sponge from the draining board into the opened microwave, which—smelly, succulent—the rat, obviously a more stupid one, seized in its yellow-fanged jaws. It then pelted out, and nimbly along the table through the avenue of coffee mugs, eventually exiting via the summer-undone back door to the yard.

"There," said Ear Rainer, as if she had managed everything perfectly. "More coffee, Dougal?"

"Er—"

"Lois! There you are. My God, you're always so late. I'm afraid breakfast's finished."

"I know." (I'd been hoovering upstairs, as *she* knew.)

"Well, never mind. You want to keep that lovely slim figure, don't you? Here's the shopping list, and cash. You'll see I've made a special note for you to collect the new CD player from Aladdins."

"Yes, Ear Rainer."

"Off you go then."

Dougal, who had stared at me in bemused distress—rather as he had at the rat—had his attention turned by Oaf tickling his neck and saying, "Is it true, you're going to teach me *history*?"

"Myth and history of the British Isles," I heard him grandly but querulously proclaim. As I, like the rat, exited into the yard.

I'd liked those subjects once.

*

THIS then, one more summer day, like all the summer days. Like all the days, which only the seasons, and the forest, gave any dissimilarity.

Two years! It could have been fifty.

I crossed the yard. Beyond the wall, where there had been a stables before it collapsed, the sloping tangle of lawn waited to lead me down to the woods.

Her crack about breakfast still rankled. Shouldn't have. I didn't eat with the family except on very rare occasions when they invited/forced me to. Sometimes I had to cook *their* breakfast, that was all. It was, "Oh, Lois, just leave that dusting for a minute and fry some eggs and bacon, would you." I cooked lots of dinners for them too, unless they all decided they wanted to cook for themselves, after a particularly telling orgy of TV home-cook programmes, or if they went out.

Additionally there was the annoying new Dougal. He seemed wet and spineless. Quite good-looking though, as per usual.

I stopped quite still. The sun was unfolding across the garden like a golden flower.

I'd stamped down as far as the steps and the statues by now, and suddenly I had a kind of horrible, truly unnerving revelation.

I realized the insane garden was beautiful.

My God, what was wrong with me? Some of that much-vaunted teenage angst I'd never had time to experience?

I glared about me, seeing the mossy trees foliaged in a heavy brocade green, dripping with fringes of unripe lemon-gold sun, the pocks and pockets of greenish water blue with sky, between the tall bars of rushes. Even the nettles were a kind of singing green—the briars had orange flowers, and wild roses (had any ever grown here before?) were spiralling magenta through the tumbled bricks of an old wall. The statues and the steps looked—picturesque. In a nearby sycamore a blackbird sang its summer territorial anthem.

It was a set some movie director could have searched half middle Europe for.

"Bloody hell," I said.

I sat down on the top step, with the shopping bags strewn around me, and gazed across to where a mother rat, with bronzy fur, was feeding her two dark mouse-like children with a slice of ham filched from the garbage.

Even they looked—well frankly, charming.

"Pretty rat," I said, with distinct disapproval.

A slowworm, like a tiny electric-blue snake, wiggled over the paving of a lower step.

This was all heartbreaking. It was as if a muddy blindfold had been wrenched from my eyes. And somehow it hurt. It made me think of Dad.

But I didn't get up. Had to wait for the slowworm to cross over, didn't I? It had right of way.

There were fairy stories I could remember, about girls like me, *stepdaughters* with a wicked stepmother, and two ugly stepsisters. (And and Oaf weren't that physically ugly, to be fair. Especially not And. But it came to the same thing.) And these woods were just like those in stories and should be full of fairies, or that fey high caste sometimes called the Folk. So now shouldn't I stumble across some magic hole in the earth, and a goblin in a pointy hat pop out, or some aged crone creep around an oak tree and apply to me for (unneeded) help—all so I could get my reward, which must be the standard one: a Way Out of this hopeless mess?

Because I was virtually a prisoner. I had no proper education or qualifications, no money and no prospects. My only alternative, if I left "home," was the streets, one way or another.

"Three wishes, that's what I'd like," I murmured to the vanishing flick of the slowworm's tail under the ivy. "Three *wishes.*" Then, before I knew I would, I stood up and shouted those two words into the treetops, at the fans and lacework of green and gilt. "THREE WISHES!"

The blackbird scolded me. A magpie jabbered from another bough. The rat mother hastily ushered her kids away into the undergrowth, casting me one frowning glance, as if I'd burped loudly in church.

"Sod it," I decided.

And went on down the steps at a sprint, because now, if I didn't watch it, I'd miss the town bus altogether.

*

WELL, I caught the bus—by the skin of my teeth. I was hot and sticky and gasping for breath, having pounded most of the mile and a half, falling over once on a tree root that, maliciously I was sure, stretched out to trip me. My knee was grazed, a smear of blood soaking through my torn jeans. But what was one more untidy stain?

Nobody on the bus said a word to me, as always. But when I'd sat down and started to breathe normally again, I heard, back along the rows, a woman say quietly, "What was that one running from?" And someone else said, "Hush."

I tried not to look out into the forest, as we trundled along to Spawdock.

But now and then I couldn't help it.

Those lush curtains of emerald on sapphire. That glitter of gold like coins drizzling through branches. . . . Wood doves, pale pinkish grey, were billing and cooing among the leaves, and a picture-book pheasant stalked out of a thicket, an impression of copper and ruby-red.

The forest was beautiful too, today. Maybe that was even why it had tripped me. Rather than sticking out a foot to bring me down, more an arm trying to halt me, make me look and *see*—

How fanciful I was getting. My instant black coffee breakfast must be causing hallucinations. I thought uneasily that I hoped no one had heard me shouting about wishes, from the house.

*

I said I had no money, but on shopping days I had the shopping money, a wad of notes, as Unmum had never trusted me with a credit card.

Having collected all the groceries, picked up the (weighty) portable CD machine, and organized a COD delivery of wine and spirits at the off-licence, I bought myself some pants, tights and Kleenex. Then I turned into the tea shop I always went to, a place too down-market for Ear Rainer or the girls to even notice. I had my usual treat, a double burger with cheese and a whole pot of clear black tea. They didn't know I did any of this, but they must know I did something like it. How else did I eat enough to stay alive, let alone equip myself with undies and the other necessities of feminine life?

Coming out again though, treat over, I was suddenly in a foul mood. It was the five o'clock bus I caught, deliberately extra late. I'd tell the witch-bitch I'd had to queue again.

In the sun-hot bus I fell asleep. The driver woke me at my stop by calling back loudly, bad-tempered as I still was, to show me up in front of the other passengers, who tittered.

"This is public transport, not a hotel," he remarked as I alighted. "Or perhaps I should say, as it's you," he elaborated, "a garbage sack."

I was struck dumb, affronted, *astounded* by this naked hostility. I stood at the roadside with the bags, scowling at him, no clever riposte coming to mind. In any case, the bus had zippered itself up and next sped away.

He'd only been an oldish faceless lump till then. Now it seemed he wanted to be part of my cosy un-fan club of enemies.

The bags weighed a ton.

Why the hell hadn't they had the CD player delivered like the booze? My aching arms felt as if they were growing longer with each step I traipsed. I was so *hot*. The woods smelled of martinis and chocolate bars and dirty washing. I located a bottle of water, undid it and gulped. I'd fill it back up from a tap when I got to the house. . . .

That was when—

How can I describe this?

It's like standing with your back to a solid wall, and abruptly the *wall* noiselessly draws itself open—like a curtain.

The thing is, no sound, not even some subtle change of light or shade.

Only a solid wall crinkling aside.

And something is there. Is there, unseen, behind you. Is waiting there, silent and still and inexplicable and fearsome—and out in the real world.

I'd put the bags down to get the water. Now I spun around so fast I sploshed half the contents of the bottle all over my trainers. It seeped in at the lace-holes. Most refreshing.

Didn't matter. What mattered was that *shape*—over *there*— about thirty strides from me off the track, in the green nearly six o'clock summer evening shadow under the trees.

What was it?

I didn't know. I thought, but without *thoughts*, It's the Beast of Spawdock—it's an escaped panther or puma—it's a wild *boar*—

I was too rattled to try to run away. Besides, they tell you not to, don't they? You're supposed to jump up and down and make a lot of noise, praying you can freak it out of thinking you're the ideal ready-snack.

Only I couldn't make a noise, or jump. I just stood there, fastened to the earth by my wet shoes. And then, oh then, the thing from the forest began to move *towards* me.

I let out this thin, utterly pathetic, girlie scream. It was disgraceful. Useless.

The moving creature passed through a series of shady dimnesses and scattered light-shafts coming down from the branches above. And as it did that it—changed. Or—it—*formed*?

The water bottle dropped out of my hand.

Three pounds' worth of water laved the grass.

He said, smiling at me a little, "That will do the ground good, there."

He was young, about twenty, it seemed. Twenty or twenty-two. Almost the age of cute drippy Dougal. Not remotely otherwise like Dougal. Not like any man I'd ever seen of any age. His hair was long, and very thick, and the colour of the moon when it's full in a cool spring. His hair shone. His eyes also shone, but were puma eyes, however, tilted at the outer corners, hazel-brown. He had a strange unknown face that might be very handsome or very—weird. It was like the images trees present in their trunks. But no, no. He *was* handsome—gorgeous. He was like a rock star. And with the body—tanned and quite tall—to match. He wore green—did he?—yes, green, like the woods, and brown like that, and just a flick of scarlet, like the red feathers the pheasant had had. He spoke with an accent. Couldn't place it. An asylum seeker?

The scents had all changed. I could smell mulberries and fresh orange, white wine, cedarwood and smoke.

"The forest," he added, smiling still, relaxed, and new as day in the morning, "thanks you for your gift."

I said, "Who the fuck are you?"

3

"MY name's Finn—or I have a longer name. But Finn will do."

"What do you want? I can't give you money." Actually I could. Or some of the groceries.

He didn't look though as if he needed anything like that.

"What am I wanting? Why, to talk with you. To walk with you. I will," he winningly said (his accented voice was light-coloured and strange as his hair), "journey a way with you."

"No."

"No harm," he said. "I'll carry your load there. It's too much for you. Any eye can see that."

"No, thanks."

"Ah, thanks given like a blow," he said. "It's far too late to see me off. Come now."

Too late to see him off—my blood went cold.

Was he an escaped and dangerous madman?

He didn't look at all mad, and I had heard it said the maddest people often come across as entirely sane.

Not taking my eyes off him I bent down to grab up all the bags. Somehow this didn't happen.

He was just there, and his brown lean hands closed on the plastic and twee hessian handles before I could get a grip. Somehow too, in this—for me—scramble, we didn't touch. He took the bags out from under my hands—and not even our fingers brushed together.

I gaped at him. And irrationally, far back in my head, thought what a divine picture *I* must make, face shiny with sweat, hair tangled, T-shirt and jeans with holes (and blood at the knee, don't forget that), plus wet, shabby, unfashionable trainers.

He'd *have* to be mad if he wanted to escort and carry the bags of an eyesore like me.

"Now you must tell me the way," he said.

His eyes gleamed. Oh, he was sumptuous.

Should I kick him? But if he was dangerously insane, that might not be the best idea.

"Er . . . up there," I faltered. Trying to appear placatory and aloof at the same time.

So we set off, he at a good pace, me keeping up. I thought, If it comes to it, I'll belt for the house. Leave the sodding shopping. Why should I die or get raped in defence of *their* property?

Then he started to sing.

That is usually embarrassing. Not with him.

He had an unbelievably wonderful voice. Well if he *was* a singer with a band—

Yet, it didn't quite have that sound. Nor the song. Older. Not folksy, not like that at all—just—miles off in the past. And I couldn't understand the words. *They* sounded ancient, too.

But then, uneducated as I was, they might only be German, or Greek.

I let him sing, couldn't stop him. But the birds, they joined in. It was nearly midsummer, when a lot of the birdsong lessens. Yet abruptly the whole of the woods was full of it, liquid trills and flutings, and all, so it seemed, *harmonizing* with his voice. A kind of fugue.

He left off as sudden as he'd started.

"It's the big house," he said.

"Oh, no," I began, attempting to evade I didn't know what.

But he said, "Come on now. I knew anyway. Where did you think I believed you were going?"

"If you know where I live," I snapped, losing patience perhaps unwisely, "why did you *ask* me?"

"Shall I say, it's how I am. I offer to assist you. I require to know where we are to travel. Later, I'll request you to let me in."

"I bloody won't!"

"Then I must request it of you again."

"Request as much as you like, mate. It isn't my house. I just—I just *work* there."

"Yes, their skivvy," he said. "The old story. Never altering. Like day and night."

He talked strangely too. But even that. . . .

I was startled. He knew a lot about me.

"You know a lot—"

"I do."

"Have you been—spying on us?"

"I have looked," he said. "But I have often better work to do than stare at those who lie in the sun, and those that are the slave to them. Nevertheless, others there are who have looked on and on."

I stopped in my tracks, and so did he, too. He regarded me calmly, still smiling a little.

"You mean—private detectives—are you from the insurance people?"

He threw back his head—yes, I'd never seen anyone do that either, thought they didn't—and laughed this golden laughter, that made the birds sing louder.

He said, "That house of yours. Eyes and spies everywhere. Hadn't you noticed? Unobservant girl."

I didn't know what he meant; for a moment I had an image of sinister agents lurking behind every door, under the stairs, dodging about round trees in the garden.

I said, "Look, I'll be straight about this. If you really do need money or food—well, take your pick. None of these goodies in the bags are for me—not many things, anyway.

They're for the three pigs. Oh, and Dopey Dougal. Oh—
and Decrepit James, if he turns up this evening. There's
money too. I'll tell her I got mugged. It's amazing I never
have been, really, prancing about with over two hundred
pounds stuffed in my pockets. So, well, go on. Have what
you like. Only if you start any violence or anything, I'll
fight. I may look thin and fragile but I'm strong as a fucking
carthorse. Nonstop housework. Better than any gym. So
watch it."

Puce in the face—I could feel it—I belligerently con-
fronted him.

"And the leaves are green," he oddly remarked. "Let's
get on."

And he turned and walked off again along the track, in
the direction of the house, swinging the bags a little, they
weighed so flimsily on his strength.

I had to follow. Or thought I did. I mean, what alternative option?

*

THERE was this other thing, and this only struck me later.
And that was itself peculiar, because I'd presumably seen
it gradually happening in front of me.

When he first—*emerged*—out of the woods, he was
mostly dressed in green, with elements of brown and red—
like Robin Hood, basically, the camouflage of the Bandit
of Sherwood. And his clothes too were . . . well, sort of—I
can't explain—because they looked all right—but they
weren't of the here and now. I don't mean he was dressed
like a minstrel or knight or prince at some battle re-creation
or Renascence Fayre. It wasn't that. I can't say *what* it was.
But he had a look of something other, and somewhere else,
and another time. Only no place or time I could pinpoint.
And I might have done, because, though an ignoramus, I
have read the odd bit of history.

Also, when he first spoke to me, and as we first trolled along, I could have sworn he had an accent. I didn't know what it was. It wasn't either posh or what Ear Rainer called "common," wasn't English, Scottish or American. Nor French, I didn't think, or German. But beyond that—well, what would *I* know? Nevertheless, it was there.

By the time we reached the outposts of the house, that is, the flint wall and the gate, I'd begun to think he must have put the accent on. Because all the while we walked, though we had talked not very much, even so it had got lighter and slighter, until he just spoke the same way I did, more or less accent*less*.

And the same thing, although I didn't realize, or not consciously, had happened about his clothes.

When we pushed into the garden, he following me straight through, argument redundant, his clothes were quite modern. Greyish jeans, a pale green shirt, and what looked like brown boots on his feet, with buckles and studs.

Just inside the gate, once I negotiated the rat-pool, I turned and faced him.

"I thought you were going to *ask* me if you could come in."

"Hey, not in here," he said. His way of talking, aside from accent, was sometimes more modern too. "This is all the same territory as the wood."

"Well, anyhow. You've been such a help. Thanks very much. But I can manage from here."

"I shall walk up to the house."

"No. If *she* sees you, she'll call the police." I wondered if she would, though, him being so gorgeous and so on.

And now he smiled, almost politely. Evidently police would be no problem for him at all. (Or he thought they wouldn't, which might amount to the same thing.)

"Look," I said.

But he simply nodded and strode forward again, up the steps between the statues, which glowed with westering sun, and seemed all jolly, nearly leaning down to greet us with their chipped and melted claws.

I scuttled behind him. Really practically running now to keep up.

And why had I mentioned that thing he'd said about his having to ask—request—entrance?

I mean, he was nuts.

That was it.

He moved through the garden-land like a technicolour hologram. You couldn't lose him, and somehow I was *impelled* to pursue—and it wasn't I felt I should, I just *had* to.

So at last we reached the nettled outskirts of the main lawn, and the house lay prolapsed before us, dilapidated and honey-gold with evening.

"From the eighteenth century," he said then, like a teacher in school or a professor at college I'd never had.

"Yes, it's 1750-something." The estate agent had told them that. "Altered in the 1800s," I went on—didn't know why, "and *she* wants to change it a lot more. But time goes by and she never does."

"I will not request," he said, reverting to his more eloquent syntax, "to enter in by that door. It must be the main door, for me."

"Forget it."

"You'll let me," he said. "In the end."

"Oh, yeah. Why?"

"You know well why, Lois my maid."

I jumped in my skin. He *knew* my name. A real fear scratched down my spine and I said, "This has gone far enough."

And precisely on cue, that was when another door opened at the side of the house, and out came Dopey Dougal and Ophelia with drinkettes, talking in some far-too friendly way, treading blithely onto the terrace, looking over the lawn, seeing—

"*There* she is!" shrieked Oaf. "You are a stupid cow, Louse. Mum's really angry! You're so *late*. She's been going apeshit."

Her voice carried like arrows all across the stones, weeds, grass tufts, and stung my ears.

Then I thought, And what will she think of *him*?

But when I turned to see too what *he* thought, *he* was gone.

He'd vanished. Swift, inaudible even to me, who'd been standing right next to him. Just the shopping sprawled about, and some grasshoppers squeaking, and the sun on my cheek like a hot flannel. Even his shadow hadn't marked the grass.

4

EAR Rainer went into one of her banshee tantrums. There was only one best way of dealing with that, as I'd learnt at fourteen, after I'd protested and she'd slapped me and shut me in the downstairs cloakroom of our earlier house for two hours. So now I went the best way, which was, "Oh, sorry, Ear Rainer, I couldn't help it," excuse, excuse, etc., etc.

I did occasionally wonder what I'd do if she hit me again now. I *was* strong. I'd had to be. So would I have hit her back? And then what?

But Decrepit was coming over at seven-thirty, and she wanted to get ready. Also not to unimpress the new Dougal too much with the disfunctionality of our "family," she cut her tirade short and went upstairs.

I unloaded the shopping and started to put everything away.

Long strips of burnt-treacle shade stretched across the kitchen, and a bee circled lazily above the coffee grinder before leaving through an opened window.

When Oaf ambled in to make another pitcher of lemonade

with a shot of vermouth (which she wasn't allowed), she gave me an amused look.

"You really are a plonker, Louse. What do you find to do in that town, anyway? Got a boyfriend? Cor, I can just picture him, some drugged-up yukko. Who else'd look at you?"

I said, idly, "I thought somebody was in the garden when I came back."

"Of *course* someone was, cretin. *I* was, and Dougal."

"No, I mean could someone have broken in?"

"Well that's not hard, with the back gate half off."

"Did you see anyone? When I came up on the lawn?"

"Only the ugly moron called *Low*-is," she replied, and splashed some more vermouth in the jug. "By the way, twat-face, don't tell mum I'm nicking her booze. I'll only say it's you. And then I'll *get* you."

"I'm not bothered what you do," I said. "You can drink the petrol out of her car for all I care."

"Really? You might care, if I decided to *really* hate you."

She swished out again in her tight little bottom-hugging skirt. She was fifteen, but looked much older than Dougal.

Once Decrepit arrived, they were all going down to the local pub, which was an hour away by Decrepit's BMW. This was great. I'd have the place to myself until at least midnight. I could take a proper bath, not the usual skimpy shower in the leaky downstairs shower room, and wash my hair. Later I too could sit on the terrace in the cool of the evening, and sip a martini. Ear Rainer never noticed her alcohol being stolen; she drank too much of it herself to ever be sure.

*

THAT evening the light was incandescent. I lay in the bath, basking.

The sun didn't set now till after eight, and then the afterglow could linger half an hour at least.

It was in the afterglow, the shadows spreading across the

garden below, and over the guest bathroom ceiling, as if trees started to grow there too, that I saw the rat sitting across from me on the lavatory cistern.

I wasn't exactly scared of rats. But I knew they were reckoned to carry disease and/or leap for your throat.

Clearing said throat, I suggested politely that the rat might like to vacate the area.

The rat gave me a long, black stare.

Its eyes were intelligent, considering me closely.

Suddenly I recalled what the Wild Man of the Woods had said to me on the way to the house: *Eyes and spies everywhere. Hadn't you noticed?*

To be honest, it wasn't that I hadn't thought about him at all until then. I'd thought about him fairly continuously, puzzling over who he'd been, what he'd wanted, what his *game* was. Remembering the exact words, though, made me jump again.

I sat slowly up and the rat didn't bat a whisker.

To my combined unease and alarm, I self-consciously heard myself announce to it, "If he sent you, you'd better go and tell him I'm having a bath."

And then—I *blushed*. That didn't happen very often any more, although I'd been a champion blusher at fourteen—I could have blushed for England.

While I was splashing there, trying to think what to do if the rat launched itself at my jugular, or somewhere worse (and also trying to think why I'd spoken to it like that and then gone crimson at the idea of *his* knowing I was naked in water), the rat pirouetted tastefully off the toilet and hopped, rather like a tiny kangaroo, out of the door.

A coincidence.

By the time I got downstairs, the dusk was moving up, palest grey-blue, from the east.

I sat on the terrace, on the lounger, swilling the drink and ice cubes round and round in my glass.

A scatter of late birds still flew about. Had I just not noticed them before? Finches and blackbirds, and little stripy ones I couldn't name. A last blue butterfly danced over the grass like a gas flame. Down below the banks and steps of the garden, the forest was putting on its second skin of darkness.

What did I anticipate? That *he'd* come striding up from the woods, from out of the wilderness of briars and trees? No. This afternoon had only been some crazy happenstance with a partly dotty young man. Perhaps a gypsy-type traveller, or even an outright criminal. Or . . .

The other notion struck me, gloomy in the gloaming, that I had somehow *imagined* all of it.

Which would mean I was going as cracked as I'd reckoned he was, handsome Finn of the Forest.

Sometimes, especially if Decrepit was there, the whole group of them would stay out on the terrace until after sunfall. I'd noticed, I now deduced, that when they did this, they put on all the house lights that side, and the two ornamental lamps stuck out on the lawn.

Even so, nobody stayed out that long, even on the hottest, most indoor-airless nights.

Nor me. Never me.

I'd rationalized about rats slinking, snakes, bats, unknown nocturnal creepy-crawlies with big pincers. It was only sensible to go in, after dark.

Tonight, however, the sky went all blue, then indigo, then navy, and the spy-eyes of stars lit up. Over the trees ghosted the wide-sailed shape of a hunting owl, and something gave a snuffly demoniac giggle away in the woods. A badger or a murderer, could be either.

And still there I was. Part of me wanted to stay out. But only part.

The dark seemed to advance on me across the expanse of open ground, through the trees, massing like an army on

the lawn—and then I saw a hundred other stars light up—
on the lawn. Like diamanté cigarettes. Had some of the plan-
ets and suns fallen off the sky? What *were* they?

I recalled that winter the year before, on the bus, and the
lights bobbing through the trees, and the bus speeding up.
And I'd pelted back to the house as if the hounds of hell
were after me. Maybe they had been. Maybe they *were.*

That did it for me.

Once I'd darted inside, slammed on lights, locked and
bolted the side door, I saw the night was still out there, staring in through every pane.

Don't be a fool, I thought. I concluded I knew what the
lights were on the grass and bushes. Glowworms. No doubt
that was what they had been too, last winter. Assuming you
get glowworms in winter . . . summer . . .

I didn't go out again.

I went upstairs to my own "room" in the attic.

Stooping double where the ceiling sloped, I peered out
through my own narrow window.

They were still there, the lights. Small as sequins now. If
they were glowworms, then it wasn't odd they were also now
moving. Though, perhaps a bit odd, because it was almost as
if, for a second, their glows spelled something—four letters—
and then, again, and again—U-O-U-S—? Then all of them
winked out.

The owl called like an unnerving factory hooter. Neither
it, nor anything else, was presently visible. Yet the whole
night was throbbing and *electric* with an *invisibly* radiant life.

Imagination. Insanity.

I wondered if a rat, or some spider hanging from a beam
in the corner, was watching to see what I did. And then
they'd be off to tell him.

I put a chair against my door, under the handle, drew a
curtain at the window, and put on my portable radio loudly.

It was all politics and bad pop music. When I got the classic station, which I couldn't always in this house, they were playing Mendelssohn's overture to *A Midsummer Night's Dream*.

I fell asleep anyhow. I'd had a busy day. I dreamed of lighted U's, O's and S's swirling about, making other words— *SO, OU*—

Woke up about one A.M. to the BMW barking home across the drive on the far side of the house. Decrepit still always drove when he'd been drinking, said he was safe as houses. But judging by the knocks some of the brickwork had taken, neither he, nor the house, was, very.

I lay there listening to these alien beings returning to their lair, at the top of which I lay captive. They had nothing to complain of. Their slave had, as instructed, cleaned the kitchen floor and put a cold supper in the larder under plates. Even the guest bathroom looked only clean, not Loisused. I knew my place.

Their rotten voices warbled over the drive. Then they were in the kitchen, vague laughter and bashings about. Then awful old-hat "music" as Unmum and the Boyfriend cavorted in a drunk reliving of their aeons-distant youth.

Dougal was quiet as a sardine. But the Twa made endless noise, showering, arguing, being shouted at from below by Ear. Then the owl started off again. Woo-woo, tirreet-woo. Over and over.

After which Oaf flung up her window screeching "Fuck-offyouowl!" And then something was thrown, missing the owl presumably, instead hitting one of the garden lamps— bang, crash, tinkle. Ah, silent night.

Two more hours and it would be dawn, at the crack of which I had better be up and about my chores.

I felt tearful. Wouldn't admit it. What was the point of tears? It was more than *them*, though. I'd been hoping—yes, hoping. Face it, Lois. For him. I'd been secretly longing over the cuckoo's nest escapee in the green shirt would dash back over the garden, and woo (woo-tirreet) me on the terrace. I'd thought he had some madman's supernatural power, too. He'd sent the little lights to charm and seduce me. Could they have been trying to say LOIS?

*

TAP-TAP, said the window.

> Girls and boys don't go out to play. . . .
> Ill-met by no moonlight, proud Oberon. . . .

Dreaming, muttering, I swung over on my back and opened my eyes to virtual blackness.

The alarm clock showed me a blurry almost three A.M.

Tap, said the window again. Tap.

Oh goody. A werewolf, vampire or ghoul has climbed up the house now, and is wanting a chat with the much-sought-after Lois.

It's a branch.

No. There were no branches that overhung my window.

Somehow, quaking, I pushed myself off the mattress, disentangled myself from the sheet, and crouched back over to the window. With a grunt of worry, I wrenched the curtain aside.

Oh God—a *thing* was out there—a levitating thing with fire-spark eyes—

No, no. Idiot. It was a bat. It was flapping about the roof, doing a circuit round the house, tipping a wing-point against the glass for some unknown batly reason. There it went, flying off again. This window was stuck, had never opened, and up here under the roof, it was in summer often like an oven. But now I was very glad the window didn't open, or it would have been open and the bat would have been in. I'd have woken up to find it sitting on my nose, staring at me—

I wasn't scared of bats, either. It was just—their over-mobile *flitteriness*.

Down below, in the garden, empty now of alphabetical glowworms, after all there was sudden big light. One of the lawn lamps, obviously the one Oaf hadn't smashed, had been turned on.

And something rather tall and dark stood before it, with the moon that had set an hour ago emblazoned over its hair.

Jesus Christ. He *had* come back. Finn the Cool, Finn of Sherwood, refugee from the funny farm.

And he'd seen me too. He was gazing right up at me, at a me bent over by the window and without clothes on, only partly hidden by my long, washed hair.

I was so shocked I just goggled down at him, and then he raised his graceful arm, and as in the most clichéd horror story, he *beckoned* me.

Oh sure. Go down into the bald-lit night-black dark to—him.

Not likely.

Oh no.

But I was pulling on my jeans, slinging on a T-shirt. *Why* was I doing this?

Outside, the light of the lamp blinked out.

Lois, you must be certifiably balmy—

I couldn't stop myself. And outlandishly, as I tiptoed down through the house towards the side door that led to the terrace and the lawn. I wasn't afraid, had even finished questioning myself; for the moment. I seemed guided. Or I was possessed. No choice after all. None.

5

WHEN I undid the side door, he was standing there, outside. I hissed, panicky only in a remote way, "I know what you said, but you can't come in."

"This isn't the door I'd request to enter at," he softly replied.

His voice. Oh.

"What do you mean?"

"A tradesman's entrance. Is that what you offer your betters? It's the main house door I'll be having opened for me, and invited over the threshold."

I said firmly, sounding rather cross, "Are you a vampire?"

Because I hadn't switched on any lights and the lawn lamp had gone out, I couldn't see him very well, only his blondness limned by starshine.

He said, so seriously he must be amused again, "No, I'm not that. But you know what I am."

"Deranged," I blurted.

"My kind," he said, "never go mad. It's your kind does that. Driven to it by all the worldly woes of life and death we never need fret over."

I slipped out and shut the door silently.

"Let's move away from the house. They sleep like concrete bollards usually, but knowing my luck, this'll be the one time they won't."

"Very well," he said.

We crossed the lawn, and as we passed between the lamps, I saw it was the *broken* one that had been lit up.

Under some trees then.

The moonless darkness, now I was out in it, had a sheen on it like polished pewter. The sky was turning all to grey, the stars fading. Dusk in reverse.

"What do you want?" I said.

Seeing him better now, was I wishing he'd say, "*You.* I want *you*"?

The idea was appalling but also utterly enticing.

I'd have liked to touch him. Didn't. Couldn't.

He said, "I want what is owed."

"*What?*"

"Owed."

"By who?"

"By you, Lois girl."

"I can't owe anything. I haven't *got* anything."

"You offered it."

"I—I bloody never offered—"

"Wait," he said, "here comes someone."

Now between two alarms, I whirled round to see who else was after me, and saw no one, and the *bat* flew straight past me, and landed, *plumpp*, on his wrist.

He spoke to it then—or sang to it. A sort of crooning murmur that made the hair go up on my neck. He looked into its eyes, and the bat folded itself up a little, and gazed at him.

Inside its small pterodactyl wings, it was furry, its face like that of a tiny rodent-cat, chin pointed, eyes full of the ending night. Was that where night stored itself—in a bat's eyes?

The crooning ceased. Finn said to me, "Come here, and take him up. He's my messenger, one of them. You may need to know him somewhat."

"Er—no thanks. It's a bat."

"Scared, are you?" He grinned. "And I thought you were a brave young modern woman."

"I'm not sc—I just—oh, all right."

I held out my arm and the bat sidle-crawled off Finn's wrist and onto my palm. Though again, Finn and I didn't touch. It glanced at me, not wary, nor interested. I felt its rough fur against my skin, and the sharp little claws like thorns.

To my surprise, I didn't mind this, standing there holding a bat.

"You see," he said.

"It's—he's pretty."

"There, *mashefla*, the lady thinks you fair." (I thought that was the word—name—*mashefla*.)

The bat preened its chest. It would have sharp teeth too, vampire fangs. I remembered Decrepit announcing all bats had rabies, they had brought it from the "Continent." But somehow, having the bat perch there was quite soothing.

"If I stroke him, will he bite me?"

"Not now."

So I ran one cautious finger over the little bat's chocolate fur. He smelled faintly like chickens and mould, and clear *navy blue* like the depths of the darkness had been.

"I like him."

"Very well. It seemed you'd prefer him to a rat."

"Your messenger. What messages?"

"While you serve me," he said.

When he said that, I felt a true and real terror. And terror was something apparently I had never felt in all my life. It wasn't like abject fear, or nauseating anxiety. It was a sweeping hugeness that turned my bones to water, blood to ash.

But I quavered, "Look, I already have to serve *them*."

"I shall be the better master. Though," he added, judicially, "perhaps less patient."

"I don't get this," I said. And idiotically too late, "Really, I'd better go in——"

"Three wishes," he said.

Something else happened. Maybe it was only the dark, sinking through the sky, a sort of fast bit of night going too quickly. Or time slipped a moment, stumbled.

Three wishes. What I'd howled at the trees yesterday morning.

My heart hammering, as if all this could really be true and not his or my delusion, I said, "You mean you're *that* kind—the Fey Folk—the—Little People—the Lordly Ones—You mean you've come to give me—*three wishes*?"

He had grown taller. He looked down and down at me with the scorn of a king for a fool he had wanted better of, and I felt ashamed of my ignorance as he told me. "No. For centuries, time out of mind, since the dawn of the first dawn, it's been that. My kind granting to your kind the boon of the Triple Trellechy. Do you think we'll settle to go unpaid forever, maiden? Does any, on this earth, mortal or un?"

"Then," I said humbly, "you mean—"

"You called out for the bargain. But the times are changed. Now you pay *me*. For all your kind, *you* pay with three wishes. Mine. For we are owed, and the debt is much in arrears." Extra unnerving, in the vernacular as it were, he added, "Better get used to it, baby."

6

"Dougal."

"Um—uh—ye-es?"

(Actually, he wasn't that cute. Beady eyes and his nose was too small.) I'd cornered him on the upper landing, while *they* were in the garden, frying.

"I need to ask you something, Dougal."

"Oh well er, I'm a bit—"

Christ, did he think I was angling for a date?

"Something about mythology and old tales. Your subject. Isn't it?"

"History and myth of—"

"Britain. Yes. I need to know—"

"You see, er, Lois? Er, I am rather—"

"You can spare me five minutes."

I'd cowed him. He wilted and waved his small artistic hands at me and said, "Well, if it can be very quick."

"I want to know about the Fey Folk—the Fair Ones—whatever they're called."

"Oh, that's a large area, Lois." Was he being evasive?

"I want to know about the Triple Trellechy."

"The—er—the *what*?"

"You've never heard of it."

"Um. I don't think . . ."

"Three wishes. The granting of three wishes to mortals."

"The word sounds like Romany, or—*Yiddish*," he lamented.

"Wouldn't it be Gaelic?"

"It's *not* Gaelic," he pronounced. Then, spineless nerd, "At least, I don't *think* it can be, but—"

"Can you recommend a book?"

"Oh, I could recommend hundreds," he said, loftily brightening at his erudition.

"Just one."

"That could be difficult."

"Why? It's simple."

"It isn't simple. There are countless fairy tales that concern three wishes, but—" he began to ramble on. He spoke of tree spirits and water-horses and goblins, and magic fish and trolls and ghosts—about everything in the realm of myth and legend that had nothing, or not much, to do with what I'd asked.

"Okay, Dougal," I said, when he paused for breath after a quarter of an hour. "Thanks."

He seemed depressed. Then annoyed. The tip of his wee nose had gone pink as he waffled on. He looked like a Burne-Jones mouse. He flounced down the stairs to join the skin fry-up. With that pale flesh, he'd *burn* Burne-Jones.

There weren't many books of any kind in the house. I was the only one who'd ever read much, and most of my books had mysteriously disappeared, like my old toys, since the move.

And it wasn't a shopping day, so I couldn't get to the town library. Besides, *that* would mean walking through the forest.

I had put him off last night. Finn. The day was coming up

in pearl layers and the birds all chirruping, and I'd said I had to hurry in and start my chores. He let me go with just a kingly nod.

Was he a king of their kind? Royalty, certainly. Some prince of the Fair Folk, the Scourges of Men. Who had fascinated and tricked and trapped and harmed humankind since the dawn of all dawns. And now, since I'd yodelled out about three wishes, right next to an ancient forest that still harboured these—*beings*—I too was to be fascinated, tricked, trapped and presumably harmed. Because how could *I* grant anyone anything they wished for—let alone a creature like *him*?

I had thought, of course, if perhaps I had made my plea a little more specific—that was, *Three wishes, I'd like to be given them*—there might have been a get-out clause on the deal. But all I'd bawled was: Three wishes, that's what I'd like. Which to the twisty lawyer mind of the Folk could be taken to mean I just wanted to be saddled with the repayment. Or maybe anyway it was only what he'd said—the times had changed. It was owed.

Despite trying for info from Dougal, I did have an idea what had generally been demanded, that was by mortals of the Folk. It normally involves, doesn't it, wealth and power, riches beyond the wildest dream, a kingdom to rule, and Heart's Desires, and other such munificence.

But why would he want anything like that? If he was what he said. What he seemed. What, let's face it, I knew he *was*.

So what on God's earth would he demand I get for him? He hadn't told me yet.

In the end I went into Dougal's room.

Despite his looks, the room was the usual boy-tutorish mess—bed unmade, pants and socks on the floor, three mugs of stale scummy coffee left on the windowsill.

His books, though, were in the bookcase.

I bent over them eagerly.

Ah. *Nights of Horror, The Waxwork Strangler, The Last of the Zombies*—the rest of the titles were comparable.

Who'd have thought it?

There was absolutely nothing on history, let alone myth (unless you counted *Curse of the Ant Pharaoh*).

I went back to hoovering.

*

I hoovered down the house, got them lunch, then put the first load of laundry in the machine. The utility area opened on the yard, and when I went out there I looked all around uneasily. Three squirrels were running along the wall. They seemed not to take any notice of me.

It would be less trying, I thought, if he *had* been a vampire—they could only call on you at night. But Finn might appear at any hour or instant.

What would he *want*? What would happen when I couldn't—as of course I *couldn't*—provide it?

*

DURING the afternoon Ear Rainer and her tribe went out again in her car. Even horror-cultist Dougal went. (Was he secretly a serial killer? Would he chop them all up in teeny pieces? Some hopes—not with those hands.)

I groped my way into the ovenous attic, fell on my mattress and slept.

Dreaming. . . .

Finn leaned over me, his face cruel and wooden. "Ill met by moonlight, humble Lois. . . ."

Bollocks.

I woke up, sat up, and cudgelled—good old word—my brains.

What did I know about—*their kind*?

Right. If he was a royal, he'd have a cup always full of wine, a cauldron always full of food, a sword that could slay nine men at a blow, a bow that could slay nine men at a blow, a harp that could entrance—literally en-*trance*—bringing sorrow or joy. He'd have a hoard of sorcerous gold, silver and priceless gems, mined and minted in the hollow hills. In that kingdom—where? *Under* the wood, or just somehow enterable through it, via an inch-wide fracture of sideways dimension. And there they laughed and sang, danced and dined, hunted and had sex and played games—forever, being immortal.

I lay down again and slept again. This time I dreamed of a tiny little Dougal, skittering up an alley after a regulation-size shrieking girl he was attempting to clobber with *The Waxwork Strangler.* Which admittedly was a hefty tome. However did he manage to carry it? A neon meanwhile flashed on and off in the sky, reading UOUS. A girl became tinier even than tiny Dougal and slipped down a crack in the road.

*

MIDNIGHT isn't black. Not really. If you're out there, in the depths of the dark, you begin to see. . . . Conceivably the pitch-black vaults of the ocean are the same. Or why else do they have such colours down there, that so far have only been shown to us through invented light? What I remember most: The arching upper ribs of trees, which gradually I began to note were metallically visible. Even—I even saw birds sleeping there inside the silk bedclothes of the leaves. And the path showed ahead, some wild track, a faint glint of tussock, and pebble on pebble, caught by the knife-edges of the stars. And then the half moon broke through, and silver fountains of ferns almost blinded me by their brilliance.

But, the deeper in I went, into the wood, away from the moon, the more some other, total, luminescence grew. It became—not like sunshine, but like a night that *could* have passed for day, only it was different. Then, all across the leaves, I noticed a sprinkle of little—well, what? They were most like stars—had been hung. They resembled the diamanté sugaring I'd seen out on the lawn the previous night. *Not* glowworms. These were static as fairy lights on a Christmas tree—the lanterns of something too ephemeral and too eternal to either doubt or believe in—

"There," he said.

I glanced into a glade, and in a ruled-straight shaft of the hot-white moon, two badgers were playing, kicking and grumbling, shaggy as unkempt dogs, their serpentine heads moon-painted in a single white strip, like an airfield for moths.

"Broc, broca," he called, and they left their fierce play and stood up. They came over to him one at a time, and across each of the striped heads he ran his hand, and where he touched them—plumes of fire seemed to rise. And then were gone. They trotted away, shoulder to shoulder.

Countless rabbits bounded through the trees.

A toad sat on a stone, congealed to jade, only its eyes swiveling.

Something else. We went by an avenue of tall, tall birches, with trunks scaled ivory. And a wolf loped along it. A wolf. I saw it. And it looked back once, and its narrow eyes glimpsed like green turquoise.

"Was it there?"

He didn't answer. But I wasn't afraid. Phantom or actual, no wolf could harm *him*. Nor me, with him, unless he changed his mind and commanded it to. Then I wouldn't stand a chance. Inevitably I considered, but far off, in a sort of buried cellar in my mind, that if I failed him, wolf-meat might well be what I'd become.

And how had I got to this stage, out in the forest with him again, seeing wolves?

I should have detailed everything in sequence. It's just that this supernal night-walk was so extraordinary, I wanted to recollect it first.

*

BASICALLY, to retrace my narrative, sufficient unto that day was the crap thereof.

After I'd woken in the attic with a headache, showered in the leaky shower and re-dressed, the monsters had come back from their trip. I didn't know or care where they'd been, but I soon knew there had been some trouble with Ear Rainer's car, a nasty bright red thing of unimportant rich make.

They wanted dinner anyway.

As I washed salad and put chicken things in the microwave, Ear Rainer and co. expatiated.

"I'll swear it was a pig!"

"Oh, Mum. You don't get *pigs* out *here*."

"That's exactly where you do get them, Ophelia. Don't be obtuse. It must have escaped from some farm."

"It wasn't a pig," said And, laconically. "It was a bear."

Ear Rainer shrieked between scorn and sudden fright. "Don't be—*was* it? An escaped *bear*—"

I didn't take a lot of notice really. They'd been through the forest, driving back. And what could you expect of the forest? (If they hadn't noticed anything about it before I could only put it down to the fact they were thick-os.)

Then apparently, reaching the drive on the front side of the house, the car had stalled. They'd had to push it, Dougal included in this activity, up the bumpy, tree-rooted track. It had been too much for Dougal. He'd now retired to bed.

"Oh where is James whenever I need him?" wailed Ear Rainer.

Soon after, though, and despite the bear, which might have followed them and still be lurking, they swayed out on the terrace with enormous drinks.

That was when, through the window, I saw the three squirrels were back, sitting on the yard wall. Mayo in one hand, french loaf in the other, I paused. You ask, how could I tell they were the same squirrels as the ones I'd seen earlier?

Well, there was something weird about them. Two were grey and one was red. A red squirrel running about, and now *sitting* about, with two greys. Doesn't happen, does it?

I thought, angrily, *Spies.*

But then I had to take the three trays of dinner carefully across to the terrace. And when I got back in the kitchen— What I saw was a line of green non-lettuce tree leaves laying, in a neat row, along the middle of the table. Nothing else was touched—well, not much. Something *had* been licking the butter.

They'd got in, and out, by one of the windows. Easy, for a squirrel.

So, this would be his message for me.

I leaned toward the leaves, and written in English, in the plainest script, impossibly clearly on the central leaf (in what looked like gold felt-tip pen): *Worldly Riches.*

I jumped back as if I'd been scalded.

He had finally deigned to tell me what I must give him for the First Wish.

And as I bent there over it, somehow I fathomed at once the unsubtle definition of the demand. I'd already puzzled over how he didn't need wealth, already being rich beyond the dreams of whatever. But of course it was *mortal* wealth— *worldly* wealth—he had stipulated. He'd blatantly required of me just what *our* kind had always avariciously begged of his. And somehow I knew it would be one- and two-pound coins, fifty- and hundred-pound notes he'd want—and plastic, oh yes, every credit card I could lay hands on.

I hadn't ever stolen from them, my unfamily. I don't know why not. (I don't count the tights or soap or the odd lunch to augment the scraps I was allowed in the house.) But now I'd have to.

Perhaps I am quite villainous underneath, or Ear Rainer had made me like that. I certainly didn't agonize over trying to oblige him, or entertain any ethical doubts. I was only scared.

The main worry was, of course, who else would Ear Rainer suspect of the theft but me?

How could I get round that? (Not that he'd care. Probably wanted to see me get caught, sent to jail. An entertaining bonus.)

Maybe I could make it look like a break-in—but also I couldn't wait for them to go out, because when they did, all the credit cards and any spare cash went with them.

God, it was a real problem. I sat brooding over the leafy table. I'd have to sneak into her bedroom when she was in one of her wine-dosed snory concrete sleeps. Would she wake up? Right at the moment I stood there with her wallet in my sweaty paw? Damn, oh damn and fuck.

"Louse, you're useless."

I nearly leapt now through the roof.

And was standing there, slenderly draped on the kitchen door frame in her tailored jeans, halter top that cost two hundred pounds, and faultless satin wave of hair.

"Yes," I mumbled.

"You didn't bring us any butter, did you?" She spoke more in sorrow than in anger, and stalked over to the butter plate. "This is melting. Where's the ice for it? Come on, hurry up. And what are all these bay leaves on the table?" she inquired. "You didn't put bloody bay leaves in the salad?"

"No, it was—er—"

"I sometimes think you were dropped on your head when you were a baby, Louse. Do you think there's a chance you were?"

"Mm," I said.

Fleerily pivotting, she swept out again. And I had a moment's respite of pleasure, thinking of them swamping their bread and new potatoes with buttery squirrel saliva.

It didn't solve my problem, however. I would simply have to get on with the theft, and get on with getting caught, if it came to it. "You ungrateful little beast," Ear Rainer would say as someone called the cops. (She had said this to me before.) "After all I've done to try and help you."

It got dark eventually, and they went quite early to bed, leaving me a relaxing mountain of washing-up. I did it to allow them time to go to sleep.

I thought, rampant with despair, I might as well rob And and Oaf as well, if I didn't manage to wake Ear Rainer. The rooms of the Twa were only just along the corridor from hers.

It was about half past eleven when I pattered upstairs, barefoot and trembling.

Outside her door I paused, listening in blackness as if my ears were raised on stalks. Her light was certainly out. Then I detected the lovely sound of snores.

I knew where, in the blacked-out room, the things would be I must take. The wallet in her handbag—either on a chair or under one, or on the dressing table among the perfumes and stay-young-forever creams. But additionally I needed the key to the bureau in the living room, where she kept extra cash for "emergencies," usually around five hundred pounds. The key meant her bedside drawer.

Softly as a shriek—it sounded like a gunshot to me—I eased open her door.

Blast. She'd drawn the curtains—or hadn't closed them properly. A ray of moonlight lit the room.

Courage, Lois! At least you'll be able to see, and not stumble over anything.

But I padded in and tripped instantly on her rotten high-heeled shoes, kicked off and lying there just for me. I fell to one knee like a romantic swain, and managed not to squeal. It was the knee I'd fallen over on yesterday in the woods.

Ear Rainier gave a horse-like snort. Waking up?

I prepared a breathless tale of an intruding bat I was sure had got in her bedroom—

But she only heaved over in the bed onto her back, and resumed her dulcet snore-music at double volume.

And there was the wallet, lying out on a chair.

As my hand closed on it, I tensed for the flying wide of the door, one of the Twa entering in a blaze of lights—Nothing.

So far so bad. Now I had to locate the bureau key.

As I quietly (again a sound like thunder) slid undone the three drawers of her bedside cabinet, I watched Ear Rainer sleeping. And I thought, clear as silver bells, My God, sod robbery, I could just murder you, couldn't I, easy as wish.

Why haven't I? I thought. Why haven't I ever killed you? Why don't I, now? *Would* I? *Could* I? Am I so wet I can't—it isn't morality, what's morality? I hate your guts, you evil bitch. So why can't I—

Ear Rainer snorted again. This time she rolled over and faced me, her awful sleeping face, smeary with nourishing cream, and open-mouthed, shut-eyed, like that of someone already dead.

Something about this terrified me. Yes, terror, the real type, rather like what I'd felt in the wood, with him.

I'd have run then—only exactly at that second I felt the key under my palm, and grabbed it. Calmer, if not very sane, I slid home the yelling drawer and picked a retreat across the room, avoiding her shoes now, and out into the passage.

I was shaking. My legs were water and I had to lean on the wall. Then, along the corridor, Oaf's door banged open in a torrent of light.

"Mum!" screamed Oaf, "there's a rat in my room—there's a *rat*, Mum! *Mum!*"

As she stood there screeching, and I cowered back into the dark as far as I could, the rat in question burst like a tiny cannonball between Oaf's horrified legs. She and I watched as it tore off in the direction of the stairs. It had been carrying something—*bright*—in its mouth—what on earth—?

7

WHAT happened next was Ear came erupting out, clutching on her "robe," about two inches away from me and yet not seeing me. Instead she blundered over to Oaf and pushed her back into her room.

Oaf's door stayed open and lit, so I could hardly now flee past it. The corridor ended in wall the other way. I was stuck.

I heard Oaf shrilling then, "It stole my necklace! Mum— listen—it *did*—a fucking rat—"

"Don't use a word like that at your age."

"*Mum*—I'm fifteen—Mum, what the fuck does saying fuck matter! It stole my *gold necklace*! Right?"

"Don't be so ridiculous, waking me up for—"

"I *saw* it. I heard a noise, *knew* it was a fucking—"

"Will you *please*—"

"—rat—and I switched on the light—and it was in my jewelry box, the one James gave me at Christmas—"

"How could a rat undo the lid—"

"I must have left it undone—how do *I* know—"

"You should take more care of—"

"Mum, *listen.* It got hold of the necklace and the silver bracelet and the gold ring with the sapphire—and it jumped on the bed and *stood there*, leering at me—with all this gold and stuff in its fucking mouth—"

"Oh for Christ's sake, Ophelia!"

Abruptly one of them slammed the door. They were both shouting as if to shout was the new black.

I took my chance and dashed by the shut door and into the other passage and up the stairs to my attic.

There I fell on the mattress and started to laugh. Still laughing I lit the bedside lamp I'd had since I was thirteen, and opened Ear Rainer's wallet. And stopped laughing. Because inside it was empty. No plastic. Not even one single five-pound note.

*

So it was the bureau or nothing, now.

I did cogitate briefly on my fellow thief, the rat. I decided perhaps they were like magpies, and sometimes stole sparkly things. But really, I knew.

The sounds from below died down. Then two doors slammed. There'd be another row in the morning, you bet. Meanwhile apparently neither And nor Dopey Dougal had registered anything, let alone emerged.

Nothing else for it then.

I crept out again and down the stairs. I had a safer story now if apprehended. My bat-intruder had changed to a rat-intruder.

Moonlight slanted through the lower storey, palpably white. The house creaked, but the night outside was very silent. Not even an owl.

When I put the key in the bureau it turned without a hitch. And the ill-met-by moon fell just right through the nearest window so I could see what I was doing.

I knew the Russian box Ear old-fashionedly kept her dosh in. I drew it out and opened that too.

Oh my.

There were neat rolls of twenties, fifties—over a thousand pounds, I was sure. At least then, I could give him, my "impatient" master, something on account. I poked about a bit more in the bureau, to see if she had also stored her credit cards there after all. But she hadn't—it was only letters and similar stuff, and a couple of boring-feeling hard things wrapped round and round in cloth. Maybe unwanted sex toys from James. I left them strictly alone.

When I glanced round, I nearly had a heart attack. Admittedly the third or fourth nearly had one that night.

All this while I'd been rummaging, I'd had a noiseless audience. They poised there, across the carpet, between me and the door, their eyes glinting like splinters of broken glass.

Thirty. I counted them.

I'd heard so many horror stories about rats, especially when grouped in large numbers. And so when the whole *battalion* launched itself right at me I nearly screamed.

But they only galloped past, and straight up into the bureau.

In astonishment that wasn't astonished, I watched as they scratched and gnawed the bureau lid, the inner cubbies, the of-course important papers and letters stored there, now and then defecating artlessly on everything.

They, like the one upstairs, had given me an alibi. I suspected I now knew, too, where and how all Ear's plastic had gone. (That hadn't been wear and tear on her wallet, but tooth marks.)

Standing in the moonlight, staring at the moon-diamond rats with their glass eyes, rivering up and down the bureau legs, shredding correspondence and ghastly, sick-making Valentine cards from Decrepit, an electric delight went through me like about five hundred volts.

After a minute, fizzing, I went to the long French doors and unbolted them.

Outside lay the night, one vast shining. That same midnight I've mentioned before, bright as some dark day. Yes, that was it. *Night* was the new black.

*

I found him. Or was taken to him.

The bat came as I was pacing across the top lawn, right between the two lamps, one of which had worked though it was smashed. The bat simply flitted from nothing, or so it looked, and settled at once on my shoulder.

I felt startled. But also sort of flattered.

"Where do I go?" I asked it. "Mashefla?" I tentatively added.

It rustled. I reviewed notions that bats got caught in long hair. But they don't, and anyhow off it fluttered, a tiny zig-zaggy bird, leading me down the garden into the trees.

(I think we went by the statues. Or were their pedestals vacant?)

Bats hold night in their eyes. But, too, they are *made* of night, I thought, poetic and somehow drunk. And owls are made of moonlight and carry the yellow autumn moon in both eyes. Badgers naturally combine both elements, and—

Poetry ended, or began, as he was *there.* He'd stepped out of shadows, or out of the trunk of a hornbeam. Or out of that other dimension where they live, the Lordly Ones.

Was he a lord? Yes.

All in black, clothed in night and scatters of silvery starriness, like metal embroidery or fringes—I couldn't be sure. Not dressed as he had been, so he'd pass as modern—or mortal. His hair—no, owls only had a little of the moon in them. The rest had all gone into the hair of Finn, who for all I knew might well be a High King.

"I got some *worldly* money," I said. "At a guess about one and a half thousand pounds. I tried to get other things but—"

"They were already removed. I have received those things."

I resisted the power of his voice and said, "If you sent the *rats* to steal from them—why ask it of me?"

"Did I ask? No. It was a demand. Which, as best you could, you fulfilled. Consider the legends and tales. It's well known my kind will send yours animal helpers, where necessary."

"But—"

"Your obedience and intention sufficed. Not so hard a task for you then, the first."

"Did they bring you the plastic too?"

"Those little cards? They did. And jewelry of a very dull and inferior design. How the jewelsmiths fail now. Where's their skill gone?"

I was so electric and elated, I couldn't worry. It all seemed, all this, quite reasonable.

I babbled, "Her credit limit all told is about twenty thousand. Maybe more."

"Then," he said, "it shall be spent."

Dazzled by the shadowy mask of his face, the talented jewelwork of his eyes, I said, "Only thing is, once she sees she's lost them, she'll cancel the cards. And you wouldn't anyway get through the security checks."

"You will do it," he said.

"*I* will?" I thought, There, just what you were afraid of. But I couldn't feel afraid. "Then I'll be caught and sent to prison."

His smile came, scimitar cut on darkness. He said no word of reassurance or denial. He would be indifferent to my little troubles.

I said, "And what do you want me to buy?"

"You," he said, "may choose."

"But what will I do with these things? I won't be able to keep them at the house—are they for you?"

"No."

"Then—"

"Do what you like also with the purchases. They must only be bought."

Then he turned, and suddenly, from off the tapestry of the glowing night, something seemed to be drawn aside. And that was when I fully saw. Saw those things I've already written about—the star lights in the trees, sleeping birds, badgers playing and coming to him to be caressed, rabbits in leaping floods, the platinum-blue solid smoke of the wolf.

We were deep in the forest by then. The moon lasted forever. The night existed out of time. Moths passed like thin flakes of bronze blown from some elder anvil. . . .

So it would be silly to question further. Even if I had been, meaningless to try to be logical.

But despite all that, it was since I saw the wolf that I understood properly how slightly I mattered. I mean, I *had* known. I'd been well-trained, after all, to recognize I amounted to nothing in any scheme of things. But when I realized he could call up such creatures as an ancient ghostly wolf, and that, if I failed, or merely *bored* him, he could give me over to them—to wolves, or bears, or other phantasmal beasts unknown, unremembered, but searingly, spiritually actual—*feed* me to them—then I became like dust. As they say we are. As we are.

But it was my own fault. Shouting about three wishes. Waking up the occult bargain so it could turn on its head.

In the stories, in *reality*, there is something terrifyingly *lawful* about the Folk. Yet their laws, of which the tales are full, are strict, and absolute—and to our kind, mostly indecipherable. Inimical. Like seeing rain fall. I know vaguely about the physics of why rain falls, but as I watch the rain, I don't grasp the physics. I only know the rain is falling. . . .

We walked, he and I, in this forest, or partly in some other world, until the sky began infinitesimally to alter, and the moon sank low.

He said very little to me. Soon I couldn't recall any of those words that hadn't touched on the bargain. I said nothing else at all.

And then not only speech—a sort of mist closes in on memory.

I *do* remember toadstools like opals. I *do* remember a

stream plaited with what looked like candle-flames. And the
moths. And the wolf. But it's like a dream you can't quite
keep hold of, only fragments, and the atmosphere, the wonder or fear—

And it was, with no warning, somehow as if I was just
waking up, widening my eyes, and he was gone. And I was
surrounded by a circle of glittering green lights about the
level of my knees.

I stood still and felt no recognizable emotion. And before
my brain could get a grip and make the adrenaline come,
the lights shifted, changed shape, and danced away. I saw it
had been a ring of foxes, grey in the predawn, a fairy fox-
ring, eyes catching the last of the moon, or the first of the
sun, and me at the centre of them, where he had left me.

But now they'd trotted away between the trees, and the
sky was filling itself in as if, before, pure outer space had been
there. Traipsing back towards the house, I found my jeans
were soaked with dew, my hair was full of fronds and tiny
feathers. I felt drained, sad, old. Eternal. A human cipher
stranded forever in a temporary, fluctuating world of hardship
and dishonour, whose suffering, to the Fair Folk, was like a
Tom and Jerry cartoon.

8

WHATEVER the credit limit was on Ear Rainer's cards, I
spent 11,962 pounds of it. From And's smaller single card I
spent 879 pounds. Also all the cash was spent. I took some
of the jewelry—a necklace, some rings—into three or four
jewellers shops, where they paid me too little for them.
Mostly I implied they'd been gifts from friends, or my father, but now I needed money for college. No one argued.
This cash I spent too.

No one argued about the cards, either.

What did I buy? Everything I could see or think of in

the glory-hole of Spawdock. Vases, books, cameras, paintings, curtains, a suite of chairs and couch, a table, clothes, a music centre, shoes, ornaments, food—a hamper was one of the items—I lost track. Really, content didn't interest me. I was only exhilarated. I wasn't afraid anymore I'd be arrested. But none of the objects meant anything. Since fourteen I'd never had much, and now I seemed to have got right out of the habit of having things. I didn't buy anything I wanted. Didn't want anything to buy. It was flatly done to obey his demand. Symbolic. Fatuous. Immensely enjoyably disturbing.

But how did I get away with any of this?

Let me—again—backtrack. The last you saw of me was wending through the grasses after my nocturnal walkabout with the Lordly Finn, in the wood, the wolf, and ring of fox eyes and so on.

Needless to say, I hadn't had any sleep, and when, dew-drenched and feather-haired, I reached the house, I made extra strong coffee. If anyone had seen me they might have thought I had been with a lover, in the forest. But no one emerged until ten, and I was by then cleaned up, and prowling with a duster for show.

And came out first, looking glamorously dishevelled. Round the kimonoed edges of her I could see a stupefied Dougal lying in her bed. Ah, so that was why they hadn't bothered to check on all the noise last night.

And stalked straight by me to the bathroom, but directly after that, Unmum sprawled out into the corridor.

"For God's sake, get me some coffee, Lois. And toast. Don't burn it. Hurry up."

But before I was halfway back down the stairs, I could hear her snarling at Oaf, and Oaf shrilling in a resumption of last night's row. And next came this alarming, wavering shriek—which turned out to be Dougal discovering that his pet watch and gold ear studs were his no more.

By the time they cascaded into the kitchen, where I was

about to empty the bin, they were mostly in uproar. Ear Rainer was in hysterics. Only And looked icily across at me and said, "We all seem to have been robbed last night. Know anything about that, Lousy?"

I heard myself say coolly, "You mean, am I missing anything?"

"Aside from brains, looks and talent? No, I meant did you have anything to do with it? I have to tell you, Louse, if *you're* the one took my gold coin necklace—"

But Oaf burst in, "It's *rats.* I *told* you. I *saw* it."

"Don't be pathetic. Rats don't steal all your money."

"Oh Christ," said Ear Rainer. She'd gone veiny white as a marble slab. She plunged out of the kitchen and away towards the living room bureau.

From whence her screams presently rocked the house.

Of course I was the obvious suspect. But then there were all the gnawings and rat shit, and all the chewed-up letters in the bureau, and Oaf chuntering on and on, until even Dougal confessed he'd seen a rat in the passage when he went to the bathroom in the night (i.e., went to And's bedroom in the night) and said rat had had something shiny in its mouth. (*"Teeth?"* And had snapped. Maybe their union hadn't been such a success?)

I then did something very odd. I just got up and drifted away, and out of the house. In the chaos no one challenged me. I thought, Ear Rainer will check her wallet now, and And's, and they'll find all the plastic's gone too. They'll call and stop the cards. But all the time, I was strolling down the nettled lawns. I was walking between the statues and seeing they seemed definitely misplaced; obviously the sun had come up before they were entirely back in the correct positions.

And then I thought, opening the gate, I'm tranced, *spelled*, I'm being *made* to do this. Only five hours ago I was out here all dreary and philosophical, and now, what *is* this I feel?

I had an immediate memory of walking home from school, when I was about twelve, and my father appeared unexpectedly, handsome and elegant and all smiles. And he said, "I'll take you to tea." And we went to tea.

Happy. That was it.

I felt happy.

Understandable then, but why now? I really must be going mad.

About ten feet into the big historic trees, I saw everything laid out ready for me on a broad sunlit stone. All the rat-got credit cards, and heaps of the jewelry he'd found so unaesthetic. All the money, including the rolled-up notes I'd brought him, which, without any contact, he had taken from me.

I bent to the hoard. It was pristine. Something was painted on the stone, too, in a sort of goldy-silvery pen again. Five words: *Spend extravagantly. Whatever you wish.*

He knew it couldn't be, any of it, for me. "*So* kind," I sarcastically muttered. "Spend extravagantly till they catch me."

But I gathered everything up, stuffed it in my pockets and in the clean plastic bag I'd been about to put into the kitchen bin. I rambled through the wood, whistling to birds and squirrels that didn't run away, smelling aftershave and ambergris—even though I don't know what that smells like—tar and roast goose and toilet cleaner. I was—relaxed.

A wasp followed me. I had no fear of it, although I recalled Dad once laughingly telling me *wasp* was an acronym: WASP, which stood for We Always Sting People.

I laughed too. Laughed and ran laughing and caught the bus, and sat there, a golden thief, in the middle of all the shut-in-tight disapproval, and with that same snotty driver, and I didn't mind. Somehow I still kept thinking of Dad, and it wasn't making me sad at all, and I thought of how he'd taken me shopping and said, "You can have whatever you want, Lois."

And even when I recollected today I'd be arrested, it made me giggle.

However.

It happened in the first store I entered.

I'd just wandered into the lingerie section, whipped up an armful of expensive frillies and plonked them down with Ear's biggest card, the platinum mega-beast. I was doomed, so a headlong charge seemed best. But they accepted everything, the card, me, my signature—which wasn't hers—only. . . .

There were mirrors all over the shop. And standing there I glanced up, and in the mirror, I saw Ear Rainer. She was *there*. She was staring at me. She was staring at me because *I* was staring at me. By which I mean, what I saw in the glass was me—but I'd taken on *her* appearance. Even to the bleach-blonde, the red lipstick, her crow's-feet eyes—her hands—and glaring at them in front of me, they *were* her hands, rings and red talons and all. And I was wearing her slumming clothes, top and trousers—and then I properly saw the signature I'd signed, and this too—was *hers*.

I hadn't cleverly faked it, hadn't even written her name but mine. But it was her name and her writing. I wondered if I'd pass out.

I thought, Don't let me stay looking like *this*—

But after I left the store, I tried And's card in the deli, and the steak sandwich they gave me—well, it was the hand of And that took the sandwich, a nice tanned young slim hand, with oval manicured nails, and that little scar she had on her thumb, where she'd said some lover bit her when she was fifteen.

Was it And's teeth biting the sandwich now?

But no. Outside the deli it was only me again. Lois. I checked out Lois's reflection in every shop window, I can tell you.

Nevertheless, I was Oaf when I flogged Oaf's jewelry.

And, when I flogged And's coin necklace. I was Ear Rainer once more when I passed over the diamond and ruby bauble James gave her, that looked like a bad Christmas tree decoration. I didn't say that time it was for college, obviously. I said, "My last boyfriend gave me this. It's vulgar. He has no taste."

Funny. My *voice* was always my own. I'd never concentrated so hard on hearing my voice. I heard it was too young for Ear, too slovenly and low for Oaf and And.

I sounded like an actress acting a part. How apt.

It was crazy. Crazy.

In the end I went into a posh pub in Ear Rainer mode and with Ear's medium card, the gold one, and got fucking bloody shit-faced drunk.

By then I'd bought all the other things, the furniture and hamper and stuff. Had them all sent to made-up addresses, some of which were probably, by the law of averages, real. What a surprise for them.

The cards hadn't been stopped, either.

Why was that?

I hiccuped onto the bus, and the driver—him again—gave me a look, and I said huskily to him, "You know, I've always fancied you rotten." And his mouth fell open and I thought, poor old geezer, he believes me.

Fell asleep, naturally. Pissed.

At my stop, he halted the bus, and came back in person to wake me up.

"You shouldn't oughta drink like that, luv," he whispered, as I wobbled off the bus and fell into a bush.

But I was in the sorcerous wood.

I ran off, calling joyously, "Finn! Finn of Sherwood! Where are you, Finn my darling dear!"

Finn didn't show, and when I reached the garden wall, I threw up all over the brink of the fey forest. But I'd done what he said—though what use that had been to him I'd no idea.

As for them, they hadn't noticed I was gone, that's how much attention they ever paid me, unless they wanted something, which for some reason they hadn't. And they'd never be able to pin any of it on me.

*

THE police were coldly patient, then quite stern with Ear Rainer. Finally they kind of suggested she see a psychiatrist, and asked did she know wasting police time was an offence?

Obviously, all the signatures were hers, or And's. People in the jewelers and elsewhere had described only And and Oaf and Ear.

The most damning extra proof of the family's mental instability was that none of the cards had been stopped. "If you believed them stolen, why exactly didn't you make that call?" the cops inquired. "The phone didn't work—" "And you have no cell phone?" "They didn't work either. None of them. Even the car—Not until that evening, when I did call, I called the card helpline at once—All this money gone. I've had to get on to my broker! And none of you will do a thing. Why do I pay taxes—" "I suggest you calm down, madam," said the police, like a death sentence. Nobody had dared try to tell them rats had thieved the money and cards. Only among themselves did I hear Oaf and Ear grumbling that someone must have trained the rats to do it. The same person who was a master of disguise and signature forgery. Obviously not the cretinous Lois.

I did wonder what would have happened if Dougal had had a credit card. Would I have looked like Dougal? (The ear studs and watch I hadn't even bothered to sell, just dumped back in the woods, with anything else superfluous.)

For me, strangely, or not, it was already fading away by that time, two days later, when the police stood frowning on us all.

Because, although I hadn't seen a flame-white hair of Finn's head after our magical walk, I had found another leaf, this one lying on my pillow. Two words again, clear in gold. *Worldly Power.*

*

THAT was my Dreamtime. Do you see? The kind of thing where you're between two worlds, and one of those not worldly at all. In a daze. *Ensorcelled.* I look back at it now and shudder, because what the hell did I think I was doing in the middle of all that—a tranced robot carrying out bizarre nonsensical orders, and, by then, glad to do so. And none of it made sense, did it? Because if he could get his other creatures to steal for him, and then didn't even *want*, or have the remotest interest in, what was done with the cash—why had he forced/seduced me into having any role in it? Besides, he was powerful enough that he could put on me the illusion of another, just as the legends tell us the Folk can. So why did he need me at all? Oh, but that was part of it, wasn't it? Some minuscule atom in my heart or soul, singing to me that he must therefore, against all odds, be fascinated in his turn by me. *Why* was the only mystery. But then. In the fairy tale, it's always the downtrodden girl, hidden in the cinders or the smelly catskin, who gets the prince.

9

THE first person who knocked on the front door the next day was the bus driver. I'd been dusting the downstairs carelessly, so I was the one who undid the door. There he stood.

Oh God. He wasn't so old, was he, only about fortyish, but to me he looked antique. And he'd dressed up tidy-casual. And he had a box of chocs, which he thrust at me.

"I just came along," he casually remarked, lighting a nonchalant fag, "to see if you were okay."

"Oh—er. Yes."

"You shouldn't drink like that. You're only—what?—twenty or so?" I didn't argue. "Anyhow. In vino veritas, eh," he surprisingly added. "Fancy going out with me, luv?"

I was frozen. Clutching the chocs like a raft in the wild ocean. Not wanting to hurt him, not really, yet annoyedly desperate to make him go away.

"I'm sorry about what I said," I said. "On your bus."

"It was fine. Cheered me up. Won't tell no one." (I thought, I bet he's told every other driver on the station. In Britain.)

"You see," I faltered. "I'm actually seeing someone. And well, he wouldn't like it."

To my consternation, the bus driver said haughtily, "I don't reckon you are. You're a real mess, girl. But *I* like you. I can see your inner light, like."

"Well that's awfully sweet, but I really am, and—"

My mouth dropped wide as if for the dentist's, my eyes popped. I choked on my own spit and bent double, coughing, still clutching the chocolates, and finally sneezing on them.

Finn said quietly, "Sorry, my unlucky man. She's telling you the truth and nothing but. I'm her bloke."

Where had he *come* from? Out of thin air, evidently. The driver hadn't heard him—Finn hadn't been there to hear—and spun round with his poor ears bright pink, thinking no doubt Finn had crept silently round the house, an aspect perhaps of some plot I and Finn had cooked up to humiliate him.

"But I agree with you," Finn said, "she *is* a mess. Despite my best efforts to smarten her up."

He was summer-unsuitably dressed, in biker-like black leathers, with a circlet of green stones round the column of his throat. Ice-wave hair. Skin brown as a flawless Caribbean tan. His eyes had pin-sharp yellow lights in them. He smelled wonderful, and looked unbearably handsome, unthinkably rich. Miraculous, like—something quite new.

"She's a bloody drunk and all," gobbled the driver viciously. "Came on to me on my bus—"

"Oh, she does that. I have to watch her like a hawk."

I'd stopped choking. I'd wiped the choc-box carefully and now handed it back to the driver. I had no right to it. He took it, too, and marched away down the drive. I could see now he had a little ordinary car parked there. He got in, and drove away.

"Here is the front door, the main entry of this house," said Finn. "Now you will ask me in."

He'd told me I must come to this, and to it I'd come. "Come in, Lord Finn," I rhymingly said, and stood back to allow him the doorway.

Something happened (again) as he did this. Something. Like so much I've tried and failed to describe here, I can't explain. Again, it was a sort of light-change—as if the sun had blinked.

And then, as the day steadied, Ear Rainer swanned through from the kitchen where I'd served their breakfasts, in her robe, unmade-up, hair like straw, and with her nail polish chipped.

It was a priceless instant. Under other circumstances, I'd always have treasured it.

She posed, a mess far worse than Lois, staring at the most beautiful man she was ever likely to see, and slowly her nasty face went red as a Turner sunset.

*

EVERYTHING, until then, had seemed to go quite slowly.

This would go quite fast.

Ear Rainer managed to speak. "Who—?"

"I am Finn," he said. "It is a longer name. But Finn will do."

"Hello, *Finn*." Striving to recover her cool. "And what can we do for you?"

"Your house," he said, "is on my land."

"Your—but surely not. It was purchased *with* the land—four acres—"

"It's mine," he said.

She didn't only look embarrassed now. She looked huffy.

"I don't think—"

"Hush now," he said. *"Huishla."* He said this quite gently.

I hated her. Still hate her, or the her she was then. But the sudden panic in her now-sallow face as she tried to speak, and scrambled her hands to her neck, her eyes all dark and scared—filled me, too, with fright. Because I could see he'd stopped her voice, simple as that.

He was a being of terror. But I'd forgotten, and she hadn't known.

"Go, sit down," he said. She shook her head, but he pointed at her, and she turned round as if something *turned* her round, and stumbled into the living room with the rat-gnawed bureau.

Worldly Power. Power over property and persons. *I'd* given it to him? Apparently.

He spoke then in that other language, the tongue that Dougal had pronounced sounded like Yiddish or Romany. What he said was *"Grom si carripeth peshpai."* Or so it sounded to me. What did it mean? A shadow fell, and fell in again and again on itself, like folds of a transparent dark cloak. A wind blew, light and green, smelling of sap and cinnamon and white wine, straight across the house. That was all.

Though from the kitchen drifted Dougal and Oaf, sort of swimmy-eyed and also staring.

Halfway down the stairs came And. And halted.

Dougal said, "Oh Jesus he's—he's—"

Oaf said, "Shut up, Dougal. Hello, you're Finn, aren't you? We've heard such a lot about you. But what is it"—her eyes had unswum and were filled by lust and delight—"you're going to teach me?"

"Your lesson," said Finn.

She thought—*Finn*—was another tutor—

How did she know he was called Finn? He must have let them all know, by occult telepathy, when he told Ear.

But Dougal, there in the hall with its damp-notched walls, elderly banisters, foul modern paintings bought for Ear by Decrepit . . . Dougal had dropped down on his knees.

Finn ignored both Dougal and Oaf.

He was looking up the stair. At And.

Something happened also to her. Her face grew beautiful (well, it always had been, rather), and she faintly, exquisitely flushed, a blush as unlike that of Ear Rainer's, or mine, as was conceivable. She lowered her eyes, her mascaraed lashes long, like the thickly multiple legs of many spiders on her cheeks.

Dougal interrupted, "Please don't make me," said Dougal, in a piteous whine, "I've really worked at this. I *liked* it, liked being this. Come on, I've been this for years. Got a degree and everything. *I've learned to read*—"

It was puzzling.

Finn only seemed, when I peered at him, dismissive.

Still gazing at And, he said, I thought to me, "He is a kind of changeling your kind took in. What shall I do, Lois?"

Sullenly I said, watching his eyes (not dismissive at all) on *her*, "Does it count, what *I* say?"

Finn glanced at me. "Every human has its secret animal side. I will show you Dougal's." (Dougal groaned, fell all the way over and went into the foetal position on the hall tiles.) "He has been this before. One day I may allow him human semblance again."

"Wait—" I cried, "are you saying Dougal isn't—I mean, what *is* Dougal—?"

Dougal, as I'd weirdly suspected, was a rodent. A small, slender, greyish mouse.

Forget all the computer effects in movies. This was neither convincing nor Oscar-worthy. It was only a young man with auburn hair curled up on the floor, and then the *illusion* ran off him like rainy dye. He sort of *washed away*. And then there was the mouse, scampering about, squeaking, so And leaned over the banister (And who had, presumably, *fucked* him) and said, astonished, "The little *cunt*."

"Was he always a mouse really?" I childishly asked Finn.

"To all intents, would you not say? Who," he said to me, "is she?"

"The other one's sister."

"Name her."

"I thought you knew all our names," I said.

"Queen over Mankind," he said.

"What?"

"Her name's meaning."

"If you know—why ask?"

Disdainful, he said, "How would I know? It's when I ask you, all the names are there."

"But then you read my mind—"

"Ah, not like that at all." But he had lost interest in me. Not that he'd ever had any. He beckoned to And—to Andromeda, Queen over Mankind. And she came shyly down the stairs.

In any case, I thought as I stood boiling with assorted, mixed feelings, he had cast her image over me, hadn't he? I mean, when I was using her card, flogging her necklace. He knew her well by sight, how she looked, and what she was. Perhaps, I thought (taking refuge in inner debate?), none of our names mean anything until one of us speaks—*thinks* them at him.

The amazing mouse-Dougal, meanwhile, went rushing

up the hallway, found a mouse-size aperture, and struggled mousefully through. I thought how he—it—had read *The Waxwork Strangler* and *Nights of Horror*. God. A literate but moronic mouse.

Other events were occurring by then.

I said the walls were damp, and stuff grew there. Out of them now was emerging this dense emerald green fur of *bearded* moss. It *swelled* out, even as I watched it, moving in a muscular and businesslike way. As that happened, other sorts of plants were beginning to glimmer down from the ceiling, polished creepers and ropes of ivy. The banister was already festooned with vines. A sharp little *crack*, and some boughs of pussy willow, still hung with their golden spring caterpillar-tails, pressed around the doorway of the dining room. Irresistibly I waded over a tiled floor now shifting and ebbing up small pools, rushes, and the occasional worm or frog, and gawked in at the big room where I'd served so many dinners. The pussy willow was already quite a sturdy young tree, growing pretty tall. And there were also lots of bushes and stands of briar and nettle making a healthy start. A decorative red shrub hung down from the ceiling like a fiery chandelier, and the table was tilting from a couple of energetic small pines, whose roots had torn the carpet.

Was all this another illusion? I touched the pussy willow, and it felt real as the plaster it had broken to get through.

After all, the house had always, clandestinely, been trying to be just like this. Moulds growing, rats tunnelling, leaks and drippings, mushrooms in the bidet. Even Dougal the Mouse had found a ready-established mouse-hole. Probably he'd soon make lots of mouse friends, telling them urgently all about the books he'd read . . . perhaps he'd scare them with *Nights of Horror* stories.

When I looked back to see what Oaf was doing about the rising of the green, she was only standing there, next to And

and crowded out by And, but still gazing with her Oaf eyes at Finn, like a sort of tranced groupie.

But Finn had seemed to notice her at last. He smiled at her tenderly, and leaning forward, kissed her on the forehead. "*Sarpa,*" he said, soft as a breath.

I thought she'd fainted. She dropped down and down—Where had she gone?

And, too, stared after her sister. She didn't look upset, only perplexed, and then she *saw*, and the most wicked smile lilted over her face.

"Did you do that?"

"It seems," he said, to And, "I did."

Between the fronds and tile fragments and madly bouncing pond life, I made out a thin dark ripple, that at first I thought was only more water—

"What kind of snake *is* she?" asked And, sounding now intrigued, but merely from a botanical or biological standpoint.

"Her bite is poison," he said.

I thought, Dead right. I thought, Oh, he's turned Oaf into an adder.

"Better watch your step," I remarked.

But no one bothered with me, and Oaf the adder was also gone. She'd eat the frogs, no doubt. She'd always been greedy.

When we three, or rather they two, and I, walked into the living room, Ear Rainer was scrabbling ratlike in the bureau.

As Finn entered she spun about, and there was a *pistol* in her shaking hands. I hadn't known she kept anything like that in the house.

Finn spoke sharply. "Lois."

That was all.

I asked myself in utter turmoil what *I* was supposed to do about any of it—but in that second Ear Rainer dropped the gun. It spurted away over the floor, red eyes winking. No more pistol, just one more rat.

Though a fraction slower than the hall and dining room, the living room was now catching up fast, wetly greenish all over as the inside of a huge marrow. As we glanced about at it, collapses and burgeonings filled the space, and from a great jagged crater in one wall, what I think was a pine marten exploded, chittering.

All so *sudden*, as they say.

I had to shift my ground. A quite mature oak tree had abruptly heaved its way up from the cellars, lifting, as it broke through the floor, the expensive carpet with it like a shawl, before dropping it in contempt. The ceiling was a writhing mass of moss and roots. Snakes or creepers snarled the curtains.

Anything Decrepit James and his Men had attempted in this room was being dismantled, especially by the pine marten. Anything anyone had ever done, through two and a half centuries.

Ear Rainer leaned there on the leafy wavering air, dumbly crying huge tears. Something worse than tears was happening to her.

While far over our heads a tremendous bang and thump announced some other flora or fauna getting the ultimate upper hand it had been rehearsing for the past two years. Counterpoint, a shower of the badly secured roof tiles flew off the roof, hailed by the windows, and smashed on the terrace. The Queen over Mankind, though, smiling into Finn's smile, now paid no attention. Ear Rainer was by then past it, too.

10

I had to take James on a kind of tour of the house later. Also, like all proper guides, had to explain to him its history, that was, how it had got like that, but mostly what things had been before metamorphosis. "And that was the dining table," for example, showing him the mass of pines and spines with a hedgehog pottering in it. Or, "And that was the downstairs shower room"—a reedy frog-pool with elaborate fountain from the fractured shower. The upstairs was unnegotiable.

Birds sang from tree limbs, cornices and leafy light fittings. They also shat everywhere.

I don't think James believed me about Oaf the Adder, or Dougal the Mouse. I don't think he believed my gushing confession about Finn, High King of the Fair People, the Lordly Ones, and the Triple Trellechy.

But about Ear Rainer he had to believe me. He could see for himself.

I'd always hated her, and I've said, with just cause. And I hated Decrepit James because he was hers. But when he went up to her that late afternoon, forcing his way through the indoor woods, with the sunlight slanted like apricot rust between the veils of ivy and daggered leaves, I stopped hating them both.

"Did she suffer—*is* she—is she *suffering?*" he pleaded.

How could I be sure? Does it hurt a lot, to be turned into a twisted, stunted, gnarly tree? Because that was what had happened to Ear Rainer. Right there in front of me in the verdant living room, as And and Finn gazed into each other's eyes.

Ear had writhed a lot, like the roots in the ceiling. But apart from writhing, she hadn't been able to move, really, certainly not to run away, and as the twigs and bark came out of the pores of her skin, and the moss powdered her face to its final makeover, she'd sort of cranked into position and petrified.

I hadn't known at first what type of tree she'd become. Then I remembered a picture in a library book. She was a crab apple. And on her clawed and tangled limbs, these little acid-hard fruit buds were growing.

Worst of all, you could almost see her face—well, you could see it, her face and her eyes, caught there frozen to wood in her trunk. I hoped James *couldn't* see.

But he stood in front of her and he must have seen, mustn't he, because obviously he credited that this was her, his true love, spelled Irene. And he started to cry.

"I think—I think she's alive," I said. "I mean, she's a growing tree. Look, her fruits are all right."

"Oh God," sobbed James. "These things don't happen."

And he seized the crab apple in his arms, rocking himself and it—her—slowly, to an ancient rhythm of grief.

An old nest tumbled from her boughs.

"Sorry, James," I said.

I'd tried to find him some vodka when he first arrived, crashing and shouting at the front door. A drink for the shock. But as we'd paddled and plunged through the undergrowth and ponds, pushing aside hanging branches and blackbirds, you couldn't really locate anything like a bottle.

He hadn't protested at the supernatural catastrophe at all. He'd just said, "What?" a few times. And then he'd waited for his brain to catch up, starting at the branched-over gap above the hall where there had been ceiling. And then he'd said, "Where's Ear Rainer? Where are the girls?" And when I told him, and added to be careful of Oaf, she was an adder now, he had only gone tripping and floundering across to the tree-wound living room doorway and swarmed through it. And found Ear Rainer. And cried.

Soon after that twilight fell on the house, and into it. Several parts of walls had by then given way, and it wasn't difficult for this last invader to invade.

When I went out on the lawns, the nettles had grown twice their height, or so it seemed. They looked—*fluffy*. Another tree was spreading from a defunct chimney. Bats circled round and round. Messengers?

All across the front of the house, definitely, there was a

message, written large, in the same gold-silvery slime used on the other messages, those on the leaves, that I'd pretended were made by clever felt-tip pens. This, however, was more like graffiti—or a repossession notice—or an estate agent's board reading *Sold*.

The moon rose early and the message shone. Four huge letters. *UOUS*. And then a mark, rather like a tick (✓).

When James came crawling out again, fighting off ivy, brushing twigs (Ear Rainer's?) from his hair, he too turned and glared at this notice written on the house. But he made no comment on it. Maybe, to him, it only looked like one more random fungus.

He presently said, "We should go to the police." And then he said, "Should we go to the police?"

"I don't know what we could say."

"Well—it's a kind of a natural disaster, isn't it? Is it? What shall I do about her?" he ended.

"Ear Rainer, do you mean?" inanely I queried.

"Well, should I dig her up—would that be what I should do? You can get big pots. Or there's the patio—"

I hesitated. "She might not—trees don't always survive transplanting."

"No." He began to bite his nails and his awful gold rings flashed like his tears. "I thought she'd be something else, if she had to be a tree—a willow perhaps. Or a cherry—" he astoundingly mused. Then, "This man," he said, "this fucker that caused all that—can't you—can't you ask him if—"

"No," I said. "That's the deal. I can't ask *him* for anything. He needs me, yes, but he doesn't have to give me anything in return. It's part of this bargain, this debt. It's so old. It's so elaborate and—straightforward. I have to help. Without me, it won't work. But I don't get rewarded. No favours. No riches. No—nothing at all."

"Then *why'd* you help the bastard?"

I shrugged. I couldn't tell him.

He said he'd drive to Spawdock, and I thought that included driving me there. But he just walked off and left me. His BMW still worked, though it made some indigestive noises when he started it. Then he drove away and left me, standing on the lawn. Did he label me a traitor to my loving stepmum and her dolls of daughters? I think actually he just forgot I'd been there. The way Finn nearly had.

*

YES, the debt was old, old as the hills. The repayment required for all those mortal centuries and eternal moments of the Folk, when humans had been given three wishes, and their puny dreams came true. And I got to pay it.

He had spelled—*(ha!) spelled*—it out for me, Lord Finn. Before he went away.

While the Folk have endless magical powers and mortals seldom have any, it's the mortal *always* who is the medium for fairy magic. Indeed, it rather seems the less magical the human, the more mileage the Folk can get out of them (think of the stories). Why? It's one more law of balance. We— think too about this one—we *earth* them, and then they can work wonders.

That's how it used to be, is still. Only hardly anyone now, at least in our neck of the woods (another pun), calls on the Folk, let alone thinks they exist. Had I? I'm fairly sure I *hadn't*. It was just a fluke I uttered those fatal words, *"Three wishes."* And I did it three times. Of course, conceivably the sorcerous forest egged me on to it, that wood reeking of delight and vileness, with its bad colours and strange tidal moods. Perhaps it wasn't chance I did what I did. Perhaps even then they *persuaded* me to do it. I was an ideal candidate. Persuadable.

And once he came to me, up out of the hollow dimension that, for all I know, may even be Hell itself, and took on the form I saw, and *fascinated* me—using all the time *my* earthing power to make *his* powers stronger and more strong—then I was his dupe forever.

So I had to obey him. Still must, if it comes to that. And no, I really do get nothing in return.

Plainly, however, he had a hidden agenda. Because what he "wished" for, even if traditionally symbolic, was rather insanely purposeless. The thieving and spending, the giving of entry by a front door and therefore control. Even the third wish, even that. Or was the third wish simply insult to injury?

I'd still been standing like a stone, gaping at Ear Rainer the crab apple tree, when Finn asked—excuse me, *demanded*—his third wish of me.

Again, it was the traditional one.

A leaf dropped into my hands, gold-written. It read: *Heart's Desire.*

Grouchy, with a foreknowing only a kid of one wouldn't have had, I scowled at him. "Which is?"

He nodded, smiling his Finn smile. "You will give me her."

He meant And. Andromeda. Perhaps in law, some other fey mad law, that was in my gift too. When Dad married Ear, he linked us all in worldly terms together.

Andromeda. Finn wanted *her.* Riches, Power, the Heart's Desire of longed-for sexual love.

In that unearthly woodland light which had already filled the greeneried house, he looked now less a man himself than some chill statue of great beauty, and she—she looked like that as well, as if she were *catching* unique glamour and strangeness from him. But her smile was like a ferret's sharp teeth. *She* had never believed in magic of any sort. But sex, authority, having only the best—naturally she believed in those.

No, And wasn't a symbol of the bargain to him, like the plastic or the opened door. Her, he *wanted*.

He sang to her then. So low I barely heard it, but every cell of me *did* hear. And her eyes flooded with a lambency . . . love? It was beyond love.

Probably he had seen her long ago, two years back, when *she* was sixteen. Desired her? Yes. And not been able to do a thing to get her, until some blithering moron started honking about three wishes under his eldritch bloody trees. And so gave him the mortal medium without which zilch could happen.

"Take her," I said. "You're welcome, mate."

And my own tears of shame and rage rolled down the back of my nose and throat to wet the edges of my shattered heart.

The last I saw of him? The instant when he took her hand. That pretty, slim, brown hand with its tiny scar. And they both vanished.

Me he had never touched.

(Sometimes I imagine them, riding together on that thing—what's it called—Dougal the Mouse would know—a *raedh*, is it? When the Lordly Ones go over the meadows and through the woods, clad in samite and stars, and on their fine white horses, whose silk manes and tails are strung with gems made from moonlight. Or is it motorbikes now? He and she, Finn and Andromeda. King and Queen.)

There are so many tales of mortals lured away underground. That's where she is. His lover. That brainless rotten waste-of-space little bitch.

Take her. You're welcome.

Even the Folk have no taste, it seems. Just as, without our cloddish cringing adoration and awe, they can't get a purchase for their power on the earth, and are *powerless*.

So what, aside from Andromeda, did he, and does he, really want me for?

It's so obvious, when you think of it. I'm his publicist, aren't I? Lois, agent to the Fair Folk—even if I don't get fifteen percent. So few of you believe in his kind now (and those that truly do are frankly fucking fey as the Folk— therefore *useless* to the Folk; you do get those sometimes, like the ones I heard on the bus, who *sense* but push it away, and wouldn't be seen dead trying to make a contact). My job, therefore, is to *make* you believe. Against your will. It's like Tinker Bell, isn't it, in the play? If you don't believe in her, she'll die. They don't die, of course. They just have to wait. Down there or in there, wherever they are, inhabiting their crystal palaces, among their purple trees, wining and dining and dancing and hunting and making love. And they are *bored* to death; worse, as they never *do* die.

But how do I spread the word then? The usual way. A whisper here, a mutter there. Weird anecdotes told at parties. Aided always by the fact the weirdness really is there— my clients, the Fair Folk. Waiting for your call.

There are surely others involved in this work too. Or so I guess.

11

I'M married now. The bus driver. His name is Ed. Old enough to be my father, though not as old as my Dad was when he died.

It was after I caught the last bus through the forest, that night when the house became part of the woods. Ed wasn't driving, but I was crying a bit, on the back seat. And at the last stop in town, when I had to get off, Ed was there, waiting to have a word with the other driver. It was after eleven-thirty. Ed stared at me. He said, "You in trouble again, eh?" Which was either sarcastic or nice of him, following what had happened with Finn and Ed. But then Ed drew me aside, into the fish-and-chip shop. We ended up at a table eating chips, and I said I'd finished with my "boyfriend." "Bit of a bully, wasn't he," said Ed thoughtfully. I nodded. Naturally. I said, "And I didn't live at that house, I just worked there and slept in the attic. And they've sacked me." And Ed said, "Well, you can kip on my couch. I won't lay a finger on you. Promise." Which promise he kept for a whole month. The bed was more comfortable anyway.

He's a good man, Ed, but not so good he gets on my nerves.

He lets me do very much whatever I want, too. And gives me generous what-he-calls Housekeeping Money. And it's okay really, doing the cooking and cleaning for just us. And he's so appreciative if I bake a cake. He got me some ID too, a copy of my birth certificate and so on, and then a passport. (My name's different now, incidentally. And I'm officially two years older than I am—twenty-eight now. He managed all that too, or a friend of his.) We take holidays in Spain and the Caribbean. He's proud of me. He always says I have such a lovely thin figure and such lovely hair, now it's always washed, conditioned and brushed. You see, I did find my prince. He even noticed me when I was still in the cinders.

Finn? Finn is my lord. No, I never see *him* now. Only the messengers, the bats. *Mashefla*—not a name, just the word they—*his* kind—use for bats. A mash flies in at the window on a summer night, when Ed is driving the last bus, or Ed is asleep because he has to start at five-thirty in the morning.

Worldly Riches, says a leaf. *Worldly Power,* says another. And then Finn-I-no-longer-see uses my medium to lend me random illusory magic, and I steal some object I don't want, nor he, or I go to another party and tell an uncanny anecdote, this peculiar thing that happened to me in the forest, or some other forest—the open door to let his kind in.

No leaf ever says *Heart's Desire.* He's got that. It's her.

What happened about the house I haven't a clue. And I never saw James again either. (Nor Dougal, nor Oaf, if it comes to that. So watch your feet!)

Sometimes I think about Ear Rainer. She used to want to fidget about such a lot, driving or eating, or rolling on the lounger, or in bed with James. Now she's a tree, and birds sit and shit in her. I should like this. But somehow it makes me uncomfortable.

It was all of ten years ago anyway, all that in the forest.

Ed and I live in another town. He's saved for years, and he's going to take early retirement. Wants us to rent a cottage in Cornwall. That's fine. I mean, who cares.

He never mentions the forest. He never has. He drove through it then, day after day. Saying nothing was the best course.

I haven't said, have I, I worked out, ages later, being rather slow (as you'll have gathered), what that notice-graffito meant on the house. *UOUS* ✓ It was last year, when Ed had borrowed some of the famous housekeeping money. But he left me a note. An IOU: *IOU, Luv, £30.*

IOU. I owe you. So *UOUS*? You Owe *Us.* And the tick put on the house, well, that meant I, in that place at least, had paid.

Bear in mind then, that because I paid, and still pay, the bargain can be made over freshly by any of you, the compact by which he, or one of his kind, will serve *you* three wishes, the Triple Trellechy. No need to thank me, then.

*

WHAT a vulgar, shoddy ending. A sales pitch! Cold-calling. I can hear you thinking it. You wanted me, the heroine, in glass slippers and a gown of cloth-of-gold, dancing in the discos of fairyland with Finnuhcai (that's one of his longer names), High King among Lords. It's what you'd like for yourself, though, is it? Riches, power, love, and/or to be abducted into Heaven?

Well, you know what to do then. *Try the woods.* My clients await you there. See if you can find them.

Look at it this way: This story I've written is the proof, the *living* proof, that it can happen. Why the hell else do you think *he* made me write it?

Grace Notes

by Megan Lindholm

Lately there appears to be an upsurge of interest in the subservience of house elves (one young woman calls it slavery), but the industrious distaff sprite of "Grace Notes" does not put up with that sort of thing; she develops a real attitude problem—but what can you expect when a brownie comes under the influence of Martha Stewart?

Megan Lindholm has been writing fantasy for over twenty years, with an occasional foray into science fiction. Under the well-known pseudonym Robin Hobb, she has written the Farseer Trilogy, the Live-ship Trilogy, and the Tawny Man Trilogy. Author of more than ten novels and several dozen short stories, she currently resides and writes in Tacoma, Washington.

"My favorite slice of the genre," she says, "is contemporary fantasy, stories that bring magic and its wonderful mayhem into modern settings. 'Grace Notes' falls into that category."

IT began with one tiny incident. Perhaps. The summer thunderstorm blew up out of nowhere, billowing his faded yellow curtains into his living room. The scent of the storm came with them, promising coolness to follow. Jeffrey sprawled on his couch that evening, watching coverage of a golf tournament that he cared nothing about. Lightning flashed. He clicked off the television and in a boyhood reflex, began counting ponderously. "One, two, three, four, five, six, seven—" The boom of the thunder rattled the glass doors in their tracks. "Seven miles away!" he announced to no one. He decided to close the door before the storm hit.

As he stood up, he heard a small sound outside, like the muffled meow of a dismayed cat.

He pulled the curtain aside. The first fat drops were starting to hit the courtyard garden in the center of the apartment complex. Maisy's orange cat was sitting on the low half-wall that separated Jeffrey's tiny concrete "patio" from the courtyard. The cat's eyes glowed lambent green for an instant as the light caught them just right. "What's the matter, Trounce? Are you shut out in the storm?" He looked across the courtyard to Maisy's apartment. The curtains were drawn behind the closed glass doors.

"You can come in, if you want," he offered the cat. The big orange tom growled low in his throat and lashed his tail. He stared down into Jeffrey's shadowy yard as if some prey had just eluded him there. He'd often seen the big cat with songbirds clamped in his jaws, but the hour and the weather seemed wrong for that sort of prey. "Is there something there?"

The cat answered with another low growl. The storm flashed again and this time the rumble of thunder followed almost immediately. "I'm shutting the door, so make up your mind. You're welcome to come in, but only if you do it now."

The cat yowled loudly and then jumped off the decorative wall and streaked off into the darkness. The wind gusted again, flapping the curtains against Jeffrey's ankles in passing. "Suit yourself!" he called after Trounce, then pulled the flapping curtains inside and shut the glass doors.

The next evening Jeffrey came home from work exhausted, his hands and face smeared with grease from lubing turnbuckles all day. He thought that he had put the tedious, grueling tasks of longshoring behind him when he earned a tech degree as a machinist. Then the Boeing gravy train had pulled out of the station and left a lot of machinists in the unemployment line, most of them with more experience than he had. He tried to be grateful that he had any job, but it was hard to find himself back on the Tacoma waterfront and paying off the student loan that was supposed to have launched his new career.

He washed most of the grease off in the bathroom sink, and then sat down on the john. He looked through a *Sports Illustrated* from February, then tossed it on the floor and reached for the toilet paper on the back of the tank. It wasn't there.

The roll was on the hanger.

He knew he hadn't put it there. For several days, the empty brown cylinder from the last roll had been on the hanger, and several others had littered the floor. The new roll had been on top of the tank. Now, the toilet paper was hung up, and the empty cardboard holders were gone. He scowled slightly as he flushed the toilet and then stripped to take a shower. Maybe his mother had paid him one of her drop-in visits, he thought as he watched grey soapsuds sluice off his arms and hands. That was probably it. She had an emergency key to his apartment. And it would be just like her to hang up fresh toilet paper and do a quick tidy if she arrived when he wasn't home.

There was no note on the table. When he opened the refrigerator, it was disappointingly bare as usual. His mother knew he didn't stock much food in the house, so she often arrived with a sack of groceries on her hip. She brought cartons of flavored coffee creamer and raspberry pastries to share with him, and sometimes tubs of Jell-O or potato salad or paper-wrapped sandwiches from the corner deli. No. She hadn't been here. Rather disappointed at the lack of goodies, he wandered into his living room, still mulling over the toilet paper.

The chance that someone had jimmied his lock and come into his apartment and done nothing except replace his toilet paper was too farfetched to consider. He strolled through his apartment, looking for other signs of tampering or mother-visits. He found the sliding-glass door to the little courtyard unlatched. Hm. He stepped out onto his minuscule patio and gazed over the half-wall into the courtyard. Too late he realized that Maisy was standing in her tiny backyard across the courtyard, her orange cat in her arms. She looked tired and her hair had gone flat in the heat. "Hello, Jeffrey," she called to him.

"Hi, Maisy. Um, did you see anyone outside my door here today?"

She shook her head. Trounce bumped his head up against her chin. She was still in her waitress uniform and the day's work had wilted her hair. "No. But I only just got home. My car died on me again. I think it's the alternator. I barely managed to get it to the service place before it just stopped dead. And then they didn't have a courtesy van available, so I had to take a bus home. I just got in the door. Trounce is starving."

She could never just answer a question without telling him her life history for the last forty-eight hours. He knew where this was leading. Her car seemed to break down at least once every two months. She was fishing for a ride to work tomorrow. She and the cat were looking at him, waiting for him to speak. He hated being cornered like that. He refused to offer. "Wow. Bummer. You really need to dump that car and buy a new one, Maisy."

"Really? You think so?" She smiled to soften her sarcastic tone. It didn't work. When he couldn't think of anything to say, she replied to his silence. "Well, maybe when I win the lottery. See you tomorrow, Jeffrey."

He was glad to get back inside his apartment and close the curtains over the glass door. He made sure the door was latched and then put the dowel in the door track for good measure. But that still didn't answer the question of the toilet paper being hung up. He decided that he must have absentmindedly done it himself and sat down to watch television for the rest of the evening. He groped for the current *TV Guide* and found it on the coffee table with the remote neatly on top of it. It was only later that he would realize that all of the outdated back issues had vanished. He should have recognized his danger then.

Jeffrey got up the next morning and got ready for work. Clean Carhartts, denim work shirt, steel-toed boots. His filthy coveralls were still in the back of his car. He wondered what they would put him to today. Longshoring wasn't what people thought it was. He spent as much time scraping and painting or stacking dunnage as he did actually loading and fastening down cargo. It was physically demanding grunt labor for the most part, without the comfort of being mindless. An error on his part could cost the company thousands of dollars, or a crewman his life. Still, he had his life in hand, even if it wasn't quite the life he'd planned. The job paid him enough to have his apartment, a car that ran reliably, basic cable with two premium channels and still pay more than the minimum payments on his credit card each month. It wasn't a bad job. It just wasn't the life he'd imagined.

When he reached his car in the parking garage below the apartment complex, Maisy was leaning up against it. She worked at the café in Uffer's Landing, down the street from the shipping yard. Its upstairs dining room offered a wide view of the working harbor and pricy lunches and dinners to a well-heeled clientele. Maisy worked in the ground-level coffee and lunch section that catered to the longshoremen, sailors and blue-collar workers of the port. She had once told him that, percentage-wise, the workers tipped better than the executives upstairs. She probably did okay at her job, yet she obviously didn't make quite enough to afford a car that ran reliably. She had on her Uffer's Landing uniform with the required high heels, and a black and gold scarf looped through the handle of her purse. She stood up straight as he approached and asked, "Can I catch a ride with you this morning, Jeffrey?"

"Yeah, I guess."

She started in right away, like he really wanted to know all the details of her life. "I thought I'd get my car back this morning. I thought it was the alternator gone bad. But the shop called and the alternator checked out fine and so did the battery. So now we're not sure. It could be something as simple as the fuel filter, or something worse like a clogged fuel pump. On the way home yesterday, I'd step on the gas, and she'd pick up speed, and then give this sort of a lurch and lose power, and then slowly gain speed again. Not much fun on a freeway."

"Not much," he agreed. He got into his car, and then leaned across the seat to unlock the other door for her. She started to get in, then made a small face. "Oh, dear," she said, and hastily gathered up the loose fast-food wrappers on the passenger seat and floor. She stuffed them into the old McD's bag. There were a few loose fries on the seat. She picked them up individually and then brushed at the salt that remained.

"Just a minute," she said and then trotted across the parking lot to the garbage can. Amazing, how women could do that in those heels. She had pretty nice legs. When she got back and hopped into the car, he put it in gear. As they pulled out of the parking garage, she buckled her seat belt and asked, "Can I catch a ride home with you, too?"

"Oh, probably. If I'm not doing something else."

"That would be great. If you could swing by the café, I mean." She gave a little sigh and leaned back in her seat. For one moment, he thought she was going to be quiet. Then, she suddenly turned to him and said brightly, "Hey, did I show you my scarf? I found it in this little secondhand store down on Sixth while I was waiting for the bus. I think it might be a Hermès! I got it for seventy-five dollars, so if it turns out to be a Hermès, that's a real deal."

He glanced at her. "Your car is in the shop and you blow seventy-five bucks on a scarf?"

"It's not just a scarf. I think it's a Hermès. If it is, then it would be worth, oh, about two hundred dollars if it were new. And I got it for seventy-five. That's amazing."

He coughed. "Spending seventy-five bucks on a scarf is amazing to me, especially for a waitress. What if it's not a Hermy?"

"Hermès." She turned to look out the window. She spoke stiffly. "Then I guess I'm as stupid as you think I am. And waiting tables is what I do, not who I am."

Oh. He'd hurt her feelings. Why had she brought up the subject if she was touchy about it? "I don't think you're stupid," he said lamely. Then he turned on the radio so he wouldn't have to make any more conversation and they drove to work.

He ended up giving Maisy a ride home from work, which meant he couldn't stop to eat. As he left the elevator and walked down the hall to his apartment, he was trying to remember if there were any chicken pot pies left in the freezer. If not, he was going to have to order pizza. Or walk down to the deli.

He opened the door and stopped where he stood. The piney scent of air freshener hung in the air. "Mom?" he called cautiously. There was no answer. He walked slowly into the living room. The remote was on the *TV Guide* in the middle of the bare table. There was no sign of the microwave popcorn bag from last night, and his empty Heineken bottle was gone from the tabletop. Strangest of all, the television was on, the volume set to a whisper, tuned to some home-decorating show. He clicked it off. "Hello?" he called cautiously. "Is someone in here?"

He peeked into his dim bedroom. Nothing amiss there.

But in the bathroom, someone had put the cap on the tooth-paste and set it beside his shaving cream and razor on top of the toilet tank. The wastebasket was empty and lined with a clean white plastic bag. He'd never even bought wastebas-ket liners. He knew he hadn't done that.

The kitchen was where the changes were most obvious. The counters were clear of dishes and empty packages. The sink was bare and polished bright. When he opened the dishwasher, the steamy waft of just-washed dishes warmed his face. Lemony fresh! He let the door of it thunk shut and looked round the small room. "Hello?" he called cautiously. "Anyone here?"

He thought he heard a small muffled sound from the bedroom, as if someone had dropped a slipper on the carpet. A shiver ran up Jeffrey's spine. "Hello?" he called again. As if in response, there was another small sound. "Who's here?" he demanded, and held his breath. Silence. It scared him and an unreasonable level of anger was his response. "I'm overreacting," he growled to himself as he eased open a kitchen drawer and took out a large knife. He didn't care. He felt better confronting whoever it was with a knife in his hand. There was no telling what sort of a wacko he was up against.

Walking softly, his heart slapping in his chest, he prowled through the living room and looked into the bathroom. Nothing. He pushed the bedroom door open slowly until it touched the wall behind it. Knife in his right hand, he snapped on the light with his left and looked around.

At first glance, the room was as he had left it. Rumpled sheets and blankets were kicked to the end of the bed, and yesterday's shorts were still on the floor. But every drawer in the dresser was closed, with not even a sock peeping out. And the closet door was shut. Aha.

He walked toward it, trying not to breathe too loudly. Then he decided on direct confrontation. "Look, I know you're hiding in there. I don't know what your problem is that you want to come into my apartment and move stuff, but I'm not angry. I just want you to leave. So, come out now and I'll let you leave. No problems!"

Silence greeted his words.

"I've got a knife!" he warned the closet door. He glanced over at the bed, wondering if perhaps he'd made an error. No. The bed was too close to the floor for anyone to be hiding under it. "I'm opening the door!" he warned the closet again. "If you just come out calmly, I won't hurt you. I'm opening it now! Stand still and no one gets hurt!"

Knife aloft in his right hand, he seized the doorknob in his left and jerked the door open. He recoiled as light spilled out toward him. The light bulb in the closet had burned out months ago; he'd never gotten around to replacing it. But even that was not what was most shocking.

Trousers to the left, crisply creased, hanging on fat hangers. Shirts to the right. All his work shirts were laundered, freshly pressed, buttoned and faced the same direction on the hangers. All the garments were grouped by colors. In the bottom of the closet, his shoes were neatly paired in a single row. His brown leather sandals had been polished. His jogging sneakers had been wiped clean and re-laced with immaculate white laces.

He spun back to face the empty bedroom. "Why are you doing this to me?" he demanded. And then, without warning, he flung himself to the floor and peered under the bed. But even in the dimness, he could see there was nothing there. Nothing but clean, freshly vacuumed carpet. Not a sock, not a dust-bunny, not a crumpled magazine. The bed concealed a perfectly clean rectangle of carpet. He got up slowly and backed out of the bedroom.

He stood in the short hallway, breathing through his mouth. "Where are you?" he shouted, but there was no reply. Knife in hand, he stalked through the apartment. He pulled down the coats in the hall closet. No one was hiding behind them. No one behind the couch in the living room. No one lurking in the dusty curtains. No one under the kitchen table or squeezed into the broom closet.

There just weren't that many places in his one-bedroom apartment that could conceal someone. In a very short time, he was confident he was alone in his apartment. He dead-bolted the door and made sure his garden doors were locked. Still shaking with suppressed nerves, he went back to the kitchen and dropped the knife into the drawer.

Okay. So someone had come into his apartment and cleaned up a few things. Someone had an obsession about him. But whoever it was, that person wasn't here now and was no threat to him. Time to calm down. Time to live his regular life.

Still pondering his mystery, he went into the kitchen and made a bologna sandwich, popped open a can of Pringles and a bottle of Heineken and took his meal to the couch in the living room. He turned on the television. The decorating show was still on. This one was a reality program about people remodeling other people's houses; how much would that suck? He switched to Cartoon Network and zoned out with the Powerpuff Girls while he waited for *Law and Order* to come on and tried to think how someone had obtained a key to his apartment. His mother had one, of course. She almost always did a bit of cleaning when she dropped in; it was her nature. But cleaning under his bed was not the sort of thing she did. Her first stop was usually to throw out anything moldy in the refrigerator. Last month she'd said he should hire a cleaning service to come in twice a month. He'd told her he couldn't afford it. Had she called one anyway, and given them her key?

He called her during a commercial. No, she had not been by to visit. No, she hadn't hired a maid for him. Why was he asking?

"I just thought it looked like someone had been in my apartment. No big deal."

What did he mean, someone had been in his apartment? Like a burglary? Was anything missing?

"I didn't even think to check, Mom. It wasn't like the place was tossed or anything. If anything, it looked like someone had tidied things up for me. Ha, ha!"

Had he called the police? Did he check with the landlord? Had he asked the neighbors if they'd noticed anyone loitering near his door or if they'd heard anything unusual? He could have a stalker, some deranged woman . . . Oh, good lord, it might be identity theft! Was his garbage gone? That was one of the first things those hackers took. Was his garbage missing?

The commercial was over, his program was coming on and she wouldn't let it go. She always made such a big deal out of everything. He told her that he'd go see if his garbage was gone or if anything valuable was missing and that he'd call her back later. "Yes, soon, Mom. Goodnight, Mom. Yes, see you soon. Got to go. Hey, Mom, my show's starting. *Law and Order.* Yes. I have to hang up now. Bye, Mom."

He set the phone down on the coffee table next to his sandwich plate. During the next commercial, he got up and went to his bedroom. He tried to think what someone would steal from him. He had no jewelry to speak of, no stamp collection, no valued art. He had started out collecting the new state quarters as they came out, but lost interest and used most of them for laundry money. The other ones were still in a sandwich bag in the top of his drawer. He opened the lock box where he kept his birth certificate, car title and emergency credit card. All of them were still there. His old album of baseball cards was still underneath it. He went and checked the kitchen garbage next, more because he was curious than because he was worried about it.

His mother was right. It was gone. The under-sink

garbage pail was lined with a clean, white, bought-specially-for-that-purpose plastic bag. Okay. So they'd stolen his garbage. What did they get? He ran through his recollections of the last few days. Takeout food containers. Empty beer and pop cans. Junk mail. He couldn't imagine that anything of value was in there, and doubted that someone trying to steal his identity would shine his shoes for him.

He didn't sleep well that night. He kept imagining soft sounds throughout the house. Each time he got up to check, he found nothing. When he showered that morning, he found that his yellow deodorant soap bar had been replaced with something brown with grit in it. As he toweled off, he noticed that the washcloth, the hand towel and the bath towel all matched. He had matching sets of towels; his mother saw to that. And it was completely possible that he'd accidentally hung up a matching set. It wasn't like he jumbled them on purpose. But the soap was suspicious, and he wished he'd looked inside the bathtub yesterday. He didn't like the idea that someone had changed his soap in the night.

He tried to dismiss the notion as foolish, but dressing in a work shirt that had been pressed, and taking a neatly matched pair of socks from a tidy row of socks in his dresser did not put him at ease. Before he left the house, he made sure the rod was in the glass door's slider. He not only locked the front door but also turned the key in the dead bolt, a security measure he had always before regarded as somewhat extreme.

When he got down to the parking lot, Maisy was waiting by his car again. "I really appreciate it. Do you mind?"

Yes. "I'm going past there anyway. Hop in."

When she climbed in, he saw that she had a bouquet of puffy red flowers. She saw him glance at it and explained, "Pom-pom dahlias from my little garden. I like to put fresh flowers out on my tables when I can."

"Why?"

She lifted one shoulder in a shrug. "Oh, you know. Just to make it nicer. A little grace note. A little touch to make the job a bit less of a drag."

"Better tips, too, I bet," he observed sagely.

She shook her head. "Most of the customers don't even know they come from me." As she settled in beside him, she observed, "You look really nice today, Jeffrey. Is that a new cologne?"

"Soap. Someone left it in my shower."

"Oh." For a moment, she seemed at a loss for words. She buckled up and smoothed her skirt over her knees before she added, "It smells like sandalwood to me. Very nice."

"I don't know. It's part of the weirdness in my apartment. New soap in the shower. Someone dumped my garbage and hung up my toilet paper, too. I don't know who it is, but they'd better damn well stop." He hadn't quite realized how pissed off he was until he heard the anger in his own voice.

"Mind if I turn on the radio?" Maisy asked hastily, and then leaned over to push the button before he could answer.

At quitting time, she wasn't waiting outside the restaurant. He stood by the hot car, the doors open to let the air move through it for a while. Then he told himself that she'd had plenty of time to come out if she needed a ride and got in and drove off. He got Two Burgers for Two Bucks at Dairy Queen. Worth every penny, he told himself grumpily as his fingers sank into the soggy buns. He stopped by Tony's for a couple of beers, and on the way home, remembered he was out of Tums and detoured past the drugstore.

He'd forgotten that he'd dead-bolted the door. He fumbled the sack with the Tums, got the second lock opened and entered the dim apartment quietly. He stood still a moment, listening, but heard nothing. He flipped on the switch and then swore.

The remote control rested on the *TV Guide* on the coffee

table. The rest of the normally cluttered surface was bare and gleaming with lemon oil. He could smell it. Martha Stewart was torturing napkins on the television. Someone had been in his apartment again. He strode over to the glass doors, clicking off the television as he passed it. The door was still locked, rod still in the tracks. He lifted the curtain and peered out. Maisy was sitting outside in her little garden, reading a book. One of those bug candles was burning on the table next to her. Trounce sprawled beside it; she petted him absently with one hand as she read. He was guiltily relieved that she'd gotten home safely. He let the curtain fall before she could think he was spying on her and made a systematic inspection of the rest of the house.

A bowl of flowers in the kitchen. Containers of food in the refrigerator, matching plastic containers with tight-fitting baby-blue lids. Not from the deli. A new shower curtain in the bathroom, white on white, a pattern of seashells on it. His Bic disposable razor was gone. A stainless-steel counterpart, the kind that took the old-fashioned flat blades, rested on a little dish on the sink corner. Another bar of brown soap filled the matching soap dish.

His bed was made and there was no dirty laundry anywhere. The sheets matched the pillowcases. The old draw curtains on the window had been replaced with drapes that looked like they were woven from grass and some filmy extra curtains behind them. He checked the bedroom window and discovered it was open a crack. He'd opened it last night, but he'd latched it this morning. Hadn't he? He couldn't remember and that made him even angrier.

He strode through the living room. Had those throw pillows been on the couch the last time he'd walked through here? They must have been and yet he suddenly wasn't sure. It was as if the rooms changed if he left them for even a moment. Ridiculous.

He picked up his phone, dialed his mother and hung up

before she could answer. That was stupid. She'd see his number on caller ID and panic. To keep from having to take her call, he called the apartment manager. He got only her voice mail and realized he hadn't planned out what he was going to say. "This is Jeffrey Horson in apartment 1E. Someone has been coming into my apartment during the day and doing stuff in here. Moving stuff. Doing my laundry and taking my garbage. I know that sounds nuts, but . . . I think I've been locking the doors and windows. Anyway. Call me back about this. Please."

He hung up, realized that he hadn't left his number and was suddenly too embarrassed by his sputtered message to call back again. The phone rang. He checked caller ID. His mom. He had to answer. She'd keep calling until he did.

"Hi, Mom. No, I mean, yes, I called, but by accident. Pushed the wrong button on the memory. No, I'm sure, everything's fine. Oh, that. No, I'd taken the garbage out and just forgotten about it. No, I'm sure, it was all a big mistake. Hey. Did you forget some Tupperware last time you were here? You know, in the refrigerator? No. Oh. Okay. No. Well, yes there is some, but it's uh, it's probably Maisy's. You know. No, you do know her, at least I told you about her. She works at the coffee shop down from the yard, sometimes I give her a ride to work when her car breaks down. No, it's nothing like that. I'm sure she just meant it as a thank you for the rides, that's all. Egg products. Okay, I'll be careful. If it has eggs and salmonella in it, I won't eat any of it. . . . Look, I'll just go throw it away now, okay? No. No, Mom, I'm sorry, I didn't mean to snap at you. I've just had a long day, that's all. Yes. That would be good. Tomorrow would be great. Sure. Sure. Bye, now."

Sweat was running down his back by the time he hung up. The closed-up apartment was stifling. He opened the curtains and his garden door. Maisy was still out there. Now she was watering the row of little potted plants she kept on top of her half-wall. The dahlias. She saw him looking at her and waved cautiously across the little courtyard. He waved back and went to investigate the stuff in the refrigerator.

One tub held some kind of chicken. Or maybe fish. It was blackened on the outside. When he bit into a piece, it tasted like lemony chicken with little bits of some leafy herb stuck on the outside of it. Well, it wasn't Kentucky Fried, but it wasn't liver either, so he ate it. In another tub, brown rice had been stirred up with some slivers of vegetables and some sliced almonds. He ate that, too. There were yellow raisins in it, but that was okay. The stuff in the third tub was brown and smooth. It turned out to be a chocolate mousse. It was actually pretty good. As he put the empty food tubs in the sink, he felt a twinge of guilt. He hated it when he put his lunch in the refrigerator at work and then returned to find someone had eaten it. But this was different; it was his refrigerator and if someone was choosing to come into his house and leave food in his fridge, then they deserved to have it eaten.

The odd act of revenge somehow lessened his anger at the intruder. He watched television with his head propped on some of the new cushions. He went to bed that night between the clean sheets after closing the grass curtains over the window. They looked and felt expensive. As he closed his eyes, he felt more smug than threatened. Someone was sneaking into his apartment, cleaning it, upgrading the furnishings and leaving palatable food in the refrigerator. Worse things could happen to him. He tried to work up a little paranoia; what if the food was drugged? What if the person showed up and demanded some sort of payment? But he didn't think either was likely. Maybe someone was mixing up his apartment with someone else's apartment in the complex and the two keys just happened to be the same. Maybe some woman was stalking him. He dozed off to a pleasant fantasy of an attractive woman coming to his door to confess that she was the one behind all the minor improvements in his life. She'd brought beer nuts.

Maisy wasn't by his car in the morning; she'd probably had her junker fixed. Well, good. He unlocked the door and slid into the seat and then gasped. Whoever had hung up the little pine tree from the rearview mirror hadn't known that you didn't take it all the way out of its plastic bag, you only tore it open a little. The scent of pine was so strong he felt like he'd eaten a tree. He held his breath while he untangled the string from the mirror and tossed it out into the parking lot. He reached across the car to open the passenger-side window, then saw it was open. No. Not open. Just so clean it looked like it was open. As clean as the windshield. As clean as the freshly shampooed carpet and the softly gleaming dashboard. He crouched down beside the car and looked under the seats. Not a McDonald's fry, not a burrito wrapper from the 7-Eleven, not even a gum wrapper. Spotlessly clean.

Jeffrey stood up slowly. He looked all around the parking lot. Was someone watching him right now, waiting for his reaction? Damned if he'd give them one. He slid in behind the steering wheel, shut the door and went to work. He spent the day chaining containers down for a trip to Japan. The partner they'd given him for the day was a temp and an idiot, and it took all his concentration to get through the day alive. He was hot and tired and all he wanted to do after work was go home and take a shower.

Maisy was waiting by his car.

"I thought you got your car fixed," he greeted her.

"I did. It just didn't last very long. The tow truck driver dropped me off here this morning." She smiled as if it was funny but desperation shone in her eyes. "Look, Jeffrey, my car's falling apart on me and you come this way every day anyway. Gas prices are going crazy, and I could probably scrape together enough each month for a car payment, but then the insurance and gas would nail me. Is there any way we could, um, sort of carpool? Just for a while, just until I can either get the piece of crap fixed or find another car that will nickel and dime me into bankruptcy. I'd kick in on the gas."

He wanted to just tell her "no." But her hair was coming out of the knot she'd twisted it into on the back of her head and dangling down her neck, sort of wilted and sweaty. She looked as weary and tired of her job as he felt. Somehow, he just couldn't do it to her. So he didn't say anything, but just unlocked the door for her and opened it.

"Thanks," she said quietly, in a discouraged voice. She'd noticed he hadn't answered her question. She sat down on the seat and then swung her feet in. "Wow!" she said in quiet awe. "This is an amazing detail job. You get it done at Pink Elephant?"

He was taking off his coveralls. She watched him climb out of them and he felt oddly self-conscious as he pulled them down past his jeans and stepped out of them. He tossed them in the trunk, got in the car and buckled his seat belt. "No. It's, um, this is sort of weird. It's like the toilet paper and the laundry and the food in my fridge. I don't know who's doing it. I just go into my apartment at night, and stuff has been done there. Cleaned up. Made pretty. This morning, I came out to my car and it was just like this. You probably think I'm crazy."

She was quiet for a minute. Then she said carefully, "I don't think I understand what you're trying to tell me."

He looked both ways before pulling out of the parking lot. "It sounds crazy," he admitted. "And half the time I wonder what I'm getting upset about. The other half of the time, I wonder why I haven't called the cops." He glanced over at her and she gave him a smile that was probably supposed to be encouraging. Oddly enough, it was.

"So. Exactly what's been happening to you?"

He told her, starting with the toilet paper and working all the way to the spotless carpets in his car. She listened and nodded and even looked intrigued. When he had finished, she said, "It sounds like a brownie."

"Like, selling Girl Scout cookies and doing good deeds?" He stopped to think. "Are there even any kids in our apartment building?" And why would one have fixated on him?

"No, no, the folklore kind of brownie. A kindly little sprite that moves into a home and does all sorts of tidying and cleaning tasks for the family there. According to the stories, the brownie will stay and work for you as long as you don't thank him or give him any gifts. Like in the story of the Shoemaker and the Elves. Those 'elves' were probably brownies, and when the shoemaker left out shoes and clothing for them, they immediately departed."

"Like that thing in the dishcloth in the Harry Potter movie?"

She winced. "Close, but again, that's an adaptation of the folklore. But they did stick to the old idea that once the homeowner gave the brownie a gift, it was free to go. Some people say that once a brownie has clothing, he thinks he's much too fine to be doing drudgery work. I always wondered if it wasn't an extended metaphor for the devaluing of women's work around the home. If you ignore all a 'homemaker' puts into keeping up a house and making it pleasant, then you can pretend it's effortless for her. It goes with the myth that if you recognize a woman's work as important, then she'll feel important and perhaps become too proud to do her work anymore."

"So. No 'Brownie Liberation,' huh?" he joked and then glanced over at her. She hadn't smiled. Quickly he asked, "So, how did you learn all that stuff, about brownies and all?"

"I majored in folklore with a minor in women's studies. There are many interesting cross connections between the two areas."

"Oh, God, you're a Greener, right? Holy cow. A major in folklore. What did you ever plan to do for a living with that degree?" He grinned as he braked for a red light.

She didn't answer.

He glanced over at her. She stared straight ahead as she replied, "Yes, I went to Evergreen College. Despite its reputation for liberal policies, or perhaps because of it, it remains one of the top colleges in the U.S. I'm proud to be a graduate of it." She sighed suddenly, her anger exhaled with her breath. She leaned back in the seat. "And I'm still paying off the student loans," she admitted.

Uh-oh. He'd stepped on her toes again. "Yeah. Tell me about it. I'm still paying off mine, too. I did my schooling at Green River Community College. I've got a technical degree as a machinist; I thought I'd graduate, work for Boeing forever and retire with a solid pension. Now look at me. Longshoring. Again. Going nowhere fast."

"At least it pays you well," she said sadly. "I'm waitressing. Putting out coffee and burgers and fries, and smiling, smiling, smiling to get those tips. Once I thought I'd travel, backpack all over the country and collect obscure folklore and write books and be, well, not famous and rich, but comfortable. Have a little house in the country, near Port Townsend or maybe Gig Harbor, with a room full of books. And maybe a horse."

Jeffrey smiled. "Sounds nice. I used to go to horse camp every summer when I was a kid. I was so sure that when I grew up, I'd have a horse of my own."

"Really? I'd never have suspected you were a horseman."

"Well, I'm not anymore. Probably never was. One week of camp every year doesn't really make you a horseman. Just a dreamer."

"Well. At least we had dreams," she said. She leaned back in the seat and looked out her side window. Thinking about something, he supposed. Probably student loans for folklore degrees. Silence fell between them. Too soon, he was pulling into the dimness of the parking garage.

She opened her door and got out. "Thanks for the ride. Um, can I, uh . . . ?"

"Sure. Just meet me here by the car tomorrow."

"Oh. Thanks. Thanks a lot. But actually, I was going to ask, could I, uh, see what your brownie has been doing to your apartment?"

He stared at her. "Are you serious? You think it's a brownie?"

She looked aside from him. "I've always maintained that all folklore has a root of truth somewhere. I've been think-ing about it all the way home. You say you've been pretty careful about keeping your place locked up, and that you can't think of anyone who'd be doing this to you. So—I just thought. . . ." She looked uncomfortable.

He wondered which would be stupider, saying "yes" or "no." "Sure. Come on up and take a look."

It felt odd to have her follow him to the elevator and ride up with him. He tried to remember the last time he'd had a woman in his apartment. He didn't meet many new women any more; longshoring just wasn't a trade that had a lot of gender mingling. It actually felt sort of good when they ran into Travis from 1D in the hallway. "Hey, Trav," Jeffrey greeted him, and "How's it going, Jeff," he replied. Travis's eyes ran over Maisy like she was the cherry on a cupcake and Jeffrey felt two inches taller.

Jeffrey shoved his key in the dead bolt and found no re-sistance. "I know I locked up this morning," he told Maisy, and eased the door open. The smell of cooking wafted out to them. "Someone's in my apartment," he told her. He put his fingers to his lips to shush her and gestured to her to fol-low him silently. Her eyes were very big; he'd never noticed before how dark they were. She tiptoed after him as he led the way through the living room to the kitchen. In passing,

Jeffrey noticed a new magazine rack at the end of the sofa. The *TV Guide* was in it, along with this month's issue of *Woodworker.* *House Beautiful* was there, too, right below *Martha Stewart Living.* Those weren't his! There was a flower arrangement on the coffee table.

Someone was definitely in the kitchen; he heard the sound of a pan being lifted from the stove. Maybe this was foolish; maybe he should just quietly go and call the cops about an intruder in his apartment. But Maisy was right behind him and he didn't want to look a coward in front of her.

He paused at the corner, and then stepped suddenly into the kitchen, demanding loudly, "What do you think you're doing in here?"

His mother spun around from the sink. The pasta in the colander she held flew out, showering the kitchen with noodles and water. She staggered back from him, to lean against the sink. "Jeffrey! Don't startle me like that!" Then she smiled a wide, hopeful smile. "I see big changes in this apartment. Tropics in the bedroom, eh? Sounds warm! Anyone special you want to tell me about?" Her wink was conspiratorial.

At that moment, Maisy stepped into view and halted at his mom's words. The two women stared at each other like startled cats. His mother's eyes were almost as big as Maisy's.

"Oh, I, um, I forgot that you were coming over today. Sorry, sorry. No, Mom, I'll clean that up, don't bother, please. Um, Mom, this is Maisy, from across the courtyard. Maisy, this is my mom, Eleanor."

"How do you do?" Maisy responded automatically. Jeffrey glanced at her as he got the broom and dustpan from the closet. Maisy looked uncomfortable but she was trying to smile.

"You don't use a broom to clean up wet spaghetti!" his

mother exclaimed. "Put that down before you make a bigger mess." She took the cleaning tools from him and then favored Maisy with an appraising look. "Men! How he managed this long on his own, I just don't know. The bedroom is just amazing. You go for that tropical look, don't you? Bamboo, grass, big bright flowers?"

"Um, it can be, um, very effective. If it's done well. I don't know that I would, um." Maisy faltered to a halt. She glanced to him for a hint but he was as mystified as she was.

His mom was unrolling a tree's worth of paper towels. She corralled the noodles on the floor as she spoke and began transferring the slippery worms to the wastebasket. A few escaped to coil on the floor again. "I think it's lovely, of course, but I don't know beans about decorating. I don't think that I'd ever have the nerve to do a whole room in it. To decorate tropical here in the Pacific Northwest, well, it just doesn't work for me." She rocked back on her heels and looked up at them both. Crouched there, she seemed to suddenly realize that she might have been tactless, because she added, "But I suppose it could be very, um, romantic. It's just sort of, well, too tropical for me."

"Well, you could always substitute totem poles and cedar bark cloth for a Northwest look," Maisy offered, and tried to laugh with his mother. It didn't take. His mom looked as if she thought she were being mocked. She glanced at him, a hurt look hidden in the back of her eyes. Then she put a stiff smile on her face. She gave a final swipe at the linoleum and came slowly to her feet, the last of the slimy paper towels in her grip. She tossed them in the kitchen garbage. "Well, that's ruined dinner. Why don't I run along? I can always see Jeffrey later."

"Oh, um, well, I wasn't expecting to stay long. In fact, I really have to go home. I haven't been there to feed Trounce yet and he'll be ravenous."

"You have a child?" His mother looked intrigued.

"Oh, no, no. Trounce is my cat. Though he can seem like as much work as a kid. Well, I've got to be going." Maisy seemed markedly uneasy now. She flapped a hand at both of them, and then said hastily to him, "Thanks for the ride, Jeffrey. I'm going to cut through the courtyard, okay?"

There was an awkward moment while his mom stood in the archway of the kitchen and watched Maisy struggle to get the glass door open. Finally, he went over and lifted the rod from the tracks and slid it open for her. "Oh, of course! I see. Well, thanks. Bye! Have a nice evening!" She all but scuttled away in relief.

He went back to the kitchen. "No need to rush off, Mom. Let's just boil up some more noodles and have dinner together. The sauce smells great."

"No, no, I don't want to be intruding. I thought you'd invited me over for tonight, but obviously you had other company in mind. I'm so glad you've finally met someone. I wish you'd mentioned her before I put my foot in my mouth."

"Mom, I think you have the wrong idea." He looked through the cupboards for the plastic sack of noodles. Couldn't find it. "Oh, oh, looks like I'm out of spaghetti noodles. Shall I run to the corner store for more, or shall we change the menu?"

"No, you've got lots of noodles. There, in the tall Tupperware thingy. Where did you buy that, anyway? Such a good way to store pasta."

He found it, a cylinder of plastic with the spaghetti standing tall inside it. He passed it up to her. She'd already refilled the saucepan with water and put it on to boil. "I don't, uh, I don't remember buying it. I don't buy those fancy doodads. Not on my budget. Are you sure you didn't bring it over to me?" Gazing into his cupboards, he knew the brownie had been at work in here as well. All the canned goods were in one section, dinner mixes in a neat row, and all the stuff that spilled after he opened it had been transferred to plastic containers. The sticky circles that usually marked where the syrup or jam had been were gone; in fact, he didn't remember having yellow shelf paper at all. He hastily shut the cupboard.

"Well, I'm sure I didn't buy it for you. If I had, I'd have bought one for myself, too. I like my 'fancy doodads.' You could use a few more in your life. Maybe it's Maisy's?"

His mom tried to ask the question delicately. Oh, damn. Time to lay that idea to rest before she got too hopeful and starting naming the grandchildren.

"No, Mom, Maisy is just a friend." At his mom's encouraged smile, he added hastily, "Barely a friend, really. Her car broke down, she needed a ride home from work. That's all."

"And she stops by your apartment just to walk through it on the way to hers. Look, Son, don't feel awkward. I think it's wonderful you've met someone. Your life seems so empty. Go to work, come home, watch TV, sleep, go to work . . . I'm glad you're seeing someone. You deserve a little happiness. I know how lonely you've been. You could use a little tropics in your bedroom."

"Mom! It's not like that!" Hastily he added, "I gotta use the john. I'll be right back."

On his way to the bathroom, he glanced into his bedroom. All was suddenly made clear. The woven grass blinds were now merely an accent to the decor. It reminded him of something. Palm trees on the lampshade. A bamboo pattern on the bedspread, and tropical prints on the big throw pillows artfully flung about the room. He suddenly recognized it: that decorating show that had been on the television. It had been reenacted in his bedroom.

He retreated hastily to the bathroom, but found no refuge there. If the bedroom was tropical, the bathroom was a spa. The old shelf rack over the toilet tank had been replaced with a tier of gleaming chrome racks in graduated sizes. Snowy white towels were precisely stacked on them in ascending order. A freshly installed shelf inside the shower held organic sponges and fat jars and bright tubes of exotic washing stuff. The tub-side mat was hand-woven hemp in Celtic knots. It was so painfully, shiningly clean that he hesitated to use it.

When he returned to the kitchen, his mother was adding noodles to the boiling water. She didn't turn to look at him as she said brightly, "I should have looked in the fridge first and realized that you two had already planned dinner. A lot fancier than spaghetti and French bread and salad."

"You know that's one of my favorite dinners. That stuff in the fridge is just leftovers. That's all."

"Leftover lobster tail. So you ate the heads last night?" His mother turned to him with a fond smile, so certain she had caught him in the midst of a clandestine romance. "So, tell me about her? Is she a local girl? What does she do for a living?"

"Mom, please. Maisy didn't cook that food or redecorate my bedroom."

She was setting out plates on the table. "Then who did?" she asked him teasingly.

"Someone else. Can we just let it go for now?"

"You're seeing two girls? At the same time? Jeffrey! No, all right, don't say another word. I'll let it go. But that explains a lot. I thought it sounded like Maisy thought the tropical bedroom was a bit much. Bit of jealousy there, I expect. Don't look at me like that! I promise, not another word about girls. How's work these days? Any prospects of anything permanent on the horizon?"

Ordinarily, that was a discussion topic he would have avoided. His mother was always able to leap unerringly from one failing area of his life to the next. Tonight he embraced it. Anything was better than the current topic. "Nope. Looks like I'm going to longshore the rest of my life."

"Oh, Jeffrey, that's scarcely the worst thing that could happen to you. At least you're out in the fresh air, getting lots of exercise. Look at Cal. High school football star and all that, and since he took that desk job, he's put on at least thirty pounds. Terrible for such a young man. Lucky for him he was already married."

"Yeah. Lucky."

All through dinner, he kept noticing small things that he didn't dare comment on. He wished he could ask her if she had brought the new salt and pepper shakers, or provided the matching sugar and creamer set, but he didn't dare. He noticed that the meal had been upscaled in other small ways. There was cream in the pitcher instead of two-percent milk, and the sugar bowl had lump brown sugar in it. The salt and pepper shakers both had built-in grinders.

After his mother finally left, he prowled the apartment, trying to decide which changes had been made today and which could have been made days ago without him noticing. Some, like the tiers of white towels in the bathroom, were obviously today's handiwork. But there were a lot of subtle changes and he was unsure when they had come about. The shades on the lamps had been dusted. Or changed. He wasn't sure which. All his back issues of *Sports Illustrated* had vanished. There were coaster-thingies under the lamps. There was no dust anywhere, not even under the couch when he moved it. The worst was opening the junk drawer and finding that it now had one of those plastic compartment liners organizing his junk. When he pushed aside the freshly washed curtains in the dining alcove and looked out the spotless windows, there was a soft yellow light burning in Maisy's apartment rather than the blue television glow that most of the other apartment windows emitted.

She was probably the type to curl up with the cat and a book in the evening instead of watching the tube. Folklore and women's studies. He shook his head. Brownies. She halfway had him believing that was the explanation. Brownies that left lobster tail in the fridge. Sure. Chic brownies.

Thinking of the food made him recall the dessert from the previous night. He went to investigate, and sure enough, there was a domed tray with six little lemon tarts, each with a cute little curl of whipped topping. He took them out and ate them all with the last two cups of coffee in the pot as he pondered his situation. The food was great, the apartment was cleaner than when he'd first moved into it, and he rather liked the elegant touches of special soap and salt grinders. In some ways, it was like having the advantages of a live-in girlfriend with none of the hassles. He decided he'd relax into it and let it go.

"Why not?" he asked the empty room aloud.

Again, there was that dull thud in the bedroom, just a soft little thump. He got up from the table and went to investigate. When he clicked on the light, there was nothing to be concerned about. The bed had been turned down and pajamas and slippers he didn't recognize awaited him. Well, why not get comfortable before settling down with the TV? He started to go back to clear up the dishes. Then he smiled smugly to himself, shrugged and changed into his pajamas, letting his dirty clothes fall to the floor.

The next morning, he minimized the events to Maisy, implying that his mother had perhaps been behind the changes. She seemed to accept that, and on the ride to work they commented only on the traffic reports and the weather. Maisy looked good in the mornings when her makeup was fresh and her hair swept smoothly up, before the day's work had taken a toll on her. He thought of telling her that, then decided it wasn't tactful, and let it go.

The rest of the month passed uncomfortably for Jeffrey.

He and Maisy grew more companionable on the daily rides. Each evening, he returned to an apartment that was spotlessly clean. A delicious and effortless meal usually awaited him, either ready to cook in the fridge or simmering aromatically in the new slow-cooker that had appeared. The table was set and the wine chilled. The brownie knew him well. There was always a cold beer or two and some snacks for evening television watching. She introduced him to new local micro-brews and tasty nibbles he would never have tried on his own. He discovered that he really liked a certain peppery pistachio nut that she stocked the new snack dishes with.

Twice he thought he caught glimpses of her. Once, rounding the threshold into his bedroom, he thought he saw her reflection in the bottom corner of the full-length mirror there. A curly head of hair, a bare brown hip and nothing at all there when he clicked on the lights. One evening, while he was watching television, he glanced aside and thought he saw a little brown face watching him from around the corner. But when he stood up to look, she was gone.

They weren't perfect roommates. There were minor annoyances. The television was always tuned to one of those decorating shows when he got home. His magazines had been replaced with copies of *Interior Today* and *House Beautiful* and *Martha Stewart Living*. A second magazine rack that had sprouted by his bedside held all sorts of catalogs for hand-woven wool rugs, organic soaps, imported cheeses and coffees, and wonderful kitchen gadgets. The new floral linen spray made him sneeze, but by the next evening, it had been replaced with one that smelled more woodsy and calming. The pots of miniature roses and the little fountain she installed on his tiny patio were nice, but they did attract bees. One night he couldn't figure out how to unfold the napkin that looked like a flower. She painted the dining room alcove a deep gold color that seemed too dark to him. But on the whole, he was living a more genteel life than he'd ever enjoyed before, and relishing it.

Then the first of the month arrived.

Jeffrey had two credit cards. There was his workaday card, for gasoline and Subway sandwiches and a new pair of socks or a haircut. When he opened that statement, he was pleased to see that the new charges on it had dropped appreciably due to dining at home. He nearly tossed aside the statement for his emergency, reserve card. He hadn't had to touch that line of credit in months. He didn't even carry that card anymore. It was strictly for unexpected, major expenses. So when he did open the envelope, he expected to find a zero balance, with at most the annual fee coming due on it.

He stared at the four figure "new balance" in shock, and then headed for the phone. Someone had been using his card. He punched in the 800 number for the card company, and while he waited through the music, he ran his gaze down the list of charges. Nordstrom. Bon-Macy. Claude's Interiors. Good Scents. David's Deliveries. Cook's Helper. The Gourmet Touch. Lighthouse Lamps.

Two of the names he recognized from the catalog rack by his bed. With a sinking heart, he waited for a human being to pick up his call. An hour later, he was explaining to the third person he'd spoken to that, no, he had not authorized Sylvia Brown to use his charge card. Yes, that was his home address. Yes, that merchandise had been delivered here, but he had assumed it was a gift. No, he had not saved the packaging. He did not think returning the merchandise was an option. No (wincing), he did not know a Sylvia Brown. Yes. Send him a copy of the authorization he had supposedly signed. Yes, cancel that card and reissue him a new one. Yes, he'd make the minimum payment while they were looking into the situation.

When he set down the phone, his head was throbbing. "There's no such thing as a free lunch," he reminded himself. He looked around the apartment. There were fresh roses in a glass vase on the table. A two-pound box of See's chocolates was on the new end table next to the couch. He noticed that several of the candies were already missing. "I can't afford to live like this!" he announced to the empty room. He waited, but there was no thud of response from the bedroom. "I'm a simple man, a hamburger-and-fries type of guy. I shop at Fred Meyers, not the damn Bon-Macy! Are you listening to me? You've got to stop. I can't afford this stuff!"

The silence that suffused the apartment had a distinct chill to it. Our first quarrel, he thought dully. He lifted his voice again. "I've canceled that charge card. I'm going to leave a note to the mailman telling him that I want all packages held at the post office. This has to stop!"

This time there was a noise, but it came from the kitchen right behind him. A crash. When he turned round, his old Seahawks coffee mug was in pieces on the floor. He'd had that mug since college. "Not funny, Sylvia!" he warned her.

He awoke the next morning to the phone ringing. It was Maisy. "What?" he asked her. Then he glanced at the unlit dial of his digital clock. "Holy cow, it's that late? My clock came unplugged. I'll be right down!"

He threw on his clothes. There was no fresh coffee in the kitchen, and he gagged when he drank a huge mouthful of sour milk straight from the carton. He dumped carton and all in the sink, wiped his mouth on a new kitchen towel with daisies on it, and headed out the door. Damn. He hadn't written the note to the postman last night and now he didn't have time. He hoped there wasn't too much expensive merchandise backed up in the delivery chute to his house. "You okay?" Maisy asked him as he stormed up to the car.

"Yeah, I'm fine. I've just made us both late and there's a bunch of stuff on my credit card that I didn't buy. That's all."

"Oh."

The ride to work that morning was silent.

He arrived home to a couch and matching end chairs. They weren't new. Worse, they were antiques, dark wood with feet and uncomfortable cushions. His old couch and comfortably broken-in TV chair had vanished. Fuming, he slammed into the kitchen for a beer. Inside the fridge, he found a small cheese pizza going stale in a cardboard box next to a plastic cup of flat cola. "Very funny!" he announced to the household in general. He dumped it in the trash. Then, in vengeance, he gathered all of the catalogs out of the magazine rack and took them out to the recycling bin. "That's it!" he announced as he came back in. "You are done here! Leave! Get out!" Impulsively, he tore his work shirt off and tossed it on the table. "Thanks! There's some clothing. Now go!"

There was no response. He wrote a note to the postman and took it down to the apartment mailboxes. He picked up the day's mail at the same time. There were invoices for five subscriptions to interior decorating magazines, a bill from a florist and a big brown envelope full of little carpet and linoleum samples. He gave in to frustration and had the satisfaction of tearing them all up and stuffing them in the garbage. Calmer, he stopped by the manager's office, to tell her not to allow UPS or any other deliveries to be made to his apartment if he wasn't home. Jeffrey asked her if she'd seen the couch being delivered. Yeah, but she hadn't noticed where it had come from. Great. There'd be no returning that, either.

He went back to his apartment, fuming. The shirt had been washed, dried, ironed and folded while he was gone. It accused him from the middle of the table. When he went for his long-delayed beer, he found only one can of Colt 45 malt liquor. He discovered other minor changes in the apartment. The bathroom was as gracious as ever, save that the toilet paper had been replaced with something the consistency of those paper towels in a grade-school bathroom. His pajamas were not laid out for him. Instead, when he opened his drawer, he found all his Calvin Klein boxers had been replaced with Fruit of the Loom tighty-whities and wife-beater undershirts. The clock was unplugged again, too. He plugged it in and reset it.

By morning, it was unplugged again, but he had slept so poorly that he was up an hour ahead of time anyway. The strongly fragranced soap in the shower was probably called something like Whorehouse in June. He had a choice of two polo shirts in his closet: one was Pepto-Bismol pink, the other a pale green. When he pulled out a pair of clean coveralls, he discovered that they had great blossoms of white on them as if someone had been careless with the bleach. "Get out!" he shouted back into his apartment before closing and locking the door behind him.

He stormed across the parking lot to his car. Maisy stood up straight when she saw him, her mouth slightly ajar. He went around the car to unlock the door for her, greeting her with, "How did you say to get rid of a brownie?"

"By thanking him. Why? What happened to you?" Then, as she slid into the car seat, she lifted a hand to her mouth, her eyes wide in feigned shock. "You made your brownie angry, didn't you? Insulted him or hurt his feelings?"

"I cut off her charge card, that's what! Lobster tails and antique end chairs! I can't afford that kind of stuff. Does she think I'm made of money?"

"I thought we were joking," Maisy observed timidly as he slammed the car door shut behind him. A few miles later she said, "You're not kidding, are you? Someone or something is really doing this to you?"

He took a deep breath through his nose. "It seemed like a good deal at first." It took most of the drive to work for him to rant through his list of grievances. He finished with, "I had no idea she was charging it all on my card. I didn't know I was going to have to pay for all that stuff!"

"Sooner or later, you always have to pay the piper," Maisy replied philosophically. She recoiled from the look he shot her, but added stubbornly, "Well, you can't expect a brownie to cook and clean all day for you and not get anything out of it for herself." She ran her fingers wistfully down the scarf on her purse. "Sometimes when it's toughest and you can least afford it is when you feel like you have to take some little corner of your life for yourself." Then she cleared her throat and sat up straighter. "Sounds to me like she has definite tastes in furniture and decorating and food and she's beginning to indulge them."

"She sure has. On my credit card. So. What do I do now? How do I get rid of her?"

He had pulled into the parking lot by Uffer's Landing. Maisy paused before getting out. "Well, traditionally, just thanking the brownie or leaving a gift would cause him to depart. But now you've made her angry. It's almost like you mocked her with that shirt and your thanks. That may make it harder."

He pondered it while he worked that day, ignoring the jibes his fellow workers made about his pinto coveralls. On his lunch break, he made a quick trip to the 7-Eleven. As he had hoped, they had a little toy rack there. No problem. He was back to work with plenty of time to spare.

When he picked up Maisy, he had the sack on the seat between them. "What's this?" she asked curiously. "Toys?"

"No, clothing. You said the shoemaker gave the elves

clothes, so I picked some up for her. What do you think? I wasn't sure of the size."

"I've no idea," she murmured, bemused. She took out the Fashion Doll Prom Queen outfit, and looked at it. Without a word, she slid it back into the bag.

"Well? What do you think?"

"Um. Well. I think you can try it. Doll clothes aren't really, um, sewn to be worn by living creatures, with arms and legs that bend. And, from what you've told me of your brownie, she may have, um, more sophisticated tastes."

"But it says it's a prom dress! What's fancier than that?" She didn't reply. Plainly she thought it wasn't going to work. "It was all I could think of," he said wearily. "I mean, where would *you* go to buy clothing for a brownie?"

"I guess I've never really thought about it," she replied, and then tried, a few moments later, to smother her giggle.

"What's so funny?"

"The thought of you shopping for your brownie."

"You wouldn't think it was so funny if she had invaded your apartment."

"Neither would she. She'd discover that I'd maxed out my credit cards before she even had a chance, and furnished most of the place from Value Village."

When they pulled into the garage, Jeffrey asked shyly, "Uh, would you mind coming and taking a look at my place with me? Maybe you'd have an idea. In case this doesn't work."

Maisy gave him a direct smile. "I wouldn't mind. All my study of folklore turns out to have been theory. This will be my first chance to do some fieldwork. Maybe my degree will turn out to be more practical than some people think it is."

"Funny," he said grouchily, but smiled in spite of himself.

She followed him silently into his apartment. "Those are

new," he said, pointing out a fan of $20-a-pop home decoration magazines on the coffee table. Someone on the television was holding wallpaper samples against paint chips. He clicked it off. "Let's see what she made for dinner today."

Inside the refrigerator was a cheap white paper plate with three greasy corn dogs wilting oil into it. Next to it was a domed cup full of melted red Slushy. "You see what I'm dealing with here?" he exclaimed angrily to Maisy. "Fancy magazines for her; corn dogs for me! And look at—"

Maisy held up a warning hand, jolting him to silence. "I just love corn dogs!" she exclaimed. "How wonderful of her to provide such a fun dinner for us. Do you have ketchup and mustard?"

"I—" He halted in astonishment that she could be enthused about such a thing. "Yeah. Mustard's there in the door of the fridge. Ketchup's in the cupboard. Knock yourself out."

"Oh, thank you!" She fairly sang the words, eyeing him all the while as if he were a slightly dim three-year-old.

"You're welcome," he replied, puzzled, and then, "Oh. Of course, you're welcome. But I'm not really the one you should thank. I really can't claim the credit. I just remembered, I left something important in my car. I'll be right back."

By the time he returned with the doll clothes, Maisy had zapped the corn dogs in the microwave. She had poured the melted Slushy over ice into two plastic cups and set it out on the table. He noticed the salt and pepper grinders had been replaced with Souvenir of Washington plastic Space Needles. As he came into the kitchen, Maisy turned to him. "Look! Western Family chocolate-flavor pudding cups for dessert! Doesn't that just perfectly complement this meal?"

"Perfect," he agreed truthfully. They sat down to eat together at the table. Cloaked in mustard and ketchup, the corn dogs weren't all that bad.

"Reminds me of when I was a kid and went to the Puyallup Fair every summer," Maisy observed thoughtfully. "Raspberry scones were my favorite, but my brother loved these. Krusty Pups were what they called them."

"Yeah, I remember those. We went every summer when I was a kid. My dad used to say a Krusty Pup sounded like a hound with a skin condition. Ow! But you're right, these are delicious. Is there any more melted Slushy?"

They finished the meal with the chocolate-flavored imitation pudding, eating right from the little plastic cups. Maisy actually seemed to enjoy the meal; at least, whenever he glanced over at her, she was smiling. Ironically, Jeffrey reflected that a month ago, he wouldn't have thought it was so bad, either. He'd just become accustomed to better, that was all. But having seen what better could do to his charge cards, he could probably re-adapt.

He cleared the debris away. Few dishes to wash; most of it went right into the garbage can. "Do you have gift wrap and paper anywhere?" Maisy called to him from the living room.

"I kind of doubt it." Did any single man have that sort of thing in a cupboard somewhere in his house?

"I'll be right back then. I've got some at my place."

What she returned with was one of those gift bags and white tissue paper and a ribbon and a thank you card. She gave the card to him while she transformed the Barbie clothes into a gift package the size of a small television. After a lot of head scratching, he wrote in the card, "Thanks, Brownie. You've taught me a lot." He signed it and wrote BROWNIE on the front of it. Maisy set it out carefully on the coffee table and then surprised him by taking his hand and saying firmly, "Let's go for a walk."

They left his apartment and went across the courtyard to hers. She made coffee for them and fed Trounce. Trounce sniffed him doubtfully, then spent several minutes carefully marking his ankles with rubs from his forehead. She had a nice place. Battered furniture, lots of books. The lamps on the end tables didn't match. Comfortable. Jeffrey leaned back in one of Maisy's armchairs and asked, "Do you think it's going to work?"

Maisy took a sip of her coffee. It looked like it was mostly creamer to him. "I don't know," she said carefully. "If she has a generous spirit, and accepts the gift as a worthy effort, then perhaps it will. But looking around your apartment at the quality of the stuff she's brought in . . ." Maisy lifted one shoulder in a shrug. "I don't know. I think her esthetics may be offended. No offense. Shopping for a brownie must have been difficult. But I don't think she sees herself as Barbie at the prom. Betsey Johnson and Prada might be more her style."

The unfamiliar names baffled him. "Oh. Well. It's all outside of my experience. How long will it take her to leave?"

"Well, in the stories I remember, the thanked brownie took the gifts and left immediately, feeling he was far too fine to do menial work anymore. Let's give her another hour and then go back. If the clothing is gone, then I think she's gone with it."

He actually stayed considerably longer. Maisy put *Romancing the Stone* in her VCR and made popcorn in a pan. "The microwave stuff is too expensive," she told him when he said he hadn't seen that done in a long time. She had Thomas Kemper root beer in her fridge.

"Isn't that a premium root beer?" he asked her teasingly as she split it between two coffee mugs for them.

"Well, for some things, I'd rather have the good stuff or nothing at all. Sometimes you have to have one really good thing to look forward to, just to get through the day."

He looked at her over his mug. "You really hate your job, don't you?"

"My job sucks." She leaned back and for a moment let her head loll onto the back of the couch. He looked at the long line of her throat. Then she straightened up and gave him a wry smile. "But that doesn't mean my life has to suck. It's up to me to put the things in my life that make it not suck. Or I deserve what I get."

Trounce climbed up on his lap and got orange cat hair all over the green polo shirt. It was close to eleven when she walked him back to his apartment. "I have to see if she took it," she confided. "Otherwise the suspense would keep me awake all night."

If he had ever doubted that he truly had a brownie, the sight of the plundered gift bag would have convinced him. Wrappings were everywhere, but the clothing and the card were gone. "Well, I guess that's it," he said, turning to Maisy.

She smiled up at him. "I suppose it is. Well. Hm. This gives me a lot to think about." She continued to stand there, looking up at him. He'd never realized he was that much taller than she was. For one crazy moment, he considered kissing her.

"Well. Good night," she said a few seconds later.

"Yeah. Good night. Thanks. For helping get rid of the brownie and everything."

"Oh. Well. You're welcome. See you tomorrow."

"Yeah, see you tomorrow. Good night, Maisy."

"Good night, Jeffrey."

She was halfway across the courtyard before he realized that if he'd walked her back to her door, maybe he could have kissed her good night. Dummy. She stopped at her patio to wave at him, and he waved back before she went inside. He shut the glass door and closed the curtain. Well, that was that. No more brownie.

His complacency lasted until he used the toilet before heading to bed. When he flushed it, the water swirled slowly, stalled and then began ominously rising. A pink Barbie high heel suddenly bobbed to the surface. A hasty resort to the plunger didn't do anything except get water all over the floor. He shut off the flow to the tank and left a message for the manager to please let the plumber into his apartment tomorrow.

When he tried to get into bed, it was short-sheeted. Cursing, he tore all the bedding off the bed, and then slept rolled up in a blanket.

He was awakened by the phone ringing. Somewhere. She'd taken the cordless phone out of its cradle and hidden it. Every clock in the house had been unplugged, even the one in the microwave. By the time he found the phone under the sofa cushions, it had stopped ringing. He used caller ID, and redial. Maisy greeted him cheerfully. "I just wanted to let you know I found your car keys on my chair this morning. In case you were looking for them."

"Thanks. I would have been. What time is it?"

"Only seven. You don't sound good."

"I'm not. She's not gone and she's really pissed off now." Tersely he recounted the events of the night and morning.

When he'd finished, she said sympathetically, "You can come over here and clean up in my bathroom if you want."

"Thanks. I'll do that. See you in a bit."

All his underwear had been starched. He put on the pink polo shirt and left a note for the plumber. He took his shave kit and crossed the courtyard and tapped on Maisy's patio door. She called to him to come in. "The bathroom's all yours. There's coffee and toast in the kitchen when you want it." She was wearing a pair of reading glasses and had five or six books open on the table. She was sitting over them with a pencil in one hand and a notebook in front of her.

"I don't know how to thank you."

She looked up with a smile. "Don't bother. This is the

first time in a long time that I've felt this intrigued and challenged. I know it's horrible for you, but I'm finding this fascinating."

"Fascinating. Yeah," he grumped, but smiled. He felt almost human after he'd shaved and brushed his teeth. The coffee wasn't too strong and she had marmalade to go with the toast. They ate together, standing in her kitchen. "So. Any new ideas?"

"A few. There are several stories here that speak of how a difficult brownie was finally laid."

"Laid?" Jeffrey was startled.

"Set free," she clarified, grinning at his expression. "Most tales about brownies are ones that tell how the brownie was finally released from servitude. Often, even when a brownie desires to be laid, it may be difficult for him. Or her. Oh. Incidentally, for a brownie to work mischief rather than be industrious because she has been insulted is nothing new. There are plenty of tales about that in the folklore. Yours has been far less violent than some in these stories."

That was scarcely reassuring. "Anything there about how to be rid of one?"

"Only hints," she said thoughtfully. "Cold iron intimidates them, it says in this book. This one says to protect yourself with holy water and then seek out a wise man learned in the ways of brownies. This one says they're fond of sweets. And beer. Some brownies were instrumental to their families' brewing operations. And this one tells a story of a brownie who could only be laid by a woman." She shrugged and took off her reading glasses. "Nothing that seems to apply to your situation." Then she smiled comfortingly at him and added, "I've a few ideas of my own. But I'd need to borrow your car this afternoon."

The look she gave him told him she didn't want to reveal why. He also sensed something of a test in her request. Would he trust her with his car, or would he demand to know why? "Okay," he replied, almost easily. "I'll leave the keys with you and walk across to work."

"Great. I'll pick you up after work, then."

He had second thoughts about it all day. What did he know about Maisy, really? Then he decided he had been foolish when she pulled into the yard's lot to pick him up. He responded to Roth's "Who's the chick?" with one lifted eyebrow, and didn't object when she leaned across the seat to unlock the passenger side for him. There was a paper bag on the seat between them. "Vintage Finds," it said. Beneath it was a fashion magazine and a little brown sack.

"I think I've got her figured," Maisy told him as they pulled out of the lot.

"What's in the bag?"

She glanced down at it, and shook her head ruefully, "Indulge me. Let me see if it works."

"Okay," he conceded. He leaned back in the seat and buckled up. It was almost relaxing. Maisy drove competently, not fiddling with the radio or looking at him while they talked. He liked that. She stopped for yellow lights, but he supposed that every driver had quirks. He could tolerate it.

They both fell silent as she pulled into the garage and parked. They got out and she tossed his keys to him over the hood of the car. He caught them neatly. "I'm dreading what I'm going to find in there today."

Maisy snagged the little paper sack out of the car. "Well. No sense in putting it off. Let's go see."

He paused at his mailbox. There were six notices for packages in his mailbox, and two notices for attempted delivery from UPS. He shook his head at them, marked, "Unordered, Return to Sender" on each of them and put them back. "At least I can cut her off here," he observed to Maisy. She shook her head, eyes large and lips pinched.

The plumber had come and gone, and left a substantial bill taped to his door. There was a plastic sack on his doorknob, full of wet doll clothes that the snake had brought up out of the line. Jeffrey left it dripping there and unlocked the door. They slipped into the dim and silent apartment. "I'll go first," Jeffrey said, as if there were danger threatening. Maisy nodded and followed him.

The apartment appeared undisturbed since he had left it. The bed was unmade, his laundry on the floor. The bathroom looked like a plumber had worked on it. When Jeffrey cautiously flushed the toilet, the water swirled and dispersed as it should. The ill-fated gift's wrapping paper still littered the living room.

When they stepped around the corner into the kitchen, all seemed normal there.

"Maybe she did leave," Jeffrey guessed. "Maybe she felt bad and left this morning."

"Somehow I doubt it," Maisy said softly. She sniffed, and so he did, too. Despite the breath of air freshener that lingered, there was an odd smell in the kitchen. She opened the refrigerator.

"Oh, my," she said softly.

Inside was a crow. It lay on its back in the serving dish, black feet curled in the air. The brownie had plucked it and gutted it before she'd roasted it for him, but she'd left the feet and head on so he'd definitely know what she was feeding him.

"She wants you to eat crow," Maisy said softly.

He looked at her, startled, "What's that supposed to mean?"

"To be forced to do something you find distasteful and demeaning. Like, perhaps, she is, when she has to cook and clean day after day. The folklore makes it clear that brownies are compelled to do their tasks. I can guess how she feels, working at something you dislike, day after day, with no end in sight or any belief it will ever get better. No wonder she wanted to indulge her own fancies." Maisy sounded almost sympathetic.

"Well, I'm not eating crow." He was suddenly angry. He snatched it up and dumped it off the plate into the garbage can under the sink. As he stood up, he hit his head on a cupboard door just as it swung open. "Damn you!" he shouted angrily. By coincidence or in response, a cup fell off the shelf and hit his shoulder. He slammed the cupboard door shut, only to have it bounce open at him again.

Maisy suddenly seized his arm. "Outside, Jeffrey," she suggested firmly. She walked him to the garden door. "I want to have a word with your brownie. Alone."

Holding his head over the rising lump on his skull, he allowed her to push him outside. She slid the glass door shut behind him and then turned back to the room. He leaned against the patio wall and watched her.

She opened the sack from Vintage Finds, and set a sparkling brooch out on the table. Next to it, she placed a gold box of Godiva chocolates and the fashion magazine. She seemed to linger there for a long time. Her back was to him. He could hear her talking softly, but he couldn't make out the words. Then, slowly, she untied the scarf from her purse. She opened the magazine and set the scarf into it as if it were a page marker. She seemed to look at it for a long time, then nodded firmly to herself and turned to the door. She came out, shutting the door firmly behind her, and took his arm.

"You're buying me dinner," she told him firmly.

"Sounds good," he said quietly. He started to take her to the car, but she steered him to the sidewalk and they walked to the corner deli. They bought sandwiches and a carton of potato salad to share and splurged on two Thomas Kemper root beers. They ate at a table on the sidewalk, watching other wage slaves trudging home for the evening. It was the nicest meal he'd had in quite a while.

"You gave her your scarf?" he said at last.

"Yes."

"It might have been a Hermy's."

"A Hermès. It was. The lady at the vintage store looked it up for me. 'Les Tuileries,' in gold and black."

"The scarf had a name?" he asked incredulously. He smiled.

She didn't. "Yes. It did." She forked up a bite from the communal salad tub, and ate it thoughtfully.

"Why did you give it to her?"

"Oh, impulse, I suppose. There was an article in the magazine, about how to drape a sarong. It suddenly just seemed too perfect to be a coincidence." She ate another forkful of potato salad. "Maybe I thought she deserved it. Needed it. A grace note to her life."

"I'll buy you another," he offered after a long silence.

She leaned back in her chair, cocked her head at him and gave him an odd look. "You can't," she said at last.

"Why not? There must be others out there. I've got a friend, he finds all sort of stuff on eBay for people."

"No. You don't understand. Some things I have to get for myself. My own grace notes. Or my life *would* suck."

"I see," he said, and he almost did. They finished their meal and walked slowly back through the summer evening to the apartment courtyard. By tacit consent, they went to his apartment door and peeked in. The gifts were gone. Just inside the patio wall, Trounce crouched over the roasted crow, eating noisily.

"Watch out for bones," Maisy warned him severely. Then they entered his apartment and walked slowly through it. It had been tidied thoroughly, but she was definitely gone. Jeffrey could feel her absence, and for a moment he felt abandoned as much as relieved. He could almost feel the dust resettling on the shelves. Idly, he moved his shaving cream from the bathroom shelf to the sink's edge, knowing it would still be there when he returned to the room. In the bedroom, he looked around and gave a small sigh. Maisy echoed it. "What are you thinking?" she asked him softly.

He smiled ruefully. "That tomorrow, I'm back to doing my own laundry, and making my own bed. When I get around to it." He turned to her. "What are you thinking? Satisfied that you finally laid the brownie?"

"Actually," she said, smiling. "I was just thinking that brownies aren't the only ones who have a hard time getting laid. Even when they desire it."

"Oh," said Jeffrey.

The Gypsies in the Wood

by Kim Newman

The unexpected is the one thing a reader may expect from a new story by Kim Newman. In his unusually plotted novella "The Gypsies in the Wood," he not only introduces us to a sinister brood of fairy folk and mortals alike, but also a brave distaff journalist and an intrepid investigator from a government agency whose very existence is kept secret from Victorian Londoners—though not from the hushed chambers of the venerable Diogenes Club. . . .

Newman, an English actor, broadcaster, film critic, and author who lives in London, has written such novels as Anno Dracula, Bad Dreams, The Bloody Red Baron, Dracula Cha Cha Cha *(aka* Judgment of Tears: Anno Dracula 1959), Jago, The Night Mayor, *and short stories collected in* The Original Dr. Shade and Other Stories, Famous Monsters, Seven Stars, Unforgivable Stories, *and* Where the Bodies Are Buried. *Under the name Jack Yeovil, he has written* Beasts in Velvet, Comeback Tour, Drachenfels, Demon Download, Genevieve Undead, Krokodil Tears, Route 666, Silver Nails, *and* Orgy of the Blood Parasites. *His fiction has been translated into German, Italian, Spanish, French, Polish, Portuguese, and Japanese.*

His nonfiction includes Horror: 100 Best Books *(with Stephen Jones), for which he won the Bram Stoker Award from the Horror Writers of America, and he also won the British Science Fiction Award; the Children of the Night Award presented by the Dracula Society; the Fiction Award of the Lord Ruthven Assembly; the International Horror Critics' Guild Award; the Prix Ozone; and the British Fantasy Award.*

ACT I: THE CHILDREN OF EYE

1: 'we take an interest'

'Mr Charles Beauregard?' asked Dr Rud, squinting through *pince-nez.*

Charles allowed he was who his *carte de visite* said he was.

'Of . . . the Diogenes Club?'

'Indeed.'

He stood at the front door. The Criftins, the doctor's house, was large but lopsided, several buildings close together, cobbled into one by additions in different stone. At once household, clinic and dispensary, it was an important place in the parish of Eye, if not a noteworthy landmark in the county of Herefordshire. On the map Charles had studied on the down train, Eye was a double-yolked egg: two communities, Ashton Eye and Moreton Eye, separated by a rise of trees called Hill Wood and an open space of common ground called Fair Field.

It was mid-evening, full dark and freezing. His breath frosted. Snow had settled thick in recent weeks. Under a quarter-moon, the countryside was dingy white, with black scabs where the fall was melted or cleared away.

Charles leaned forward a little, slipping his face into light-spill to give the doctor a good, reassuring look at him.

Rud, unused to answering his own front door, was grumpily pitching in during the crisis. After another token glance at Charles's card, the doctor threw up his hands and stood aside.

A Royal Welsh Fusilier lounged in the hallway, giving cheek to a tweeny. The maid, who carried a heavy basin, tolerated none of his malarkey. She barged past the guard, opening the parlour door with a practiced hip-shove, and slipped inside with an equally practiced flounce, agitating the bustle-like bow of her apron-ties.

Charles stepped over the threshold.

The guard clattered upright, rifle to shoulder. Stomach in, shoulders out, eyes front, chin up. The tweeny, returning from the parlour, smirked at his tin soldier pose. The lad blushed violet. Realising Charles wore no uniform, he relaxed into an attitude of merely casual vigilance.

'I assume you are another wave of this *invasion?*' stated the doctor.

'Someone called out the army,' said Charles. 'Through channels, the army called out us. Which means you get me, I'm afraid.'

Rud was stout and bald, hair pomaded into a laurel-curl fringe. Five cultivated strands plastered across his pate, a sixth hanging awry—like a bell-pull attached to his brain. Tonight, the doctor received visitors without ceremony, collarless, in shirtsleeves and waistcoat. He ought to be accustomed to intrusions at all hours. A country practice never closed. Charles gathered the last few days had been more than ordinarily trying.

'I did not expect a curfew, sir. We're good, honest Englishmen in Eye. And Welshmen too. Not some rebellious settlement in the Hindu Kush. Not an enemy position, to be taken, occupied and looted!'

The guard's blush was still vivid. The tweeny put her hands on her broad hips and laughed.

'Your "natives" seem to put up a sterling defence.'

'Major Chilcot has set up inspection points, prohibited entry to Hill Wood, closed the Small Man . . .'

'I imagine it's for your protection. Though I'll see what I can do. If anything is liable to lead to mutiny, it's shutting the pub.'

'You are correct in that assumption, sir. Correct.'

Charles assessed Rud as quick to bristle. He was used to being listened to. Hereabouts, he was a force with which to be reckoned. Troubles, medical and otherwise, were brought to him. If Eye was a fiefdom, the Criftins was its castle and Dr Rud—not the vicar, Justice of the Peace or other local worthy—its Lord. The doctor didn't care to be outranked by outsiders. It was painful for him to admit that some troubles fell beyond his experience.

It would be too easy to take against the man. Charles would never entirely trust a doctor.

The bite-mark in his forearm twinged.

Pamela came to mind. His wife. His *late* wife.

She would have cautioned him against unthinking prejudice. He conceded that Rud could hardly be expected to cope. His usual run was births and deaths, boils and fevers, writing prescriptions and filling in certificates.

None of that would help now.

This sort of affair rang bells in distant places. Disturbed the web of the great spider. Prompted the deployment of someone like Mr Charles Beauregard.

A long-case clock ticked off each second. The steady passage of time was a given, like drips of subterranean water forming a stalactite. Time was perhaps subjectively slower here than in the bustle of London—but as inevitable, unvarying, inexorable.

This business made the clock a liar. Rud did not care to think that. If time could play tricks, what *could* one trust?

The doctor escorted Charles along the hallway. Gas lights burned in glass roses, whistling slightly. Bowls of dried petals provided sweet scent to cover medical odours.

At the parlour door, the soldier renewed his effort to simulate attention. Rud showed the man Charles's card. The fusilier saluted.

'Not strictly necessary,' said Charles.

'Better safe than sorry, sah!'

Rud tapped the card, turning so that he barred the door, looking up at Charles with frayed determination.

'By the bye, how precisely does membership of this institution, this *club*—with which I am unfamiliar—give you the right to interview my patient?'

'We take an interest. In matters like these.'

Rud, who had probably thought his capacity for astonishment exhausted, at once caught the implication.

'Surely this case is singular? Unique?'

Charles said nothing to contradict him.

'This has happened before? How often?'

'I'm afraid I really can't say.'

Rud was fully aghast. 'Seldom? Once in a blue moon? Every second Thursday?'

'I really can't say.'

The doctor threw up his hands. 'Fine,' he said, 'quiz the poor lad. I've no explanation for him. Maybe you'll be able to shed light. It'll be a relief to pass on the case to someone in authority.'

'Strictly, the Diogenes Club has status rather than authority.'

This was too much for Rud to take aboard. Even the mandarins of the Ruling Cabal could not satisfactorily define the standing of the Diogenes Club. Outwardly, the premises in Pall Mall housed elderly, crotchety misanthropes dedicated only to being left in peace. There were, however, other layers: sections of the club busied behind locked steel doors, *taking an interest.* Gentlemanly agreements struck in Whitehall invested the Diogenes Club as an unostentatious instrument of Her Majesty's government. More often than the public knew, matters arose beyond the purview of the police, the diplomatic service or the armed forces. Matters few institutions could afford to acknowledge even as possibilities. *Some* body had to take responsibility, even if only a job-lot of semi-official amateurs.

'Come in, come in,' said Rud, opening the parlour door. 'Mrs Zeals has been feeding the patient broth.'

The Criftins was low-ceilinged, with heavy beams. Charles doffed his hat to pass under the lintel.

From this moment, the business was *his* responsibility.

2: 'my mother said I never should'

The parlour had fallen into gloom. Dr Rud turned the gas-key, bringing up light as if the play were about to begin. *Act I, Scene 1: The parlour of the Criftins. Huddled in an armchair by the fire is . . .*

'Davey Harvill?'

The patient squirmed at the sound of Charles's voice, pulling up and hugging his knees, hiding his lower face. Charles put his hat on an occasional table and took off his heavy ulster, folding it over a high-backed chair.

The patient's eyes skittered, huge-pupilled.

'This gentleman is . . .'

Charles waved his fingers, shutting off the doctor's pre-amble. He did not want to present an alarming, mysterious figure.

The patient's trousers stretched tight around thin shanks, ripped in many places, cuffs high on the calf-like knee-britches. He was shirtless and shoeless, a muffler wrapped around bird-thin shoulders. His calloused feet rested in a basin of dirtied water. His toenails were like thorns. Many old sores and scars made scarlet lakes and rivers on the map of his very white skin. His thatch of hair was starched with clay into the semblance of an oversized magistrate's wig; his beard matted into pelt-like chest-hair, threaded through with twigs; his moustaches hung in twisted braids, strung with bead-like pebbles.

Glimpsing himself in a glass, Rud smoothed his own stray hair-strand across his scalp.

Charles pulled a footstool close to the basin.

The patient looked like Robinson Crusoe after years on the island. Except Crusoe would have been tanned. This fellow's pallor suggested a prisoner freed from an *oubliette*. Wherever he had been marooned was away from the sun, under the earth.

An animal smell was about him.

Charles sat on the stool and took the patient's thin hands, lifting them from his knees. His fingernails were long and jagged.

'My name is Charles. May I talk with you?'

The eyes fixed on him, sharp and bright. A tiny flesh-bulb, like a drop of fresh blood, clung to the corner of the right eyelid.

'Talk, mister?'

The voice was thin and high. He spoke as if English was unfamiliar, and his native tongue lacked important consonants.

'Yes, just talk.'

'Frightened, mister. Been so long.'

The face was seamed. Charles would have estimated the patient's age at around his own, thirty-five.

Last week, Davey Harvill had celebrated his ninth birthday.

The patient had a child's eyes, frightened but innocent. He closed them, shutting out the world, and shrank into the chair. His nails pressed into the meat of Charles's hands.

Charles let go and stood.

The patient—Davey, he had to be called—wound a corner of the muffler in his fingers, screwing it up close to his mouth. Tears followed runnels in his cheeks.

Mrs Zeals tried to comfort him, with coos and more broth.

'Rest,' said Charles. 'You're safe now. Talking can wait.'

Red crescents were pressed into the heels of Charles's hands, already fading. Davey was not weak.

The patient's eyes flicked open, glittering in firelight. There was a cunning in them, now. Childlike, but dangerous.

Davey gripped Charles's arm, making him wince.

'My mother said I never should . . . play with *the gypsies in the wood* . . . if I did, she would say, *"naughty girl to disobey"!*'

Davey let him go.

The rhyme came in a lower voice, more assured, almost mocking. Not a grown-up voice, though. A feathery chill brushed Charles's spine. It was not a boy's rhyme, but something a girl would sing. Davey smiled a secret smile, then swallowed it. He was as he had been, frightened rather than frightening.

Charles patted his shoulder.

'Has he an appetite?' he asked the housekeeper.

'Yes, sir.'

'Keep feeding him.'

Mrs Zeals nodded. She was part-nurse, probably midwife too. The sort of woman never missed until she was needed, but who then meant life or death. If a Mrs Zeals had been in the Hill Country, Charles might still be a husband and father. She radiated good sense, though this case tested the limitations of good sense as a strategy for coping.

'We shall talk again later, Davey. When you're rested.'

Davey nodded, as much to himself as Charles.

'Dr Rud, do you have a study? I should like to review the facts.'

The doctor had hung back by the door, well out of reach.

'You're in charge, Mrs Zeals,' he said, stepping backwards out of the room, eyes on the patient. 'Mr Beauregard and I have matters of import to discuss. Have Jane bring up tea, a light supper and a bottle of port.'

'Yes, doctor.'

Rud shot a look at the soldier. He disapproved of the invasion, but at present felt safer with an armed guard in his home.

'It's this way,' he told Charles, indicating with his hands, still watching the patient. 'Up the back stairs.'

Charles bowed to Mrs Zeals, smiled again at Davey, and followed the doctor.

'Extraordinary thing, wouldn't you say?' Rud gabbled.

'Certainly,' Charles agreed.

'Of course, he can't be who he says he is. There's some *trick* to this.'

3: 'pebble in a pond'

Rud's consulting room was on two levels, a step running across the floor raising a section like a small stage. One wall was lined with document-boxes. Locked cabinets held phials of salves, balms, cures and patent potions. A collection of bird and small mammal skeletons, mounted under glass domes, were posed upon items—rocks, branches, green cloth representing grass—suggestive of natural habitat.

On the raised area was a desk of many drawers and recesses. Above this, a studio photograph of Dr and Mrs Oliver Rud was flanked by framed documents, the doctor's diploma and his wife's death certificate. Glancing at this last item, careful not to be seen to do so, Charles noted cause of death was down as *diphth.* and the signature was of another physician. He wondered if it was prominently displayed to caution the doctor against medical hubris, or to forewarn patients that miracles were not always possible.

Where was Pamela's death certificate? India?

Rud sat by the desk, indicating for Charles an adjustable chair in the lower portion of the room, obviously intended for patients. Charles sat down, suppressing a thought that straps could suddenly be fixed over his wrists, binding him at a mad surgeon's mercy. Such things, unfortunately, were within his experience. The doctor rolled up the desk-cover and opened a folder containing scrawled notes.

'Hieroglyphs,' he said, showing the sheaf. 'But I understand them.'

A maid came in with the fare Rud had ordered. Charles

took tea, while the doctor poured himself a full measure of port. A plate of precisely cut sandwiches went untouched.

'If you'll start at the beginning.'

'I've been through this with Major Chilcot, and . . .'

Charles raised a finger.

'I know it's tiresome to rehash over and over, but this is a tale you'll retell for some years, no matter how it comes out. It'll be valuable to have its raw, original form before the facts become, as it were, *encrusted* with anecdotal frills.'

Rud, vaguely offended, was realist enough to see the point.

'The yarns in circulation at the Small Man are already wild, Mr Beauregard. By the end of the month, it'll be full-blown myth. And heaven knows what the newspapers will make of it.'

'We can take care of that.'

'Can you, indeed? What useful connections to have . . . at any rate, the facts? Where to begin?'

'Tell me about Davey Harvill.'

Rud adjusted his *pince-nez* and delved into the folder.

'An ordinary little boy. The usual childhood ailments and scrapes, none fatal. Father was well set-up for a man of his stripe. Cabinet-maker. Skilled craftsman. Made most of the furniture in this room.'

'*Was* well set-up? Past tense.'

'Yes, cut his arm open with a chisel and bled out before anything could be done. Two years ago. Undoubtedly an accident. Risk of the trade, I understand. By the time I was summoned, it was too late. Davey and his sisters, Sairey and Maeve, were raised by their mother, Mrs Harvill. Admirable woman. Her children will have every chance in life. Would have had, rather. Now, it's anyone's guess. Sairey, the eldest child, is married to the local baker, Philip Riddle. She's expecting her first this spring. Maeve . . . well, Maeve's an unknown quantity. She is—was—two years older than her brother. A quiet, queer little girl. The sort who'd rather play by herself. Davey, or whoever this vagrant might be, says Maeve is still "in the wood".'

Charles sipped strong tea.

'Tell me about Davey's birthday.'

'Last Wednesday. I saw him early in the morning. I was leaving Mrs Loll. She's our local hypochondriac. Always dying, secretly fit as a horse. As I stepped out of her cottage, Davey came by, wrapped up warm, whipping a hoop. A new toy, a birthday present. Maeve trailed along behind him. "If I don't watch him, doctor, he'll get run over by a cart," she said. They were walking to school, in Moreton.'

'Along Dark Lane?'

Rud was surprised. 'You know the area?'

'I looked at the map.'

'Ah, *maps*,' said Rud, touching his nose. 'Dark Lane is the road to Moreton *on the map*. But there's a cart-track through Hill Wood, runs up to Fair Field. From there, you can hop over a stile and be in Moreton. Not everything is on the map.'

'That's an astute observation.'

'Davey was rolling his hoop. There was fresh-fallen snow, but the ruts in Fair Field Track were already cut. I saw him go into the wood, his sister following, and that was it. I had other calls to make. Not something you think about, is it? Every time someone steps out of your sight, it could be the last you see of them?'

'Were you the last person to see the children?'

'No. Riddle, Sairey's husband, was coming down the track the other way, with the morning's fresh-bake. He told them he had a present to give Davey later, when it was wrapped— but gave both children buns, warm from the ovens. Then, off they went. Riddle hasn't sold a bun since. In case they're cursed, if you can credit it. As we now know, Davey and Maeve didn't turn up for school.'

'Why weren't they missed?'

'They were. Mrs Grenton, the teacher, assumed the Harvills were playing truant. Giving themselves a birthday treat. Sledging on Fair Field or building a snowman. She told the class that when the miscreants presented themselves, a strapping would be their reward. Feels dreadful about it, poor woman. Blames herself. The Harvills had perfect attendance records. Weren't the truant sort. Mrs Grenton wants me to prescribe something to make her headaches go away. Like a pebble in a pond, isn't it? The ripples. So many people wet from one splash.'

Rud gulped port and refilled the measure. His hand didn't shake, but he gripped the glass-stem as if steadying his fingers.

He whistled, tunelessly. Davey's rhyme.

'*Are* there gypsies in the wood?' asked Charles.

'What? Gypsies? Oh, the rhyme. No. We only see Romanies here at Harvest Festival, when there's a fair on Fair Field. The rhyme is something Maeve sings . . . used to sing. One of those girls' things, a skipping song. In point of fact, I remember her mother asking her not to chant it during the fair, so as not to offend actual gypsies. I doubt the girl took any notice. The gypsies, neither, come to that. No idea where the song comes from. I doubt if Violet Harvill ever had to warn her children against playing with strangers. This isn't that sort of country.'

'I've an idea the gypsies in the rhyme aren't exactly gypsies. The word's there in place of something else. Everywhere has its stories. A ghost, a dragon, a witch's ring . . .'

Rud thought a moment.

'The local bogey tale is *dwarves*. Kidnapping children to work in mines over the border. Blackfaced dwarves, with teeth filed to sharp points. "Say your prayers, boyo, or the Tiny Taffs will away with you, into the deep dark earth to dig for dirty black coal." I've heard that all my life. As you say, everywhere has its stories. Over Leintwardine way, there's a Headless Highwayman.'

'All Eye lives in fear of Welsh dwarves?'

'No, even children don't—didn't—pay any attention. It came up again, of course. When Davey and Maeve went missing. There was a stupid scrap at the Small Man. It's why the Major closed the pub. English against Welsh. That's the fault-line that runs through the marches. Good-humoured mostly, but sharp-edged. We're border country, Mr Beauregard. No one is wholly one thing or the other. Everyone has a grandparent in the other camp. But it's fierce. Come Sunday, you might hear "love thy neighbour" from the pulpit, but we've three churches within spitting distance, each packed with folk certain the other congregations are marching in step to Hell. The Harvills call themselves English, which is why the children go to school in Moreton. The Ashton school is "Welsh," somehow. The school-master is Welsh, definitely.'

Charles nodded.

'Of course, all Eye agrees on something now. Welsh soldiers with English officers have shut down the pub. I'm afraid the uniting factor is an assessment of the character and ancestry of Major Chilcot.'

Charles considered this intelligence. He had played the Great Game among the squabbling tribes of India and Afghanistan, representing the Queen in a struggle with her Russian cousin to which neither monarch was entirely privy, exploiting and being exploited by local factions who had their own Byzantine causes and conflicts. It was strange to find a Khyber Pass in Herefordshire, a potential flashpoint for an uprising. In border countries the world over, random mischief could escalate near-forgotten enmities into riot and worse.

'When were the children missed in Ashton?'

'About five o'clock. When they didn't come in for their

supper. Because it was the lad's birthday, Riddle had baked a special cake. Davey's friends came to call. Alfie Zeals, my housekeeper's son, was there. Even if brother and sister *had* played truant, they'd have been sure to be home. Presents were involved. The company waited hours. Candles burned down on the cake. Mrs Harvill, understandably, got into a state. Riddle recounted his story of meeting the children on Fair Field Track. Alfie also goes to Moreton School and admitted Davey and Maeve hadn't been there all day. Mrs Harvill rounded on the boy, who'd kept mum to keep his friend out of trouble. There were harsh words, tears. By then, it was dark. A party of men with lanterns formed. They came to me, in case a doctor was needed. You can imagine what everyone thought.'

Charles could.

'Hill Wood isn't trackless wilderness. It's a patch between fields. You can get through it in five minutes at a stroll. Even if you get off Fair Field Track and have to wade through snow. The children couldn't be *lost* there, but mishaps might have befallen. A twisted ankle or a snapped leg, and the other too afraid to leave his or her sibling. The search party went back and forth. As the night wore on, we ventured further, to Fair Field and beyond. We should have waited till morning, when we could see tracks in the snow. By sun-up, the wood was so dotted with boot-prints that any made by the children weren't noticeable. You have to understand, we thought we'd find them at any moment. A night outside in March can be fatal for a child. Or anyone. We run to bone-freezing cold here. Frost forms on your face. Snow gets hard, like a layer of ice. Violet Harvill had to be seen to. Hysteria in a woman of her age can be serious. Some of our party had come directly from the Small Man and were not in the best state. Hamer Dando fell down and tore a tendon, which should put a crimp in his poaching for months. Came the dawn, we were no better off.'

'You summoned the police?'

'We got Throttle out of bed. He's been Constable in Eye since Crimea. He lent his whistle to the search. The next day, he was too puffed to continue, so I sent for Sergeant High, from Leominster. He bicycled over, but said children run off all the time, dreaming of the South Seas, and traipse back days later, crying for mama and home cooking. I don't doubt he's right, usually. But High's reassurances sat ill with these circumstances. No boy runs away to sea when he has a birthday party to go to. Then, Davey's new whip was found in the wood, stuck into a snow bank.'

'A development?'

'An unhappily suggestive one. The mother began insisting something be done, and I was inclined to support her. But what more *could* be done? We went over the ground again, stone cold sober and in broad daylight. My hands are still frozen from dismantling snowdrifts. Every hollow, every dead tree, every path. We looked. Riddle urged we call out the army. Stories went round that the children had been abducted by foreign agents. More foreign than just Welsh. I had to prescribe laudanum for Violet.'

'This was all five days ago?'

Rud checked his notes. 'Yes. The weekend, as you can appreciate, was a terrible time. Riddle got his way. Major Chilcot's fusiliers came over from Powys. At first, they just searched again, everywhere we'd looked before. Violet was besieged by neighbours offering to help but with no idea what to do. I doubt a single soul within five miles has had a night's uninterrupted sleep since this began.'

Rud's eyes were red-rimmed.

'Then, yesterday morning,' said the doctor, 'Davey—or whoever he might be—came to his mother's door, and asked for his blessed cake.'

Rud slapped his folder on his desk. An end to his story.

'Your patient claims to be Davey Harvill?'

'Gets upset when anyone says he can't be.'

'There is evidence.'

'Oh yes. Evidence. He's wearing Davey's trousers. If the army hadn't been here, he'd have been hanged for that. No ceremony, just hanged. We're a long way from the assizes.'

Charles finished his tea and set down the cup and saucer.

'There's more than that,' he said. 'Or I wouldn't be here. Out with it, man. Don't be afraid of being laughed at.'

'It's hard to credit . . .'

'I make a speciality of credulousness. Open-minded, we call it.'

Gingerly, Rud opened the file again.

'The man downstairs. I would put his age at between thirty-five and forty. Davey is nine years old. *Ergo*, they are not the same person. But, in addition to his own scars, the patient has *Davey's*. A long, jagged mark on his calf. Done hauling over a stile, catching on a rusty nail. I treated the injury last year. The fellow has a perfect match. Davey has a growth under the right eye, like a teardrop. That's there, too.'

'These couldn't be new-made.'

'The scar, just maybe—though it'd have to be prepared months in advance. The teardrop is a birthmark. Impossible to contrive. It's not a family trait, so this isn't some long-lost Harvill popping up at the worst possible moment.'

Upon this development, Chilcot, like all bewildered field commanders, communicated with his superiors, who cast around for some body with special responsibility for changelings.

Which would be the Diogenes Club.

'Where does he claim to have been?'

'Just "in the wood".'

'With the gypsies?'

'He sings that rhyme when the mood takes him, usually to end a conversation he's discomfited by. As you said, I don't think gypsies really come into it.'

'You've examined him. How's his general health?'

Rud picked up a note written in shiny new ink. 'What you'd expect from a tramp. Old wounds, untended but healed. Various infestations—nits, lice, the like. And malnutrition.'

'No frostbite?'

Rud shook his head.

'So he's not been sleeping out of doors this past week? In the cold, cold snow?'

Rud was puzzled again. 'Maybe he found a barn.'

'Maybe.'

'There's another . . . ah, anomaly,' ventured the doctor. 'I've not told anyone, because it makes no sense. The fellow has good teeth. But he has two missing at the front, and new enamel growing through the gums. Normal for a nine-year-old, losing milk teeth and budding adult choppers. But there is no third dentition. That's beyond freakish.'

Rud slipped the paper back into the folder.

'That's Davey Harvill's file, isn't it?'

'Yes, of course . . . oh, I see. The patient should have a fresh folder. He is not Davey Harvill.'

Rud pulled open desk drawers, searching for a folder.

'Follow your first instincts, Dr Rud. You added notes on this patient to Davey's folder. It seemed so natural that you didn't even consider any other course. Logic dictated you proceed on an assumption you know to be impossible. So, we have reached the limits of logic.'

4: 'Silas Gobbo'

In the snug of the Small Man, after breakfast, Charles read the riot act to the army. Though the reason for closing the pub was plain, it did not help Major Chilcot's case that he had billeted himself on the premises and was prone to 'requisitioning' from the cellar.

'Purely medicinal,' Chilcot claimed. 'After a spell wandering around with icicles for fingers, a tot is a damn necessity.'

Charles saw his point, but suspected it had been sharpened after a hasty gulp.

'That's reasonable, Major. But it would be politic to pay your way.'

'We're here to *help* these ungrateful bounders . . .'

The landlord glared from behind the bar.

'Just so,' said Charles.

The Major muttered but backed down.

The landlord, visibly perked, came over.

'Will the gentleman be requiring more tea?'

'No, thank you,' said Charles. 'Prepare a bill for myself and the Major. Keep a running tally. You have my word you will not be out of pocket. Tonight, you may re-open.'

The landlord beamed.

'Between sunset and ten o'clock,' insisted Chilcot.

A line appeared in the landlord's forehead.

'That's fair,' said Charles.

The landlord accepted the ruling. For the moment.

The Major was another local bigwig, late in an undistinguished career. This would be the making or breaking of a younger, more ambitious officer.

While he stayed cosy in the Small Man, his men bivouacked on Fair Field under retreat-from-Moscow conditions. They were diamond-quality. Sergeant Beale, an old India hand, had rattled off a precise report of all measures taken. It wasn't through blundering on the part of the fusiliers that Maeve Harvill still hadn't turned up.

Charles left the pub and walked through Ashton Eye. Snow lay thick on roofs and in front gardens. Roads and paths were cleared, chunky drifts stained with orange mud piled at the sides. By day, the occupation was more evident. Soldiers, stamping against the cold, manned a trestle at the bottom of Fair Field Track. Chilcot, probably at Beale's prompt, had established a perimeter around Hill Wood.

At the Criftins, Charles was admitted—by a manservant,

this time. He joined a small company in the hallway. A fresh fusilier stood guard at the parlour. Dr Rud introduced Charles, vaguely as 'from London,' to a young couple, the woman noticeably with child, and a lady of middle years, obviously in distress.

'Philip and Sairey Riddle, and Mrs Harvill . . . Violet.'

He said his good mornings and shook hands.

'We've asked you here to put the man purporting to be Davey to the test,' Charles explained. 'Some things are shared only among family members. Not great confidences, but trivial matters. Intelligence no one outside a home could be expected to have. Remarks made by someone to someone else when they were alone together. An impostor won't know that, no matter how carefully he prepared the fraud.'

Mrs Harvill sniffled into a kerchief. Her daughter held her shoulders.

'He is still in the parlour?' Charles asked Rud.

'Spent the night there. I've got him into a dressing gown. He's had breakfast. I had my man shave him, and make a start on his hair.'

The doctor put his hand to the door.

'It is best if we hold back,' said Charles. 'Allow the family to meet without outsiders present.'

Rud frowned.

'We'll be here, a moment away, if needs arise.'

The doctor acquiesced and held the door open.

'Mam,' piped a voice from inside. Charles saw Davey, in his chair, forearms and shins protruding from a dressing gown a size too small for him. Without the beard, he looked younger.

Mrs Harvill froze and pulled back, shifting out of Davey's eye-line.

'Mam?' almost a whine, close to tears.

Mrs Harvill was white, hand tightly gripping her daughter's, eyes screwed shut. Her terror reminded Charles of

Davey's, last night, when he felt threatened. Sairey hugged her mother, but detached herself.

'You stay here, Mam. Me and Phil'll talk with the lad. The gentlemen will look after you.'

Sairey passed her mother on to Rud.

Mrs Harvill embraced the practitioner, discomfiting him, pressing her face to his shoulder. She sobbed, silently.

Sairey, slow and graceful in her enlarged state, took her husband's arm and stepped into the parlour. Davey started out of his seat, a broad smile showing his impossible teeth-buds.

'Sairey, Phil . . .'

Charles closed the door.

Rud sat Mrs Harvill on a chair and went upstairs to fetch a something to calm her. The woman composed herself. She looked at Charles, paying him attention for the first time.

'Who are you?' she asked, bluntly.

'Charles Beauregard.'

'Oliver said that. I mean what are you?'

'I'm here to help.'

'Where are my children? Are they safe?'

'That's what we are trying to determine, Mrs Harvill.'

The answer didn't satisfy. She looked away, ignoring him. In her petishness, she was like Davey. Charles even thought he heard her crooning 'My mother said . . .' under her breath. She had found a fetish object, a length of rope with a handle. She bound her hand until the fingers were bloodless, then unwound the rope and watched pink seep back.

Rud returned and gave Mrs Harvill a glass of water into which he measured three drops from a blue bottle. She swallowed it with a grimace and he rewarded her with a sugar-lump. If her son *had* been transformed into an adult, this business had turned her—in some sense—into a child.

A muffle of conversation could be heard through the door.

The temptation to eavesdrop was a fish-hook in the mind. Charles saw the doctor felt the tug even more keenly. Only the soldier was impassive, bored with this duty but grateful to be inside in the warm.

'What *can* be keeping them?' said Mrs Harvill.

She fiddled again with her fetish, separating the rope into strands as if undoing a child's braid. The rope was Davey's new whip, which had been found in Hill Wood.

Charles could only imagine how Violet Harvill felt.

Pamela had died, along with their new-born son, after a botched delivery. He had blamed an incompetent doctor, then malign providence, and finally himself. By accepting the commission in the Hills, he had removed his family from modern medicine. A hot, hollow grief had scooped him out. He had come to accept that he would never be the man he was before, but knew Pamela would have been fiercely disappointed if he used the loss as an excuse to surrender. She had burst into his life to challenge everything he believed. Their marriage had been a wonderful, continuous explosion. In the last hours, clinging to him—biting deep into his forearm to staunch her own screams—and knowing she would die, Pamela had talked a cascade, soothing and hectoring, loving and reprimanding, advising and ordering. In London fog, he had lost the memory for a while. An engagement to Pamela's cousin, Penelope Churchward, had been his first effort at re-forming a private world, and its embarrassing termination the spur to think again on what his wife had tried to tell him. As he found himself deeper in the affairs of the Diogenes Club, Pamela's voice came back. Every day, he would remember something of hers, something she had said or done. Sometimes, a twinge in his arm would be enough, a reminder that he had to live up to her.

Looking at Mrs Harvill, he recalled the other loss, eclipsed by Pamela's long, bloody dying. His son, Richard Charles, twelve years dead, had lived less than an hour and opened his eyes only in death, face washed clean by the *ayah*. If he had been a girl, she would have been Pandora Sophie. Charles and Pamela had got used to calling the child 'Dickie or Dora.' As Pamela wished, he had served mother and child in the Indian manner, cremating them together. Most of the ashes were scattered in India, which she had loved in a way he admired but never shared. Some he had brought back to England, to placate Pamela's family. An urn rested in the vault in Kingstead Cemetery, a proper place of interment for a proper woman who would have been disowned had she spent more time at home expressing her opinions.

But what of the boy?

Losing a child is the worst thing in the world. Charles knew that, but didn't *feel* it. His son, though born, was still a part of Pamela, one loss coiled up within the other. If he ached for Dickie or Dora, it was only in the sense he sometimes felt for the other children Pamela and he would have had, the names they might have taken. The Churchwards ran to Ps and there had yet to be a Persephone, Paulus, Patricia or Prosper.

Now he thought of the boy.

It was in him, he knew, wrapped up tight. The cold dead spot. The rage and panic. The ruthlessness.

Violet Harvill would do *anything*.

She seemed to snap out of her spell, and tied Davey's whip around her wrist, loose like a bracelet. She stood, determined.

Rud was at the parlour door.

'If you feel you're up to this, Violet . . .'

She said nothing but he opened the door. Sairey was laughing at something Davey had just said. The lad was smiling, an entirely different person.

'Mam,' he said, seeing Mrs Harvill.

Charles *knew* disaster was upon them. He was out of his

chair and across the hall, reaching for Mrs Harvill. She was too swift for him, sensing his grasp and ducking under it. A creak at the back of her throat grew into a keening, birdlike cry. She flew into the parlour, fingers like talons.

Her nails raked across Davey's face, carving red runnels. She got a grip on his throat.

'What've you done with them?' she demanded.

A torrent of barrack abuse poured from her mouth, words Charles would once have sworn a woman could not even know—though, at the last, Pamela had used them too. Violet Harvill's face was a mask of hate.

'What've you *done?*'

Sairey tried to shift from her chair, forgetting for a moment her unaccustomed shape. With a yelp, she sat back down, holding her belly.

Riddle and Rud seized Mrs Harvill and pulled her away. Charles stepped in and prised the woman's fingers from Davey's throat, one by one. She continued to screech and swear.

'Get her out of the room,' Charles told the doctor. 'Please.'

There was a struggle, but it was done.

Davey was back in his huddle, knees up against his face, eyes liquid, sing-songing.

'Naughty girl to disobey . . . dis-o-*bey*! Naughty girl . . .'

Sairey, careful now, hugged him, pressing his head to her full breast. He rocked back and forth.

Charles's collar had come undone and his cravat was loose.

He was responsible for this catastrophe.

'He'm Davey, mister,' said Sairey, softly. She didn't notice she was weeping. 'No doubt 'bout it. We talked 'bout what you said. Family things. When I were little, Dad do made up stories for I, stories 'bout Silas Gobbo, a little wood-carver who lives in a hollow tree in our garden and makes furniture for birds. Dad'd make tiny tables and chairs from offcuts, put 'em in the tree and take I out to the garden to show off Silas's new work. Dad told the tales over, to Davey and Maeve. Loved making little toys, did Dad. No one but Davey could've known 'bout Silas Gobbo. Not 'bout the tiny tables and chairs. Even if someone else heard the stories, they couldn't *love* Silas. Davey and Maeve do. With Dad gone, loving Silas is like loving him, remembering. Maeve used to say she wanted to marry Silas when she grew up, and be a princess.'

'So you're convinced?'

'Everythin' else, from last week and from years ago, the boy still has in 'en. Mam'll never accept it. I don't know how I can credit it, but it's him.'

She held her brother close. Even shaved, he seemed to be twice her age.

Charles fixed his collar.

'What does he say about Maeve?'

'She'm with Silas Gobbo. He'm moved from our tree into Hill Wood. Davey says Maeve be a princess now.'

5: 'filthy afternoon'

It was a dreary, depressing day. Clouds boiled over Hill Wood, threatening another snowfall. The first flakes were in circulation, bestowing tiny stinging kisses.

Charles walked down Dark Lane, towards Fair Field Track. A thin fire burned in a brazier, flames whipped by harsh, contradictory winds. The fusiliers on guard were wrapped in layers of coat and cloak. The youth who had tried to make time with Rud's tweeny was still red-cheeked, but now through the beginnings of frostbite.

Sergeant Beale, elaborately moustached and with eyebrows to match, did not feel the cold. If ordered to ship out, Beale would be equally up for an expedition through Arctic tundra or a trail across Sahara sands. Men like Major Chilcot only thought they ran the Empire; men like Beale actually did.

'Filthy afternoon, sir,' commented the Sergeant.

'Looks like snow.'

'Looks and feels like snow, sir. Is snow.'

'Yes.'

'Not good, snow. Not for the little girl.'

'No.'

Charles understood. If this Christmas card sprinkle turned into blizzard, any search would be off. Hope would be lost. The vanishing of Maeve Harvill would be accepted. Chilcot would pack up his soldiers and return to barracks. Charles would be recalled, to make an inconclusive report. The Small Man could open all hours of the night.

An April thaw might disclose a small, frozen corpse. Or, under the circumstances, not.

Charles looked over the trestle and into the trees.

The men of Eye and the fusiliers had both been through Hill Wood. Now, Charles—knowing he had to make sure—would have to make a third search. Of course, he wasn't just looking for the girl.

'I'll just step into the wood and have a look about, Sergeant.'

'Very good, sir. We'll hold the fort.'

The guard lifted the trestle so Charles could pass.

He tried to act as if he was just out for a stroll on a bracing day, but could not pull it off. Pamela nagged: it was not just a puzzle; wounded people surrounded the mystery; they deserved more than abstract thought.

Footprints were everywhere, a heavy trample marking out Fair Field Track, scattering off in dispersal patterns to all sides. Barely a square foot of virgin white remained. The black branches of some trees were iced with snow, but most were shaken clean.

Charles could recognise fifteen different types of snake native to the Indian sub-continent, distinguishing deadly from harmless. He knew the safest covert routes into and out of the Old Jago, the worst rookery in London. He understood distinctions between spectre, apparition, phantasm and revenant—knowledge the more remarkable for being gained first-hand rather than through dusty pedantry. But, aside from oak and elm, he could identify none of the common trees of the English countryside. Explorations of extraordinary fields had left him little time for ordinary ones.

He was missing something.

His city boots, heavily soled for cobbles, were thin and flexible. Cold seeped in at the lace-holes and seams. He couldn't feel his toes.

It was a small wood. No sooner was he out of sight of Beale than the trees thinned and he saw the khaki tents pitched on Fair Field. Davey and Maeve had been *detained* here, somehow. Everyone was convinced. Could the children have slipped out unnoticed, into Fair Field and over the stile or through a gate, disappearing into regions yet to be searched? If so, somebody should have seen them. No one had come forward.

Could they have been stolen away by passing gypsies?

In Eye, gypsies or any other strangers would be noticed. So, suspicion must range closer to home. Accusations had begun to run around. Every community had its odd ones, easy to accuse of unthinkable crimes. P.C. Throttle still said it was the Dandos, a large and unruly local clan. Accusing the Dandos had solved every other mystery in Ashton and Moreton in the last thirty years, and Throttle saw no reason to change tactics now. The fact of Davey's return had called off the witch-hunt. Even those who didn't believe Davey was who he claimed assumed he was at the bottom of the bad business.

If Davey was Davey, what had happened?

Charles went over the ground again, off the track this time, zigzagging across the small patch. He found objects trampled into muddy snow, which turned out to be broken pipes, a single man-sized glove, candle-stubs. As much rubbish was tossed here as in a London gutter. The snowfall was thickening.

Glancing up, he saw something.

Previous searches had concentrated on the ground. If Maeve had flown away, perhaps Charles *should* direct his attention upwards.

Snowflakes perished on his upturned face.

He stood before a twisted oak. A tree he could identify, even when not in leaf. An object ringed from a branch, just out of his reach. He reached up and brushed it with his fingers.

A wooden band, about eighteen inches in diameter, was loose about the branch, as if tossed onto a hook in a fairground shy. He found footholds in the trunk and climbed a yard above the ground.

He got close enough to the band to see initials burned into its inner side. *D.H.* Davey's birthday hoop.

Charles held the branch with gloved hands and let go his knee-grip on the trunk. He swung out and the branch lowered, pulled by his weight. His feet lightly touched ground, the branch bent like a bow. With one hand, he nudged the hoop, trying to work it free. The branch forked and the hoop stuck.

That was a puzzle.

The obvious trick would be to break the hoop and fix it again, around the branch. But there was no break, no fix. In which case, the toy must have been hung on the tree when it was younger, and become trapped by natural growth.

The oak was older than Davey Harvill, by many human lifetimes. It was full-grown when Napoleon was a boy. The hoop had not been hung last week, but must have been here since the Wars of the Roses.

He let go of the branch. It sprang back into place, jouncing the hoop.

Snow dislodged from higher up.

The tree creaked, waving branches like a live thing.

Charles was chilled with more than cold.

About twenty feet from the ground, packed snow parted and fell away, revealing a black face. A pattern of knot-holes, rather, shaped into a face.

We see faces in everything. It is the order we attempt to put on the world—on clouds, stains on the wallpaper, eroded cliffs. Eyes, a nose, mouth. Expressions malign or benevolent.

This face seemed, to Charles, puckish.

'Good afternoon to you, Mr Silas Gobbo,' he said, touching his hat-brim.

'Who, pray, is Silas Gobbo?'

Charles turned, heart caught by the sudden, small voice.

A little girl stood among the drifts, braids escaping from a blue cap, coat neatly done up to her muffler.

His first thought was that this was Maeve!

It struck him that he wouldn't recognise her if he saw her. He had seen no picture. There were other little girls in Eye.

'Are you looking for Maeve Harvill?' he asked. 'Is she your friend?'

The little girl smiled, solemnly.

'I am Maeve,' she said. 'I'm a princess.'

He picked her up and held her as if she were his own. Inside, he melted at this miracle. He was light-headed with an instant, fast-burning elation.

'This is not how princesses should be treated, sir.'

He was holding her too tight. He relaxed into a fond hug and looked down at the fresh footprints where she had been standing. Two only, as if she was set down from above, on this spot. He looked up and saw a bramble-tangle of black branches against dirty sky.

He cast around for the face he had imagined, but couldn't find it again.

Maeve's Dad would have said Silas Gobbo had rescued Maeve, returned her to her family.

It was the happy ending Charles wanted. He ran through his joy, and felt the chill again, the cold chill and the bone chill. He shifted the little girl, a delicate-boned miniature woman, and looked into her perfect, polite face.

'Princess, have you brothers and sisters?'

'David and Sarah.'

'Parents? Mam and Dad.'

'Father is dead. My mother is Mrs Violet Harvill. You would do me a great service if you were to take me home. I am a tired princess.'

The little bundle was warm in his arms. She kissed his cheek and snuggled close against his shoulder.

'I might sleep as you carry me.'

'That's all right,' he told her.

He trudged along Fair Field Track. When the guards saw him, they raised a shout.

' 'E's gone and done it!'

Charles tried a modest smile. The shout was taken up, spread around. Soon, they became hurrahs.

6: 'something about the little girl'

Dr Rud's parlour was filled with merry people, as if five Christmases had come along together and fetched up in a happy, laughing pile.

Mrs Harvill clung to her princess, who had momentarily stopped ordering everyone as if they were servants. Philip and Sairey, stunned and overjoyed, pinched each other often, expecting to wake up. Sairey had to sit but couldn't keep in one place. She kept springing up to talk with another well-wisher, then remembering the strain on her ankles. Philip had made another cake, with Maeve's name spelled out in currants.

Rud and Major Chilcot drank port together, laughing, swapping border war stories.

People Charles had not met were present, free with hearty thanks for the hero from London.

'We combed Hill Wood and did all we could,' said the Reverend Mr Weddle, Vicar of Eye. 'Too familiar, you see, with the terry-toree. Could not see the wood for the trees, though acts of prayer wore the trews from our knees. Took an outsider's eye in Ashton Eye, to endeavour to save the Princess Maeve. Hmm, mind if I set that down?'

Weddle had mentioned he was also a poet.

P.C. Throttle, of the long white beard and antique uniform, kept a close eye on the limping, scowling Hamer Dando—lest thieving fingers stray too close to the silverware. Hamer's face was stamped on half a dozen other locals of various ages and sexes, but Throttle was marking them all.

Charles's hand was shaken, again, by a huge-knuckled, blue-chinned man he understood to be the Ashton schoolmaster, Owain Gryfudd.

'Maeve's coming to the Welsh school now,' he said, in dour triumph. 'No more traipsing over the stile to that Episcopalian booby in Moreton. We shall see a great improvement.'

Charles gathered Gryfudd captained an all-conquering rugby team, the Head-Hunters. They blacked their faces with coal before going onto the pitch. The teacher still had war paint around his collar and under his hairline, from frequent massacres of the English.

Cake was pressed upon Charles. Gryfudd clapped his back and roared off, bearing down on a frail old lady—Mrs Grenton, of Moreton Eye school—as if charging for a match-winning try.

Whenever Mrs Harvill saw Charles, she wept and—if Maeve wasn't in her arms—flung an embrace about him. She was giddy with joy and relief, and had been so for a full day.

Her princess was home.

As Sairey had said, she would never accept Davey as Davey. But Maeve's return ended the matter.

That, among other things, kept Charles from entering into the spirit of this celebration.

In this room, he sensed an overwhelming desire to put Davey and the mystery out of mind. Davey was upstairs, shut away from the celebration.

All's well that ends well.

But Charles knew nothing had ended. And nothing was well.

He could do no more. In all probability, his report to the Ruling Cabal would be tied with pale green ribbon and filed away forever.

He left the parlour. In the hallway, soldiers and maids sipped punch. Smiles all round.

But for Sergeant Beale.

'I suppose you'll be back to London now, sir?'

'I see no other course.'

'There's something about the little girl isn't there?'

'I fear so.'

'Where *were* those kids? What happened to the boy?'

'Those, Sergeant, are the questions.'

Beale nodded. He took no punch.

Charles left the Sergeant and walked to the door. A tug came at his arm. Sairey held his sleeve. The woman was bent almost double. It was nearly her time. That was all this party needed: a sudden delivery and a bouncing, happy baby.

'Phil and I'll take in Davey.'

'I'm glad to hear that, Sairey. I know it won't be easy.'

She snorted. 'Neither one'll take him in class, not Gryfudd nor Grenton. So that's an end to his schooling. And he's a clever lad, Davey. Give him a pencil and he can draw anything to the life. Mam . . . she's daffy over Maeve, hasn't any left for Davey. Won't have him in the house.'

Charles patted her hand, understanding.

'And what *is* it about Maeve? She calls I "Sarah." I've been "Sairey" so long I forgot what my name written down in the family Bible were.'

'She doesn't know Silas Gobbo.'

Sairey closed her eyes and nodded.

'She frightens I,' she said, so quietly no one could overhear.

Charles squeezed her fingers. He could give no reassurance.

Riddle came into the hallway, looking for his wife. He escorted her back into the warmth and light. A cheer went up. Someone began singing . . .

'A frog he would a wooing go . . . *Heigh-ho, says Rowley!* And whether his mother would let him or no . . .'

Other voices joined. One deep bass must be Gryffud. 'With a roly poly gammon and spinach . . . *Heigh-ho, says Anthony Rowley!*'

Charles put on his hat and coat and left.

ACT II: UNCLE SATT'S TREASURY FOR BOYS AND GIRLS

1: 'Lady of the Leprechauns'

'If that's the Gift,' commented a workman, 'I'd likes ter know as 'oo gave it, and when they're comin' ter fetch it back.'

Kate jotted the words into a notebook, in her own shorthand. The sentiment, polished through repetition, might not be original to the speaker. She liked to record what London thought and said, even when the city thought too lightly and said too often.

'Dunno what it thinks it looks like,' continued the fellow. In shirtsleeves, cap on the back of his head, he perspired heavily.

Freezing winters and boiling summers were the order of the '90s. This June threatened the scorch of the decade. She regretted the transformation of the parasol from an object of utility into a frilly aid to flirtation. As a consequence of this social phenomenon, she didn't own such an apparatus and was just now feeling the lack—and not because she wished the attention of some dozy gentleman who paid heed only to females who flapped at him like desperate moths. Like many blessed (or cursed) with red hair, too much sun made her peel hideously. Her freckles became angry blood-dots if she took a promenade *sans* veiled hat. Such apparel invariably tangled with her large, thick spectacles.

At the South end of Regent's Park, the Gift shone, throwing off dazzles from myriad facets. Completed too late for one Jubilee, it was embarrassingly early for the next. To get shot of a White Elephant, the bankrupt company responsible made a gift of it (hence the name) to the Corporation of London. Intended as a combination of popular theatre, exhibition hall and exotic covered garden, the sprawling labyrinth had decoration enough for any three municipal eyesores. The thing looked like a crystal circustent whipped up by a colour-blind Sunday painter and an Italian pastry-chef.

It was inevitable that someone would eventually conceive of a use for the Gift. That visionary (buffoon?) was Mr Satterthwaite Bulge, 'Uncle Satt' to a generation of nieces and nephews, *soi-disant* Founder of Færie and Magister of Marvells (his spelling). This afternoon, she had an invitation to visit Bulge's prosperous little kingdom.

'Katharine Reed, daredevil reporter,' called a voice, deep and American.

A man in a violently green checked suit cut through gawping passers-by and wrung her hand. He wore an emerald bowler with shining tin buckle, an oversize crepe four-leafed clover *boutonniere*, a belt of linked discs painted like gold coins and a russet beard fringe attached to prominent ears by wire hooks.

'Billy Quinn, *publicist*,' he introduced himself, momentarily lowering his false whiskers.

She filed away the word. Was it a coinage of Quinn's? What might a publicist do? Publicise, she supposed. Make known personalities and events and products, scattering information upon the public like lumps of lava spewn from Vesuvius. She had a notion that if such a profession were to become established, her own would be greatly complicated.

'And, of course, Oi'm a leprechaun. Ye'll be familiar with *the leettle people.*'

Quinn's Boston tones contorted into an approximation of Ould Oireland. Inside high-button shoes, her toes curled.

'There's not a darter of Erin that hasn't in her heart a soft spot for Seamus O'Short.'

She was Dublin-born and protestant-raised. Her father, a lecturer in Classics at Trinity College, drummed into her at an early age that *pots o' gold* and *wee fair folk* were baggages which need only trouble heathen Papists dwelling in the savage regions of dampest bog country. Whenever anyone English rabbited on about such things (usually affecting speech along the lines of Quinn's atavistic brogue), she was wont to change the subject to Home Rule.

'You're going to love this, Kate,' he said, casually assuming the right to address her by a familiar name. She was grateful that he had reverted to his natural voice, though. 'Here's your fairy sack.'

He handed over a posset, with a drawstring. A stick protruded from its mouth, wound round with tinsel.

'That's your fairy wand. Inside, there's magic powder

(sherbet) and a silver tiara (not silver). Tuppence to the generality, but *gratis* to an honoured rep of the Fourth Estate.'

Rep? Representative. Now, people were *talking* in short-hand. At least, people who were Americans and *publicists* were.

Quinn led her towards the doors of the Gift.

A lady in spangled leotards and butterfly wings attracted a male coterie, bestowing handbills while bending *just so* to display her *décolletage* to its best advantage, which was considerable. The voluptuous fairy had two colleagues, also singular figures. Someone in a baggy suit of brown fur and cuirass, sporting an enormous plaster bear's head surmounted by an armoured helm. A dwarf with his face painted like a sad clown.

'Come one, come all,' said Quinn. 'Meet Miss Fay Twinkledust, Sir Boris de Bruin and Jack Stump.'

The trio posed *en tableau* as if for a photograph. Miss Fay and Jack Stump fixed happy grimaces on their powdered faces. Sir Boris perked up an ear through tugging on a wire. In this heat, Kate feared for the comfort and well-being of the performer trapped inside the costume.

Children flocked around, awed and wondered.

Jack Stump was perturbed by affections bestowed on him by boys and girls taller and heftier than he. Kate realised she'd seen the dwarf, dressed as a miniature mandarin, shot out of a cannon at the Tivoli Music Hall. This engagement seemed more perilous.

In the offices of the *Pall Mall Gazette*, she had done her homework and pored through a year's worth of *Uncle Satt's Treasury for Boys and Girls.* She was already acquainted with Miss Fay Twinkledust, Sir Boris de Bruin, Jack Stump, Seamus O'Short and many others. Gloomy Goat and his cousins Grumpy (her favourite) and Grimy; Billy Boggart of Noggart's Nook; Bobbin Swiftshaft, Prince of Pixies; Wicked

Witch-Queen Coelacanth. The inhabitants of Uncle Satt's Færie Aerie were beloved (or deliciously despised) by seemingly every child in the land, to the despair of parents who would rather their precious darlings practiced the pianoforte or read Euripides in the original in exactly the way they hadn't when they were children.

Kate was out of school, and near-disowned for following her disreputable Uncle Diarmid into 'the scribbling trade,' well before the debuts of Miss Fay *et al.*, but her younger brother and sisters were precisely of an age to fall into the clutches of Mr Satterthwaite Bulge. Father, whose position on the *wee fair folk* was no longer tenable, lamented he was near financial ruin on Uncle Satt's account, for a mere subscription to the monthly *Treasury* did not suffice to assuage clamour for matters færie-related. There was also *Uncle Satt's Færie Aerie Annual*, purchased in triplicate to prevent unseemly battles between Humphrey, Juliet and Susannah over whose bookshelf should have the honour of supporting the wonder volume. Furthermore, it was insisted that nursery wall-paper bear the likenesses of the færie favourites as illustrated by the artist who signed his (or her?) works 'B. Loved,' reckoned by connoisseurs to be the true genius of the realm which could properly be termed Uncle Satt's Færie Empire. In addition, there were china dolls and tin figures to be bought, boardgames to be played, pantomime theatrical events to be attended, sheet-music to be performed, Noggart's Nook sugar confections to be consumed. Every penny doled out by fond parent or grandparent to well-behaved child was earmarked for the voluminous pockets of Uncle Satt.

As a consequence, Bulge could afford the Gift. On his previous record, he could probably turn the White Elephant into the wellspring of further fortunes. Pots of gold, indeed.

The Gift was not yet open to the general public, and excited queues were already forming in anticipation. No matter how emetic the Uncle Satt *oeuvre* was to the average adult, children were as lost to his Færie as the children of Hamelin were to the Pied Piper.

A little girl, no more than four, hugged Sir Boris's leg, rubbing her cheek against his fur, smiling with pure bliss.

'We don't pay these people,' Quinn assured her. 'We don't have to. To be honest, we would if we did but we don't. This is all gin-u-wine.'

Some grown-ups were won over to the enemy or found it politic to claim so, lest they be accused of stifling the child-ish heart reputed to beat still in the breasts of even the hard-est cynics. Many of her acquaintance, well into mature years and possessed of sterling intellects (some *not even parents*), proclaimed devotion to Uncle Satt, expressing admiration if not for the literary effulgences then for the talents of the mysterious, visionary 'B. Loved.' Even Bernard Shaw, whose stinging notice of *A Visit to the Færie Aerie* led to a splashing with glue by pixie partisans, praised the illustrations, hail-ing 'B. Loved' a titan shackled by daisy-chains. The pictures, it had to be said, were haunting, unusual and impressive, simple in technique, yet imbued with a suggestiveness close to disturbing. Their dreamy vagueness would have passed for *avant-garde* in some salons but was paradoxically em-braced (beloved, indeed) by child and adult alike. Aubrey Beardsley was still sulking because B. Loved declined to contribute to a færie-themed number of *The Yellow Book*, though it was bruited about that the refusal was mandated by Uncle Satt, who had the mystery painter signed to an ex-clusive contract. It was sometimes hinted that Bulge *was* B. Loved. Other theories had the illustrator as an asylum in-mate who had sewn his own eyes shut but continued to cover paper with the images swarming inside his broken mind, a spirit medium who gave herself up to an inhabitant of another plane as she sat at the board, or a factory in Aldgate staffed by unlettered Russian immigrants overseen by a knout-wielding monk.

'Come inside,' said Quinn. 'Though you must first pass these Three Merry Guardians.'

The publicist opened a little gate and ushered Kate into an enclosure that led to the main doors. The entrance was painted to look like the covers of a pair of magical books. Above was a red-cheeked, smiling, sparkle-eyed caricature of Uncle Satt, fat finger extended to part the pages.

Envious glares came from the many children not yet admitted to the attraction. Cutting comments were passed by parents whose offers of bribes had not impressed The Merry Guardians. Kate had an idea that, if his comrades were looking the other way, Jack Stump would not have been averse to slipping a half-crown into his boot and lifting a tent-corner.

'This is a Lady of the Leprechauns,' said Quinn, to appease the crowds, 'on a diplomatic visit to Uncle Satt. The Gift will open to one and all this very weekend. The Færie Aerie isn't yet ready to receive visitors.'

A collective moan of disappointment rose.

Quinn shrugged at her.

Kate stepped towards the main doors. Long, hairy arms encircled her, preventing further movement. Sir Boris de Bruin shook with silent laughter.

This was very irritating!

'I had almost forgotten,' said Quinn. 'Before you enter, what must you do?'

She was baffled. The bear was close to taking liberties.

'What must she do, boys and girls?' Quinn asked the crowd.

'Færie name! Færie name!'

'That's right, boys and girls. The Lady of the Leprechauns must take her færie name!'

'Katharine Reed,' she suggested. 'Um, Kate, Katie?'

'*Nooooo,*' said Quinn, milking it. 'A new name. A true name. A name fit for the councils of Bobbin Swiftshaft and Billy Boggart.'

'Grumpia Goatess,' she ventured, quietly. She knew her face was red. The bear's bristles were scraping.

'I have the very name! Brenda Banshee!'

Kate, surprised, was horrified.

'Brenda Banshee, Brenda Banshee,' chanted the children. Many of them booed.

Brenda Banshee was the sloppy maidservant in the house of Seamus O'Short, always left howling at the end of the tale. It struck Kate that the leprechaun was less than an ideal employer, given to perpetrating 'hi-larious pranks' on his staff then laughing uproariously at their humiliations. In the real world, absentee landlords in Ireland were *boycotted* for less objectionable behaviour than Seamus got away with every month.

'What does Brenda Banshee do?' asked Quinn.

'She howls! She howls!'

'If you think I'm going to howl,' she told Sir Boris quietly, 'you're very much mistaken.'

'Howl, Brenda,' said Quinn, grinning. 'Howl for the boys and girls.'

She set her lips tight.

If Brenda Banshee was always trying to filch coins from her employer's belt o' gold, it was probably because she was an indentured servant and received no wages for her drudgery.

'I think you'd howl most prettily,' whispered Sir Boris de Bruin.

It dawned on her that she knew the voice.

She looked into the bear's mouth and saw familiar eyes.

'Charles?'

'If I can wear this, you can howl.'

She was astounded, and very conscious of the embrace in which she was trapped. Her face, she knew, was burning.

'Please howl,' demanded Quinn, enjoying himself.

Kate screwed her eyes shut and howled. It sounded reedy

and feeble. Sir Boris gave her an encouraging, impertinent squeeze.

She howled enough to raise a round of applause.

'Very nice, Brenda,' said Quinn. 'Howl-arious. Shall we go inside?'

The book-covers opened.

2: 'details, young miss'

What *did* Charles Beauregard think he was about?

She scarcely believed an agent of the Diogenes Club would take it into his head to supplement his income by dressing up as a story-book bear in the service of Mr Satterthwaite Bulge. She recalled John Watson's story in the *Strand* of the respectable suburban husband who earned a healthy living in disguise as a deformed beggar. Kate wondered at the ethics of publicising such a singular case; it now served as an excuse for the smugly well-off to scorn genuine unfortunates on the grounds that 'they doubtless earn more than a barrister.' Money would not come into this. Charles was of the stripe who does nothing for purely financial reward. Of course, he could afford his scruples. He did not toil in an underpaid calling still only marginally willing to accept those of her sex. The profession Neville St. Clair had found less lucrative than beggary was her own, journalism.

Sir Boris hung back as Quinn escorted her along a low-ceilinged tunnel hung with green-threaded muslin. Underfoot was horsehair matting, dyed dark green to approximate forest grass.

'We proceed along the Airy Path, to Noggart's Nook . . .'

Quinn led her to a huge tree-trunk which blocked the way. The plaster creation was intricate, with grinning goblin faces worked into the bark. Their eyes glowed, courtesy of dabs of luminous paint. An elaborate mechanical robin chirruped in the branches. Quinn rapped three times on the oak. Hidden doors opened inwards.

'. . . and into the Realm of Bobbin Swiftshaft, Prince of the Pixies . . .'

Kate stepped into the tree, and down three shallow steps. Cloth trailed over her face.

'Mind how you go.'

She had walked into a curtain. Extricating herself, she found she was in a vaulted space: at once cathedral, Big Top and planetarium. The dome sparkled with constellations, arranged to form the familiar shapes of B. Loved creatures. Miss Fay, Bobbin Swiftshaft, Jack Stump, Sir Boris, Seamus and the rest cavorted across the painted, glittering ceiling. Tinsel streamers hung, catching the light. All around was a half-sized landscape, suitable for little folk, created through tamed nature and theatrical artifice. Kate, who spent most of her life peering up at people, was here taller than the tallest tree—many were genuine dwarves cultivated in the Japanese manner, not stage fakery—and a giant beside the dwellings. The woods were fully outfitted with huts and palaces, caves and castles, stone circles and hunting lodges. Paths wound prettily through miniature woodland. Water flowed from a fountain shaped like the mouth of a big bullfrog, whose name and station escaped her. The respectable torrent poured prettily over a waterfall, agitated a pond beneath, and passed out of the realm as a stream which disappeared into a cavern. An iron grille barred the outflow, lest small persons tumble in and be swept away.

All around were strange gleams, in the air and inside objects.

'The light,' she said, 'it's unearthly.'

Looking close, she found semi-concealed glass globes and tubes, each containing a fizzing glow-worm. Some were tinted subtle ruby-red or turquoise. They shone like the eyes of ghosts.

'We're mighty proud of the lighting,' said Quinn. 'We use only Edison's incandescents, which burn through the wizardry of the age, *electricity*. Beneath our feet are vast dynamos, which churn to keep the Aerie illuminated. The Gift quite literally puts the Savoy in the shade.'

Mr d'Oyly-Carte's Savoy Theatre had been fully electrified for over a decade. Some metropolitan private homes were lit by Edison lamps, though the gas companies were fighting a vicious rearguard campaign against electrification, fearing the fate of the candle-makers. Despite scare stories, the uninformed no longer feared lightning-strikes from new-fangled gadgetry. They also no longer gasped in wonder at the mere use of an electrical current to spin a wheel or light a room. There was a risk that electric power would be relegated to quack medicinal devices like the galvanic weight-loss corset. In America, electrocution was used as a means of execution; in Britain, the process was most familiar from advertisements for the miracle food Bovril—allegedly produced by strapping a cow into an electric chair and throwing the switch. From H.G. Wells, the *Pall Mall Gazette*'s scientific correspondent, Kate gathered the coming century would be an Era of Electricity. At present, the spark seemed consigned to trivial distraction; that was certainly the case here.

A bulb atop a lantern-pole hissed, flared and popped. A tinkling rain of glass shards fell.

'Some trivial teething troubles,' said Quinn.

A lanky fellow in an overall rushed to attend to the lantern. He extracted the burned-out remains, ouching as his fingers came into contact with the hot ruin. He deftly screwed in a replacement, which began at once to glow, its light rising to full brightness. Another minion was already sweeping the fragments into a pan for easy disposal.

'Unusual-looking elves,' she commented.

'It takes a crew of twenty-five trained men to keep the show going,' said Quinn. 'When the Gift is open, they *will* be elves. Each will have their own character and place.'

Uncle Satt was insistent that in Færie, as in mundane society, there was a strict order of things. If a woodsman wed a fairy princess, it was a dead cert. he was a prince in disguise rather than a real peasant. The reader was expected to guess as much from a well-born character's attention to personal cleanliness. Children knew the exact forms of protocol in Uncle Satt's imaginary kingdom, baffling adults with nursery arguments about whether a knight transformed into a bear by Witch-Queen Coelacanth outranked a tiger-headed maharajah from Far Off Indee.

Charles had shambled in and was sitting on a wooden bench, head inclined so he could talk quietly with one of the worker elves. Quinn had not noticed that Sir Boris had abandoned the other Merry Guardians.

When Mr Henry Cockayne-Cust, her editor, sent Kate to the Gift, she had considered it a rent-paying exercise, a story destined for the depths of the inside pages. Much of her work was fish-wrap before it had a chance to be read. It was a step up from 'Ladies' Notes'—to which editors often tried to confine her, despite an evident lack of interest in the intricacies of fashionable feminine apparel or the supervision of servants—but not quite on a level with theatre criticism, to which she turned her pen in a pinch, which is to say when the *Gazette*'s official reviewer fell asleep during a first night.

An item ('puff piece') about the Færie Aerie seemed doomed to fall into the increasingly large purview of Quinn's profession. She lamented the colonisation of journalism by organised boosterism and the advertising trade. In some publications, people were deemed worthy of interest because of a happenstance rather than genuine achievement. The day might come when passing distraction was valued higher than matters of moment. She held it a sacred duty to resist.

If Mr Charles Beauregard, if *the Diogenes Club*, took an interest in the Gift, an interest was worth taking. Some aspect of the endeavour not yet apparent would likely prove, in her uncle's parlance, 'news-worthy.'

Quinn's jibe about 'daredevil' lady reporters had niggled. Now, she wondered whether there might not be a Devil here to dare.

'This, dear Kate, is Uncle Satt.'

While she was thinking, Mr Satterthwaite Bulge had come up out of the ground.

Illustrations made Bulge a cherubic fat man, a clean-shaven Father Christmas or sober Bacchus, always drawn with gleam a-twinkle in his bright eye and smile a-twitch on his full, girlish lips. In person, Bulge was indeed stout but with no discernible expression. His face was the colour of thin milk, and so were his long-ish hair and thin-ish lips. His eyes were the faded blue of china left on a shelf which gets too much sun. He wore sober clothes of old-fashioned cut, like a provincial alderman who stretches one good suit to last a lifetime in office. Bulge seemed like an artist's blank: a hole where a portrait would be drawn. More charitably, she thought of actors who walked through rehearsals, hitting marks and reciting lines without error, but withheld their *performance* until opening night, saving passion for paying customers.

Bulge had climbed a ladder and emerged through a trapdoor, followed by another elf, a clerkish type with clips on his sleeves and a green eyeshade.

'This is Katharine Reed, of the *Pall Mall Gazette*,' said Quinn.

'What's the circulation?' asked Bulge.

'Quite large, I'll wager,' she said. 'We're under orders not to reveal too much.'

That, she knew, was feeble. In fact, she had no idea.

'I know to the precise number what the *Treasury* sells by the month. I know to the farthing what profit is to be had from the *Annual*. Details, young miss, that is the stuff of my enterprise, of *all* enterprises. Another word for *detail* is *penny*. Pennies are hard to come by. It is a lesson the *dear children* learn early.'

She did not think she would ever be able to call this man 'Uncle.' The instant Bulge used the phrase 'the *dear children*' and slid his lips into something he fondly imagined to be a smile, Kate knew his deepest, darkest secret. Mr Satterthwaite Bulge, Uncle Satt of *Uncle Satt's Treasury for Boys and Girls*, greatly disliked children. It was an astonishing intuition. When Bulge used the word 'dear,' his meaning was not 'beloved' but 'expensive.' Some parents, not least her own, might secretly agree.

'Do you consider the prime purpose of your enterprise to be educational?' she asked.

Bulge was impatient with the attempt at interview.

'That's covered in the, ah, what do you call the thing, Quinn . . . the *press release*. Yes, it's all covered in that. Questions, any you might ask, have already been answered. I see no purpose in repeating myself.'

'She has the press release, Mr Bulge,' said Quinn.

'Good. You're doing your job. Young miss, I suggest you do yours. Why, all you have to do to manufacture an article is pen a general introduction, copy out Quinn's *release* and sign your name. Then you have your *interview with Uncle Satt* at a minimum of effort. A fine day's work, I imagine. A pretty penny earned.'

The flaw, of course, was that she was not the only member of the press to receive the 'release.' If an article essentially identical to her own appeared in a rival paper, she would hear from Mr Harry Cust. The editor could as devastatingly direct disapproval in person at one tiny reporter as, through editorial campaign, at an entire segment of society or tier of government. For that reason, the excellent and detailed brochure furnished by Quinn lay among spindled documents destined for use as tapers. The 'press release' would

serve to transfer flame from the grate to that plague of cigarettes which rendered the air in any newspaper office more
noxious than the streets during the worst of a pea-soup fog.

'If I could ask a few supplementary questions, addressing
matters touched upon but not explored in the release . . .'

'I can't be doing with this now,' said Bulge. 'Many things
have to be seen to if the Gift is to open to the *dear children* on
schedule.'

'Might I talk with others involved? For instance, B.
Loved remains a man of mystery. If the curtain were lifted
and a few facts revealed about the artist, you could guaran-
tee a great deal of, ah, *publicity.*'

Bulge snorted. 'I *have* a great deal of publicity, young
miss.'

'But . . .'

'There's no mystery about Loved. He's just a man with a
paint-box.'

'So, B. Loved *is* a man then, *one* man, not . . .'

'Talk with Quinn,' Bulge insisted. 'It's his job. Don't
bother anyone else. None can afford breaks for idle chatter.
It's all we can do to keep everyone about their work, without distractions.'

Quinn, realising his employer was not making the best
impression, stepped in.

'I'll be delighted to show Kate around.'

'You do that, Quinn.'

'She has her fairy sack.'

Kate held it up.

'Tuppence lost,' said Bulge. 'Quinn's extravagances will
be the ruin of me, young miss. I am surrounded by spend-
thrifts who care nought for *details.*'

'Remember, sir,' said Quinn, mildly, 'the matter we
discussed . . .'

Bulge snorted. 'Indeed, I do. More jargon. *Public image*,
indeed. Arrant mumbo jumbo and impertinence.'

If Uncle Satt wrote a word published under his name, Kate would be astounded. On the strength of this acquaintance, she could hardly believe he even *read* his own periodicals.

Which begged the question of what exactly he did in his empire.

See to details? Add up pennies?

If B. Loved was a man with a paint-box, was he perhaps on the premises? If not painting murals himself, then supervising their creation. She had an intuition that the trail of the artist might be worth following.

A nearby tower toppled, at first slowly with a ripping like stiff paper being torn, and then rapidly, with an almighty crash, trailing wires that sparked and snapped, whipcracking towards the stream.

Bulge looked at Kate darkly, as if he suspected sabotage.

'You see, I am busy. These things *will* keep happening . . .'

Wires leaped like angry snakes. Elves kept well away from them.

'Accidents?' she asked.

'Obstacles,' responded Bulge.

Bulge strode off and stared down the cables, which died and lay still. The electric lamps dimmed, leaving only cinder ghosts in the dark. Groans went up all around.

'Not again,' grumbled an elf.

Someone struck a match.

Where the tower had fallen, a stretch of painted woodland was torn away, exposing bare lath. Matches flared all around and old-fashioned lanterns lit. It was less magical, but more practical.

'What is it this time, Sackham?'

'Been chewed through, Uncle,' diagnosed the clerk, examining the damage. 'Like before.'

Bulge began issuing orders.

Kate took the opportunity to slip away. She hoped Bulge's attention to details would not extend to keeping track of her.

These things will *keep happening.*

That was interesting. That was what they called a lead.

3: 'goblins'

'Is this a common event?' she asked an idling elf.

'Not 'arf,' came the reply. 'If it ain't breakin' down, it's fallin' down. If it ain't burnin' up, it's messin' up.'

This particular elf was staying well out of the way. Several of his comrades, under the impatient supervision of Uncle Satt, were lifting the fallen tower out of the stream. Others, mouths full of nails and hammers in their hands, effected emergency repairs.

'They says it's the *goblins.*'

Kate wanted to laugh, but her chuckle died.

'No, ma'am,' said the elf, 'it's serious. Some 'ave seen 'em, they say, then upped and left, walkin' away from good wages. That's not a natural thing, ma'am, not with times as they are and honest labour 'ard to come by.'

'But . . . goblins?'

'Nasty little blighters, they say. Fingernails like teeth, an' teeth like needles. Always chewin' and clawin', weaken' things so they collapse. Usually when there's someone underneath for to be collapsed upon. The craytors get into the machinery, gum up the works. Them big dynamos grind to a 'alt with a din like the world crackin' open.'

She thought about this report.

'You mean this is sabotage? Has Satterthwaite Bulge deadly rivals in the færie business? Interests set against the opening of the Gift?'

'What business is it of yours?'

The elf realised for the first time he had no idea who she was. Her relative invisibility was often an aid in her profession; many forgot she was there even as they talked to her. Now, her spell of insignificance was wearing off.

'Miss Reed is a colleague, Blenkins,' came a voice.

They had been joined by a bear. His presence reassured the elf Blenkins.

'If you say so, Sir Boris,' he allowed. 'My 'pologies, ma'am. A bloke 'as to be careful round 'ere.'

'A bloke always has to be careful around Miss Reed.'

She hoped that, in the gloom, Charles could not discern the fearful burning of her cheeks. When he first strolled into her life, Kate was thirteen and determined to despise the villain set upon fetching away her idol, Pamela Churchward. Father was lecturing at London University for a year and Kate found herself absorbed into the large, complicated circle of the Churchwards. The beautiful, wise Pamela was the first woman ever to encourage Kate's ambitions. Her engagement seemed a treacherous defection, for all the bride-to-be insisted marriage would not end her independent life. Penelope, Pamela's ten-year-old cousin, said bluntly that Kate's complexion meant she would end up a governess or, at best, palmed off as wife to an untenured, adenoidal lecturer. Just then, as Kate was trying in vain not to cry, Pamela introduced her princely fiancé to her protégé.

Of course, Kate had fallen *horribly* in love with Charles. She doubted she had uttered a coherent sentence in his presence until he was a young widower. By then, courtesy of interesting, if brief, liaisons with Mr Frank Harris, another editor, and several others, none of whom she regretted, she was what earlier decades might have branded *a fallen woman*.

Now, with Pamela gone and pernicious Penelope in retreat, she knew the thirteen-year-old nestled inside her thirty-two-year-old person remained smitten with the Man from the Diogenes Club. As a grown-up, she was more sensible than to indulge such silliness. It irritated her when he pretended to think she was still a tiny girl with rope braids down to her waist and cheeks of pillar-box red. It was, she knew, *only* pretence. Like his late wife (whom she still missed *so*), Charles Beauregard was among the select company who took Katharine Reed seriously.

'Sir Boris, you do me an injustice.'

The bear-head waved from side to side.

For once, she was not the most ridiculous personage in the room.

'Still, I'm sure you intended to be a very gallant bear.'

She reached up and tickled the fur around his helm. It was painted plaster and she left white scratches. She stroked his arm, which was more convincing.

Blenkins slipped away, leaving them alone.

'There's a catch at the back,' Charles said, muffled. 'Like a diver's helmet. If you would do me the courtesy . . .'

'You can't get out of this on your own?'

'As it happens, no.'

She found the catch and flipped it. Charles placed his paws over his ears and rotated his head ninety degrees so the muzzle pointed sideways, then lifted the thing free. A definite musk escaped from the decapitated costume. Charles's face was blacked like Mr G.F. Elliott, the music hall act billed as 'the Chocolate-Coloured Coon.' She found Elliott only marginally less unappealing than those comic turns who presented gormless, black-toothed caricatures of her own race. Charles's make-up was to prevent white skin showing through Sir Boris's mouth.

He whipped off a paw and scratched his chin.

'I've been desperate to do that for hours,' he admitted.

He used his paw-glove to wipe his face. She took pity, produced a man-size handkerchief from her cuff and set about properly cleaning off the burnt cork. He sat on a wooden toadstool and leaned forwards so she could pay close attention to the task.

'Thank you, mama,' he teased.

She swatted him with the blacked kerchief.

'I could leave you looking like a Welsh miner.'

He shut up and let her finish. The face of Charles Beauregard emerged. Weary, to be sure, but recognisable.

'You've shaved your cavalry whiskers,' she observed.

His hand went to his neatly-trimmed moustache.

'A touch of the creeping greys, I suspect,' she added, wickedly.

'Good grief, Katie,' said Charles, 'you're worse than Mycroft's brother!'

'I'm right, though, am I not?'

'There was a certain *tinge* of dignified white,' he admitted, shyly, 'which I estimated could be eliminated by judicious barbering.'

'Considering your calling, I'm surprised every hair on your person hasn't been bleached. It's said to be a common side-effect of stark terror.'

'So I am reliably informed.'

He undid strings at the back of his neck and shrugged the bear-suit loose, then stepped out of the top half of the costume. The cuirass, leather painted like steel, unlaced down the back to allow escape from straitjacket-like confines. Underneath, he wore a grimy shirt, with no collar. High-waisted but clownishly baggy furry britches stuck into heroic boots that completed the ensemble.

'The things you do for Queen and Country, Charles.'

He looked momentarily sheepish.

'*Charles?*'

'I'm at present acting on my own initiative.'

This was puzzling and most unlike Charles. But she knew what had brought him here. She had seized at once on the 'news-worthy' aspect of the Gift.

'It's the *goblins*, isn't it?'

He flashed a humourless smile.

'Still sharp as ever, Kate? Yes, it's Blenkins's blinkin' goblins.'

The hammering and tower-raising continued. The electric lights fizzled on again, then out. Then on, to burn steady. Charles instinctively stepped back, into a shadowed alcove, drawing Kate with him.

Bulge flapped a list of 'to do' tasks at the elves. Mr Sackham was presently at the receiving end of the brunt of Uncle Satt's opprobrium.

'What do you know that I don't?' she asked Charles.

'That's a big question.'

She hit him on the arm. Quite hard.

'You deserved that.'

'Indeed I did. My apologies, Katie. Life inside a bear costume is, I'm afraid, a strain on any temperament. When the Gift opens to the public, I should not care to let a child of my acquaintance within easy reach of anyone who is forced, as the "show-business" slang has it, "to wear a head." An hour of such imprisonment transforms the most patient soul into Grendel, eager for a small, helpless person upon whom to slake his wrath.'

'You have my promise that I shall write a blistering exposé of this cruel practice. The cause of the afflicted "head-wearers" shall become as known as, in an earlier age, was that of the children employed as human chimney-brushes or, as now, those drabs sold as "maiden tributes of modern Babylon." A committee shall be formed and strong letters written to Members of Parliament. Fairies will chain themselves to the railings. None shall be allowed to rest in the Halls of Justice until the magic bears are free!'

'Now *you're* teasing *me*.'

'I have earned that right.'

'That you have, Katie.'

'Now this amusing diversion is at an end, I refer you back to my initial question. What do you know that I don't?'

Charles sighed. She had sidestepped him again. She wondered if he ever regretted that she was no longer tongue-tied in his presence.

'Not much,' he admitted, 'and I can't talk about it here. If you would meet me outside in half an hour. I am acting on my own initiative and honestly welcome your views.'

'This goblin hunt?'

'That's part of it.'

'Part only?'

'Part only.'

'I shall wait half an hour, no longer.'

'It will take that to become presentable. I can't shamble as a demi-bear among afternoon promenaders.'

'Indeed. Panic would ensue. Men with nets would be summoned. As an obvious chimera, you would be captured and confined to the conveniently nearby London Zoo. Destined to be stuffed and presented to the Natural History Museum.'

'I'm so glad you understand.'

He kissed her forehead, which reddened her again. She was grateful her blushes wouldn't show up under the electric lamps.

4: 'a pale green ribbon'

A full forty-five minutes later, Kate was still waiting in the park. On this pleasant afternoon, many freed from places of employment were not yet disposed to return to their homes. A gathering of shop-girls chirruped, competing for the attention of a smooth-faced youth who sported a cricket cap and a racy striped jacket. Evidently quite a wit, his flow of comments on the peculiarities of passersby kept his pretty flock in fits.

'With her colourin' and mouth,' drawled the champion lad, 'it's a wonder she ain't forever bein' mistook for a pillar box.'

Much hilarity among the *filles des estaminets*.

'Oh Max, you are so *wicked* . . . you shouldn't ought to say such things . . .'

Kate supposed she *was* redder than usual. The condition came upon her when amused, embarrassed or—as in this case—annoyed.

'I 'magine she's waitin' to be emptied.'

'The postman's running late today,' ventured the boldest of the girls.

'Bad show, what. To leave such a pert post-box unattended.'

Charles emerged from the Gift at last, more typically clothed. Most would take him for a clubman fresh from a day's idleness and up for an evening's foolery.

As he approached, the girls' attention was removed entirely from Max. Their eyes followed Charles's saunter. He did such a fine job of pretending not to notice that only Kate was not fooled.

'He must have a letter that *desperately* needs postin',' said the amusing youth.

'If you will excuse me,' said Charles, raising a finger.

He walked over to the group, who fluttered and gathered around Merry Max. Charles took a firm grip on the youth's ear and dragged him to Kate. The cap fell off, revealing that his cultivated forelock was a lonely survivor on an otherwise hairless scalp.

'This fellow has something to say to you, Kate.'

'Sorry,' came the strangled bleat, 'no 'ffence meant.'

Now someone was redder than she. Max's pate was practically vermilion.

'None taken.'

Charles let Max go and he fell over. When he sat up again, his congregation was flown, seeking another hero. He snatched up his cap and slunk off.

'I suppose you expect me to be grateful for your protection, Sir Boris?'

Charles shrugged. 'After a day in the bear head, I had to thump *someone*. Max happened to be convenient. He was making "short" jokes about Jack Stump earlier.'

'I believe you.'

He looked at her, and she was thirteen again. Then she was an annoyed grown-up woman.

'No, really. I do.'

Charles glanced back at the Gift.

'So, Mr Beauregard, what's the story? Why take an interest in Uncle Satt?'

'Bulge is incidental. The mermaid on the front of the ship. Oh, he's the one who's made the fortune. But he's not the treasure of the *Treasury*. That's the other fellow, the mysterious cove . . .'

'B. Loved?'

Charles tapped her forehead. 'Spot on. The artist.'

'What does the B stand for?'

'David.'

'Beloved. From the Hebrew.'

'Indeed. Davey Harvill, as was. B. Loved, as is.'

The name meant nothing to her.

'Young Davey is a singular fellow. We met eight years ago, in Herefordshire. He had an unusual experience. The sort of unusual that comes under my purview.'

It was fairly openly acknowledged that the Diogenes Club was a clearing house for the British Secret Service. Less known was its occult remit. While the Society for Psychical Research could reliably gather data on cold spots or fraudulent mediums, they were hardly equipped to cope with supernatural occurrences which constituted a threat to the natural order of things. If a spook clanked chains or formed faces in the muslin, a run-of-the-mill ghost-finder was more than qualified to provide reassurance; if it could hurt you, then the Ruling Cabal sent Charles Beauregard.

'Davey was lost in the woods and found much older than

he should be. I don't mean aged by terrible experience, your "side effects of stark terror." He disappeared a child of nine and returned a full-grown man, as if twenty years had passed over a weekend.'

'You established there was no imposture?'

'To my satisfaction.'

Kate thought, tapping her teeth with a knuckle. 'But not to everyone's?'

Charles spread his hands. 'The lad's mother could never accept him.'

She had a pang of sympathy for this boy she had never met.

'What happened after he was returned?'

'Interesting choice of words. "Was returned"? Suggests an agency over which he had no control. Might he not have *escaped*? Davey was taken in by his older sister, Sarah Riddle. Maeve Harvill, Davey's other sister, also went into the woods. She came out like her normal self and was embraced by the mother. Sadly, Mrs Harvill died some time afterwards. I have questions about that, but we can get to them later. Sarah, herself the mother of a young son, became sole parent to both her siblings. By then, Davey was drawing.'

'The færie pictures?'

'They poured from his pencils,' said Charles. 'He does it all with pencils, you know. Not charcoal. The pictures became more intense, more captivating. You've seen them?'

'Who hasn't?'

'Quite. That's down to Evelyn Weddle, the vicar of Eye. He took an interest, and brought Davey's pictures to the attention of a Glamorgan printer.'

'Satterthwaite Bulge?'

'Indeed. Bulge, quite against his nature, was captivated. The pictures have strange effects, as the whole world now knows. Bulge put together the first number of his *Treasury*. It made his name.'

'Who writes the copy?'

'At first, Weddle. He's the sort of the poet, alas, who rhymes "pixie" with "tipsy" and "færie" with "hurry." Don't you hate that diphthong, by the way. It's one step away from an umlaut. What's wrong with f-a-i-r-y, I'd like to know? The vicar was so flattered to see his verses immortalised by type-setting that he cared not that his name wasn't appended. He fell by the wayside early on. Now, Bulge has many scribbling elves—though he oversees them all, and contrives to imprint his own concerns upon the work. All that business about washing your hands, respecting princes and punishing servants. Leslie Sackham, whom you saw dancing attendance, is currently principle quill-pushing elf. They are interchangeable and rarely last more than a few months, but there's only one B. Loved.'

'Is this golden egg-laying goose chained to an easel?'

Charles shook his head. 'His artistry is of a *compulsive* nature. The *Treasury* can't keep up with the flow. Even under a hugely unfair personal contract the Harvills knew no better than to accept, Davey has become very well off.'

She thought of the illustrations, wondering if she would see them differently now she had some idea about their creator. They had always seemed portals into another, private world.

'What does Davey say about the time he was away?'

'He *says* little. He claims an almost complete loss of memory.'

'But he draws. You think not from imagination, but from life?'

'I don't suppose he is representing a literal truth, no. But I am certain his pictures spring from the place he and his sister were taken—and I do believe they were *taken*—whether it be a literal Realm of Færie or not.'

'You know the stories . . .'

Charles caught her meaning. '. . . of the little people, and babies snatched from their cribs? Changelings left in their stead? Very Irish.'

'Not in the Reed household. At least, not until the rise of Uncle Satt. But, yes, those stories.'

'They aren't confined to the emerald isle. Ten years ago in Sussex, a little girl named Rose Farrar was allegedly spirited away by "angels." That's an authenticated case. We took an interest. Rose is still listed among the missing.'

'It's not just leprechauns. Someone is always accused of child abduction. Mysterious folk, outsiders, alien. Dark-complected, most like. Wicked to the bone. There are the stories of the Pied Piper and the Snow Queen. Robbers, imps and devils, Red Indians, the gypsies . . .'

'Funny you should mention gypsies.'

'Tinkers, in Ireland. Have they ever *really* stolen babies? Why on earth would they want to? Babies are bothersome, I'm given to understand. Nonsense is usually spouted about strengthening the blood-stock of a small population, but surely you'd do better taking grown-up women for that. No, it seems to me that the interest of the stories is in the people who tell them. There is a *purpose*, a lesson. Don't go wandering off, children, for you might fall down a well. Don't talk to strangers, for they might eat you.'

Afternoon had slid into evening. One set of idlers had departed, and a fresh crowd come upon the scene. This was a park, not wild woods. Nature was trimmed and tamed, hemmed in by city streets and patrolled by wardens. Treetops were black with soot.

A shout went up nearby, a governess calling her charge.

'Master Timothy! Timmy!'

Kate felt a clutch of dread. Here, in the press of people, was more danger than in all the trackless woods of England. Scattered among the bland, normal faces were blood-red, murderous hearts. She had attended enough coroner's

courts to know imps and angels were superfluous in the
metropolis. Caligula could pass, unnoticed, in a celluloid
collar.

Master Timothy was found and smothered with tearful
kisses. He didn't look grateful. Catching sight of Kate, he
stuck out a fat little tongue at her.

'Beast,' she commented.

Charles looked for a moment as if he was going to serve
the ungracious little perisher as he had Merry Max. She laid
a hand in the crook of his arm. She did not care to be complicit with another assault. Charles laid his hand on hers and
tapped, understanding, amused.

'The Diogenes Club has a category for everything,' he said,
'no matter how outré. Maps of Atlantis—we have dozens of
them, properly catalogued and folded. Hauntings, tabulated
and sub-categorised, with pins marked into ordnance survey
charts and patterns studied by our learned consultants.
Witch-Cults, ranked by the degree of unpleasantness involved
in their ritual behaviour and the trouble caused in various
quarters of the Empire. There's also a category for mysteries
without solution. Matters we have looked into but been unable to form a conclusion upon. Like the diplomat Benjamin
Bathurst, who "walked around the horses" and vanished without trace. Or little Rose Farrar.'

'The *Mary Celeste*?'

'Actually, we did fathom that. It remains under the rose
for the moment. We've no pressing desire to go to war with
the United States of America.'

She let that pass.

'Unsolved matters constitute a large category,' he continued. 'Most of my reports are inconclusive. A strategy has
formed for such cases. We tie a pale green ribbon around the
file and shelve it in a windowless room behind a door that
looks like a cupboard. The Ruling Cabal, which is to say

you-know-who, disapproves of fussing with green-ribbon files. As he says, "When you are unable to eliminate the impossible, don't waste too much time worrying about it." The ribbons are knotted tight and difficult to unpick—though, from time to time, further information comes to light. Of course, it's easier to work in the green-ribbon room, you think of *people* as *cases*.'

'And you can't?'

'No more than you can. No, I don't mean that, Katie. You, more than anyone, are immune to that tendency. I am not. I concede that sometimes it helps to consider mysteries purely as puzzles. Pamela would nag me about it. She always thought of *people* first, last and always.'

Pamela's name did not come up often between them. It did not need to.

'So, in her memory and for fear of disappointing you, I tied the pale green ribbon loosely around Davey Harvill. I had thought the whole thing buried in Eye, a local wonder soon forgotten. However, here we are in the heart of London, before Davey's færie recreated. There are the goblins to consider. Blenkins's goblins. How did they creep into the picture?'

Kate snapped her fingers. 'That's how B. Loved draws goblins, hidden as if they've crept in. You have to look twice, sometimes very closely, to see them, disguised against tree-bark or peeping out of long grass. In the *Annual*, there's a plate entitled, "How many goblins are being naughty in this picture?" It shows a country market in an uproar.'

'There are twenty-seven goblins in the picture. All being naughty.'

'I found twenty-nine.'

'Yes, well, that's a game. This is not. Workmen have been injured. Nipped as if by tiny teeth. Rats, they say. The thing is, when it's rats, parties involved usually say it isn't. *That's* when they talk about mischievous imps. No one who wants to draw in crowds of children likes to mention the tiniest rat problem. But here everyone says it's rats. Except Blenkins, and he's been told to shut up.'

'. . . if it can hurt you . . .'

'I beg your pardon.'

'Just something I was thinking of earlier.'

There was another commotion. Kate assumed Timmy had fled his governess again, but that was not the case.

'Speak of the Devil . . .'

Blenkins was running through the crowds, clearly in distress.

He saw Charles and dashed over, out of breath.

'Mr B,' he said, 'it's terrible what they done . . .'

Police whistles shrilled nearby.

'I can't credit it. 'appened so quick, sir.'

Cries went up. 'Fire!' and 'Murder!'

'You better take us in,' said Charles.

'Not the lady—beggin' your pardon, ma'am—it's too 'orrible.'

'She'll be fine,' said Charles, winning her all over again— though the casual assumption of the strength of her constitution in face of the truly horrible gave her some pause. 'Come on, quick about it!'

Blenkins led them back towards the Gift.

5: 'the scene of the occurrence'

There was a rumble, deep in the ground, like the awakening of an angry ogre. The doors of the Gift were thrown open, and people—some in costume—poured through. Bulge, collar burst and a bruise on his forehead, was carried out by a broken-winged fairy and a soot-grimed engineer.

Charles held Kate's arm, holding her back.

Bulge caught sight of her and glared as if she were personally to blame.

Blenkins took off his cap and covered his face with it.

Something big broke, deep inside the Gift. Cries and screams were all around.

*

QUINN, beard awry and hat gone, staggered into the evening light, dazed.

The elves stumbled into an encircling crowd of curious spectators. Kate realised she was in danger of belonging to this category of nuisance.

A belch of smoke escaped and rose in a black ring.

The doors clattered shut.

Breaths were held. There was a moment of quiet. No more smoke, no flames or explosions. Then, everyone began talking at once.

The police were on the scene, a troop of uniformed constables throwing up a picket around the Gift. Kate recognised Inspector Mist of Scotland Yard, a sallow man with a pendulous moustache.

Mist caught sight of Charles and Kate. He shifted his bowler to the back of his head.

'Again we meet in unusual circumstances, Inspector,' said Charles.

'Unusual circumstances are an expected thing with you, Mr Beauregard,' said the policeman. 'I suppose you two'll have the authority of a certain body to act as, shall we say, observers in this investigation.'

Charles did not confirm or deny this, a passive sort of mendacity. She had a pang of worry. Her friend stood to lose a hard-to-define position. She had dark ideas of what form expulsion from the Diogenes Club might take.

'We're not sure any crime has been committed,' she said, distracting the thoughtful Mist. 'It might be some kind of accident.'

'There is usually a crime somewhere, Miss Reed.'

Mist might look the glum plodder, but was one of the sharpest needles in the box.

'Hullo, Quinn,' said the Inspector, spotting the publicist. 'Not hawking patent medicines again, are we?'

Quinn looked sheepish and shook his head.

'I'm relieved to hear it. I trust you've found respectable employment.'

The former leprechaun was pale and shaking. His green jacket was spotted with red.

Mist ordered his men to disperse only the irrelevant crowds. He told the elves not to melt into the throng just yet. Questions would have to be answered. More policemen arrived, then a clanking, hissing fire engine. Mist had the Brigade stand by.

'Let's take a look inside this pixie pavilion, shall we?'

Quinn shook his head, insistently.

Mist pulled one of the book-covers open, and stepped inside. No one from Bulge's troupe was eager to join him. Blenkins hid behind Miss Fay, whose wand was snapped and leotards laddered. Kate followed the Inspector, with Charles in her wake. In the murk of the tunnel, Mist was exasperated. He pushed the main door back open.

'Who's in charge?' he called out.

Some elves moved away from Uncle Satt, who was fiddling with his collar, trying to refasten it despite the loss of a stud.

'Mr Bulge, if you would be so kind . . .'

The Inspector beckoned. Bulge advanced, regaining some of his composure.

'Thank you, sir.'

Bulge entered his realm, joining the little party.

'If you would lead us to the scene of the occurrence . . .'

Bulge, even in the shadows, blanched visibly.

'Very well,' he said, lifting a flap of black velvet. A stairwell wound into the ground. Smell hung in the air, ozone and machine oil and something else foul. Arrhythmic din boomed from below. Kate felt a touch of the quease.

Mist went first, signalling for Bulge to follow. Kate and Charles waited for them to disappear before setting foot on the wrought-iron steps.

'Into the underworld,' said Charles.

'I didn't realise Noggart's Nook harboured circles of damned souls.'

'Children who don't wash their hands before *and* after meals, maids who sweep dust under the carpets . . .'

Beneath the Gift were large, stone-walled rooms, hot and damp. Electric lamps flickered in heavily-grilled alcoves.

'Good God,' exclaimed Inspector Mist.

The dynamos were still in motion, though slowed and erratic. Huge cast-iron engines, set in concrete foundations, spat sparks and water-droplets as great belts kept the drums in motion. Wheels and pistons whirled and pounded, ball-valves spun and somewhere below a hungry furnace roared. The central dynamo was grinding irregularly, works impeded by a limp suit of clothes filled with loose meat.

Kate gasped and covered her mouth and nose with her hand, determined not to be overcome.

Flopping from the suit-collar was a deflated ball with a bloody smear for a face.

'Sackham,' cried Bulge.

She could not recognise this rag as the clerkish elf she had seen earlier, scurrying after his master.

'What's been done to you?!' howled Bulge, with a shocking, undeniable grief.

The human tangle was twisted into the wheels of the machine, boneless legs caught in cogs. A ball-valve whined to a halt and shook off its spindle. With a mighty straining and gouts of fire, the central dynamo died. Its fellows flipped over inhibitors and shut down in more orderly fashion. The lamps faded.

In the dark there was only the *stench*.

Kate felt Charles's arm around her.

ACT III: FÆRIE

1: 'events have eventuated'

After a day as Sir Boris and a night at a police station, Charles needed to sleep. The situation was escalating, but he was no use in his present state. He had told Inspector Mist as much as he could and done his best to spare Kate further distress.

He was greeted at the door of his house in Cheyne Walk.

'Visitors, sir,' said his man, Bairstow. 'I have them in the reception room. Funereal gentlemen.'

He considered himself in the hall-mirror. Unshaven, the grey Kate—clever girl!—had deftly intuited was evident about his gills.

These visitors would not care about his appearance.

'Send in tea, Bairstow. Strong and green.'

'Very good, sir.'

Charles stepped into his reception room, as if he were the intruder and the others at home.

The two men were dressed like undertakers, in long black coats and gloves, crepe-brimmed hats and smoked glasses.

'Beauregard,' said the senior, Mr Hay.

'Gentlemen,' he acknowledged.

Mr Hay took his ease in the best armchair, looking over the latest number of the *Pall Mall Gazette*, open to an article by Kate. Not a coincidence.

Mr Effe, younger and leaner, stood by a book-case, reading spines.

Charles, not caring to be treated like a schoolboy summoned before the beak for a thrashing, slipped into a chair of his own and stretched out, fingers interlaced on his waistcoat as if settling down for a nap.

(Which would be a good idea.)

Two sets of hidden eyes fixed on him.

'Must you wear those things?' Charles asked.

Mr Hay lowered his spectacles, disclosing very light-coloured, surprisingly humorous eyes. Mr Effe did not follow suit. Charles amused himself by imagining a severe case of the cross-eyed squints.

At this hour in the morning, a maid would have opened the curtains. The visitors had drawn them again, which should make protective goggles superfluous. He wondered what his visitors could actually see. It was no wonder Mr Effe had to get so close to the shelves to identify books.

'The salacious items are under lock and key in the hidden room,' said Charles. 'Have you read *My Nine Nights in a Harem*? I've a rare *Vermis Mysteriis*, illustrated with brass-rubbings that'd curl your hair.'

'That's a giggle,' snarled Mr Effe. 'Of course, you *do* have hidden rooms.'

'Three. And secret passages. Don't you?'

He couldn't imagine Mr Hay or Mr Effe—or any of their fellows, Mr Bee, Mr Sea and Mr Dee, all the way to Mr Eggs, Miss Why and Mr Zed—*having* homes, even haunted lairs. He assumed they slept in rows of coffins under the Houses of Parliament.

Mr Effe wiped a line down a mediocre edition of *The Collected Poems of Jeffrey Aspern* and pretended to find dust on his gloved finger.

Charles knew Mrs Hammond, his housekeeper, better than that.

'You've been acting on your own initiative,' said Mr Hay. 'That's out of character for an active member of the Diogenes Club. Not that there are enough of you to make general assumptions. Sedentary bunch, as a rule.'

'Did you think we wouldn't notice?' sniped Mr Effe.

Mr Hay raised a hand, silencing his junior.

'We're not here for recriminations.'

Millie, the second-prettiest maid, brought in the tray.

He approved; Lucy, the household stunner, was in reserve for special occasions. After thanking the by-no-means unappealing Millie, he let her escape. Mr Effe's attempt at a charming smile had thrown a fright into the girl. Charles poured a measure of Mrs Hammond's potent brew into a giant's teacup, but did not offer hospitality.

'Events have eventuated,' said Mr Hay. 'Your Ruling Cabal was shortsighted to green-ribbon the Harvill children. You, however, were perceptive in continuing to take an interest. Even if *unsanctioned*.'

'Bad business under Regent's Park,' commented Mr Effe.

Charles expected these fellows to be up on things.

'Your assumption is that this is the same case?' asked Mr Hay.

He swallowed tea. The Undertaking knew full well this was the same case.

'Mr Effe, if you would do the honours,' said Mr Hay, snapping his fingers.

Mr Effe unbuttoned his coat down the front, and reached inside.

Charles tensed, ready to defend his corner.

Mr Effe produced a pinch of material, which he unravelled and let dangle. A pale green ribbon.

'Removed from the Harvill file,' said Mr Hay. 'With the full co-operation and consultation of the Ruling Cabal.'

'You're official again, pally,' snapped Mr Effe.

Charles relaxed. He would have to make explanation to the Cabal in time, but was protected now by approval from on high (rather, down below). There was a literal dark side to this. For all its stuffinesses and eccentricities, he understood the Diogenes Club: it was a comfort and shelter in a world of shadows. The Undertaking was constituted on different lines. Rivalry between the Club and the men in smoked glasses held a potential for outright conflict. It had been said of Mycroft Holmes, chairman of the Ruling Cabal, that sometimes he *was* the British Government; the troubling thing about the Undertaking was that sometimes it *wasn't*.

'We'll see your report,' said Mr Hay.

He remembered how tired he was. He closed his eyes.

When he opened them again, he was alone.

Something tickled on his face. He puffed it away, and saw it was the ribbon.

2: 'thrones, powers and principalities'

Kate's story dominated the front page of the *Pall Mall Gazette*. An affront to a national treasure (for so Uncle Satt was reckoned), a gruesomely mysterious death and rumours of supernatural agency meant Harry Cust had no choice but to give her piece prominence. However, it was rewritten so ruthlessly, by Cust himself at the type-setting bench, that she felt reduced to the status of interviewee, providing raw material shaped into journalism by other hands.

She was cheered, slightly, by a telegram of approval from Uncle Diarmid, who *ought* to be reckoned a national treasure. It arrived soon after the mid-morning special was hawked in the streets, addressed not to the *Gazette* offices but the Cheshire Cheese, the Fleet Street watering hole where Kate, and four-fifths of the journalists in London, took most meals. Uncle Diarmid always said half the trick of newspaper reporting was getting underfoot, contriving to be present at the most 'news-worthy' incidents, gumming up the works to get the story.

The image conjured unpleasant memories. She had ordered chops, but wasn't sure she could face eating—though hunger pangs had struck several times through the long night and morning.

Reporters from other papers stopped by her table, offering congratulations but also soliciting unrefined nuggets of information. Anything about Satterthwaite Bulge was news.

Back-files were being combed to provide follow-up pieces to fill out this afternoon and evening editions. The assumption was that the notoriously close-mouthed Inspector Mist would not oblige with further revelations about the death of Mr Leslie Sackham in time to catch the presses.

Kate had little to add.

The story about the goblins was out, and sketches already circulated ('artists' impressions,' which is to say unsubstantiated, fantastical lies) depicting malicious, oval-headed imps tormenting Mr Sackham before tossing him to the dynamo. Most of Uncle Satt's elves had come forth with tales of goblin sightings or encounters in the dark. Blenkins was charging upwards of ten shillings a time for an anecdote. The rumour was that Scotland Yard was looking for dwarves. Jack Stump was in hiding. Kate wondered about other little people— like Master Timothy, the obnoxious child. How far could such a prankster go? Surely, nursery ill-manners did not betoken a heart black enough for murder. It made more sense to look for goblins. The sensation press had already turned up distinguished crackpots willing to expound at length about the vile habits of *genus goblinus*. Soon, there would be organised hunting parties, and rat-tail bounties offered on green, pointed ears.

Kate's chops were set before her. She had ordered them well-cooked, so that no red showed. Even so, she ate the baked potato first.

There was the problem of Mr Sackham's obituary, which was assigned to her. The most interesting thing about the man's life was its end, already described at quite enough length. His injuries were such that it was impossible to tell whether he had been thrown (or fallen) alive into the dynamo. Indeed, the corpse was mutilated to such an extent that if the incident were encountered in a penny dreadful, the astute reader would assume Mr Sackham not to be dead at all but that the body was a nameless tramp dressed in his clothes and sacrificed in order to facilitate a surprise in a later chapter. The second most interesting thing about Sackham was that he had penned many of the words recently published under the by-line of Uncle Satt, but Cust forbade her to mention this. Exposing hypocrites was all very well, but no newspaper could afford to suggest that Satterthwaite Bulge was less than the genial 'Founder of Færie and Magister of Marvells' for fear of an angry mob of children invading their offices to wreak vengeful havoc. She was reduced to padding out a paragraph on Sackham's duties at the Gift and the fact that he very nearly could legitimately call Uncle Satt his uncle; Leslie Sackham had been the son of his employer's cousin.

She finished her copy and her chops at about the same time, then gave a handy lad tuppence to rush the obit. to the *Gazette* in the Strand. As Ned made his way out of the Cheese, he was entrusted with a dozen other scribblings—some on the reverse of bills, most on leaves torn from notebooks—to drop off at the various newspapers on his route.

Now, she might snatch a snooze.

'Kate.'

She looked up, not sure how long (or if) she had dozed in her chair.

'Charles.'

He sat down.

'Scotland Yard is saying it was an accident,' he said.

Kate sensed journalistic ears pricking up all around.

'That doesn't sound like Mist,' she observed.

'I didn't say "Mist," I said "Scotland Yard".'

She understood. Decisions had been made in shadowed corridors.

'The Gift is declared "unsafe" for the moment,' he continued. 'No grand opening this weekend, I'm afraid. There'll be investigations, by the public health and safety people and anyone else who can get his oar in. It turns out that the Corporation of London still owns the site. Uncle Satt is lessee of the ground, though he has deed and title to all structures built on and under it. There'll be undignified arguments over whose fault it all is. In the meantime, the place is under police guard. As you can imagine, Regent's Park is besieged by aspirant goblin hunters. Some have butterfly nets and elephant guns.'

She looked around. The cartoonist responsible was lurking somewhere.

'I was given this,' he said, producing a length of green ribbon.

'The Ruling Cabal want you to continue to take an interest?'

'They've no choice. Another body has made its desires known. There are thrones, powers and principalities in this. For some reason beyond me, this matter is important. My remit is loose. While the police and the safety fellows are concerned with Sackham's death, I am to pull the loose ends. I have leeway as to whom I choose to involve, and I should like to choose you.'

'*Again?* You'll have to put me up for membership one day.'

She was teasing, but he took it seriously. 'In a world of impossibilities, that should be discussed. I shall see what I can do.'

Previously, when Charles involved her (or, more properly, allowed her to become involved) in the business of the Diogenes Club, she had gathered stories that would make her name if set in type but which wouldn't even pass the breed of editor willing to publish 'artist's impressions,' let alone Henry Cockayne-Cust. Still, she had an eternal itch to draw back the curtain. Association with Charles was interesting on other levels, if often enervating or perilous.

'If the Gift is being adequately investigated, where should we direct our attentions?'

Charles smiled.

'How would you like an audience with B. Loved?'

3: 'the Affair of the Dendrified Digit'

'So this is the house that Færie built?' said Kate.

'Bought,' he corrected.

'Very nice. Pennies add up like details, indeed.'

They were on a doorstep in elegant Broadley Terrace, quite near Regent's Park and a long way from Herefordshire.

'What's that smell?' asked Kate, nose wrinkling like a kitten's.

'Fresh bread,' he told her.

The door was opened by a child with flour on his cheeks and a magnifying glass in his hand. The boy examined Charles's shoes and trouser-cuffs, then angled his gaze upwards. Through the lens, half his face was enlarged and distorted.

'I be a 'tective,' he announced.

'What about the flour?' asked Charles.

Kate had slipped a handkerchief out of her tightly-buttoned cuff, possessed of a universal feminine instinct to clean the faces of boys who were perfectly happy as they were.

The boy touched his forehead, then examined the white on his fingertips.

'I be a baker too, like my Da. I be baker by day, 'tective by night.'

'Very practical,' said Kate. 'In my experience, detectives often neglect proper meals.'

'Are you a 'tective too, mister?'

Charles looked at Kate, for a prompt.

'Sometimes,' he admitted. 'But don't tell anyone. Affairs of state, you know.'

The boy's face distorted in awe.

'A *secret agent* . . . Come in and have some of my boasters. I made them special, all by myself. Though Da helped with the oven.'

Charles let Kate step into the hallway and followed, removing his hat.

A woman bustled into the hall.

'Dickie,' she said, incipiently scolding, 'who've you let in now?'

The woman, neat and plump, came to them. Sairey Riddle, well shy of thirty, had grey streaks. In eight years, she had filled out to resemble her late mother.

She remembered him.

'It's you,' she said, face shaded. 'You found *her*.'

'Maeve.'

'Her.'

He understood the distinction.

'This is my friend, Miss Katharine Reed. Kate, this is Sairey Riddle.'

'Sarah,' she said, careful with the syllables now.

Dickie was clinging to his mother's skirts. Now, he looked up again at Charles.

'You be *that* 'tective. Who found Auntie when she were lost? In the olden days?'

'He means before he were . . . was born. It's all olden days to him. Might as well a' been knights in armour and fire-breathing dragons.'

'Yes, Dickie. I found your Aunt Maeve. One of my most difficult cases.'

Dickie looked through his magnifying glass again.

'A proper *'tective*,' he breathed.

'I do believe you've found a hero-worshipper,' whispered Kate, not entirely satirically.

Charles was intently aware of a sudden responsibility.

'Don't mind our Dickie,' said Sarah. 'He's not daft and he means well.'

For the first time in months, Charles felt the ache in his forearm, in the long-healed bite. It was the name, of course. By now, his son would have been almost an adult; he would have been Dickie as a child, Dick as a youth and be on the point of demanding the full, respectful Richard.

'Are you all right?' enquired Kate, sharp as usual.

'Old wound,' he said, not satisfying her.

'Have you come about the business in the park?' prompted Sarah. 'We heard about poor Mr Sackham.'

'I'm afraid so. We were wondering if we might see Davey?'

Sarah bit her lower lip. He noticed a worn spot, often chewed. She glanced up at the ceiling. The shadow that had fallen over this family in Hill Wood had never been dispelled.

'It's not been one of his good days.'

'I can imagine.'

'We never did find out, you know, what *happened* to him. To them both.'

'I know.'

Sarah led them into a reception room. She left Dickie with them while she went to look in on her brother.

'Do you want to see my *clues?*' asked the boy, tugging Charles's trouser-pocket.

Kate found this hilarious but stifled her giggles.

Dickie produced a cigar-box and showed its contents.

'This button 'nabled me to solve the Case of the Vanishing Currant Bun. It were the fat lad from down the road. He snitched it from the tray when Da weren't looking. This playin' card, a Jack of Hearts with one corner bent off, is the key to the Scandal of the Cheatin' Governess. And this twig that looks 'zactly like a 'uman finger is a mystery whose solution no man yet knows, though I've not 'bandoned my inquiries.'

Dickie examined the twig, which did resemble a finger.

'What do you call the case?' he asked the boy.

'It hasn't a name yet.'

'What about the Affair of the Dendrified Digit?' suggested Kate.

Dickie's eyes widened and he ran the words around his mouth.

'What be a "dendrified digit"?'

'A finger turned to wood.'

'Very 'propriate. Are you a 'tective too, lady?'

'I'm a reporter.'

'A *daredevil* reporter,' Charles corrected.

Kate poked her tongue out at him while Dickie wasn't looking.

'Then you must be a 'tective's *assistant*.'

Kate was struck aghast. It was Charles's turn to be amused.

Dickie reached into his box and produced a rusty nail.

'This be . . .'

He halted mid-sentence, swallowed, and stepped back, positioning himself so that Kate stood between the door and him.

The handle was turning.

Into the room came a little girl in blue, as perfectly dressed as a china doll on display. She had an enormous cloud of stiff blonde hair and a long, solemn, pretty face.

Beside her, Dickie looked distinctly shabby.

The girl looked at Charles and announced, 'We have met before.'

'It's Auntie,' whispered Dickie. Charles saw the wariness the lad had around the girl; not fear, exactly, but an understanding, developed over years, that she could hurt him if she chose.

'Maeve,' Charles said. 'I am Mr Beauregard.'

'The man in the wood,' she said. 'The hero of the day. *That* day.'

Kate's mouth was open. At a glance from Charles, she

realised her lapse and shut it quickly. Dickie wasn't quite hiding behind Kate's skirt, but was in a position to make that retreat if needed.

Maeve wandered around the room, picking up ornaments, looking at them and putting them down in exactly the same place. She didn't look directly at Charles or Kate, but always had a reflective surface in sight to observe their faces.

Instinctively, Charles wanted to know where she was at any moment.

If Dickie were seven or eight, Maeve should be nineteen or twenty. She was exactly as she had been when he first saw her, in Hill Wood.

'I thought you'd be taller,' said Kate.

The girl arched a thick eyebrow, as if she hadn't noticed Kate before.

'Might you be *Mrs* Beauregard?'

'Katharine Reed, *Pall Mall Gazette*,' she said.

'Is it *common* for ladies to represent newspapers?'

'Not at all.'

'Oh, really? I rather thought it was. Most *common*.'

She turned, as if dismissing a servant.

Maeve Harvill did not act like a carpenter's daughter or a baker's niece. She was a princess. Not an especially nice one.

'You'll have come to see poor David.'

'Poor' David owned this house and was the support of his whole family. Charles wondered if Davey even knew that.

'About the unpleasantness in the park.'

'You know about that?'

'It was in the *newspapers*,' she said, tossing a glance at Kate. 'Do you know Mr Satterthwaite Bulge? He's *ghastly*.'

That was the first child-thing she had said.

'Does Uncle Satt call here often?' asked Kate.

'He's not *my* uncle. He stays away unless he absolutely can't help it. Will he go to jail? I'm sure what happened to Leslie is all his fault.'

'You knew the late Mr Sackham?' he asked.

Maeve considered Kate and then Charles, thinking. She pressed an eye-tooth to her lower lip, carefully not breaking the skin, mimicking Sarah—whom it was hard to think of as the princess's sister.

'Is this to be an *interrogation?*'

'They be 'tectives, Auntie' said Dickie.

'How exciting,' she commented, as if on the point of falling asleep. 'Are we to be arrested?'

She held out her arms, voluminous sleeves sliding away from bird-thin wrists.

'Do you have hand-cuffs in my size?'

She spied something on a small table. It was Dickie's twig-clue. She picked it up, held it alongside her own fore-finger, and snapped it in half.

'Dirty thing. I can't imagine how it got in here.'

Dickie didn't cry but one of his eyes gleamed with a tear-to-be.

Maeve made a fist around the twig fragments as if to crush them further, then opened her hand to show an empty palm. With a flourish she produced the twig—whole—in her other hand.

Kate clapped, slowly. Maeve smiled to herself and took a little bow.

'I be a 'tective,' said Dickie, tears gone and delight stamped on his face. 'Auntie Maeve be a *conjurer.*'

'She should go on the halls,' said Kate, unimpressed. 'Mystic, Magical Maeve, the Modern Medusa.'

The girl flicked the twig into a grate where no fire would burn till autumn. Neither of her hands was dirty, the neatest trick of all.

'She makes things vanish, then brings 'em back,' said Dickie.

'That seems to happen quite often in this family,' commented Charles.

'More things vanish than come back,' said Maeve. 'Has he told you about the Bun Bandit from two doors down?'

'A successful conclusion to a baffling case?'

Maeve smiled. 'Sidney Silcock might not think so. He was thrashed and put on bread and water. Dickie has to keep out of the way when Sidney pays a call. A retaliatory walloping has been mentioned. There's a fellow who knows how to bide his time. I shouldn't be surprised if he waits *years*, until everyone else has forgotten what it was about. But the walloping will be *heroic*. Sidney is one to do things on an heroic scale.'

'He sounds a desperate villain.'

'He's desperate all right,' said Maeve, smiling her secret smile again.

'Greedy Sid's sweet on 'er,' said Dickie.

She glared calmly at her nephew.

Sarah came into the room, took in the scene, and nipped her lip again.

'Sarah, dear, I have been renewing a friendship. This, I am sure you realise, is Charles Beauregard, the intrepid fellow who rescued me from the *gypsies in the wood*.'

'Yes, Maeve, I realise.'

Sarah was not unconditionally grateful for this rescue. Sometimes she wished Charles had left well enough alone, had not lifted the princess from the snow, not carried her out of the wood.

'Davey says he'd like to see you,' Sarah told Charles, quietly—like a servant in her mistress's presence. 'And the lady.'

'You are privileged,' said Maeve. 'My brother rarely likes to see me.'

She was playing with a glass globe that contained a miniature woodland scene. When shook, it made a blizzard.

'Happy memories,' she commented.

'Davey's upstairs, in his studio,' said Sarah. 'Drawing. He's better than he was earlier.'

Sarah held the door open. Kate stepped into the hall, and Charles followed. Sarah looked back, at her son and her sister.

'Dickie, come help in the kitchen,' she said.

Dickie stayed where he was.

'I can see he stays out of trouble while we have visitors,' said Maeve. 'I've been practicing new tricks.'

Sarah was unsure. Dickie was resigned.

'I be all right, Ma.'

Sarah nodded and closed the door on the children. A tear of blood ran down the groove of her chin, unnoticed.

'Maeve hasn't changed,' said Charles as Sarah led them upstairs.

'Not since you saw her,' she responded. 'But she *did* change. When she were away. As much as Davey, not that anyone do listen to I. Not that Mam listened, God rest her.'

From the landing, Charles looked downstairs. All was quiet.

'Come through here,' said Sarah. 'To the studio.'

4: 'industry is a virtue'

Kate was expecting Ben Gunn—wild hair, matted beard, mad eyes. Instead, she found a presentable man, working in a room full of light. Beard he had, but neatly-trimmed and free of beetles. One eye was slightly lazy, but he did not seem demented. Davey Harvill, B. Loved, sat on a stool, over paper pinned flat to a bench. His hand moved fast with a sharp pencil, filling in intricate details of a picture already sketched. To one side was a neat pile of papers, squared away like letters for posting. By his feet was a half-full waste-paper basket.

This was the neatest artist's studio she had ever seen: bare floorboards spotless, walls papered but unadorned. Uncurtained floor-to-ceiling windows admitted direct sunlight. The expected clutter was absent: no books, reference materials, divans for models, props. Davey, in shirtsleeves, had not so much as a smudge of graphite upon him. He might have been a draper's clerk doing the end-of-day accounts. It was as if the pictures were willed into being without effort, without mess. They came out of his head, whole and entire, and were transmitted to paper.

Mrs Riddle let Kate and Charles into the room, coughed discreetly, and withdrew.

Davey looked up, nodded to Charles and smiled at Kate. His hand moved at hummingbird-speed, whether his eye was upon the paper or not. Some mediums practiced automatic writing; this could be automatic drawing.

'Charles, hello,' said Davey.

As far as Kate knew, the artist had not seen Charles in eight years.

'How have you been?' asked Charles.

'Very well, sir, all things considered.'

He finished his drawing and, without looking, freed it from its pinnings and shifted it to the pile, neatening the corners. He unrolled paper from a scroll, deftly pinned it in place and used a pen-knife to cut neatly across the top. A white, empty expanse lay before him.

'Busy, of course,' he said. 'Industry is a virtue.'

He took a pencil and, without pause, began to sketch.

Kate moved closer, to get a look at the work in progress. Most painters would have thrown her in the street for such impertinence, but Davey did not appear to mind.

Davey's pencil-point flew, in jagged, sudden strokes. A woodland appeared, populated by creatures whose eyes showed in shadows. Two small figures, hand in hand, walked in a clearing. A little boy and a girl. Watched from the trees and the burrows.

'This is my friend Kate Reed,' said Charles.

Davey smiled again, open and engaging, content in his work.

'Hello, Kate.'

'Please forgive this intrusion,' she ventured.

'It's no trouble. Makes a nice change.'

His pencil left the children, and darted to the corners of the picture, shading areas with solid strokes that left black shadows, relieved by tiny, glittering eyes and teeth. Kate was alarmed, afraid for the safety of the boy and the girl.

'I still haven't remembered anything,' said Davey. 'I'm sorry, Charles. I have tried.'

'That's all right, Davey.'

He was back on the central figures. The children, alone in the woods, clinging together for reassurance, for safety.

'What subject is this?' she asked.

'I don't know,' said Davey, looking down, seeing the picture for the first time, 'the usual.'

Now his eyes were on the paper, Davey stopped drawing.

'Babes in the Wood?' suggested Charles. 'Hansel and Gretel?'

Something was wrong about the children. They did not fit either of the stories Charles had mentioned.

'Davey and Maeve,' said the artist, sadly. 'I know everything I draw comes from *that time.* It's as if it never ended, not really.'

Charles laid a hand on the man's—the boy's—shoulder.

Davey began to work again on the children, more deliberately now.

Kate saw what was wrong. The girl was not afraid.

As Davey was doing the girl's eyes, the pencil-lead broke, scratching across her face.

'Pity,' he said.

Rather than reach for an india-rubber and make a minor change, he tore the paper from the block and began to make a ball of it.

'Excuse me,' said Kate, taking the picture from its creator.

'It's no use,' he said.

Kate spread the crumpled paper.

She saw something in it.

Charles riffled through the pile of completed illustrations. They were a sequence. The children entering the woods, taking a winding path, walking past færie dwellings without noticing, enticed ever deeper into the dark.

Kate looked back at the rejected picture.

The girl was exactly the child-woman Kate had met downstairs, Maeve. Her brother had caught the sulky, adult turn of her mouth and made her huge brush of hair seem alive. A princess, but a frightening one.

In the picture, the children were not lost. The girl was *leading* the boy into the woods.

'This is your sister,' said Kate, tapping the girl's scratched face.

'Maeve,' he said, not quite agreeing.

'And this is you? Davey?'

Davey hesitated. 'That's not right,' he said. 'Let me fix it . . .'

He reached for his pencil, but Charles stayed his hand.

They all looked closely at the boy in the picture. He was just beginning to worry, starting to consider unthinkable things—that the girl who held his hand was, in a real sense, a stranger to him, a stranger to *everyone*, that this adventure in the woods was taking a sinister turn.

It *might* be Davey, as he was when he went into the woods eight years ago, as a nine-year-old.

But it looked more like Dickie, as he was now.

5: 'Richard Riddle, Special Detective'

'If *I* were a real detective,' said Auntie Maeve, 'I shouldn't be content to waste my talents tracking down bun-thieves. For my quarry, I should choose more desperate criminals. Fiends who threaten the country more than they do their own trouser-buttons.'

Dickie trailed down the street after his aunt.

'I should concentrate exclusively on cases which constitute a challenge, on mysteries *worth* solving. Murders, and such.'

Maeve led him past the Silcock house, which gave him a pang of worry. Greedy Sid was, like the Count of Monte Cristo, capable of nurturing over long years an impulse to revenge. Behind the tall railings, bottom still smarting, the miscreant would be brooding, plotting. Dickie imagined Sidney Silcock, swollen to enormous size, become his lifelong nemesis, the Napoleon of Gluttony.

'The mystery of Leslie Sackham, for instance.'

The name caught Dickie's mind.

He remembered Mr Sackham as a bendy minion, hair floppy and cuffs ink-stained, trailing after Mr Bulge in attitudes of contortion. A tall man, he tried always to look up to his employer, no matter what kinks that put into his neck and spine. Sometimes, Mr Sackham told stories to children, but got them muddled and lost his audience before he reached the predictable endings. Dickie remembered one about Miss Fay Twinkledust, who put all her sparkles into a sensible investment portfolio rather than tossing them into the Silver Stream to be gobbled by the Silly Fish. Mr Sackham had been a boring grown-up. Now he was dead, the limits of his bendiness reached inside the works of a dynamo, Dickie felt guilty for not having liked him much.

It would be fitting if he were to solve the mystery.

Everyone would be grateful. Especially if it meant the Gift could open after all. Mr Bulge's business would be saved from the Silly Fish. Dickie understood the fortunes of the Harvill household depended in some mysterious way on the enterprises of 'Uncle Satt'—though only babies and girls read that dreary *Treasury* for anything but Uncle Davey's pictures.

Maeve took his hand.

'Where are we goin'?'

'To the park, of course.'

'Why?'

'To look for *clues*.'

At this magic word, Dickie was seized by the *rightness* of the pursuit. Whatever else Maeve might be, she was clever. She would make a valuable detective's assistant, with her sharp eyes and odd way of looking at things. Sometimes, she frightened people. That could be useful too.

Though it was too warm out for caps, scarves and coats, Maeve had insisted they dress properly for this sleuthing expedition. They might have to go *underground*, she said.

Dickie wore his special coat, a 'reversible' which could be either a loud check or a subdued herringbone. If spotted by a suspected criminal one was 'tailing,' the trick was to turn the coat inside-out and so seem to be another boy entirely. He even had a matching cap. In addition, secret pockets were stuffed with the instruments of his calling. About his person, he had the magnifying glass, measuring callipers, his catapult (which he was under strict orders from Ma not to use within shot of windows), a map of the locality with secret routes pencilled in, a multi-purpose penknife (with five blades, plus corkscrew, screwdriver and bradawl) and a bottle of invisible ink. He had made up cards for himself using a potato press, in visible and invisible ink: 'Richard Riddle, Special Detective.' Da approved, saying he was 'a regular Hawkshaw.' Hawkshaw was a famous detective from the olden days.

Maeve, with a blue bonnet that matched her dress, was a touch conspicuous for 'undercover' work. She walked with such confidence, however, that no one thought they were out on their own. Seeing the children—not that Aunt Maeve was *exactly* a child—in the street, people assumed there was a governess nearby, watching over them.

Dickie didn't believe in governesses. They came and went so often. Ma lamented that most found it difficult to work under a baker's wife, which proved the stupidity of the breed. He might bristle at parental decrees, especially with regards to the overrated virtues of cleanliness and tidiness, but Ma knew best—better than a governess, at any rate. Some were unaccountably prone to fits of terror. He suspected Maeve worked tricks to make governesses vanish on a regular basis, though she never brought them back again. He even wondered whether his aunt hadn't had an unseen hand in one of his greatest triumphs, the Mystery of the Cheating Governess. Despite overwhelming evidence, Miss MacAndrew had maintained to the moment of her dismissal that she had done no such thing.

In the park, children were everywhere, playing hopscotch, climbing anything that could be climbed, defending the North-West Frontier against disapproving wardens, fighting wild Red Indians with Buffalo Bill. Governesses in black bombazine flocked on the benches. Dickie imagined a cloud of general disapproval gathering above them. He pondered the possibility that they were in a secret society, pledged to make miserable the lives of all children, sworn to inflict *etiquette* and *washes* on the innocent. They dressed alike, and had the same expression—as if they'd just been made to swallow a whole lemon but ordered not to let it show.

He shouldn't be at all surprised if governesses were behind the Mystery of the Mangled Minion.

Mr Sackham had died in the park. There were always governesses in the park. They could easily cover up for each other. In their black, they could blend in with the shadows.

He liked the theory. Hawkshaw would have found it sound.

A pretty child with gloves in the shape of rabbit-heads approached, smiling slyly. She had ribbons in her hair and to her clothes. She was overdecorated, as if awarded a fresh ribbon every time she said her prayers.

'Little boy, my name is Becky d'Arbanvilliers,' said the girl, who was younger than him by a year or more. 'When I gwow up and Papa cwoaks, I shall be *Lady* d'Arbanvilliers. If you do something for me, I'll let you kiss my wabbits.'

Maeve took the future Lady d'Arbanvilliers aside, lifted a curtain of ribbons, and whispered into her ear. Maeve was insistent but calm. The girl's face crumpled, eyes expanding. Maeve finished whispering and stood back. Becky d'Arbanvilliers looked up at her, trembling. Maeve nodded and the girl ran away, exploding into screams and floods of tears.

'Hey presto, Hawkshaw,' she told Dickie. 'Magic.'

Becky d'Arbanvilliers fled to the coven of governesses, too hysterical to explain, but pointing in the direction where Maeve had been.

An odd thing was that two men dressed like governesses, not in long skirts but all in black with dark spectacles and curly hat-brims, were nearby. Dickie pegged them as sinister individuals. *They* paid attention to the noisy little girl.

'How cwuel,' said Maeve, imitating perfectly. 'To be named "Rebecca" and yet pwevented by nature fwom pwonouncing it pwoperly.'

Dickie laughed. No one else noticed his aunt could be funny as well as frightening. It was a secret between them.

Maeve led him towards the Gift.

A barrier of trestles was set up all around the building, hung with notices warning the public not to trespass. A policeman stood by the front doors, firmly seeing away curiosity-seekers. Dickie and Maeve had visited while Uncle Davey was helping Mr Bulge turn the Gift into the Færie

Aerie, and knew other ways in and out. Special Detectives always had more information than the poor plods of the Yard.

Maeve led Dickie round to the rear of the Gift. A door there supposedly only opened from the inside, so the used-up visitors could leave to make room for fresh ones. Unless you knew it was there, you wouldn't see it. The wall was painted with a big, colour copy of one of Uncle Davey's drawings, and the door hid in a waterfall, like goblins in a puzzle.

They slipped under an unguarded trestle.

Commotion rose in the park, among governesses. Becky d'Arbanvilliers had been able to explain. Though the governess instinct was to distrust anything a child told them, *something* had upset the girl. A hunt would have to be organised.

The men dressed like governesses took an interest.

Dickie was worried for his aunt.

Maeve smiled at him.

'I shall spirit us to safety, with more magic,' she announced. 'Might I borrow your catapult?'

He was reluctant to hand over such a formidable weapon.

'I shall return it directly.'

Dickie undid his secret pocket and produced the catapult.

Maeve examined it, twanged the rubber appreciatively and pronounced it a fine addition to a detective's arsenal.

She made a fold in the rubber and slipped it into the crack in the falling waters that showed those who knew what to look for where the door was. She worked with her fingers for a few moments.

'This is where a conjurer chats to the audience, to take their minds off the trick being done in front of their eyes.'

Dickie watched closely—he always did, but Maeve still managed tricks he could not work out.

'I say, what are you children doing?'

It was a *governess*, a skeleton in black.

'Have you seen a horrid, *horrid* little girl . . . ? Dipped in the very essence of wickedness?'

Maeve did one of her best tricks. She put on a smile that fooled everyone but Dickie. She seemed like all the sunny girls in the world, brainless and cheerful.

'I should not like to meet a wicked little girl,' she said, sounding a little like Becky d'Arbanvilliers. 'No, thank you very much.'

'Very wise,' said the governess, fooled entirely. 'Well, if you see such a creature, stay well away from her.'

The woman stalked off.

Maeve shrugged and dropped the smile.

'I swear, Hawkshaw, these *people*. They're so *stupid*. They deserve . . . ah!'

There was a click inside the wall. Maeve pulled the catapult free and the door came open.

She handed him back the catapult and tugged him inside, into the dark.

The door shut behind them.

'This is an adventure, isn't it?'

He agreed.

6: 'intelligence reports'

Sarah Riddle, over the first shock, slumped on a hall settee, numb and cried out.

Charles understood.

The worst thing was that this was a *familiar* anxiety.

Maeve and Dickie were missing.

'It's *her*,' said Sarah. 'I always knew . . .'

The house had been searched. Kate turned up Bitty, a maid who recalled noticing Dickie and his aunt, dressed as if to go out. That she had not actually seen them leave the house saved her position. Charles knew that even if Bitty had been there, she would not have been able to intervene. Maeve treated her family like servants; he could imagine how she treated servants.

'It's like before,' said Philip Riddle, standing by his wife. 'Only then it were Hill Wood. Now, it's a whole *city*.'

Charles reproached himself for not considering Dickie. He had given a lot of thought to Davey and Princess Cuckoo, but rarely recalled this household harboured one proper child. When Charles was in Eye, Dickie had not been born, was not part of the story.

Now, Charles saw where Dickie fit.

Davey had escaped *something*. Dickie would do as replacement.

'Charles,' said Kate, from the top of the stairs. 'Would you come up?'

He left Sarah and Philip, and joined Kate. She led him into the studio.

Davey was still drawing.

Kate showed him finished pictures in which the children ventured deeper into the woods. A smug bunny in a beribboned pinafore appeared in a clearing. The girl, more Maeve than ever, loomed over the small, terrified rabbit. In one picture, her head was inflated twice the size of her body, hair puffed like a lion's mane. She showed angry, evil eyes and a toothy, dripping shark's maw. The rabbit fled, understandably. In the next picture, Maeve was herself again, though it would be hard to forget her scary head. She was snatching the boy, Dickie, away from a clutch of old-womanish crows who sported veiled hats and reticules. Then the children came to a waterfall. Maeve used long-nailed fingers to unlock a door in the cascade—a door made of *flowing* water, not ice—to open a way into wooded underworld.

'What does this mean, Davey?'

He drew faster than ever. Tears spotted his paper, blotching the pencil-work. His face shut tight, he rocked back and forth, crooning.

'*My mother said . . . I never should . . . play with the gypsies . . . in the wood.*'

Another picture was finished and put aside.

The children were in a forested tunnel, passing a fallen tower. Goblins swarmed in the undergrowth, ears and tongues twitching, flat nostrils a-quiver.

'I know that ruin,' said Kate. 'It's in the Gift. We were there when it collapsed.'

'And *I* know the waterfall door.'

Kate began searching the studio.

'What are you looking for?' he asked her.

'A sketch-pad. Something he can carry. We have to take him to the park. All this is happening *now*. The pictures are like *intelligence reports*.'

Kate opened a cupboard in the work-bench and found a package of notebooks. She took several and shoved one opened under Davey's pencil, whispering to him, urging him to shift to a portable medium. After a beat of hesitation, he began again, drawing still faster, pencil scoring paper. Kate gathered the completed pictures into a sturdy artist's folder.

'Stay with him a moment,' Charles told her, leaving the study.

Dickie's parents were at the foot of the stairs, looking up.

'Is this household on the telephone?' he asked.

'Mr Bulge insisted,' said Philip Riddle. 'The apparatus is in the downstairs parlour.'

'Ring up Scotland Yard and ask for Inspector Henry Mist. Tell him to meet us at the Gift.'

Riddle, a solid man, didn't waste time asking for explanations. He went directly to the parlour.

Kate had Davey out of his studio and helped him downstairs. He still murmured and scribbled.

'Bad things in the woods,' Kate reported. 'Very bad.'

Charles trusted her.

'Have you called a cab?' she asked.

'Quicker to walk.'

Sarah reached out as Kate and Charles helped Davey past, pleading wordlessly. Her lip was bleeding.

'There's hope,' he told her.

She accepted that as the best offer available.

On the street, he and Kate must have seemed the abductors of a lunatic. When Davey finished a picture, Kate turned the page for him.

From a window peered the fat face of a sad little boy. He alone took notice of the peculiar trio. People on the street evaded them without comment. Charles did his best to look like someone who would brook no interference.

Every pause to allow a cart or carriage primacy was a heart-blow.

The streets were uncommonly busy. People were mobile trees in these wilds, constantly shutting off and making new paths. London was more perilous than Hill Wood. Though it was a sunny afternoon and he walked on broad pavement, Charles recalled snow underfoot.

'What's in the pictures now?' he asked.

'Hard to make out. Children, goblins, woods. The boy seems all right still.'

Maeve and Dickie must have taken this route, perhaps half an hour earlier. This storm had blown up in minutes.

If it weren't for Kate's leap of deduction, the absences might have gone unnoticed until tea-time. Another reason to propose her for membership.

In the park, there was the expected chaos. Children, idlers, governesses, dogs. A one-man band played something from *The Mikado*.

'The crows,' said Kate.

Charles saw what she meant. Some governesses gathered

around a little girl, heads bobbing like birds, veiled hats like those in Davey's illustration.

'And that's the frightened bunny,' he pointed out.

He remembered Maeve's temporary scary head. Davey's drawings weren't the literal truth, he hoped. They hinted at what really happened.

'Ladies,' he began, 'might I inquire whether you've seen two children, a girl of perhaps eleven and a slightly younger boy? You would take them for brother and sister.'

The women reacted like Transylvanian peasants asked the most convenient route to Castle Dracula, with hisses and flutterings and clucks very like curses.

'That horrid, *horrid* girl . . .' spat one.

Even in the circumstances, he had to swallow a smirk.

'That would be the miss. You have her exactly.'

The governesses continued, yielding more editorial comment but no hard news.

'Why is that man dwawing?' asked the ribboned girl.

'He's an artist,' Charles told her.

'My name is Becky d'Arbanvilliers,' she said proudly. 'When I gwow up and Papa cwoaks, I shall be *Lady* d'Arbanvilliers.'

Few prospective heirs would be as honest, he supposed. At least, out loud. In cases of suspicious death, the police were wont to remember such offhand remarks.

'Did you meet a bad girl, Becky?'

She nodded her head, solemnly.

'And where is she now?'

Becky frowned, as angry as she was puzzled.

'I *told* Miss Wodgers, but she didn't believe me. The bad girl and the nasty boy went to the waterfall in that house.'

She pointed to the Gift.

'There was a girl,' said the governess, whose name he presumed was Miss Rodgers. 'But not the one who so upset Becky. This was a nice, polite child.'

Becky looked at Charles, frustrated by her governess's gullibility.

'It was her,' she insisted, stamping a tiny foot.

Davey finished one notebook and started on the next. Kate took the filled book and leafed through, then found a picture.

'*This* girl?' she asked. 'And this boy?'

'That's them,' said Becky. 'What a pwetty picture. Will the man dwaw me? I'm pwettier than the bad girl.'

'Miss Rodgers,' he prompted.

The governess looked stricken.

'Yes,' she admitted. 'But she *smiled* so . . .'

Recriminations flew around the group of governesses.

'*Will the man dwaw me?*'

Kate leafed through the folder and found a picture of the children meeting the ribboned rabbit, the one in which Maeve was not showing her scary head. She handed it over. Becky was transported with delight, terrors forgotten.

Miss Rodgers saw the picture, puzzled and disturbed.

'How did he do this? It was drawn before he set eyes on Rebecca . . .'

They left the governesses wondering.

From the corner of his eye, Charles glimpsed a couple in black who weren't governesses. Mr Hay and Mr Effe. Since this morning, he had been aware of their floating presence. The Undertaking was playing its own game and had turned up here before he did. He would worry about that later, if he got the chance. Right now, he should be inside the Gift.

By the time they found the door concealed in the water-fall design, Inspector Mist was on the scene.

'Mr Beauregard, what is all this about?'

7: 'stage snow'

Kate knew Charles would make a token attempt to dissuade her from continuing. The argument, a variation on a theme with which she was bored, was conducted in shorthand.

Yes, it might be dangerous.

Yes, she was a woman.

No, that wouldn't make a difference.

Settled.

Mist of the Yard was distracted by Davey's compulsive sketching.

'Is this fellow some sort of psychic medium?'

'He has a connection with this business,' Charles told Mist. 'This is Davey Harvill.'

'The boy from Eye.'

The Inspector evidently knew about the Children of Eye. She was not surprised. Whisper had it that Mist was high up in the Bureau of Queer Complaints, an unpublicised Scotland Yard department constituted to deal with the 'spook' cases.

Mist posted constables to keep back this afternoon's crowds. Rumours circulated. The Gift was about to be opened to the public. Or razed to the ground. No one was sure. Helmeted bobbies assumed their usual attitudes, bored resignation to indicate nothing out of the ordinary taking place behind the barriers and truncheon-tapping warning that no monkey business would be tolerated. Popular phrases were recited: 'move along, now' and 'there's nothing to see 'ere.'

Two men in black clothes augmented by very black spectacles sauntered over. At the flash of a card, they were admitted to the inner circle.

The crowd chimed with another whisper, about funereal officials seen pottering about new-made meteor craters or the sites of unnatural vanishments. Another high-stakes player at this table, in competition or alliance with the Diogenes Club and the BQC. The poor plodders of the Society for Psychical Research must feel left out, stuck with only the least-mysterious of eternal mysteries, trivial table-rappings and ghosts who did nothing but loom in sheets and say 'boo!' to handy geese.

Charles made rapid introductions, 'Mr Hay and Mr Effe, of the Undertaking. Mist you know. Katharine Reed . . .'

Mr Effe bared poor teeth at her. Even without sight of his eyes, she could gauge his expression.

'Do we need the press, Beauregard?' he asked.

'*I* need *her.*'

Argument was squashed. She was proud of him, again. More than proud.

'The missing boy is in there,' said Mist. 'And his . . . sister?'

'*Aunt,*' corrected Charles. 'Maeve. Don't be taken in by her. She's not what she seems. The boy is Richard. Dickie. He's the one in danger. We must get him out of the Gift.'

'The girl too,' prompted Mr Hay.

Charles shook his head. 'She's long lost,' he said. 'It's the boy we want, we *need* . . .'

'That wasn't a suggestion,' said the Undertaker.

Charles and Mist exchanged a look.

'Get that door kicked in,' Mist told two hefty bobbies.

They shouldered the waterfall, shaking the whole of the Gift.

'It's probably unlocked and opens outwards,' she suggested.

The policemen stood back. The dented door swung slowly out, proving her point. Inside, it was darker than it should be. This was a bright afternoon. The ceiling of the Gift was mostly glass. It should be gloomy at worst.

White powder lay on the floor, footprints trodden in.

'Is that snow?' asked Mist.

'Stage snow,' said Charles. 'Remember, nothing in there is real. Which doesn't mean it's not dangerous.'

'We'll need light. Willoughby, hand over your bull-lantern.'

One of the bobbies unlatched a device from his belt. Mist

lit the lamp. Charles took it and shone a feeble beam into the dark. Stage snow fell from a sky ceiling. It was a clever trick—reflective sparkles set into wooden walls. But she did not imagine the cold wind that blew from the Gift, chilling through her light blouse. She was not dressed to pay a call on the Snow Queen.

Charles ventured into the dark.

Kate helped Davey follow. He had stopped chanting out loud but his neck muscles worked as he sub-audially repeated his rhyme.

In his pictures, goblins gathered.

Mist came last, with another lamp.

Mr Hay and Mr Effe remained outside, in the summer sunshine.

This was not a part of Færie she had seen yesterday, but Charles evidently knew his way. The walls were theatrical flats painted with convincing woodlands. Though the corridor was barely wide enough for two people side by side, scenery seemed to extend for miles. In the minimal light, the illusion was perfect. She reached out. Where she was sure snow fell through empty air, her fingers dimpled oiled canvas.

They could not be more than fifty feet inside the Gift, which she knew to cover a circle barely a hundred yards across, but it seemed miles from Regent's Park. Glancing back, she saw the Undertakers, scarecrows against an oblong of daylight. Looking forward, there was night and forest. Stars sparkled on the roof.

The passage curved, and she couldn't see the entrance any more.

Of course, the Gift was a fairground maze.

Charles, tracking clear footprints, came to a triplicate fork in the path. Three sets of prints wound into each tunnel.

'Bugger,' said Mist, adding, 'Pardon me, Miss.'

She asked for light and sorted back through Davey's pictures. She was sure she had seen this. She missed it once and had to start again. Then she hit on sketches representing this juncture. On paper, Maeve led Dickie down the left-hand path. In the next picture, goblins tottered out of the trees on stilts tipped with child-sized shoes which (horribly) had disembodied feet stuffed into them. The imps made false trails down the other paths, smirking with mean delight, cackles crawling off the paper.

Kate was beginning to *hate* Davey's goblins.

Charles bent low to enter the left-hand tunnel, which went under two oaks whose upper branches tangled, as if the trees were frozen in a slapping argument. Disapproving faces twisted in the bark.

Even Kate couldn't stand up in this tunnel.

They made slow, clumsy progress. It was hard to light the way ahead. All Charles and Mist could do was cast moon-circles on the nearest surface, infernally reflecting their own faces.

The tunnel angled downwards.

She wondered if this led to the dynamo room. The interior of the Gift was on several levels. Yesterday, it had been hot here. Now snowflakes whisped on her face like ice-pricks.

'That's not likely,' said Mist, looking at snowmelt in his palm.

Davey stumbled over an exposed root. Kate reached out to catch him. They fell against a barbed bramble and staggered off the path, tumbling into a chilly drift. Painted walls had given way to three-dimensional scenery, the break unnoticed. The snow must be artificially generated—ice-chips sifted from a hidden device up above—but felt unpleasantly real.

Mist and Charles played their lamps around.

Kate assumed they were in the large, central area she had visited, but in this minimal light it seemed differently shaped. Everything was larger. She was now in proportion with trees that had been miniature.

A vicious wind blew from somewhere, spattering her spectacles with snow-dots. The waterfall was frozen in serried waves, trapping bug-eyed, dunce-capped Silly Fish in a glacier grip.

Charles took off his ulster and gave it to her. She gratefully accepted.

'I never thought I'd miss my Sir Boris costume,' he said.

Mist directed his lamp straight up. Its throw didn't reach any ceiling. He pointed it down, and found grass, earth and snow—no floorboards, no paving, no matting. In the wind, trees shifted and creaked.

'Bloody good trick,' said the policeman.

Davey hunched in a huddle, making tinier and tinier pictures.

There was movement in the dark. Charles turned, pointing his light at rustles. Wherever the lantern shone, all was stark and still. Outside the beam, things were evilly active. The originals of Davey's goblins, whatever they might be, were in the trees. The illustrations, satirical cartoons, were tinged with grotesque humour. She feared there would be nothing funny about the live models.

'*Dickie,*' shouted Charles.

His echo came back, many times. Charles's breath plumed. His shout dissipated in the open night. She could have sworn mocking, imitative voices replaced the echo.

'There's a castle,' said Kate, looking at Davey's latest drawings. 'No, a *palace.* Maeve is leading Dickie up steps, to meet . . . I don't know, a prince?'

Davey was still working. His arm was in the way of a completed picture. Gently, she shifted his wrist.

In a palatial hall, Dickie was presented to a mirror, looking at himself. Only, his reflection was different. The boy in the glass had thinner eyes, pointier ears, a nastier mouth.

Davey went on to another book.

Kate showed Charles and Mist the new sequence.

'We have to find this place, quickly,' said Charles. 'The boy is in immediate danger.'

8: 'the game is up'

Maeve had turned her ankle. Dickie's aunt did not usually act so like a girl. After helping as best he could, he left her wrapped up by the path. She kept their candle. When the mystery was solved, he could find his way back to her light. Bravely, Maeve urged him on, to follow the clues.

In the middle of the Gift, she said, was a palace.

Inside the palace was the *culprit*.

Steeled, Dickie made his way from clue to clue.

Moonbeam pools picked them out. A dagger with the very tip sheared away, a half-burned page of cipher, a cigarette end with three distinctive bands, a cameo brooch that opened to a picture of a hairy-faced little girl, an empty blue glass bottle marked with skull and crossbones, a bloodied grape-stem, a dish of butter with a sprig of parsley sunk into it, a dead canary bleached white, a worm unknown to science, a squat jade idol with its eyegems prised out, a necklace crushed to show its gems were paste, a false beard with cardboard nose attached.

Excellent clues, leading to his destination.

When he first glimpsed the palace through the trees, Dickie thought it a doll's house, much too small for him. When, at last, he found the front door, spires rose above him. It was clever, like one of Maeve's conjuring tricks.

Who *was* the culprit?

Mr Satterthwaite Bulge (he had known the dead man best, and could have been blackmailed or have something to gain from a will) . . . Uncle Davey (surely not, though some said he was 'touched'; he might have another person living in his head, not a nice one) . . . the clever gent and the Irish lady who had called this afternoon (Dickie had liked them straight off, which should not blind him to sorry possibilities) . . . Greedy Sid Silcock (too obvious and convenient, though he could well be in it as a minion of the true mastermind) . . . Miss MacAndrew (another vengeance-plotter?) . . . Bitty, the rosy-cheeked maid (hmmmn, something was *stirring* about her complexion) . . . Ma and Da (*no!*) . . .

He would find out.

The palace disappointed. It was a wooden façade, propped up by rough timbers. There were no rooms, just hollow space. The exterior was painted to look like stone. Inside was bare board, nailed without much care.

He could not see much. Even through his magnifying glass.

'Hello,' he called.

''lo?' came back at him, in his own voice.

Or something very like.

'You are found out.'

'Out!'

The culprit was here.

But Dickie was still in the dark. He must remember to include a box of lucifers in his detective apparatus, with long tapers. Perhaps even a small lantern. Having left his candle with Maeve, so she wouldn't be lonely, he was at a disadvantage.

'The game is up,' he announced, sounding braver than he felt.

'Up?'

'This palace is surrounded by *special detectives*. You are under arrest.'

'Arrest?'

The culprit was an *echo*.

The dark in front of his face gathered, solidified into coherence. He made out human shape.

Dickie's hand fell on the culprit's shoulder.

'Ah hah!'

A hand gripped his own shoulder.

'Hah,' came back, a gust of hot breath into his face.

He squeezed and was squeezed.

His shoulder hurt, his knees weakened. He was pushed down, as if shrinking.

The hand on his shoulder grew, fingers like hard twigs poking into him. His feet sank into earth, which swarmed around his ankles. His socks would get muddied, which would displease Ma.

Shapes moved all around.

The culprit was not alone. He had minions.

He imagined them—Greedy Sid, Miss MacAndrew, Uncle Satt, an ape, a mathematics tutor, a defrocked curate. The low folk who were part of the mystery.

'Who are you?'

'You!'

9: 'two jumps behind'

There was light ahead. A candle-flame.

Charles pointed it out.

The light moved, behind a tree, into hiding.

Charles played his lantern over the area, wobbling the beam to indicate where the others should look, then directing it elsewhere, hoping to fool the candle-holder into believing she was overlooked.

Charles was sure it was a *she*.

He handed his lantern to Kate, who took it smoothly and continued the 'search.'

Charles stepped off the track.

Whatever was passing itself off as snow was doing a good job. His shins were frozen as he waded. He crouched low and his bare hands sunk into the stuff.

He crept towards the tree where the light had been.

'Pretty princess,' he breathed to himself, 'sit tight . . .'

He had picked up night-skills in warmer climes, crawling

over rocky hills with his face stained, dressed like an untouchable. He could cross open country under a full moon without being seen. In this dark, with so many things to hide behind, it should be easy.

But it wasn't. The going was treacherous. The snow lay lightly over brambles that could snare like barbed wire.

Within a couple of yards of the tree, he saw the guarded, flickering spill of light. He flexed his fingers into the snow, numbing his joints. Sometimes, he had pains in his knuckles—which he had never mentioned to anyone. He stood, slowly.

He held his breath.

In a single, smooth movement, he stepped around the tree and laid a hand on . . .

. . . *bark!*

He summoned the others.

The candle perched in a nook, wax dribbling.

Clear little footprints radiated from a hollow in the roots. They spiralled and multiplied, haring off in all directions as if a dozen princesses had sprung into being and bolted.

Kate showed Charles a new-drawn picture of Maeve skipping away, tittering to herself.

'Have you noticed he never draws us?' he said.

'Maybe we're not in the story yet.'

'We're here all right,' said Mist. 'Two jumps behind.'

Mist supported Davey now. The lad was running out of paper. His pictures were smaller, crowded together—two or three to a page—and harder to make out.

'Let me try something,' said Kate.

She laid her fingers on Davey's hand, halting his pencil. He shook, the beginnings of a fit. She took his chin and forced him to look at her.

'Davey, where's the palace?'

He was close to tears, frustrated at not being able to draw, to channel what he knew.

'Not in pictures,' she said. 'Words. Tell me in words.'

Davey shook his head and shut his eyes. Squeaks came from the back of his throat.

'. . . mother said . . . never should . . .'

'Dickie's in the woods,' said Kate.

'With the gypsies?'

'Yes, the naughty, naughty gypsies. That bad girl is taking Dickie to them. We can help him, but you have to help us. Please, Davey. For Dickie. These are *your* woods. You mapped them and made them. Where in the woods . . .'

Davey opened his eyes.

He turned, breaking Kate's hold, and waded off, snow slushing around his feet. He pressed point to paper and made three strokes, then snapped the pencil and dropped the notebook.

'This way,' he said.

Davey walked with some confidence towards a stand of trees. He reached up and touched a low-hanging branch, pushing a bird's nest, sending a ripple through branch, tree and sky. He took out his pen-knife, opened the blade and stuck it into the backdrop. With a tearing sound, the knife parted canvas and sank to the hilt. Davey drew his knife in a straight line, across the branch and into the air. He made a corner and cut downwards, as if hacking a door into a tent. The fabric ripped, noisily.

Charles thought he could see for hundreds of yards, through the woods. Even as Davey cut his door, Charles could swear the lad stood in a real landscape.

Davey slashed the canvas, methodically.

There was a doorway in the wood.

Beyond was gloom but not dark. It looked like the quarter where backstage people worked, where Sir Boris had got dressed and prepared or took his infrequent meal and rest-breaks.

'Through here,' said Dickie.

They followed. Beyond the door, it wasn't cold any more. It was close, stifling.

Dickie cut a door in an opposite wall.

'I know where you're hiding,' he said, to someone beyond.

A screech filled the passage. A small person with wild hair tore between their legs, launching a punch at Davey's chest, clawing at Kate's face, sinking a shoulder into Mist's stomach.

Charles blocked her.

The screech died. The girl's face was in shadow, but could no longer be mistaken. This was not—*had never been*—Maeve Harvill. This was Princess Cuckoo, of Pixieland. Rather, of the shadow realm Davey recreated in his pictures, which Satterthwaite Bulge had named Færie and built in the real world. That was what she had wanted all along.

'Where is he?' Charles asked. 'Dickie?'

The little face shut tight, lip buttoned, chin and cheeks set. This close, she seemed a genuine child. No Thuggee strangler or Scots preacher could be as iron-willed as a little girl determined not to own up.

'I know,' said Davey. 'It's where she took me, where I got away from.'

The girl shook her head, humming furiously.

'That's an endorsement,' Charles commented. 'Lead on, Davey.'

10: 'holes'

They descended into the ground. Brickwork tunnel walls gave way to shored earth and flagstones. Kate could not believe Regent's Park was only a few feet above their heads.

She squirreled through, following Davey. Charles dragged Maeve after him. Inspector Mist held the rear.

The place smelled of muck.

They emerged in the dynamo chamber, site of the sacrifice that had kept the throngs away from the Gift so Maeve could make her private exchange. Roots thick as a man's torso burst through, spilling bricks on the floor, entwining like angry prehistoric snakes. A canvas cover over the dynamos, stained with red mud, was partially lifted. Ivy grew like a plague, twining into ironwork, twisting around stilled pistons and bent valves. The weed grip had cracked one of the great wheels.

Green sparks nestled in nooks. Fairy lights, little burning pools which needed no dynamos.

Dickie sat in front of the machine, knees together, cap straight.

'There he is,' said Maeve. 'No harm done. Satisfied?'

Charles shone his lantern. Emerald light-points danced in the boy's eyes. He raised a hand to shield his face.

'Princess,' said the boy. 'Is that you?'

They were here in time! Kate wanted to hug the errant special detective.

'Dickie,' said Charles, off-handedly. 'Tell me, what clue enabled you to solve the Baffling Business of the Cheating Governess?'

Dickie lowered his hand. His eyes were hard.

Ice brushed the untidy hair at the nape of Kate's neck.

'Who was the Bun Bandit?' she asked.

No answer. The lightpoints in his eyes were fixed. Seven in each. In the shape of the constellation Ursa Major.

'That's not D-Dickie,' said Davey. 'That's . . .'

'I think we know who that is,' said Charles.

Kate's insides plunged. She looked at the boy. He was like Maeve, but new-made. Clean and fresh and tidy, still slightly moist. He did not yet have the knack of passing among people.

Davey whirled about the chamber, tapping roots, tearing off covers.

Maeve and the boy exchanged gazes and kept quiet.

Kate knew Sarah Riddle would not be happy with a boy who merely *looked* like her son.

'So, it's another one,' said Inspector Mist, walking around the boy.

He looked up at the policeman, unblinking, head rotating like an owl's.

'That's a good trick,' Kate said.

The boy experimented with a smile of acknowledgement. It did not come off well.

Charles was with Davey, talking to him quietly, insistently.

'Think hard, Davey . . . this is that place, the place that was under Hill Wood . . .'

'Yes, I know. But this is London.'

'The place where you were taken is *somewhere else*, Davey. Somewhere that travels. Somewhere with holes that match up to holes here. I don't know how the hole was made in Eye. Perhaps it was always there. But the hole here, in the Gift, you made.'

Davey nodded, to himself.

'I thought I'd got away, but I brought it with me, in my head. The drawing, the dreams. That was it, pressing on me. I cheated *them*, by their lights. I owed them.'

He felt his way around now, carefully. He began humming his rhyme—his long-lost sister's rhyme—then caught himself, and was quiet, chewing his lip like a Harvill.

'A hole,' he said, at last. 'There's a hole. Something like a hole.'

Davey took out his pen-knife. He shook his head and threw it away.

'Would this be any use?' suggested Inspector Mist.

The policeman pulled a giant-sized spanner from the clutches of greenery and handed it over.

Davey took the length of iron, felt its heft, and nodded.

Charles stood back. Davey took a swing, as if with an axe. The spanner clanged against exposed root. The whole chamber rung with the blow. Kate's teeth rattled. Old bark sloughed, exposing bone-yellow woodflesh. Davey struck again, and the wood parted.

There was an exhalation of foul air, and a vast inpouring of soft, insect-inhabited earth. Almost liquid, it slurried around their ankles, then grew to a tidal wave that threatened to fill the chamber. Some of the lights winked out. She found herself clinging to Charles, who held onto a dangling chain to steady his footing. Mist hopped nimbly out of the way.

The sham children paid no mind.

In the dirt, something moved. Charles deftly shifted Kate's grip to the chain and weighed in, with Davey, shovelling earth with cupped hands.

A very dirty little boy was disclosed, spitting leaves.

Charles whispered in his ear.

'Jack of Hearts, with one corner bent off,' Dickie shouted.

Davey hugged his nephew, who was a bit embarrassed.

The dirty boy looked at his clean mirror image. Dickie had a spasm of fear, but got over it.

'You'd better leave,' Charles told the impostor.

The failed changeling stood, lifted his shoulders at the girl in a well-I-*tried* shrug, and stepped close to the fissure in the wall. The gap seemed too narrow. As the faux Dickie neared the hole, he seemed to fold thinner, and be sucked beyond, into deeper, frothing darkness. The stench settled, but remained fungoid and corpse-filthy.

Everyone looked at Maeve.

'So, Princess Cuckoo,' said Charles, hands on hips, 'what's to be done with you?'

She regarded him, blankly.

11: 'you might not know what you get back'

The place was changing. The roots withdrew. The crack in the wall narrowed, as healing. A machine-oil tang cut through the peaty smell.

'The holes are closing,' said Davey.

Charles considered the Princess. It had been important that there be *two* cuckoos, Prince and Princess. Davey's escape from the realm beyond the holes had stalled some design. If Dickie had been successfully supplanted, it would have started again, rumbling inexorably towards its end. Charles did not even want to guess what had just been thwarted. Plans laid in a contingent world were now abandoned—which should be enough for the Ruling Cabal.

That unknown place rubbed against thinning, permeable walls. Davey's drawings were not the first signs that barriers could be breached. Everywhere, he once said, has its stories. Many places also had their holes, natural or special-made. It was difficult, but travellers could pass through veils that separated there from here and here from there.

This girl-shaped person was one such.

'Princess, if I may call you that . . .'

She nodded. Her face was thinner now, cheekbones more apparent, pupils oval, skin a touch green in the lamplight.

'. . . outside the Gift are two men dressed in black.'

She knew the Undertaking.

'They would like me to hand you over to them. You are a *specimen* of great interest. As you once had *plans* for us, they have plans for you. Which you might not care for.'

'It doesn't matter,' she said.

'You say that now. You're disappointed, of course. Your life for the past eight years—and I can imagine it has been utterly strange—was geared up to this moment. And it's proven a bust.'

'No need to rub it in, Mr Detective.'

'I am just trying to make you realise this might not be the *worst* moment of your sojourn here.'

The girl spat out a bitter little laugh.

She *was* like a child. Perhaps they all were. That child-ishness was evident in all the impressions that came through the holes, dressed up and painted in and cut about by Davey

Harvill and Uncle Satt and Leslie Sackham and George MacDonald and Arthur Rackham and many, many others. They were the *little* people, small in their wonderments, prone to spasms of sunlit joy and long rainy afternoon sulks.

'Mr Hay and Mr Effe might tire of asking questions. It can be boring, not getting answers. In the end, the Undertaking might just *cut you up* in the name of science. To find wings folded inside your shoulder-bones, then spread them on a board and pin you like a butterfly. There's a secret museum for creatures like you. It's possible you'd be under glass for a long time.'

A thrill passed through her. A horror.

That was something to be proud of. He had terrified the Medusa.

'What do you want?' she said, quietly.

'His sister,' he said, nodding at Davey.

She thought it over.

'There's a balance. She can't be here if I am. Not for long. You saw, with Dickie. Things bend.'

'You're not going to *let her go*?' said Kate.

Charles sympathised with Kate's outrage. Mist, as well. This girl was responsible for at least one murder. Sackham, obviously—to keep the Gift shut, so her business could proceed. Almost certainly, she had contrived the death of Violet Harvill, who could not be fooled forever. (Did Davey know that? How could he not?) Charles was certain the Princess would answer for her failure to the powers she served or represented.

'It is for the best,' he told Kate.

Mist gave him the nod. Good man.

'I should warn you,' said the Princess, 'you might not know what you get back. Time passes differently.'

He understood. If thirty years fly past in three days, what might not transpire in eight years?

The Princess stood by the fissure, which pulsed—almost like a mouth.

She looked at them all.

'Good-bye, Hawkshaw,' she said. 'The Dickie who was almost is less fun.'

Dickie frowned. Kate had most of the dirt off his face.

'Auntie,' he said. 'I know you didn't mean it.'

The Princess seemed sad but said nothing. Suddenly boneless and flimsy, she slid into the slit as if it were a post-box and she a letter. Long seconds passed. The fissure bulged and creaked. An arm flopped out.

Davey took hold of the hand and pulled.

Charles grabbed Davey's waist and hauled. Mist and Kate lent their strength. Even so, it was hard going. Davey's grip slipped on oily skin. Charles's forearm ached, as he felt the old bite.

A shoulder and head, coated with mud, emerged. Eyes opened in the mask of filth. Bright, alive eyes.

Then, in a long tangle, a whole body slithered out. She drew breath, as if just born, and gave vent to a cry. Noise filled the dynamo chamber.

'Let's take the quickest way out,' he said.

Kate went ahead with the lanterns. The three men carried the limp, adult length of the rescued girl between them. Dickie, magnifying glass held up, followed.

When they banged out of the waterfall door, Mist ordered a constable to fetch water from the horse-trough in Regent's Crescent. The new-found girl lay on the ground, head in Davey's lap. A drapery wound around her, plastered to her body like a toga, but her bare, gnarled feet stuck out.

Kate held Dickie back.

Mr Hay and Mr Effe exchanged dark glances, unreadable. When Charles looked again, they were gone. A worry for another day.

Philip and Sarah Riddle got past the cordon and bustled

around, too relieved at the return of Dickie to ask after the new arrival. They took their son, scolding and embracing him.

Mist had his men round up buckets of water, and had to stop P.C. Willoughby from dashing one in the woman's face.

'Looks like she's been buried alive, sir,' said the constable.

'It's not so bad,' said Dickie, bravely.

Charles requisitioned a flannel from a stray governess, soaked it, and cleaned the face of the woman who had come back.

A beautiful blank appeared with the first wash. She was exactly like the Princess. Then a few lines became apparent, and a white streak in her hair.

'Maeve,' said Davey.

The woman looked up, recognising her brother.

Charles would have taken her for a well-preserved forty or a hard-lived thirty. He stood back, and looked at the family reunion.

'How long's it been?' she said.

'Not but a moment,' said Davey.

She closed her eyes and smiled, safe.

Charles found Kate was holding his elbow, face against his sleeve. He suspected a manoeuvre to conceal tears. A pricking in his eyes suggested discreet dabbing might be in order to repair his own composure.

A crowd began to assemble. There was still interest in the Gift. It occurred to Charles that it might even be safe to open the place, though Mist would have to write up the Sackham case carefully for the BQC files.

Maeve rolled in Davey's grasp and flung her arms around his neck.

Sarah Riddle noticed her sister, recognised her at once. She gasped, in wonder. Her husband, puzzled at first, caught on and began to dance a jig.

Charles slipped his own arm around Kate's waist. Her

hands were hooked into his coat. They had been through a great deal together. Again. Pamela had been right about Katharine Reed; she was an extraordinarily promising girl. No, that was then. Now, she was an extraordinarily delivering woman.

He lifted her face from his arm and set her spectacles straight.

'What should a fairy tale have?' he asked.

Kate sniffed. 'A happy ending,' she ventured.

He kissed her nose, which set her crying again.

She arched up on tip-toes and kissed him on the lips, which should not have been the surprise it was.

Mist gave a nod to Willoughby.

The constable raised big hands to his belt, thumb tapping the handle of his truncheon.

'Move along, now,' he told the gathering crowds. 'There's nothing to see 'ere.'

The Kelpie

by Patricia A. McKillip

Patricia A. McKillip was born in Salem, Oregon, received a master's degree in English literature from San Jose State University, California, and has been a writer ever since. Primarily known for her fantasy, she has published novels both for adults and young adults. Her YA novel The Forgotten Beasts of Eld *won the first World Fantasy Award in 1975. Among other YA fantasy novels are* The Changeling Sea *and the* Riddle-Master Trilogy, *as well as the science fictional* Moon-Flash *and* The Moon and the Face. *Lately she has been writing fantasy novels for adults, among them* The Tower at Stony Wood *and* Winter Rose, *both of which received Nebula Award nominations, and* Ombria in Shadow, *which won the World Fantasy and the Mythopoeic awards for 2003. She has also written a number of short stories, again both for adults and young adults. Her latest published novel is the fantasy* Solstice Wood. *She and her husband, the poet David Lunde, recently moved from the "wilds of upstate New York" to be closer to their families in Oregon.*

The origins of the following story trace back to early 2003. Ms. McKillip explains, "I was asked to write a novella for a collection of fantasy stories; the only stipulation was that there would be some sort of romance in the tale. I chose to write about a sort of pseudo-Victorian world in a city much like London, with characters who were very like the Pre-Raphaelite painters and their circle. I decided to return to a similar milieu for 'The Kelpie.'" And she does so with great éclat; her delicious prose reminds me of Oscar Wilde, and I don't believe the comparison hyperbolic. Her witty tale is also deeply poignant, as its heroine struggles in the coils of a dilemma that contains no whisper of the world of Faerie—but just wait!

NED met Emma Slade at her brother Adrian's new lodgings, the night Bram Wilding brought the monkey and it set fire to the veils in which Euphemia Bunce was posing for Adrian's painting. Ned had come to the party with some friends who knew Adrian, and had been invited to help him celebrate his new studio. Drink in hand, trying to remember people's names in the lively, disorganized gathering, Ned watched Bram catch the monkey with one elegant hand and, with the other, dump a vase full of water and drooping lilies—a prop for the painting—onto the flaming veils, which were now down around Miss Bunce's ankles. There had not been much under them. The model, a flame-haired stunner with a body the color of fresh cream, grabbed the tapestry covering the piano and wrapped herself in it, spitting some choice language at Bram. He threw back his head and laughed. She picked up the candle the monkey had dropped on her veils and flung it at him. Then Adrian's housekeeper, cooing soothingly, bundled a cloak over her and drew her away to dress.

Ned spotted a familiar face, with a beard like a hedgehog sprouting from its chin. The face belonged to a tall, vigorous poet by the name of Linley Coombe.

"What did she call him?" Ned asked, raising his voice above the din.

"Ah, Bonham. I didn't know you were acquainted with Adrian."

"I'm not; I followed some friends here. A clabber-brained—something?"

"A clabber-brained jabbernowl," Linley said, relishing the syllables.

"Meaning?"

"Pretty much what he is," a young woman commented tartly, "bringing a monkey into this jungle."

Hers was another recognizable face, Ned saw with pleasure; the lovely Sophie Burden, another model. He had painted her a year earlier as Cassandra prophesying some dire event in the marketplace and being ignored. With her storm-grey eyes and long black hair, she made a marvelous doom-laden figure, barefoot among the cabbages while lightning flashed above her. Now she smiled at him cheerfully. "Hello, Mr. Bonham. Have you got me hung yet?"

"I'm touching up the painting for the spring exhibit. You look wonderful, but the cabbages seem strangely lurid under the lightning."

"Lurid cabbages," Coombe murmured with delight, then eyed Sophie quizzically. "Was that a note of disparagement I heard toward the incomparable Wilding? I thought all his models fell in love with him."

She made a wry face, flashing the dimples that kept plaguing Ned at odd moments as he painted the dour Cassandra. "He's careless of people," she said briefly, and did not elaborate.

The monkey had escaped from Bram's hold. A tiny, golden, spidery-limbed creature, it was sitting on the mantelpiece now, chattering at the party. Some very fine pieces of blue and white pottery stood near it. Ned wondered how long it would be before the little monkey started heaving them across the room. Someone else had foreseen disaster, and was moving through the crush toward the monkey. Ned watched her. She was very tall; it made her movements somewhat tentative, uncertain, as though she didn't quite know what disorders her rangy limbs might cause. Like a wood-nymph at a tea party, he thought. She scooped up the monkey easily with her long fingers and turned, looking for its owner. Ned saw her face and blinked. She really was a nymph, he thought dazedly. Or one of the minor goddesses, a forgotten sister or daughter of one of those deities who attract all the attention and cast their relatives into obscurity. Obviously she had gotten lost on her way to some ethereal gathering; here she was, minding a monkey in an artist's rackety studio instead.

"Who is that?"

"Which?" Linley Coombe asked.

"Which? Which, indeed! That fair-haired young Amazon carrying the monkey."

"Oh. That's Miss Emma Slade, Adrian's sister."

They watched her ease back through the crowd with that odd, cautious manner, as though she walked on water but didn't understand by what grace.

"Coltish," Coombe commented.

"She probably grew tall very fast," Sophie said shrewdly. "Country living might do that to a girl. All that fresh air and rambles across the cow pastures. She only just came to the city recently to help Adrian get organized. I've heard Adrian's encouraging her to paint."

"I'd love to paint her," Ned said fervently.

Sophie flung him a mischievous glance. "Maybe she'd like to paint you."

Miss Emma Slade resembled her brother Adrian, Ned thought. Both had curly golden hair and wide-set eyes beneath broad, untroubled foreheads. He couldn't see the color of her eyes; they were lowered, intent on the monkey. Then, as he watched, they lifted, turned to gaze at someone. It was Bram Wilding, Ned saw, come to take his monkey from her. Their eyes were at a level. His, dark as a horse's, seemed transfixed by the airy azure of hers.

Ned, who had opened his mouth to ask Coombe for an introduction, closed it. As usual, Bram had wasted no time getting acquainted with the charming newcomer. His paintings had power and discipline; his reputation grew daily, it seemed. He would ask her to pose and who would resist? Slightly older than the roisterous young men in Adrian's circle, he had an aura of experience and was, with his black flowing locks and profile like a Greek statue that had been lightly toasted by the sun, remarkably handsome. Some said devilishly so. Ned could claim his own amount of manly attributes: muscles where they were needed, nutmeg curls, hazel eyes, an open, modest demeanor often sought after by his painter friends when they needed someone to pose for the friend of the dying knight, or the rejected suitor.

He found the poet's hand on his shoulder. "Have you met Adrian yet?"

He shook his head. "The friends I came with pointed him out, and then we all got distracted by the fire."

Coombe grinned at the memory. "Come with me. Why should Bram have all the fun?"

Adrian was found sitting on a crate of unpacked books, opening a bottle of wine. He recognized Ned's name, and, to Ned's delight, even remembered where he'd seen it.

"You painted that marvelous landscape with the white owl and the full moon shining over the snow: *Winter Solstice*," he said, rising to grasp Ned's hand. "I wished I had thought of it first."

"I would like to have done your *Last Roman Soldier Standing Watch on Hadrian's Wall*."

Adrian shook his head, drawing the cork out of the bottle. "No, you wouldn't. It rained every single day while I was painting the wall, and when it wasn't raining, the mosquitoes surrounded me in droves. Most miserable experience I've ever had. I came home with a massive cold and painted the soldier in my studio, between sneezes. Where's your glass?" Ned held it out; Adrian refilled it, then turned to Coombe. "I hope you brought some poetry to read."

"An epic," Coombe assured him.

"Oh, good. I thought we might scatter some of these crates around, since there won't be enough chairs. Ah, there you are, Buncie." He reached quickly for another glass, peering at his model, who had reappeared. She was dressed now, and, but for her reddened eyes, a bit more composed. "Are you all right? You didn't get hurt, did you?"

"I hate your Mr. Wilding," Miss Bunce said between her teeth.

"Try to forgive him; he's not entirely right in the head. I won't make you work any longer tonight." He gestured toward a long plank table painted cherry red, on which the housekeeper was piling platters and bowls of cold meats and fruits, pies and puddings and punch. "Have a sausage. Mr. Coombe is going to read to us soon." He cast an upraised brow at Sophie. "Perhaps you and Miss Bunce should corner a comfortable place to sit before all the chairs get taken. Nelly," he called to his housekeeper, a wiry young woman with a cheerful face and a good deal of energy, "I just remembered all those cushions—Where were they last seen?"

"You shoved them all in a cupboard, Mr. Slade."

"Well, we'll just shove them out again, and line them up along the walls. I'll ask my sister to play the piano while everyone's filling a plate. That'll quiet them down. Where is she?" he asked, standing on the crate to peer over the crowd. "Emma? Coombe, have you—"

"When last seen," the poet said drily, "she was speaking to Bram Wilding."

Adrian closed his mouth over a toneless "Mmm." He stepped off the crate, added briskly, without elaborating, "Well."

"I can help you with the cushions," Ned offered, "if you'll tell me where they're hiding."

"That cupboard by the door, I think. Thank you." He paused, his eyes flicking over the crowd again. "Ah. There's Emma in a corner, showing Wilding her drawings."

He vanished into the crush, and Ned went to set the cushions free.

The new lodgings were on Carmion Street, in an apartment building on a corner; it had an oblique view of the river if you stood at the right window. The building was a staid brick block with large windows tidily painted white and unadorned with fripperies. The fripperies had all followed Adrian in, it seemed. They lay scattered everywhere: brilliant carpets and shawls he'd picked up on the streets, ancient tiles, pieces of costume to use as props for his paintings, plates and cups, bulky chairs, a horsehair sofa, massive chests and sideboards, even the odd piece of armor and broken statuary. It looked, Ned thought, like the sorting room in a museum basement. Paintings leaned against the walls. Ned recognized a few of them from exhibits, or visits to other friends' studios. The chaos, he noted as he opened the cupboard, extended into the next room as well, and was even strewn all over the massive, canopied bed.

He found a stack of round, oversized cushions covered with faded crewelwork. Wedged into a square cupboard, they resisted Ned's efforts until one popped out near the middle of the stack, exuding a puff of antique dust. What exactly they had been intended for, Ned could not imagine. He began strewing them hither and yon, which became easier as the party gathered around the table, leaving him some bare floor. People, plates and cups in hand, wandered back and sat upon them as soon as he dropped them. Adrian appeared beside him suddenly while he wrestled with another.

"Here we are," he said cheerfully, taking the cushion out of Ned's arms after he staggered back from the tug-of-war with the cupboard.

"It's like dancing with a drunken costermonger," Ned muttered. "What were these in their previous lives?" He hauled out another cushion and turned to find himself face to face with the nymph.

He blinked at her, startled, wondering how Adrian had turned into his sister. Then Adrian rejoined them, dusting his hands.

"You must meet my sister," he declared. "Emma, this is Edward Bonham, who painted that wonderfully chilly painting with the owl in it."

"Oh yes." She spoke, Ned thought dazedly, as she walked: carefully and delicately, as though she had just turned from a graceful poplar into a woman and was uncertain about the effects she might have on people. "I loved that painting, Mr. Bonham." There was an unnymph-like smile in her eyes, perhaps left by the wake of his costermonger comment.

"You should show him your drawings," Adrian suggested, hauling the last cushion out and giving it a hearty shove with one boot to an empty spot along the wall.

"I've just been showing them to Mr. Wilding," she told them. "He said that technically I show promise, but that thus far passion seems to have eluded me. He offered to give me a lesson or two." Adrian's mouth opened abruptly; she continued with unruffled composure, "I told him that I understood what he meant, but that true passion in painting could only be expressed by true mastery of technique; without it passion looked sentimental, trite, and in the end ridiculous."

Adrian grinned. "Good for you. What did he say?"

"That most women painters should confine themselves to watercolors, since they have not the breadth of soul to express the fullness and complexity of oils, though he had seen one or two come close enough to counterfeit it."

Adrian rolled his eyes. "What did you say to that?"

"That I would do my best to prove him wrong," she answered simply. "And then the monkey had an accident on his hair and he went off to wash."

Ned loosed an inelegant guffaw. A corner of Emma's long mouth crooked up. "What are your thoughts on the breadth of a woman's soul, Mr. Bonham?"

"I think," he said fervently, "I could travel a lifetime in one and never see the half of it."

She regarded him silently for a heartbeat, out of eyes the color of a fine summer day, and in that moment he caught his first astonished glimpse of the undiscovered country that was theirs.

Adrian cleared his throat. His sister looked suddenly dazed, herself, as though she had forgotten where she was.

"Come and eat," Adrian said, smiling. "Then you can show Bonham your drawings."

*

EMMA played the piano after supper while the party, clustered into little groups on cushions and crates, argued intensely about the nature of Art, or languished, satiated, over their coffee and listened to Emma. She scarcely heard what her fingers were doing. She was still lost in that little moment when she had looked into Mr. Bonham's hazelnut eyes and seen her future. They say it happens that way sometimes, she thought, amazed. I just never thought it would happen now. I never thought that it would actually happen, only that it was always something to be expected, to hope for, never that it would suddenly happen and I would be wondering: What happens next?

Then Mr. Bonham drifted over and smiled at her. She smiled back. That was what happened next. He lingered to listen; she played, simply content with his nearness. There was nothing extraordinary about his looks; there were half-a-dozen young men in the room, including her brother and the irritating Mr. Wilding, she would have chosen over Ned to pose for the hero of her painting. True eye-stoppers, they were. But hers had stopped at a boyish face with a determined jawline and a sweet, diffident expression, behind which a busy, talented brain conceived pictures like the simple mystery of that winter night, and crafted them with a great deal of ability. She had come to the city to learn to paint; perhaps she could learn something from him.

Perhaps that was next.

She was trying to conceive a painting around him, idly wondering which role might suit him best, when Adrian came up to her. She softened her playing, lifted her brows at him questioningly.

"Emma, this is Marianne Cameron. She wants to ask you to pose for her, but she is too shy."

The young woman in question snorted at the idea, making Adrian laugh. She was short and stocky, with frizzy, sandy hair and truly lovely violet eyes. Her pale lavender dress, sensibly and elegantly plain, suited those eyes.

"You," she said to Emma, "are the most beautiful thing in this room, with the possible exception of Bram Wilding, who can't be bothered to pose for anyone. Several of us rent a room on Tidewater Street; we'd love you to come and pose for us. Adrian says you paint, too. If you like, we can make a space for you to work. It's a bit quieter than this place; we don't have monkeys and poets swinging from the rafters there."

"Speaking of which," Adrian murmured, "I wonder where that monkey has gotten to?"

"Us?" Emma asked.

"We women," Marianne said briskly. "We have made our own band of painters, and we refuse to be convinced of our inferiority. We learn from one another. Would you like to come and see?"

"Oh, yes," Emma said instantly. "I would very much." She remembered Adrian then; her eyes slid to him. "That is—I came to help Adrian get settled—"

"Go ahead," Adrian urged. "We both must work; we can deal with this clutter in the evenings."

"Good!" Marianne said with satisfaction. "I'll come for you tomorrow at noon then. We work all day, but the afternoon light is best."

"Miss Cameron paints quite well," Adrian said, propping himself against the piano as Marianne moved away. "She has even had one or two paintings exhibited: *Love Lies Bleeding* and *Undine*—that one has marvelous watery lights in it."

"It's strange," Emma sighed. "I always feel such a great country gawk, and here I am to be painted."

"You're as far from a gawk as anyone can get without turning into something completely mythical."

She smiled affectionately at her brother. "You didn't say such things when we were younger."

"I don't recall that I was ever less than perfectly well behaved."

"You called me a she-giant once and warned that I would never stop growing; I'd be tall as a barn by the time I was twenty, and there would be nobody big enough to marry me."

"I'm sure I never said any such thing, and anyway you were probably taller than me, then, which as your older brother I found completely unacceptable. Now I'm taller, so I can be magnanimous." He straightened, glancing at the party; the noise-level had ratcheted upward considerably when Emma stopped playing. "We'd better have Coombe read now that Nelly has finished clattering plates. I do wonder where that monkey is; I hope it isn't burning up the beds."

"I'll go and look," Emma said, and slipped through the crowd as Adrian began describing the unutterable delight yet to come: an epic of epic proportions by the brilliant Linley Coombe on the subject of—what was the subject again? Emma heard them all laugh at something the poet said as she opened the kitchen door.

The kitchen, along with the small dark rooms attached to it, was the domain of Nelly and the cook, Mrs. Dyce. Nelly, who had a thoroughly practical and unflappable nature, was Adrian's treasure; she could conjure beds out of books and floorboards for any number of unexpected guests, he said, and she did the work of five servants without turning a hair. Now the housekeeper was being scullery-maid, helping Mrs. Dyce with the mountain of dirty dishes. Earlier that day, Emma had helped her unpack the crates, dust furniture for the party, find silverware and candlesticks and lamps among the boxes, and summon food and wine for an unknown number of guests, all before she vanished into the kitchen to help Mrs. Dyce cook the elaborate supper.

Mrs. Dyce, a gaunt, mournful woman who could turn out a fragrant shepherd's pie with one hand while she was wiping away a tear for her dead husband with the other, only sighed and shook her head at the notion of monkeys in the kitchen.

Nelly wiped her hands on her apron, said calmly. "I'll have a look, Miss."

She took a lamp into the inner sanctums of bedchamber and pantry, while Emma checked the high shelves and cupboards.

"I don't see it, Miss Emma," Nelly said, reappearing. "Maybe Mr. Wilding shut it up in a cupboard after it set Miss Bunce on fire."

"I doubt that Mr. Wilding would think of doing anything so sensible."

"You may be right, Miss. But one can hope."

"One can, indeed, hope. I'll ask him."

But, reluctant to put herself again under that powerful, discomfiting gaze, she looked first into Adrian's bedroom, expecting she might find the little monkey curled up and napping among the sheets. Her lamplight, sliding over the room, revealed only its familiar chaos. Finally she glanced into the room, hardly bigger than the pantry, where she slept.

No monkey.

She turned back into the hallway, perplexed, and jumped. Bram Wilding stood in her lamplight with the golden monkey on his shoulder reaching for the lamp.

She moved it hastily. "Mr. Wilding. You startled me."

"You were looking for me."

"I was looking for your monkey."

"Ah. Well, I've come in search of you. Please forgive my earlier rudeness, Miss Slade; the last thing I would want is to discourage you or anyone from painting. The truth is that I am so distracted by you that any amount of idiocy can come out of my mouth without me hearing a word of it. From the moment I saw you, I knew I must paint you. I see you as the great, doomed Celtic Queen Boudicca, in silk and fur and armor, with her long fair hair flying free as she faces her conquerors, knowing that she will lose the final battle but ready to fight until she can no more for her lost realm. Will you pose for me?"

"I'm sorry, Mr. Wilding," she said with relief. "I've already promised Marianne Cameron that I would pose for her—"

"Put her off."

"Tomorrow."

He was silent. The monkey chattered at her, wanting her flame, its great eyes filled with it. Bram's dark eyes seemed impenetrable; light could not reach past them.

"I'll talk to her," he said finally.

"Mr. Wilding, I wish you wouldn't. She has offered me a place to paint. I want to go there."

He only smiled cheerfully. "I'm sure you will be welcome in any case, Miss Slade."

There was a step behind Bram. She lifted the lamp higher and caught Ned Bonham's face in her light. She gazed at him a moment, smiling upon him and wondering how his face, which she had never seen before that night, could give her so much pleasure.

"Miss Slade," he said, smiling back.

"Mr. Bonham."

"I see you found the monkey."

Bram Wilding, who must have felt invisible, moved abruptly. His face, which until then seemed genial and imperturbable, had grown mask-like; Emma could not guess at his thoughts.

"You might say it found me."

"We are all found," Bram said lightly, moving ahead of them into shadow. "I suppose we must go and hear Coombe read. What is the subject this time?"

"A mortal straying into the realm of Faery and how he gets himself out again—something like that."

"I didn't think you could," Emma said. "Aren't you lost forever if you wander out of the world?"

"It depends, I think, on how you actually got there. If you're taken by a water sprite, an undine, or by La Belle Dame Sans Merci, you're sunk. But others have found a way to freedom—Thomas the Rhymer, for instance, and Tam Lin."

They were walking more and more slowly, Emma realized. Bram Wilding had already vanished back into the party. Light and Linley Coombe's sonorous voice spilled through the studio doors Wilding had left open.

> Through mists and reeds he ran,
> Through water grey as cloud
> And air that grasped him with unseen hands,
> And clung closer than a shroud.

They stopped before they reached the doors. Their eyes met above the lamp in Emma's hand. She searched, curious, hoping to find the reflection of her strange feelings in his eyes.

He said softly, huskily, "Miss Slade, I don't mean to offend, but I've never—I've never felt this way before about anyone. As though all my life I have been on my way to meet you."

A smile seemed to shine through her as though she had swallowed the lamplight. "Oh, yes," she whispered. "Yes. I feel it, too."

"Do you?" he whispered back with an amazed laugh. "Isn't it strange? We hardly know each other."

"I suppose that's what comes next."

"What?"

"Getting to know one another," she answered. "For example, you should know that my second name is Sophronia."

"Really? Emma Sophronia?"

"After my mother's great aunt."

"Well," he said, drawing breath. "It won't be easy, but I think I can bear it. Mine's Eustace."

"Edward Eustace Bonham. How terribly respectable."

"I try to live above it."

> Until at last he saw the day
> Green and gold around him spread,
> The timeless, changeless land of Fay,
> And he was seized with mortal dread.
> "Would I were with the dead instead,"
> he cried, then saw the Fairy Queen.

"Any other dreadful secrets?" he asked.

"I once threw an aspidistra at Adrian."

"Did you hit him?"

"Yes."

"Good shot. I'm sure he deserved it."

"And you?"

"I suppose you should know," he said reluctantly, "that I can never be that romantic figure, the struggling artist in the garret, much as I wish I could deceive you. I was an only child, and my father died several years ago, leaving me more money than is good for anyone, a house in the city, and another on a lake in the north country."

"Oh," she said, amazed. "Mr. Bonham, how have you managed to stay unattached?"

"How have you?" he countered, "looking the way you do, like a young goddess who got stranded among mortals?"

She felt her cheeks warm. "Really? I always see myself as

such a hobbledehoy of a girl. Fashionable young women are supposed to look delicate and spiritual. That's hard to do when you're nearly as tall as most men. In the country, I have a reputation for being eccentric. I wander around in a pair of big rubber boots and a huge hat, carrying my easel and paints. I bribed the milkmaid to pose for me dressed in ribbons and lace among the sheep, and the old gardener to wear a cloak and a tunic and pose as a druid on top of a ruined tower. He never heard the end of that."

> And oh, she was as fair as fair
> Can be, with hair spun out of gold
> And emerald eyes without a cloud or care,
> Just a smile to make the mortal bold
> And walk into her lair. She said,
> "Come into my bower and tarry with me . . ."

"Miss Slade."

"Yes, Mr. Bonham?"

"Should I ask you to marry me now, or would you like me to wait a bit?"

She felt no great surprise, only a deepening of the strange peace she felt upon first looking into his eyes. "I suppose," she said reluctantly, "you should wait, otherwise people will think we are completely frivolous. Perhaps you should invite me for a walk in the park instead. Tomorrow afternoon when I finish posing for Miss Cameron. There should be time before dark."

"Do you think I am frivolous?"

"No," she said quickly, surprised. "How can you ask that? You must know that my heart has already answered you."

He started to speak, did not, only held her eyes and she felt the warmth of the smile on his lips like a phantom kiss.

She scarcely slept after the party had broken up in the

early hours of the morning, and the house finally quieted. It was difficult, she discovered, to smile and sleep at the same time. When she heard the housekeeper stirring, she rose and dressed, went into the kitchen to ask for a cup of tea.

"You're up early, Miss," Nelly said.

"I thought I would do some unpacking, rid our lives of a few more crates."

"It will be nice not to have to walk around them. I'll give you a hand as soon as I tidy up from the party."

Mrs. Dyce produced Scotch eggs and cold ham and toast; after breakfast they worked so hard that when Marianne Cameron rang the bell at noon, most of the books had been unpacked and shelved, and Adrian's collection of oddities and props had found places to reside that were not the floor or his bed. He had come out of his room at midmorning, helped them pile empty crates and hang paintings. By the time Miss Bunce came to pose and he began to paint, there was an empty island of polished floorboards around his easel.

"I'll get the door," Emma told Nelly, whose arms were full of costumes out of a crate that needed to be folded and put away. "It'll be Miss Cameron, come for me."

But, opening the door, she found Bram Wilding instead.

Surprised, she glanced behind him down the hall, hearing bells striking noon all through the city.

"Good day, Miss Slade," he said. "I have good news. I was able to persuade Miss Cameron to let me paint you first."

She stared at him, still bewildered by the unwelcome sight of his face instead of the one she expected.

"How?" she asked incredulously.

"I offered to speak to a gallery owner who exhibits my work about doing an exhibit of work by the women's studio. Miss Cameron found my suggestion irresistible."

Emma found his suggestion awoke a childish impulse in her to stamp her foot at him. "I wished," she said coldly, "to pose for her."

"And I wish you to pose for me."

"Do you always get your wishes, Mr. Wilding?"

"In this case, I believe I do. I don't see why I should bother to persuade the gallery owner to hang an exhibit of little-known, though possibly talented, women painters if you do not pose for me."

She opened her mouth, stood wordless a moment, too astonished to speak. Then her eyes narrowed. "Mr. Wilding," she said softly, "I believe this is what they call blackmail."

"Do they?" he said indifferently. "Well, no matter, as long as I can have my Boudicca. I'll just step in and let Adrian know where you're going. Join me when you're ready."

*

NED painted feverishly all day in his own comfortable studio on the top floor of his house. He had enlarged and added windows on all sides of the studio; he could see the river to the east, city to the north and south, and the park to the west, where, when the sun came to roost like a great genial bird on the top branches of the trees, he intended to be strolling with Miss Emma Sophronia Slade. Or, as would be as soon as respectably possible, Mrs. Emma Bonham.

He whistled while he tinkered with a painting that he never seemed to get right. He had been working on it for several years, shutting it away in exasperation when he got tired of reaching his limitations. The subject was along the lines of Linley Coombe's poem: a man lost in a wood and glimpsing in a fall of sunlight the Fairy Queen and her court riding toward him. The figures emerging through the light could barely be seen; some of them he conceived as only half human, figures of twig and bark on horseback, with faces of animals, perhaps, or exotic birds. The look on the man's face, of astonishment tinged with dawning horror as he realized he had walked out of the world, never seemed convincing. Most of the time he looked simply pained, as though berries he had eaten earlier were beginning to make themselves known. The fairy figures were no less difficult; color had to be suggested rather than shown, and the strange faces, part human, part fox or bluebird, were extraordinarily elusive.

A good thing, he reminded himself, I'm not doing this for a living.

At last the sun sank within an inch of the trees in the park. Shafts of lovely, dusty-gold fairy light fell between the branches, gilded the grass below. It was one of those spring days that revealed how much more ease and warmth and loveliness there was to come. A perfect mellow dusk for a first walk into the future. He cleaned and put things away quickly, slipped on his coat and went around the block to Adrian's apartment.

Adrian, who was in the midst of paying Euphemia Bunce, received Ned with pleasure and without surprise.

"Come at the same time tomorrow, Buncie," he requested. "Maybe I can finish those veils and we can start on the platter you're holding. Ned, I don't suppose you would let me borrow your head. You've got exactly that combination of innocence and strength in your face that I need."

"Doesn't sound like it helped me much if my head winds up on a platter."

"You can bask in the company of Miss Bunce and me for a couple of weeks. And Mrs. Dyce's cooking."

"Might Miss Slade be basking with us?" He glanced around. "Has she returned from the women's studio? We had plans to walk."

"Oh." Adrian's amiable smile diminished slightly. "I'm afraid she's been snared by Wilding."

"What?"

"He apparently talked Miss Cameron into letting my sister pose for him first. That's what he told me, at any rate. I doubt that's the full story. But we'll have to wait for Emma to tell us the rest. She should be here soon." He folded Miss Bunce into her shawl. "Tomorrow morning, then, Buncie."

"That Mr. Wilding is a mischief-maker," she said tersely. "I'd keep your eye on him."

"I will do just that with both eyes," Adrian promised, opening the door for her.

"Thank you, Mr. Slade. Goodnight, Mr.—Bonham, was it?" She flashed him a smile. "I hope your head will join us."

"So that's what she was doing in those veils," Ned murmured. "Salome dancing about with the severed head. I wondered. Do you suppose the public will appreciate it?"

"They will appreciate Miss Bunce. And your guileless and saintly head, cut so tragically short from its body, will affect them deeply, I'm sure. There won't be a dry eye at the exhibit." He was cleaning his brushes with a great deal of energy, glancing down at the street now and then.

Ned paced a step or two, then stopped and said simply, "Where is Wilding's studio? I'll go and meet her there."

"Yes," Adrian said emphatically. "Good idea. It's straight down Summer Street beside the river, a yellowish villa-ish sort of thing with red tiles on the roof. You can't miss it."

Even if he had missed the eye-catching villa at the corner of Summer Street and River Road, the monkey chattering at him on the wall beside the gate would have alerted him to Wilding's domain. The monkey wore a thin gold chain around its neck, long enough for it to reach the ground, but too short for it to do more than climb back up. Ned opened the gate cautiously, wondering what other wildlife roamed Wilding's garden.

The only wildlife he found on the other side of the wall was Emma and Bram Wilding, walking together toward the gate.

"Ah, Bonham," Wilding said, with a faint smile in his eyes. "How good of you to come and visit me. Miss Slade is just leaving."

Ned looked at her. She had colored at the sight of him, but other than a trifle embarrassed, she seemed quite pleased to see him.

"I'm sorry I can't stay," he told Wilding with satisfaction. "I have an appointment to escort Miss Slade through the park."

"So she told me when I tried to persuade her to accept some supper. Another time, perhaps, Miss Slade. I will see you tomorrow at noon?"

"Unless my brother needs—"

"Now, Miss Slade," Wilding interrupted gently. "We discussed this. I need my Boudicca. I will be more grateful than you can imagine for your time."

"I would be happy to join you, Miss Slade," Ned offered. "I would like to see Mr. Wilding's work."

"Oh, yes—"

"Alas, I find it difficult to work when I'm watched. You understand, Mr. Bonham."

"Perfectly," Ned assured him, watching the monkey rise on the wall behind Wilding and fling what looked like a chestnut from last autumn's crop at Wilding's head. It bounced off its target with a satisfying thump.

"Mr. Wilding," Emma said, her hands flying to her mouth. Her voice wobbled. "Are you hurt?"

Wilding turned briefly to stare at the monkey as he rubbed his head. "Perfectly fine, I assure you." He added, his eyes on Ned, "I should tell you that there are occasionally creatures in the garden who might be dangerous if surprised. I need to know exactly when my guests are coming or leaving so that I can have them put away. You were fortunate that I'd already done so before you came in. Didn't Slade tell you?"

"He did not," Ned answered, surprised. "Perhaps he thought I would find Miss Slade on the street."

He offered his arm to Emma, whose face had lost expression.

"Miss Slade," Wilding said with his charming smile.

"Goodnight, Mr. Wilding," she said perfunctorily, and went through the gate without a backward glance. "I don't believe in his dangerous animals," she whispered when the gate closed behind them. "I think he just said that to keep you away."

"Why—"

"Mr. Bonham, do you know where Marianne Cameron's studio is?"

"Yes, I do."

"Will you please take me there now?"

"Not the park?" he said wistfully.

"I'm sorry." Her fingers tightened a little on his arm; she added ruefully, "I know none of this makes much sense. But when I speak to Miss Cameron, you'll understand."

The women's studio, which Ned had visited several times, was the second floor of an old warehouse along River Road. Ned smelled paints and turpentine, mold and the lingering odors of mud flats as they climbed the creaky flight of stairs. The stairs ended at a long sweep of floorboard beneath unpainted rafters. Light came from tall windows overlooking the river, inset where doors had once opened in midair for goods to be grappled and winched up for storage off boats in the full tide below. Older windows on the other side gathered the morning light. The vast room was filled with easels, canvases, paints and paper, stools with stained smocks hanging over them. The painters had vanished into the fading light; only Marianne was there, lighting lamps to continue her work.

She looked stricken when she saw Emma, and came to her quickly. "Oh, Miss Slade, I do apologize. It was an offer I couldn't refuse. I'm so glad you came here. Hello, Mr. Bonham. Have a stool."

"Hello, Miss Cameron." He sat, looking at them puzzledly. "I wish someone would explain what I've missed."

"Mr. Wilding—" Emma began.

"I invited Miss Slade to pose for us—"

"And then Mr. Wilding begged me to pose for him, and I refused because I had promised Miss Cameron, and anyway I wanted to come here and paint—He knew that, and yet he found a way to sabotage our plans."

Miss Cameron's broad face flushed. "He offered us an exhibit, Mr. Bonham. A promise to talk to the owner of a new gallery about a women's show. If we let him have Miss Slade first."

"Will he keep his promise?" Emma asked grimly.

"As long as he gets what he wants, he will. I felt dreadful giving you up like that, but—it was too much to refuse. I've been trying for years to get someone to agree to exhibit us. And he paints wonderfully well; you'll be pleased with what he makes of you."

Emma sighed. "But I have to endure his company for hours. I thoroughly dislike him. I didn't know why at first, but now I do."

"Has he been rude to you?" Ned asked abruptly. "If he has, he'll be wearing his painting around his neck."

"No. He hasn't. I just feel a bit trapped."

"And so you have been, and I've been complicit in your entrapment," Miss Cameron said ruefully. "How can I make it up to you? Can you find time to come and paint with us? I won't charge you for studio space; you can come and go as you please, and see what the rest of us are doing."

"Yes," Emma said emphatically. "That's why I came to talk to you. I would love a corner here to work in. I feel underfoot at my brother's, and his friends, though terribly interesting, are so terribly distracting. I could paint here in the mornings, then pose for Mr. Wilding in the afternoons . . ." Her voice trailed away; Ned found her blue eyes on his face as though she had sensed his sudden pang of distress. She was silent a moment, conjecturing; then she added softly, "And in the evenings, Mr. Bonham, you and I can draw one another."

He said, his odd heartache gone, "I can think of nothing I would like better. Well, actually I can, but that will wait until the fullness of time."

Miss Cameron eyed them speculatively. "I see you have outplayed us all, Mr. Bonham," she murmured. "Even the paragon, Mr. Wilding."

"I was the more fortunate," he admitted. "Speaking of posing, your brother wants my head for Salome's platter. Shall I give it to him?"

"What a wonderful idea," Emma said, laughing. "Yes, I think you should indulge my brother. You can get to know him better and meet all of his disreputable friends."

"And what is Mr. Wilding making out of you?" Marianne asked her curiously.

"I am Queen Boudicca, about to plunge into my last battle."

"I wouldn't have pictured you as a warrior queen," Marianne said thoughtfully. "May Queen, maybe, or Queen of the Fairies, something with a lot of flowers."

"Mr. Wilding prefers to set me off with a musty bearskin rug over my shoulders. He claims he shot it in some wilderness or another. Oh, and he says he must put a horse in the painting as well, as soon as he finds the right one."

She was looking at Ned speculatively as she spoke. So, he realized uneasily, was Miss Cameron.

"Perhaps," Marianne mused slowly, "when your brother is finished with him."

"Yes. As what, do you think?"

"Something with dignity," Ned pleaded, envisioning himself barelegged on a pedestal with a bow in his hand, dressed fetchingly as Cupid, the object of intense and critical female scrutiny.

"The young knight errant, going forth into the world to

rescue maidens and do battle with wicked knights who look like Wilding?"

"Can't I be evil? Just once?"

"Can't you settle for being triumphant?" Emma asked with such affection and trust in her eyes that he could only be grateful for his fate.

He bowed his head and acquiesced.

"For you."

*

EMMA found herself whirling through her days like a leaf in a sluice. In the mornings, she went to Marianne's studio, where she had set up her easel. She drew whatever caught her eye in the endless supply of still life on the studio's shelves, which held everything from old boots to exotic draperies and vases in which dried grasses, seed pods, and flowers purloined from the park could be arranged. Occasionally, as she worked, someone would come to sketch her. She scarcely noticed. Sometimes she herself drifted through the room, watching the other women work in ink and watercolor, pencil and oil. She confined herself to sketching for a while, to improve her technique. Miss Cameron moved among them now and then, gently suggesting, never criticizing. She was in the midst of an oil, mostly whites and greys and browns, of the river beyond the window, beneath lowering sky, and the boats and ships that moved ceaselessly along it, the buildings on the far shore, and the stone bridge in the distance, tiny figures crossing it the only flecks of brightness in the painting.

While Emma drew, she let her thoughts wander about, searching for a compelling subject to paint. Something simple, she wanted, like Ned's solstice or Marianne's river. But with a human face in it, drawing the viewer's eye and kindling emotions. Whether the face was male or female, mortal or mythical, and what emotions it should evoke, Emma could not decide. She was content for the moment just to be in the company of painters, watching and learning from them, her mind an open door to inspiration, not knowing what face it would wear when it finally came knocking.

Somewhere around midday, the contentment would fray. Mr. Wilding would enter her thoughts and refuse to go away. Finally time would force her to put away pencil and paper, take off her smock, and say goodbye to Miss Cameron, who always looked a little guilty when she left.

"Don't fret," Emma told her. "When Mr. Wilding procures the exhibit for us, I'll be in it, too. That will make up for everything."

She would return to her brother's for one of Mrs. Dyce's excellent and very informal lunches: Adrian fed anyone who happened to be there. Invariably, he and Ned would make her laugh. And then Ned would walk with her through the streets to Wilding's villa.

Sometimes Mr. Wilding met her at the gate; more often it was a silent, wraithlike servant whose eyes would dart nervously about the garden as he escorted her to the house. He carried a roughhewn walking stick carved out of a tree limb; the polished burl at the top looked formidable.

Curious, she commented on it once; he answered briefly, "In case they left one out of their cages, Miss."

"One what?" she said incredulously.

He rasped his prickly white chin. "Can't rightly say, can I, Miss? Whatever they are, he gets them from far away."

"Are they like the monkey? Or more like big cats?"

"Big," he conceded. "That they are. But I wouldn't say either monkey or cat. More like—like—Well, I couldn't say that either, Miss, since I've never seen anything like them in my life. Not even at the zoological gardens, where I have been a time or two in my youth."

She was silent, willing to doubt they were real, but disturbed by the thought that Wilding was terrifying his servants with mythological monsters.

Mr. Wilding only laughed when she expressed her doubts. "Do you think I've conjured up a garden full of harpies and manticores? Of course they're real. Most are harmless, though they might not look it. Most would run from old Fender."

"Most?"

"I'm very careful," he assured her. "I value my friends too much to want them eaten by beasts."

Friends by the dozens might come to visit, but never, it seemed, while he was working. At mid-afternoon the villa was as still as though it stood in one of the countries whose houses it emulated; the ones that drowsed in heat and light and came alive at night. Mr. Wilding himself painted silently much of the time. From what Emma saw of the painting, it could become a masterwork. Each hair on the bearskin hanging across her shoulders was meticulously recorded by a brush as fine as an eyelash; as a whole the painted pelt, thick and glossy, made her want to run her hand over it, feel its softness.

Her own face emerging out of the canvas slowly, like a figure from a mist, astonished her. It was fierce and lovely, nothing tentative about it that she could recognize.

"That doesn't look like me at all," she protested.

He smiled tightly. "Oh, yes, it does. When you look at me."

"Really?"

"You dislike me, Miss Slade. Your face is quite expressive. Luckily, Boudicca didn't like her enemies, either; that makes you perfect."

Her eyes narrowed. "Did you do that deliberately, Mr. Wilding? Make me dislike you for this?"

"No," he said, surprised. "Turn your head again; you're out of position. I want very much for you to like me. A little more. Lift your chin. Stare me down. Because I think you are the most beautiful woman I have ever seen in my life, and one of the most intelligent and interesting. I hoped— Chin up, Miss Slade; I have come to steal your realm and slay your people. I hoped you would confess to some truer feeling about me."

"Truer," she said through rigid jaws.

"You are afraid of me because you are drawn to me. That makes you dislike me. So you turn to the much safer and predictable Mr. Bonham."

Her jaw dropped; so did her spear-arm. "Mr. Wilding—"

"You asked, Miss Slade," he said evenly. "Chin up, spear up. Remember the exhibit."

"You take advantage, Mr. Wilding!"

"No, no. You, after all, have the spear; you can throw it at me any time. I tell you what is in my heart. Can you blame me for that?"

He left her wordless. She could only stare at him as he requested, at once furious and vulnerable, willing to skewer him yet unable to move, while he touched her constantly with his eyes, and his brush stroked every hair on her head and every contour of her body.

Toward the end of the session, when she was drained, angry, and thoroughly confused, he would tell her some improbable yet fascinating story about how he had acquired one or another of his animals. One had been found floating in the middle of the sea, surrounded by the flotsam of a sunken ship, alone in a rowboat but for a litter of fishbones and a bloody pair of boots. Explorers had come across another on a tropical island; it had chased them up a tree, then settled into a vigil among the roots, waiting for them to fall one by one like coconuts. Such things colored her weary thoughts, painted bright images; imagining them, she forgot that she had been angry.

So when Ned, waiting at the gate, saw them across the garden, she and Mr. Wilding would seem to be amiably chatting like friends and her smile might seem for him rather than in expectation of Mr. Bonham's face. Even this,

Wilding used as a weapon, she knew. The truth lay in his painting: the warrior queen fighting her strong-willed adversary over a realm to which he had no claim.

The evenings belonged to Ned.

Tired and content in his company, she had little to say on their walk to Adrian's apartment. She didn't encourage questions; she might inadvertently tell him something that would make her posing for Mr. Wilding impossible, and ruin all expectations of the prized exhibit. I must go through this, she told herself adamantly. I will have my reward.

So she kept her comments light, asked about Ned's painting day, about his posing with Miss Bunce, and which of her brother's friends he had met that day.

"Valentine DeMorgan," he answered with awe one evening. "He wears a cloak lined with purple satin and yellow gloves. He keeps in one pocket a slim volume of his poems, all of which are so dreadfully sweet you could stir them into your tea." Or: "Eugene Frith, the reformed pickpocket turned bookseller. He taught himself to read, Adrian said. And now he is an expert on rare editions. Your brother must know half the city."

But she did not fool his painter's eye, which caught the troubled expressions on her face at odd moments, and the faint lines and shadows left by her never-ending days.

"You're tired," he told her one evening after a few weeks of the inflexible routine.

"A little," she confessed.

"Has Wilding been—"

"No," she said quickly. "He wants his painting too much to drive me away."

"Or do you want that exhibit too much?" he guessed shrewdly.

"He's working very fast," she temporized. "And his painting will be wonderful. I have been working hard, but that part of my day will come to an end." She smiled at him brightly. "Then I can pose for you, if you like."

He didn't answer her tactless suggestion, just gazed at her, frowning a little. They were sitting in a comfortable corner of Adrian's studio; Ned was sketching her as she leaned back in her chair, too weary herself to draw. Beyond their little lamp-lit world, Adrian and Linley Coombe, Miss Bunce and Marwood Stokes, another painter who had brought a couple of friends with him, sat around the table cracking nuts and drinking and telling stories. Their laughter rolled across the room, but somehow didn't disturb what lay within the intimate circle of light.

"I know," Ned said abruptly. "I'll take you up north for a rest. To my house on the lake. It's lovely there, this time of year."

She stared at him. "But we can't just go away together, as if we were—as if we were—"

"We are," he said simply, "in our hearts. Anyway, I'm not suggesting that. We'll take your brother with us. Slade!" he called abruptly, turning toward the merry group. "Let's take our paints north to my lake house for a week or two. Your sister needs a rest. The scenery is amazing, and we can live on fat salmon and grouse. The house is big enough for everyone."

Adrian, who had reached an affectionate understanding with his wine, raised his glass promptly. "Brilliant. Coombe can come and catch fish for us. And Stokes here can shoot. But—"

"No," Emma said firmly, raising her voice. "No, no, no. I can't go now."

"But we won't invite Wilding," Adrian finished, then peered at her. "No?"

"I can't go now. Please." She straightened, nearly took Ned's hand, stopped herself. "I would love to go," she told him softly. "But I'd rather do it when I can truly relax and not have any worries. Anything complicated," she amended quickly, "like the exhibit or Mr. Wilding's painting to come back to."

"All right," Ned agreed reluctantly. Their hands and fingers and knees were very close as they leaned in their chairs towards one another. The company around the table watched them owlishly. "But promise to tell me the moment you change your mind."

"I will."

At the oddly silent table, someone hiccuped. "Slade," Stokes said excitedly. "What is this we're seeing? Can it be—"

"Mr. Stokes, I forbid you to mention my sister's name in the company of other gentlemen."

"Her name will not leave my lips, on my solemn oath," Stokes said earnestly, hiccuping again. "But are we to understand that this—this goddess and this young painter of the most exciting potential—"

"No," Adrian said firmly. "We are to understand nothing of the sort until we are given permission to understand it. Fill your glass and be quiet. Coombe is going to recite all nine hundred lines of his latest masterpiece."

*

"You look tired," Marianne Cameron said brusquely a few days later, as Emma arranged two pears from Mrs. Dyce's pantry and a bunch of wildflowers from the park on a platter. "You're too pale, and there are smudges under your eyes. You'll make yourself ill. Go home and put your feet up. Or go and buy yourself a bonnet. Get some sunlight."

Emma shook her head. "Don't worry," she said absently, trying the pears in different positions. "I think this needs something else . . . What do you think?"

"You've got ovals and circles and horizontal lines," Marianne said, gazing at it, and forgot her advice. "You need a vertical. How about a candlestick? Or your brushes in a cup?"

"My brushes. The very thing. A bouquet of brushes in a jar."

She drew contentedly until noonday sun spangled the river with light, and Mr. Wilding's face insinuated itself into her thoughts.

"You've got interesting shadows under your eyes," Mr. Wilding commented that afternoon as, in bearskin and tunic, she took her position. "They make you look even more heroic and doomed. Perhaps I'll use them . . . Has your brother been keeping you awake with his late hours?"

"I haven't been sleeping well. But Adrian is never less than thoughtful."

"You mustn't get ill. Perhaps you should stop going to Miss Cameron's studio until I finish my painting."

"I will be fine," Emma said stolidly, shifting her grip on the spear until it balanced properly. "I have no intention of giving up my studio time."

He reached out, gently shifted hair away from her eyes. "Your hair has such lovely shades of saffron in it. Perhaps I'll take forever with this painting," he added. "What I weave by day I will unravel by night, like Penelope . . . Miss Slade, you look positively horrified. Where has your fighting spirit gone?"

"I hope you are joking, Mr. Wilding."

"Perhaps," he said lightly. "Perhaps not. I don't intend to stop seeing you." Her hand tightened on the spear. "That's better. The hawk's glare rather than the hare's stare of terror."

Emma didn't answer. He painted a while, mercifully silent. Her thoughts strayed to Mr. Bonham. Edward, she thought fondly, remembering his face in the lamplight as he sketched her. Edward Eustace. My Ned.

"Perhaps your sleep is troubled by foreboding," Wilding commented after a while. "No, don't answer. Don't move an eyelash. Foreboding of the future. A house full of caterwauling children, a husband who, no matter how good his intentions, cannot, for the sake of his own art, put your work before his needs. You are equals now. But marriage has a way of altering the scales. He will tend to his art. You will tend to everything else." His eyes flicked to her frozen face. "You think I am cruel. I am only thinking of you."

"I can't imagine why," she said sharply. "You have told me that no matter what I do, my art will be inferior."

"I did not say that," he answered calmly. "I said that most female painters lack depth. Surely not all. But I can't know what your art might become."

"No."

"Don't speak. And neither will you know, if you marry. You simply won't have time. What is regarded as novel and intriguing and perhaps is important in you now will be looked upon as irrelevant when you have a household and a husband to look after. I'd think very hard about those things, if I were a woman. Don't speak. I'm doing your mouth." He concentrated on it for a while, then went on smoothly, "I never wanted children around. Noisy, messy, ignorant little barbarians who must be taught the slightest thing . . . Nor do I need a wife to make myself seem respectable. What I have longed for is a companion. An equal, in wit and temperament and of course in beauty. Free to indulge herself in whatever she might consider important. She would not need my permission to do as she pleased because legally I would have no claim on her. Consider that, Miss Slade."

She did, straightening so suddenly with a whirl of spearhead that he blinked. "Mr. Wilding," she said icily, her voice trembling, "what kind of monster are you, trapping me and then tormenting me?"

He raised his brows, gazed at her perplexedly for a moment. Then he put down his brush. "I think, Miss Slade, that I will send you home early today. You must be very tired to be imagining such things. Tell your brother that you need a good night's sleep. Forego the studio in the morning just this once. Try to come back refreshed tomorrow."

"Mr. Wilding—"

"It's all right. I've just given you some things to think about, that's all. They may seem a bit confusing now, but they're worth examining. Get dressed. I'll walk you out and send you home in my carriage. Fender had an unfortunate encounter in the garden this morning; it will be a while before he'll be up and about."

Emma flung open Adrian's studio door and said tersely to the group of startled faces—Ned, Euphemia Bunce, and Adrian—around his easel, "Mr. Bonham, I have changed my mind. I really do need to get away. Can we leave for your house in the north as soon as possible?"

*

NED didn't ask questions. He didn't dare. There was tension in his beloved's voice and in her movements that told him simply to do what must be done as quickly as possible. He sent word to his caretaker and housekeeper in the north to prepare for a full house, perused the train schedules, and started packing. Beneath his alarm for her, he was delighted, and afraid that if he delayed or discussed her reasons for the abrupt decision, she might change her mind again. Long hours rambling through the country was what she needed: sun and rain on her face, work whenever she wanted, laughter in the evenings, fish out of the rivers, fresh cream and strawberries, and long, peaceful, dreamless sleeps.

Two days later, when the train to the north country began to move out of the station, Ned saw the tension suddenly melt out of Emma like something palpable. She turned to look at him with wonder. Around her, friends and her brother and their older female cousin Winifred, whose art lay in her embroidery threads, chatted and laughed. Aisles and racks were piled with their luggage, as well as baskets of provisions, sketchbooks to record the journey, blankets, books and a great trunk full of the paraphernalia of their art.

"We're moving," she said incredulously. "I thought it wouldn't be possible. Something would happen to prevent it."

"Is Wilding that difficult?" he asked her, appalled.

She thought, watching the city flow past her, before she answered. "He is playing a game to make me feel like Boudicca. But, unlike her, I will win. I just needed to retreat for a week or two." She smiled at him, the shadows like bruises under her eyes. He could not find a smile to give back to her.

"You will not go there again," he said flatly. "I will explain that to Mr. Wilding."

Her smile faded; he glimpsed a look in her eyes that Wilding must have put there: fierce and inflexible.

"You will not fight my battles for me," she said softly. "If I can't fight for myself and my art, then what kind of an artist can I be? Only what you will permit me to be."

He blinked at her, startled at this stranger's face. Then he thought about what she said, and answered haltingly, "I think I understand. This is that important to you."

"Yes."

"More important than me or Wilding."

Her face softened; she touched his hand, held it unexpectedly. "No. As important as you. The only important thing about Wilding is what we will get from him when this is finished."

He opened her fingers, let his own explore her long bones and warm, softer skin, roughened here and there by a callous from her pencil, or by scrubbing to remove dried paint. Though their hands were tucked neatly out of sight beneath her skirt, he felt that warmth against his lips, as though longing, for an instant, had made it so.

"Miss Slade," he said huskily.

"Mr. Bonham?"

"Will you please marry me so that I might have the privilege of putting my arms around you?"

She nodded, sighing audibly. Then she added quickly, "I mean no. I mean not yet. Soon. I meant that—I dearly wish you could. How long have we known each other?"

"One month, three weeks, four days and some odd hours. Surely that's long enough."

"Surely it must be," she agreed, "in some countries. You would bring my father half a dozen cows and he would give you his blessing and me. If he were still alive."

"If I had any cows. Perhaps I should offer some to Adrian."

"Perhaps that would be proper."

"How soon," he begged, "is soon?"

"Not soon enough." She held her breath, thinking, then looked at him helplessly. "Do you think two months might be considered within the pale of propriety?"

"Miss Slade, may I remind you that as an artist you are already beyond the pale?"

She laughed breathlessly, a sound he had heard only rarely during the past weeks.

"Then when two months have passed since the night we met you may ask me again, and I will answer with all my heart."

"Well, then," he said, clasping her fingers gently in both hands and smiling mistily down at them. "That's settled. I'll start collecting some shaggy northern cattle from the hills the moment we get there."

The lake house, a great square four stories high, was built of stone as grey as the water. It stood alone near the edge of the water, its lawns and gardens surrounded on all sides by wild shrubs, gorse and heather, and juniper twisted by the winds. A stony hill rose behind it, hiding the village on the other side. The road that wound up and over the hill from

the village to the house was an ancient thing; stones run-
neled with archaic letters and odd staring faces appeared out
of the shrubbery now and then as though they watched all
who journeyed along the road.

"What are those peculiar stones?" Winifred wondered.
She was a paler version of Adrian and Emma, rather tall and
bony without Emma's grace, her hair more sandy than gold.
But she shared their even temperament and fearless interest
in unusual things.

"No one really knows," Ned answered. "The locals have
various tales about them: they mark graves, or once gave directions to travelers, or even that they're doorposts into
fairyland."

"Really?" Coombe said. "How wonderful. I intend to see
if they work. If I vanish, you'll know where I've gone."

"You'd better not," Adrian told him. "You're in charge of
catching our fish."

"My caretakers, Mr. and Mrs. Noakes, know a lot of local
tales. Mrs. Noakes is housekeeper and cook; she can do uncanny things with a grouse. Mr. Noakes tends the gardens
and keeps the house from falling down. Sometimes I think
they're as old as it is. They're its household gods."

The crowd, smelling hot bread and savory meat as soon as
Noakes opened the door to the rattle of wagons, seemed willing to worship. Mrs. Noakes, round as an egg with a crown
of grey braids, greeted them all calmly, unperturbed by the
numbers. She dispatched them to various rooms, pointing
directions with the wooden spoon in her hand. Noakes, a
burly old man with eyebrows like moth wings, began hauling their baggage upstairs.

"You gave us short notice," he remarked to Ned. "But
Mrs. Noakes managed to air out the rooms and find beds for
everyone. You came just in time for the strawberries in the
garden. I've checked the boats; they're both sound, and all
the fishing gear is in order. Word is that the sky should clear

up soon; all the signs are there, they say, though I couldn't tell that myself."

"You are a paragon, Noakes. I'm sorry we didn't give you much time to prepare. We made up our minds very suddenly."

His eyes, grey as the stone walls around them, crinkled with a smile. "It's good for the house to be full, makes it feel young again."

Inside, the house was as simple as its outer lines suggested. The whitewashed rooms were large and full of light; windows and doors were framed with solid oak; thresholds were worn and polished with age. The odd unframed oil or strip of embroidery hung here and there; beyond that, only the views of water and blooming heather and rocky hills adorned the rooms. The party spent some time exploring, watching the sunset out of different windows, exclaiming over the solitude, the colors, the potential for their brushes. A herd of wild ponies galloping through the gorse rendered them nearly incoherent.

Then the last piece of luggage found its place, the sun vanished, and they clattered down the stairs to supper.

Afterwards, they rearranged the vast drawing room, pulled chairs and couches and cushions taken from other rooms as close to the enormous fireplace as possible. They took turns reading out of ancient volumes they had discovered around the house: obscure poetry, a farmer's journal, a collection of local folktales. Marwood Stokes, who had a fine and fruity voice, was reading about a pesky household hobglobin whose tricks could drive people to leave their homes, and who would pack itself in among their possessions and follow them along to the next, when someone pounded at the door.

Ned, half-listening, heard Noakes' footsteps on the flagstones, and then a brief exchange. Then the drawing room opened and there stood Bram Wilding, smiling genially upon them.

"Sorry I'm late."

They all stared at him wordlessly. Then Adrian threw a cushion at him. "You weren't invited, Wilding. Go away."

"I know," he said imperturbably. "I've got a room in the village. But I couldn't let you have all the fun without me. Nor did I want my Boudicca out of sight, though I promise—" He held up his hand as Ned and Adrian protested vigorously and incomprehensibly at once. "I promise I won't ask her to work as long as she is here." He looked at her; she sat motionless in an old rocking chair, her face colorless and expressionless. "May I stay?" he asked her. "I only came to paint a landscape."

She shifted slightly, let her hand slip beneath the chair arm to rest lightly on Ned's shoulder, where he sat on a cushion beside her. "Here I am not Boudicca," she said softly. "I am Emma Slade, whom you barely know. You are my brother Adrian's friend; it is of no interest to me if you stay or go."

"Oh, Adrian, let him stay," Winifred, who hardly knew him, said kindly. "He has come so far. And country darkness is so—dark."

Adrian cocked a brow at Bram. "If my sister says you go, you go. Is that agreed?"

Wilding bowed his head, added cheerfully, "I brought gifts of appeasement from the city. Bottles of brandy, baskets of fruit, and Valentine DeMorgan's latest book of poetry, fresh from the press."

They all exclaimed at that. "Produce it," Coombe demanded. "Read and prove your worthiness."

Mrs. Noakes put her head through the doorway. "Pardon me, Mr. Bonham, am I to make up another bed?"

"Mr. Wilding has a room in the village," Ned said firmly.

"Oh, dear. Mr. Noakes misunderstood and sent the wagon on its way back to the village. Should he wait up, then, to take Mr. Wilding back?"

Ned sighed. "He's liable to be waiting all night." He hesitated a moment, then said tersely to Wilding, who was trying to look meek and penitent and not succeeding well at either, "You can stay tonight, if Mrs. Noakes can find you a bed."

"There's a narrow bed in an attic room," Mrs. Noakes suggested doubtfully. "It leaks in the rain."

"That sounds perfect."

"You are too kind," Wilding murmured.

"I," Emma said, rising abruptly, "think I will say goodnight. I'm very tired. Come with me, Winifred?"

Her cousin joined her with a rather wistful glance back at the party and the fascinating newcomer. He smiled cordially at them, then stretched out on the carpet in front of the fire as the door closed behind them, and promptly began to read about a young woman wasting away from a broken heart as the violets He had given her withered before her eyes in their vase, a poem of such sweet and lugubrious melancholy that Wilding had most of the party weeping with laughter within a dozen lines. Adrian, sipping port and watching Wilding, did not find him amusing; nor did Ned.

But there was nothing to be done that night, and Emma, he reminded himself, might prefer to find her own ways of dealing with Wilding in the light of day.

Ned rose early, trying to be quiet as he gathered his sketchbook and watercolors and boots and took them all downstairs. As always, Mrs. Noakes was earlier; the sideboard was laden with hot tea and scones, boiled eggs, smoked salmon and sausages and strawberries from the garden.

As Ned stood in his stockings, drinking scalding tea and eating a sausage with his fingers, the door opened and delighted him with the unexpected vision of Emma.

"I heard someone creep past my door, and looked to see who it was," she said. "I hoped it might be you."

She had brought her sketchbook down as well, her pencil case and a broad, well-weathered hat. He happily poured her tea, brought it to her as she sat.

"I'm going down to the lake to see what I can make of the water and those rocky hills in the distance," he said.

"Oh, good. I'll come with you."

"Yes."

"We could take a boat," she suggested eagerly. "Row out onto the water and draw. Shall we?" She rose, began filling the pockets of her painting smock with scones, strawberries wrapped in a napkin, and a couple of eggs. "Let's go now before anyone else is up; the sun is rising and it's so beautiful out there now."

"All right," he said, managing to gulp tea and put his boots on at the same time. Like children trying to be quiet, they only succeeded in dropping things and snorting with laughter as they made their way out of the house into the morning.

A low mist still hung over the lake, obscuring the water, but the clouds were fraying above their heads, and sunlight broke through from behind the hills, illumining the jagged slopes. Raindrops sparkled on every tree branch and grass blade. The air smelled of strawberries and bracken. Ned took deep, exuberant breaths of it as they made their way across the lawn toward the water. In the boathouse, someone moved. Noakes, Ned saw, as the old man raised a hand; he had probably brought the fishing gear down.

Emma came to a sudden stop, gripping Ned. "I saw something," she breathed.

"That's just Noakes."

"No, something in the mist—something white moving across the water."

"A wild swan, maybe."

"Maybe." She started moving again, her long strides free and confident, he saw, when she was in the open. Sunlight touched her hair, turned it into an aura of gold around her face, and his breath caught. Entranced, he stood still, watching her move across the morning. Missing him, she turned, laughing, walking backwards and beckoning him on.

Then her face changed, became guarded, inexpressive; he guessed at what she had seen behind him and sighed.

He turned. Wilding, his own steps lithe and quick, was gaining on them. He, too, had a sketchbook under his arm, a pencil case in his pocket.

"Good morning," he called cheerfully.

"It was," Ned muttered. Emma had already started on her way again, firmly ignoring the interloper. She went down the path to the boathouse, causing Wilding to ask promptly when he caught up with Ned, "Are you rowing out? What a splendid idea." He clapped Ned lightly, irritatingly on the shoulder, his eyes following Emma. "Thanks for the bed, by the way. Creaky thing; my feet hung over the end. But amusing." He had continued his brisk walk before he finished talking, leaving Ned in his wake. "I just need a word with Miss Slade—"

"Wilding!" Ned protested, hurrying after him. "She came here to rest."

"I know," Wilding called soothingly over his shoulder. "I know. Miss Slade!"

She didn't answer. She had nearly reached the lake, where the mist, beginning to burn off, revealed reeds near the boathouse, a strip of water, and a flock of baby ducks paddling after their mother. Ned, flushed and angry, caught up with Wilding, nearly plowing into him as Wilding stopped abruptly.

"Look at that," he said breathlessly.

Nick, seeing for the moment only Wilding's excellently tailored back, stepped aside and looked over his shoulder.

A horse as white as the mist stood on the shoreline. Emma had seen it, too; she walked toward it slowly, one hand outstretched. Ned heard her speaking to it, half-laughing, half-crooning, and remembered the country girl she was, raised among all kinds of creatures and not likely to be afraid of a wild pony.

It looked quite a bit bigger than the local hill ponies; Ned wondered if it had escaped from someone's pasture. It stood very still, watching Emma come, mist snorting out of its nostrils. It looked like a hunter, Ned guessed, realizing how big it was as Emma, his rangy goddess, moved closer to it.

"It's perfect," Wilding whispered.

"What?"

"I wanted a horse just like that to put behind Boudicca."

"Good. You've found it. You paint it while Miss Slade and I go rowing."

"No, I need her—" He started walking again, calling, "Miss Slade!"

She shook her head as though at a midge. The horse nuzzled her fingers; she stepped closer, running her hands along its mane. Wilding, hurrying so quickly he was nearly running, cried her name again.

"Miss Slade!"

She glanced at him finally, her face set and colorless. Then someone else shouted—Noakes, who never raised his voice. She gripped the thick mane, pulled herself up as she must have done countless times as a child, riding the placid farm horses bareback, with an eye-catching flash of knee above her boot before she settled her skirts.

The horse gathered its muscles, turned, and leaped so cleanly into the mist over the lake that Ned did not hear a sound from the water, and the hatchling ducks floated serenely by, undisturbed. The silence seemed to spread over the world, through Ned's heart; he couldn't find a word, a sound, for what he had seen. Beside him, Wilding was as still; he didn't breathe.

Only Noakes made noises, dropping something with a clatter, calling incoherently and puffing as he ran out of the boathouse. He stared at the quiet water and cried again, a shocked, harsh noise. Ned moved then, trembling, stumbling, his heart trying to outrace him as he reached the boathouse.

"Noakes—" he said, gripping the old man. "Noakes—"

"What was—What happened?" Wilding demanded raggedly.

"We must go out there—You take one boat, Noakes, we'll take the other—Hurry!"

"No time to hurry," Noakes said, wiping his twitching face. "No place to hurry to. Never," he added in a whisper, "saw that before in my long life. Heard about them but never thought I'd live to see one."

"One what?" Ned cried.

"Kelpie," Noakes said. He wiped at his brow, trembling, too; his cap fell on the ground. "I'm sorry, lad."

"Kelpie—What's a kelpie?" Ned asked wildly.

"What you saw. That white horse. A water sprite. No mercy in them. They lure you onto their backs with their beauty, they carry you into the water, and then—and that's the end."

"What end?" Wilding asked sharply.

The old eyes, grey as the water, gazed back at Ned with a sheen of tears over them. "In all the tales I ever heard, you drown."

*

EMMA, after the first gasp of shock from the horse's sudden plunge into the cold water, was holding her breath. They were going down, she realized, down and down, deeper than the shallows of the lake had any right to be. She had slid off the horse's back, but her fingers were still locked into its mane. Water weeds trailed past her, and schools of startled fish. The horse, which was behaving like no horse she had ever met in her life, dragged her ruthlessly. It galloped in water effortlessly; she was as buffeted, roiling around its body, as she would have been on land. Sometimes, flung over its outstretched head, she glimpsed a black, wicked eye, a widened nostril, its great muscular neck snaked out, teeth bared. It shook its head now and then, trying to loosen her grip, she thought; she only clung tighter, her lungs on fire, her eyes strained open, round and staring like a fish's, unable not to look at what could not be possible.

If I must breathe, so must it, was her only coherent thought; she clung to that as well, ignoring all the implications of the horse's magic. Beneath that thought lay a confused impulse, a fragment from some fairy tale or another, the only thing shaken to the surface of her mind as the monstrous horse surged into impossible depths and she twisted in the water like an eel clamped to a writhing fish.

Don't let go.

And then the pain spilled through her, burst out of her until it must have filled the world, for she felt nothing else, not water nor motion nor the coarse mane, long and wet as sea grass, in her fingers. She closed her eyes at last, and drowned in pain.

She woke again, at which she felt vaguely surprised. Drenched and limp as a bundle of beached sea kelp, she lay on sand in what must have been the bottom of the world. A hollow of rock rose around her; a cave, holding air like a bubble. Beyond it, she saw the grey-green glimmer of water, shadowy things moving among trailing weeds.

The great horse loomed over her, its long white head with its onyx eyes and great dark nostrils swooping down as though to bite. Its mouth stopped an inch from her cheek. It only scented her, once, fastidiously, as though it were uncertain what she was.

"Am I dead?" she asked. Her voice had no more strength than a tendril of water moss.

"You should be," its eye told her, or its thoughts; she couldn't tell exactly where the voice came from.

She sat up slowly, pulling herself together in piecemeal fashion, bone by bone off the fine white sand. It crusted her hair, her clothes; she tasted it on her lips. The horse backed, stood watching her motionlessly. She saw a glimmering, moving reflection in its eye, and turned stiffly; her bones might have been there for centuries, they felt that creaky.

A man entered the cave. Some manlike creature, at any rate, if not truly mortal. His skin seemed opalescent, wavery grey-green, like the water; his green hair floated like sea-grass around his head. He wore a coronet of gold and pearl and darkly gleaming mother-of-pearl. In his tall grace and beauty, in his eyes the shade of blue-black nacre, he bore a startling resemblance to Bram Wilding.

She sighed. "Out of the frying pan . . ." she whispered. Her throat hurt, as though she had tried to scream under water. "Who are you?"

He gave her a look she couldn't fathom before he spoke. "You are in my realm," he answered, a lilt in his voice like the lap of waves against the shore. "This water is my kingdom."

"How do you understand me?" she asked with wonder.

"I am as old as this water. I have been hearing the sounds that mortals make since before they learned to speak."

"What happens now?"

He gave a very human shrug. "I have no idea." She stared at him. "No one has ever ridden my kelpie and lived."

"I'm still alive?"

"So it seems."

"I wasn't sure. I feel as though I have gotten lost in someone else's dream. Why did the kelpie come to kill me?"

"It's the way of things," he answered simply. "To ride the kelpie is to drown."

"But I didn't."

"No."

She thought a moment; her mind felt heavy, sluggish with water, thoughts as elusive as minnows. "You could," she suggested finally, "have the kelpie take me back."

He scratched a brow with a green thumbnail; a tiny snail drifted out. "I could just leave you in here; you would die eventually. But the kelpie kills, not I. Perhaps you were not meant to die. Every other mortal dragged underwater lets go of the kelpie to swim. It swims too deep, too quickly; they can never reach the surface again before they drown. But you would not let go."

"I think I got my tales confused," she answered fuzzily.

"Are there rules for such things?" the lake king asked curiously. "What happens in other tales at times like this?"

She tried to remember. Her childhood seemed very distant, on the far side of the boundary between water and air, stone and light. Inspiration struck; she felt absurdly pleased. "We might bargain," she told him. "You could ask me for something in return for my life."

He grunted. "What could you possibly have that I might want?"

She felt into the pockets of her smock, came up with a soggy handkerchief, some crumbled charcoal, sand, an unfortunate carp, a few crushed strawberries. "Oh," she breathed, a sudden flame searing her throat.

"What is that?" the lake king asked.

"It was part of our breakfast."

"No. Not that in your hand. That in your voice, your eye."

She blinked and it fell. "A tear," she told him. "I just remembered how happy we were, running out into the morning. We were going to row onto the lake, eat scones and strawberries, paint the world. And then Wilding came. And then the kelpie. And now here I am, and Mr. Bonham might as well be on the moon for all we can see of one another." She wiped away another tear. "He must think I am dead. In no conceivable circumstances would it occur to him that I might be sitting in a cave under water talking to the king of the lake."

The king came to kneel beside her, his eyes like the kelpie's, wild and alien, as he studied her.

"You have words I don't know," he said. "I hear them in your voice. What are they?"

"Sorrow," she told him, her voice trembling. "Joy. Eagerness. Dislike. Astonishment. Anger. Love."

"Are they valuable?"

"As air."

He was silent, his strange eyes fixed on her, his beautiful underwater face so like and unlike Wilding's it made her want to laugh and weep with rage: even there, that far beyond the known world, she could not get away from him.

"Give me those words," the lake king said, "and I will send you back."

She gazed at him mutely, wondering at the extraordinary demand; it was as though a trout had asked her to define joy. Slowly, haltingly, having no other way but words in that underwater world to explain such things, she began a tale. She started with her brother, and then Bram Wilding came into it, and then painting, and Boudicca, and the women's studio, and Edward Eustace Bonham, and how he and she had so unexpectedly fallen together into the depths of a word. All that had made her understand the words the lake king had heard in her voice, she told him, having no idea how much he understood, and not daring to hope that they might be worth more to him than a handful of pretty pebbles she might have picked up on the shore and lightly tossed into his realm.

*

ON the shore, the assembled houseparty stared numbly across the water. They had spent the morning rowing frantically over the lake, searching for any sign of Emma. Noakes had summoned villagers, who carried more boats over the hill on their wagons. Ned had refused to come in until the oars slipped out of his aching hands, and one of the villagers pulled him and his boat ashore. Adrian tried to persuade him to rest. But he could only pace along the water's edge, tormented by visions of Emma floating among the reeds in a lonely, distant stretch of shoreline.

Adrian, his eyes reddened, his face white and set with shock, kept asking reasonably, "How could she possibly have been taken by a kelpie? It's not real. How could it be real? These things belong in tales and paintings, not in life. We imagine them! They have no power over us."

"Yes, they do," Wilding finally said. "They have power. They force art out of us."

His imperturbable composure had not only been shaken; it had dissolved. He looked as stunned and wretched as any of them; for once in his life he had not a tactless word to say. He had very little to say, Ned noticed dimly. He was just there, whenever a hand was needed to push a boat out, when a trek to one cove or another was planned, when Coombe, searching the murky water under the boathouse, came defeated to shore and needed a blanket.

What Wilding said to Adrian worked its way finally into Ned's thoughts. Winifred came among them with a tray of mugs and fresh tea. He took one, warmed his hands and took a burning sip. Then he looked at Wilding. "What we paint is real. That's what you're saying?"

"You saw," Wilding reminded him inarguably.

He shook his head, took another swallow. "I never thought such things were real," he said huskily. "But if we—if we see these realms and paint them, then why can't we—why should we not be able to find our way into them? Find their doorways, cross their borders? Why can't we?" Wilding didn't answer. Ned turned his eyes back to the lake. He was gathering strength to resume his search, along the shore or on the water or in it, any way he could.

"We can't breathe water," Wilding said gently. "That's the boundary we can't cross."

"Neither can horses," Ned reminded him. "Yet nobody saw the kelpie come back up for air."

"It's a symbol," Adrian said heavily. "Kelpie means death. That's what Noakes said." He dropped his hand on Ned's shoulder, left it there a moment. On the lake, in shallower waters, the villagers had dropped grappling hooks. So far they had pulled up only weeds.

"If it's only a symbol, then how could it kill Emma?" His voice shook, and then his face; he turned blindly away from them, staring at the stony hills. "There must be a way," he whispered when he could. "There must be a way in. Those standing stones—doorposts, they're said to be—All those tales of people coming and going, taken and then finding their way back—"

"It's never anyone you or I know," Adrian said, "who finds their way back out of fairyland. It's always someone in a tale."

"This time it's Emma," Ned said fiercely. "Where there's a way in, there must be a way out. I'm going to find it." He dropped his cup on the grass, went towards the water. All the boats were in use. But they were no good anyway, he thought. They only sat on the surface of the water, keeping you safe and ignorant. How to find the place where tale becomes truth . . . He pulled off his shoes, felt the water on his feet, and then around his knees. And then, before he could reach the depths and glide beneath the surface, seek out the true kingdom of water, someone caught at him, pulled him back.

It was Wilding. Ned broke free of him, stumbled back. Wilding lost his balance, splashed down among the reeds.

"All this is your fault!" Ned shouted at him furiously. "You hounded her—you drove her up here, and even then you couldn't leave her alone, you had to come here yourself and drive her away from you again—she rode that kelpie to get away from you!"

"I know." Wilding was shivering in the water. His face, without its mask of arrogance and irony, was nearly unrecognizable. "Do you think," he asked Ned huskily, "that I will ever forgive myself? But the kelpie didn't come for me or you. You won't find it this way."

"I might," Ned said stubbornly, wading out again. "I can swim so close to death I might see its white mane and its black eye. I'll ride that kelpie then, and I will never let it go until it shows me where it has taken Emma. We paint such things because it's safe—we see them without danger—Our canvas is the boundary between worlds."

"It's all we know of them," Wilding said. "All we can ever know. Emma is gone."

"Emma—"

There was a sudden roil in the placid surface of the lake in front of them. Water streamed upward, splashed everywhere. Some said later they glimpsed in the bright jets raining back into the lake, a mane as white as spume, a spindrift tail, hooves like opalescent shell, eyes blacker than the nothing between stars. All anyone saw for certain as the strange eddy calmed, was someone swimming away from it toward the shore.

Ned, waist deep in the water, knew then that a heart could break with joy as well as grief, and twice in the same day.

He dove into the water and swam to meet her.

Later, they curled together under blankets on a sofa beside the great hearth, their wet heads close, their hands clasped. The group had sat around them mutely listening to Emma tell her tale. Then, in the face of such intimacy, the gathering broke up to marvel with one another, to eat and drink, to wander off and stare at the surface of the quiet lake, or up the hillside to gaze at the ancient stones. Then they strayed back to marvel again at Emma and ask for the tale again.

Adrian finally asked the obvious. "Are you planning to marry my sister, Mr. Bonham, or merely trifle with her affections?" They laughed at him. He reached out, his eyes widening with remembered pain and wonder, and lightly touched Emma's drying hair. "No one," he breathed, "will believe this. I still don't."

"No," Emma said. "They won't. But now I have a use for Mr. Wilding."

Wilding, who had been hovering at the door, unable to come in or go away, asked her hesitantly, "What is that?"

She gestured to him; he came to the fire, held out his hands to it. He hadn't changed his clothes, Ned saw; water moss and mud and bits of lake grass clung to his damp suit. Emma regarded him thoughtfully, without a trace of trouble in her eyes.

"I have bargained for my life with the king of the lake and won. Surely I can do the same with you."

"You don't have to," he answered painfully. "I won't ask you to pose again."

"But I will," she said. "And in return, I want you to pose for me."

He was silent, not in protest, Ned saw, but perplexed. He inclined his head. "Yes, of course. Anything. But—as what? A very great fool?"

"No. As the king of the lake. He looked exactly like

you," she sighed. "It wasn't funny," she told Adrian, who had loosed a bark of laughter. "It was, in fact, extremely annoying to think that Mr. Wilding's might be the last face I saw in my life."

"I'm sure it was," Wilding said ruefully.

"And I'll paint the kelpie beside you: that's another face I'll never forget for as long as I live. I intend to hang you, Mr. Wilding, in the women's exhibit." She turned to Ned then, as though she felt his pang of uncertainty, his resignation: never the hero, always the squire, the spear-bearer. She took his hands, held them very tightly. "You will be in it, too," she told him softly. "The man on the lake shore waiting beyond hope. The one to whom I will always find my way back."

He smiled, stroking her damp mermaid's hair, and wondered briefly how many worlds she might chance into, how often he might have to wait in terror and wonder at the edge of the unknown. But it would not matter, he decided. As long as she wanted, he would be there waiting.

An Embarrassment of Elves

by Craig Shaw Gardner

Back in 1976 when Ted White edited the late lamented magazine Fantastic Stories, *one issue contained the first installments of two humorous fantasy series: my own "Incredible Umbrella" tales and Craig Shaw Gardner's risible adventures of Ebenezum, a wizard with a sneezing allergy to magic.*

For years I kept saying that his series deserved a much wider readership, but no one listened. One editor—no longer in publishing—went so far as to explain that "humor doesn't sell," a charge I've also heard leveled at anthologies (oh, really?). But something in the wind must have shifted because suddenly Craig was turning out popular Ebenezum stories right and left. To date, there have been six books in the series, sequentially: A Malady of Magicks, A Multitude of Monsters, A Night in the Netherhells, A Difficulty with Dwarves, An Excess of Enchantments, *and* A Disagreement with Death.

I am pleased to present this brand-new Ebenezum story, "An Embarrassment of Elves," which features Craig's usual suspects: grumpy dwarves and demons, a dragon with a theatrical flair, a riff on Michael Moorcock's Eternal Champion and his accursed sword ("Doom! Doom!"), and of course the great wizard himself, at last cured of his magical affliction, and his apprentice, Wuntvor, not yet cured of his virginity.

Craig writes, "I've published thirty-one books and a whole bunch of short stories. I currently review books for H.P. Lovecraft's Magazine of Horror. *My most recent opus is* A Little Purple Book of Peculiar Stories, *a collection from Borderlands Press. I should have a website within a month or so, too: CraigShawGardner.com. It will be somewhat silly."*

1

"It's always darkest before the dawn, the sages say. And they further remind you that every cloud has a silver lining. But a truly successful wizard needs to remind his customers that a bit of silver is surrounded by an awful lot of grey, and a few hours after dawn, it's going to be getting awfully dark all over again."

—From *The Teachings of Ebenezum, Volume XXVI*

NEVER stand too close to a distraught dragon.

That, of course, is only one of the many lessons I have learned in my time as an apprentice to Ebenezum, the greatest mage in all the Western Kingdoms. But at the moment it was a very important one.

Hubert the dragon's large blue body landed rather heavily upon the far side of the clearing. I took a step away an instant before a great gout of flame shot straight up into the sky.

"Why do I bother?" the dragon called to the heavens. "What is the use?"

My other companions both made their opinions known.

"Why does he bother? What is his use? Many is the time I have asked those very questions," said one.

"Doom," spoke the other.

I glanced at each of the fellows who had already accompanied me on untold adventures. For I had come to accept my own particular talent—as some were good with the sword or bow, and others were destined to be heads of state or a bard of world renown—I was destined to have companions. Lots and lots of companions. I was told of this by no greater authority than that Spectre Death itself, who called me "The Eternal Apprentice." It was a decent enough title, I supposed, if only I might gain some inkling as to what it actually meant— besides the fact that I would seldom be alone.

On my one side stood one of my most regular companions—Snarks, a demon from the Netherhells far below us all, but he was a demon with a difference. It seemed his mother had been traumatized by a demonic politician shortly before Snarks was born, a shock of such force that Snarks was forever after forced to tell the truth—or at least the truth as Snarks saw it. As he wandered through the Western Kingdoms, far from his fiery home, Snarks always kept his countenance hidden beneath a monastic hood, but his opinion was always fully in the open.

On my other side stood the massive bulk of another companion—the warrior Hendrek, who rested one hand on his cursed club Headbasher, cursed because he had obtained it from a demonic dealer in used weaponry, only to discover it was a club which no man could own, but could only rent—a fact which no doubt contributed to the warrior's continued sour disposition.

But Hubert the dragon—who was still another companion—took no notice of these comments. Instead he continued to call on-high, flapping his wings for emphasis. "Did I ask for a golden horde? A fair princess whom I might hide in a cave so that I would have a neverending line of knights to slay? No! I just wanted a little song, a bit of dance, a tiny smidgen of applause from a grateful audience."

"Not asking for much, is he?" Snarks murmured close by one side.

"Doom," Hendrek added upon the other.

I cleared my throat in a manner that I had learned from my master.

"Pardon me, Hubert. Is there something we might do for you?"

Hubert swept about to stare down at me. Maybe it was his many years in the theater—while others of his kind burned and pillaged, Hubert the dragon preferred song and dance. No doubt it was that natural flair for melodrama that set him apart from others of his kind—but even in something as simple as looking around, he certainly commanded the entire clearing.

"Oh?" the dragon asked in a much quieter voice. "Was I talking aloud? I had hoped to keep these distressing feelings to myself."

"Indeed?" I asked, thinking that there might be some way to reassure the large blue fellow.

"But now that's out in the open," Hubert continued quickly, "I may as well tell you the rest of it!" Smoke unfurled from his nostrils as he sighed. "It's about Alea, of course. Maybe it was always about Alea."

He folded his wings behind him and sat heavily in the dirt. "She seemed so fair, so innocent when I first met her. And I considered myself a dragon-about-town. I had my way with damsels before. Love 'em and eat 'em Hubert, they used to call me. But I had tired of my old dragon life. I was looking for something new, something dramatic. And then, the first time I heard Alea scream—oh, what a purity of tone! I knew I had found my true singing partner at last!"

The dragon chuckled sourly. "We were an immediate sensation. When people see a damsel and dragon together, they know they'd better applaud! We had bookings for months! And what does she do? She runs off with a giant! Why? I ask you. Why?"

I didn't have an answer for that one. Apparently, though, Hubert didn't need one.

"Does a giant have magnificent blue scales?" the dragon continued, barely taking time to draw a breath. "Or can he simultaneously sing and blow smoke rings from his handsome snout? I think not. And what kind of name is Richard, anyways? Rather common, isn't it? It has none of the royal richness of Hubert, does it?"

"Quick!" another very soft voice said by my side. "Who do I have to strangle?"

I glanced over to see that we had been joined by the Dealer of Death, a professional assassin who specialized in strangling anything and everything. While we had once been upon opposite sides in one of my master's earlier struggles, he was thankfully working with us at the moment. Which meant he was yet another companion.

I waved at Hubert by way of explanation.

"It sounded like a struggle," the Dealer continued, flexing his arms, his legs, his back and every other conceivable body part. His every muscle was a finely honed instrument of murderous strength. Until I had met the Dealer, I had never seen anyone flex his hair. "I so need a struggle. I haven't killed anything in days."

"Thank goodness!" another voice of almost unimaginable beauty chimed in. "I thought your lap might be in danger." It was the unicorn, a magnificent beast whom I had met early on in my adventures, and who now followed me around simply because I was, well, inexperienced in certain matters of the heart. Well, the heart and certain other areas.

"Doom," Hendrek remarked. "Hubert is drawing a crowd."

"And I thought there was nothing worse than his singing!" Snarks added. The demon made a yelping sound, backing away from a small explosion by his feet.

"Nothing is too big for Brownie Power!" the very-small Tap the Brownie exclaimed.

Snarks took a deep breath, overcoming his initial horror to speak quickly. "But I thought you were back in the good graces of His Brownieship," the demon said, referring to the ruler of all Browniedom. "And were going back to, well, wherever it was that brownies come from!"

Tap did a little dance of joy in reply. "We're rebuilding Vushta! Somebody's got to watch to make sure the shoe shops come out right!"

Of all my companions, Tap was the liveliest, the most cheerful, and after the mighty wizard Ebenezum and my beloved witch Norei, the most filled with magic. But being a brownie made Tap a bit more specialized than the others. Every lively, cheerful, magical bit of him had to do with—shoes.

"Shoe shops?" Snarks whispered.

"It's an exacting task, but who better to do it than brownies?"

Even Snarks didn't have an answer for that. For Tap was correct. We were indeed rebuilding the City of a Thousand Forbidden Delights. While my master Ebenezum and my beloved Norei went about curing the rest of the wizard population from an unfortunate malady that had robbed them of their power, my companions and I were in charge of general clean-up and reconstruction.

The great city had fallen upon hard times. What with the recent war with the Netherhells, and the malady that seemed to have effected the entire local wizard population, the city was but a shadow of its former self. It hardly lived up to its name. Most of the forbidden delights had long since fled. The ones that were left were, at worst, hardly forbidden at all. Many were only in questionable taste, and one or two of them might be downright wholesome. Or so I had been told by the others in my party. I, of course, had no time to sample such things.

Any time I had left after rebuilding would be spent in the company of my beloved Norei. As soon as she might find some time herself. It was not an easy situation for any of us. My part of it called for the occasional simple spell with plenty of muscle in between. It was the best I could do. For, while I was apprenticed to the greatest mage in all the

Western Kingdoms, recent catastrophic events had kept me from learning much but the most basic of spells. Attempts to perform more difficult magics had resulted in rather less satisfactory results, in part because, under stress, I had an unfortunate tendency to drop things, or trip over my own feet, or slightly misremember a mystical word or two. I sighed. No matter what my problems, I did have many companions to aid my efforts, companions who now appeared to be talking all at once.

"Alea!" Hubert cried.

"You know, I've never strangled a dragon," the Dealer remarked.

"Doom!" Hendrek replied.

"Everything would be so much calmer," the unicorn added meaningfully, "with the proper lap to rest my heavy head!"

"I'm so happy to be back with my pal Snarks!" Tap called from below. "We're going to have the best adventures ever!"

"Tell me," Snarks casually asked the Dealer, "have you ever strangled a brownie—wait a minute." He looked across the clearing. "I haven't seen one of those in quite a while!"

"Doom," Hendrek replied. "One of what?"

"Over there," Snarks pointed. "They used to be quite popular in the Netherhells."

Everyone, Hubert included, looked to where Snarks pointed a sickly green finger. There, upon the far hillside, was a rider upon a horse. But this was no ordinary horseman, for the rider's clothing, and the color of his steed, and even the color of his great battle-axe, were of such a deep shade of obsidian that they seemed to suck the very light from the sky.

There was a certain awe in Snarks' voice. "Now *that's* a dark rider."

"Are we in danger?" the Dealer of Death asked, flexing his muscles in anticipation. "Will he attack?"

Snarks shook his head. "Dark riders never attack."

"Doom." Hendrek's frown deepened. "Then what do they do?"

"Basically, what this one's doing. They just appear on hillsides, looking ominous."

"Doesn't seem to be much of a profession," Tap piped up. "Nowhere near as good as making shoes!"

"No, you don't understand. The dark rider is a harbinger."

"Indeed?" I had heard of harbingers. "Sort of like the first robin of spring?"

Snarks nodded. "Sort of like the first robin of spring, if the robin was six feet tall, and totally devoid of any color save black, and was carrying a weapon designed to cleave people in two."

"Doom."

"Exactly," Snarks agreed.

I was still trying to understand. "So the dark rider is here to announce—something not too good?"

"Far worse than that. Dark riders are never employed by springtime festivals. Not that he'll stick around to tell us. After everyone notices how ominous he is he'll just—ride away."

Snarks' explanation even upset the brownie. "That's it?" Taps demanded. "No explanations? Just, here I am, looking evil, you'd better watch out—oh, time to go! Have a nice day?"

"Basically," Snarks agreed.

"I think not," Hubert rumbled as he got to his feet.

"What are you going to do?" Snarks asked. "He's leaving already." And indeed the rider was tugging upon the reins of his jet-black steed.

Hubert flapped his wings. "I need something to occupy my talons—get my mind off of—other things. Dark riders might be fast, but dragons are faster." Hubert took off as the horseman began to ride away. The dark rider never had a chance.

2

"You'll never beat a dragon to the punch.
By the time you've swung you'll be the dragon's lunch.
Your nobility's divested
For you're now being digested
For that's just the way the dragon likes to munch!"
  —Allegedly entertaining ditty "Forty Ways to Feed Your
    Dragon," as once performed by Damsel and Dragon
                                                    (Verse 12)

THE crowd around me gasped.

The dark rider barely had time to twist its hooded form around before Hubert was upon it. The creature tried to raise its great battle-axe in defense. It was a weapon fully twice as long as Hendrek's massive warclub, with a blade as wide as your average door. Hubert flexed a single claw and snapped the axe in two.

The crowd whistled.

The rider roared in frustration, the breath emerging from its great mouth as a congealed puff of frigid blue, as though the creature exhaled a hoarfrost that might freeze anything it touched.

In answer, Hubert breathed a single gout of fire, and the frigid breath melted into drops of dew.

The crowd cheered.

The rider twisted away from the dragon hovering above it, spurring its steed to make haste away. The steed was soon running at full gallop, a moment after Hubert had plucked the rider from its saddle.

The crowd applauded with gusto.

Hubert calmly flew back to his waiting audience, the

dark rider held gently in his claws. He deposited the rider, slightly singed and soiled, some few yards before us, then landed gently with the slightest of bows.

The dark rider groaned beneath its voluminous cloak. Its voice seemed to rumble through the dirt beneath our feet.

The audience greeted the dragon with a hearty chorus of "Well done!" "That's the way to go!" and "That'll show those harbingers!"

"Thank you," Hubert said with a smile. "It was nothing."

The rider thrashed about, throwing aside the heavy folds of its costume, finally raising its head, if you could call it that, to look at our company. For where its head should be was a swirl of darkness, save for two glowing embers where other beings sported eyes, and two rows of glowing, razor fangs when it opened its mouth. Which it did, to cry:

"HOWWWW DARRRE YOUUUUU!"

Its voice was so loud and deep it shook the surrounding trees.

That quieted the crowd for the moment. But I found I was curious.

"Indeed?" I asked politely. "How dare we—what exactly?"

"YOU HAVE INTERFERED WITH MY DUTIES!" the rider roared. "YOU TAMPER WITH FORCES BEYOND YOUR MORTAL KEN!"

"Some of us might not be exactly—mortal," the unicorn sniffed.

"I used to know a brownie named Ken," Tap added brightly. "He specialized in really shiny shoes!"

These replies seemed to enrage the rider even further. "A GREAT EVIL IS COMING!" he screamed. "I AM BUT THE FIRST SIGN. I WILL SMITE YOU WITH MY—" He paused, glaring wildly about.

"You're looking for that thing I snapped in two?" Hubert asked casually.

"MY GREAT AND POWERFUL BATTLE-AXE? SNAPPED?" A

great shudder went through the creature's robes. "YOU FORCE ME TO MEASURES EVEN MORE DIRE! I WILL FREEZE YOU WITH MY—"

The rider paused as Hubert laid one talon gently against the creature's shoulder. "Thinking about that breath thing? You've forgotten about my dragon fire."

But the rider wasn't done. "I WILL CALL THOSE TERRIBLE BEINGS WHICH I SERVE. SOON YOU WILL BE SURROUNDED BY HUNDREDS—"

"You'll do no such thing," Hubert replied, leaning just the slightest bit on that talon which touched the rider. The rider swayed under the weight. "Another outburst and I'll sit on you."

"SIT?" the rider demanded.

"Sit," Hubert confirmed.

The rider closed its glowing mouth with an audible snap.

"Much better," Hubert agreed. He looked to the rest of the assemblage. "You know. That was surprisingly satisfying. Perhaps there's a future for me in show business after all."

"Let's hope it's better than your past," Snarks remarked.

"Pardon?" Hubert's tail twitched as he blew the slightest bit of smoke from his nostrils.

"Nothing!" Snarks seemed to withdraw deeper within his monkish robes. At times like this, the demon's compulsion to tell the truth was truly a curse. "Surprisingly good work you did out there!" his voice called out from deep within the folds.

The dragon nodded happily. "I thought so, too. Of course, I'd have to change the nature of my act. Sort of a spectacle thing, I suppose. I'd miss the dancing, though. Not to mention the snappy patter."

"Indeed!" I quickly interjected, for while I was sure we were all quite grateful that Hubert had brought us the dark rider, I thought it more important to question the new arrival rather than listen to show business nostalgia. "I think we would be best served if we asked a few questions of the rider."

The creature turned its two glowing orbs in my direction, but said nothing. All the others gathered about looked to me as well.

It seemed best that I ask the first question. "What is your purpose here?"

"I AM THE THREAT UPON YONDER HILL," the rider replied.

"Even I had figured that much," the Dealer of Death spoke from where he stood at the back of the group, his every muscle tensed for instant action, "and I often tend to strangle before I even think. This rider does not have much of a face. I wonder if he has a neck."

"Doom," Hendrek agreed. "Surely you must do more than threaten."

The rider nodded what passed for a head. "I RUMBLE WITH EVIL."

"No doubt a worthwhile skill," I added, eager to keep the newcomer talking. "Do you have other duties as well?"

The rider shrugged its dark clothed shoulders. "I RUMBLE. I THREATEN. THAT'S PRETTY MUCH IT."

"That's all?" Snarks demanded, reemerging from his robes. "A big guy like you? Talk about overkill!"

"WE ALL HAVE OUR JOB IN THESE QUESTS. THAT IS MINE."

"This is a quest?" Tap asked excitedly. "I've always wanted to do a quest. 'Search for the Missing Shoe,' maybe. Ooh! How about 'The Look for the Lost Laces!' Or 'The Curse of the Slippery Slipper!' Or—"

I frowned as the brownie prattled on. A quest, the rider had said. This seemed important. Perhaps we should find my master Ebenezum and my beloved Norei and tell them of our discovery. While the two of them were busy curing the remaining wizardly population hereabouts, this seemed the sort of thing my master would want to know. And as for

the young witch who aided him—well, I was always eager
for a chance to see Norei.

"Or we could call it 'Raiders of the Lost Boot!'" Tap
continued. "Or—"

"Indeed," I interrupted. "I believe this business is important enough that we should inform my master. Tap, you can
probably find him the fastest."

"Brownie power is always ready!" the small fellow agreed.

"Could you go then," I further explained, "and tell
Ebenezum we could use his assistance?"

"Boots and laces!" Tap exclaimed. "I'm already gone!"

And with that, he disappeared.

Snarks sighed heavily. "We don't have to hear about any
more shoe quests? That brownie needs to be sent on many,
many more errands."

For a change, the rest of the company appeared to agree.

"Magic."

The word hung in the air, spoken by some unseen female
voice. But what a voice! The words seemed to contain music,
and sunshine, and the first flowers of spring.

"Ah!" the wonderful voice continued, "surely you are
worthy of the party!"

And with that, a single ray of sunlight seemed to pierce
the sky above. And in the center of the light appeared a single, glowing figure.

Did this have anything to do with the dark rider? I was
doubly glad I had sent for Ebenezum. Not to mention Norei.
I sighed.

The glowing figure gained definition. I could see that it
was female.

Norei. We had been through so many adventures
together—and she still liked me. Or even more than liked
me. My heart quickened in my chest to realize she might be
near. How long had it been—

The newcomer was a particularly shapely female. The

glow faded, and I could see that she had long, auburn tresses, the fiery red of a perfect sunset. Her eyes were the color of the morning sky, her skin as pale as the moon, her tight-fitting gown the green of the first leaves of summer.

Nor—er—no—uh—

What was I thinking about? I only wanted to look at the woman before us. And she regarded us in turn.

"My, you certainly are an interesting group."

Interesting? She had called us interesting? My heart leapt within my chest.

"But I have not introduced myself," the most magnificent of women continued. "I am a princess of the Elvin. My name, which mere mortals cannot pronounce, is—"

She then spoke a phrase that combined all joy and comfort, music and silence, beauty and mystery. She smiled when it was done.

"But since none of you can pronounce that, you may call me Lalala."

"Lalala," the whole company said as one—well, except for the unicorn, who seemed a bit out of sorts.

The princess' eyes widened in delighted surprise. "What a wonderful group you are! I detected magic. I detected special gifts. Truly, you are worthy of an invitation."

No one appeared to disagree. The unicorn pawed at the ground distractedly.

"Then you will come?" The beauty clapped her hands with joy. "Oh, this will be the most unusual celebration!"

And with that, she vanished.

I blinked. I forced myself to breathe. My arms and legs felt like lead weights. The woman was gone. There was a hole at the center of my life. When would I see her again?

If only I could call her true name. Surely, I could pronounce those sounds, and bring that feeling back.

"Naga—" I began. That wasn't right. "Saburoga—Vitnog—" I saw others in my company doing the same.

"Sceegbaj!" the Dealer muttered. "Wagagaforx!" Hubert sang tentatively. Even Snarks muttered something like "Wanalanadingbop." All of us were trying to find a way back to that magnificent name.

I swallowed and stilled my tongue. It was useless. I was only a mortal. Her name, and all that it represented, was far beyond my pitiful grasp. How could I possibly see her again?

I fell to my knees.

"Lalala!" I cried.

"Wuntvor?" another woman's voice replied. I looked up. It was Norei.

3

"A wizard needs to fit in well in society. For those in society have the communication tools, also known as gossip, which will increase the wizard's fame. And those in society have problems of such a rarified and elite nature as to test the wizard's skills. But most important, of course, is that those in society have the sort of money that can make a wizard's life truly worthwhile."

—From *The Teachings of Ebenezum*,
third annual supplement

"N-N-NOREI?" I managed to say her name with some difficulty as the young witch helped me to my feet. It was the sort of contact with my beloved that I usually longed for. Now, however, I seemed strangely out of place, as if I had taken a single step into some brand-new world, and was having trouble stepping back into Vushta proper.

"What has happened to you?" she asked with a frown. It was a lovely frown, as she was a lovely witch, with a pleasing oval face framed by the curly, red-tinged hair common to much of witchkind. What had I been thinking of, looking at that elf, when I could have been looking at Norei instead?

She waved impatiently at the dark rider sprawled by my side. "And who is this?"

Indeed, most of my company, Hendrek, the Dealer of Death, Snarks, even Hubert, seemed to be in the same dazed condition that currently bothered me.

Only one of our number was still on its feet. It shook its horn magnificently as it trotted forward.

"I suppose I will have to explain. Unicorns are above such petty things as what has just occurred." The creature studied Norei for an instant with its beautiful pale blue eyes. "And while you and I may have some difficulties concerning"—the magnificent beast glanced meaningfully in my direction—"well, you know—I fear we both face a much greater threat."

"Another threat?" Norei frowned. "What is it this time?"

"Elves," the unicorn replied. "All these poor mortals and near mortals. They are all victims of Elvin enchantment."

Norei shook her head in disapproval.

"All of you? Enchanted by elves?" She spoke to the group, but her gaze was fixed upon me. "I don't know how you allow yourself to become ensorcelled so easily."

The Dealer was the first to find his voice. "She was so beautiful, I had no urge to strangle her at all!"

"Doom," Hendrek agreed a moment later. "She did invite us to a party."

"A party? How strange. What sort of party?" Norei surveyed the assemblage. "Did any of you bother to ask?"

The Dealer seemed to bristle a bit at that. "Ask? Who needs to ask? She invites, we attend."

"How could I even speak?" Snarks added with a heavy sigh. "There was nothing to criticize."

"Lalala." Hubert breathed a contented smoke ring. "Her name was Lalala."

"Lalala?" If anything, my beloved's frown deepened.

"And she did nothing more than invite you to a party that she told you nothing about?"

I nodded my head at last. "I thought it was very generous of her."

Norei's frown stretched deeper still. "This enchantment might be worse than I thought. We'd best wait here for Ebenezum. He sent me on ahead while he worked on curing the dean of the wizards' school. This restoration of magic is delicate work."

Still frowning, she waved at the newcomer among our ranks. "But nothing you've said explains this—thing."

The dark rider seemed to awaken from a trance.

"LALALA," the creature rumbled. "I WONDER IF SHE WOULD MIND IF I—THREATENED HER? VERY GENTLY, OF COURSE." The dark rider sighed. "A WOMAN OF HER BREEDING WOULD SURELY APPRECIATE A GOOD, EVIL RUMBLE OR TWO."

"That's a dark rider," Snarks explained. "Though I don't think he's a particularly dangerous example of his breed."

As though in reply, the dark rider sighed again.

"He does not appear to be an immediate threat," Norei agreed.

There was a small, popping noise by her feet. "Buckles and laces! What have I missed?"

"The magical rabble seems to be everywhere," Snarks muttered.

"Doom," Hendrek agreed. "Vushta just seems to attract them."

"That's the reason I'm still here, plying my trade," the Dealer of Death added. "Vushta seems to attract just about everything."

"Demons, biting insects, brownies," Snarks agreed. "Why not elves?"

"Elves? I missed elves?" Tap the Brownie seemed genuinely upset.

"But this event they will be holding—" Norei insisted.

"It'll be a going-away party," Snarks explained. "It's the only kind they ever have. Elves are always leaving someplace. They left the Netherhells eons ago."

"What a pity," Tap continued. "Elves always wear the very best shoes. Especially to parties."

Hendrek frowned, attempting no doubt to assimilate all this Elvin information behind his broad warrior's brow. "Doom. So what happens after the elves have left—everywhere?"

Snarks snickered. "Oh, I imagine they'll just start coming back—and spend another eon or two arriving! It will be nothing more than an excuse for yet more celebrations. An excuse for the most important of all the elves—the most revered among Elvinkind—the most . . ."

Snarks' voice faltered.

"What aren't you telling us about the elves?" Norei asked pointedly.

"What aren't you telling us about Lalala?" the Dealer of Death added with a certain undertone of menace.

"She is the most pleasant of their kind," Snarks said quickly with the slightest of cringes. "There are others—"

His body was shaken by a spasm of fear. What, I wondered, might be so terrible that it would make a demon shudder?

"She's here!" Snarks whispered, retreating even more deeply beneath his monkish cowl.

I sensed the change as well. When Lalala had arrived, the air about us had seemed alive with warmth and promise, as if her presence brought forth the finest hour of spring. Now the air seemed charged again, but in a different and much less pleasant way. The whole field about us had become unnaturally still, as if every animal, insect and blade of grass had paused, waiting, like that quiet moment that comes before the arrival of the mother of all storms.

"Doom—oom—oom—oom!" Hendrek's voice echoed in the stillness.

"I should have expected something like this," the most incredibly critical of voices replied. "Lalala has no judgment whatsoever!"

I blinked. Two new elves stood before us. And it was obvious from everything about them that one was far superior to the other.

The more prominent among the two was a woman of advanced years, a truly imposing older elf, with a gaze that seemed to peer into your inner secrets and out the other side. One look from her and you knew you were guilty, and would be guilty forever. Guilty of what? you might ask. I was quite sure she would come up with something.

All but Norei took a step away from this daunting dame. The young witch tried to stare back at the elfess with equal concentration as she asked:

"Snarks? You know this intruder?"

"C-certainly," the truth-telling demon said in an unusually uncertain tone. "She is truly the most powerful of all the elves."

"What is she, the queen?" Norei continued. "Or the all-too-influential mother of the Elvin king?"

"Worse, far worse," Snarks continued in a voice that seemed to grow closer to a whisper with every word. "She is the social director!"

"Your small, green, hideously ugly friend is correct. I am she who shows the elves the way." She glanced at the elf behind her.

With that, the much shorter and humbler, though still thoroughly magnificent elf stepped forward. His clothes were of more muted colors than the other elves', yet they seemed trimmed with gold. His face, though downturned in a gaze of humility, was fine-boned and handsome, and when he briefly smiled at me and my fellows, I involuntarily raised my hand to shield my eyes from the glare. With a single glance at his mistress, this quiet elf raised a small trumpet to his lips and blew three notes of such grandeur that the surrounding trees seemed to bow before the music.

The elfess nodded in satisfaction. "It is my responsibility to plan the parties!"

The other elf blew three further notes of equal stature and beauty, then put the trumpet away.

"But where are my manners?" the woman continued. "We have not been introduced. I am—" She opened her mouth to speak her Elvin name, as complicated as Lalala's, but where the younger elf's name was made of spring and sunshine, this older woman's seemed made of speed and industry, the syllables rushing forward like a hawk intent upon its prey. I had no desire to repeat those sounds. She had the sort of name not to be tampered with, much less pronounced.

She paused and smiled condescendingly. "But my name among mere mortals is Shamalama. Dame Shamalama to all of you." She waved at the elf who trailed behind her. "This small but noble fellow who accompanies me is—" She proceeded to enunciate a new series of astonishing sounds, different still from either of the earlier names. Rather than reflect the beauty of the first name or the onrushing grandeur of the second, the latest collection seemed composed of very small and discrete noises, with each noise very fine and individually polished. "But," she added when she was done, "you may refer to him as Ding Dong."

This latest announcement was met by a moment of silence. Most of the others seemed overwhelmed by these newest arrivals, though for somewhat different reasons than they had had with Lalala. I realized, as apprentice to the great wizard Ebenezum, it was therefore my turn to step forward and reply.

"Indeed," I began, "we are most pleased to make your acquaintance. If I may be so bold as to introduce this humble company, we are—"

The Dame Shamalama stopped my speech with a single glance. "Oh, who cares about you? Do you think someone of my stature would bother to remember any of your names? Lalala was foolish enough to invite you to the party. So you will be coming to the party." She looked away abruptly, as if it might be too painful to look at those before her. "I swear the girl has no standards at all."

"Oh, please!" Norei exclaimed. Apparently, she continued to be much less impressed than the rest of us. "I'm sure you give wonderful celebrations, but it's not as if anyone asked you here. I'm afraid we're rather busy at the moment."

Norei's words only made the dame more agitated. "You weren't too busy to listen to Lalala, were you?"

"I wasn't even here!" Norei exclaimed.

The dame sniffed, as though it was beneath her to listen further. "I try not to pass judgment on her choices." She surveyed those standing before her, much like one might study a particularly noxious fungus. "I never lower my expectations quite enough."

Tap had stepped to the front of the crowd. "Would you mind if I took a closer look at your shoes?"

Dame Shamalama looked down—way down—at the brownie. "There are reasons we are leaving. Some of them should be painfully obvious."

The elf woman's tone seemed to increase Norei's anger in turn. "Really! We will see if she takes that superior tone when the wizard arrives!"

Dame Shamalama rewarded that remark with a superior smile. "There are few wizards who are equal to the elves!"

As though on cue, a small patch of darkness appeared before us, accompanied by a silent flash of lightning, as the darkness billowed out into a man-sized cloud in a very attractive shade of green.

Now that my master had been cured, I imagined that

I would see far more of this kind of thing. It was the sort of properly dramatic arrival worthy of a great wizard.

"Indeed," the wizard Ebenezum intoned as he stepped from the dissipating cloud.

He looked at Dame Shamalama for a long moment. And she looked at him.

"Wait," my master said. "Aren't you?"

The dame gave a hesitant nod. "It's been so long. I never thought . . ."

"Shammikins?" my master asked in a voice barely above a whisper.

"Ebbybooboo?" she replied with equal uncertainty.

Apparently, they knew each other rather well.

4

"I'm a damsel in distress!
And I'll do my very best!
To find a man who'll love me 'til the end!
Now I don't trust that squire
So I'll set his pants on fire!
You can do that when a dragon is your friend!"
   —Verse Seven (of sixteen) of "A Fiery Lament"; another
      song formerly performed by Damsel and Dragon. (Be
      thankful you don't have to watch the dance routine.)

DAME Shamalama's surprise seemed to go the slightest bit sour.

"Say," she said to the wizard. "Weren't you supposed to send a spell or two my way?"

"Indeed?" Ebenezum tugged a bit at this robes. "Unfortunately, I became rather busy."

"And the social director of the elves has all this free time?" The dame stopped herself and took a deep breath.

"Oh, dear. We meet for the first time in close to a century—has it been that long?—and immediately start to argue. We didn't end on the best of terms, did we?"

"Indeed not," Ebenezum agreed. "I had always thought that such a shame, considering what we meant to each other before . . ."

Shamalama smiled at that. It made her look decades younger. "We used to have such fun together. Remember the night we scandalized the fairies?"

Ebenezum nodded with a wry chuckle. "Until that night, I hadn't thought that possible. They were taken aback by that spell that gave us those temporary wings—"

"In all the wrong places?" She winked at the wizard. "Or all the *right* places, should I say?" They both laughed heartily at that. "And that night that shocked half of Vushta? I mean, those giant bananas and tangerines—"

Dame Shamalama stopped abruptly when she realized everyone else in the clearing was watching her, some with open mouths. I snapped mine shut.

The dame's pale skin flushed the slightest shade of pink. "Oh, my. I didn't mean to get so carried away. Perhaps we should take this someplace else."

"Indeed." The wizard raised a single eyebrow in the general direction of the rest of our party. "If you will excuse us?" He waved his hands about, shouting three quick words of power. The green smoke enveloped both wizard and elf, and they were gone.

I took a deep breath. This was a side of my master that I had never seen. Of course, I realized Ebenezum must once have had a personal life, but in recent months the wizard had been too busy sneezing to do much else. Now that his allergy to magic had finally been cured, I would no doubt see many sides of my master that would be new to me. I hoped someday soon he might resume his full-time instruction, finally introducing me to the deeper secrets of magic.

Magic? I gasped. I had been so taken aback by Ebenezum's social life, I had forgotten to show my master the dark rider! I looked over to where the newcomer still glanced warily at Hubert the dragon, who for his part would occasionally send a lazy smoke ring wafting in the rider's direction. It appeared, then, that the rider wasn't planning much in the way of immediate escape. No doubt I would have the opportunity to mention the creature the next time my master happened by.

As I studied the others in my party, I noticed the unicorn push itself to the front of the crowd. The creature sighed splendidly.

"Thank goodness she's gone!"

I realized this was the first time I had seen the beast since the arrival of Dame Shamalama.

"Indeed?" I asked. "Do you have a problem with the elves?"

The creature shook its incredibly tawny mane and rolled its stunningly blue eyes. "Problem? Elves always want to make a unicorn the center of their parties. You know, put the magnificent beast on a pedestal, festoon the unicorn with garlands, leave the beast standing there for hours on end to be relentlessly admired." The wondrous animal shuddered. "Do you know what it feels like to be festooned?"

I had to admit that the thought had never crossed my mind.

"Pedestals? Relentless admiration?" Hubert jumped to the center of the clearing. "What am I thinking? We have a party coming! And not just any party! An elf party! That's as big as parties get!"

"They certainly have the best shoes," Tap agreed.

The dragon beat his tail against the ground with a resounding thump. "Maybe I could entertain? Who needs a partner who's run off with a giant? This could be a real solo career opportunity!"

"Doom," Hendrek agreed.

I wondered if the dragon's song and dance was the best way to wish the elves farewell. Still, it was good to see some of the old fire back in Hubert's attitude. It certainly wouldn't hurt to encourage him.

"Indeed," I therefore said. "We should suggest this to Dame Shamalama."

"A dragon instead of a unicorn?" the magnificent beast said skeptically. "Well, I suppose it would be easier for some of us."

Hubert flexed his wings. "Do you think she would?"

I had no idea, but I still didn't wish to dampen his spirits. "Well, my master certainly seems to have a certain influence with her."

"Hmmpphh," Norei remarked. "Well, if we have to have this elf party, at least someone will get something out of it." The young witch smiled ruefully in my direction. "Who would object to being entertained by a dragon?"

"Who indeed?" Snarks asked softly.

"Still, you sound critical of the elves." The Dealer of Death looked first to Norei, then to the rest of us, as he casually flexed the muscles in his neck. "I don't think this woman has the right attitude. You'd feel different if you had met Lalala."

"Lalala?" Norei replied. "What kind of name is—"

The assassin flexed the muscles in his arms and legs as he took a step towards the young witch. "Be careful!" The Dealer's feelings for the elf maiden seemed to be quite intense.

"We should all be careful," Norei replied evenly. She placed her hands in basic conjuring position, ready to defend herself if necessary. "As we should be considerate of each other's feelings. I am tired from working long hours with the wizard. I apologize for making assumptions about the newcomers."

"Perhaps I am overreacting." The Dealer took a step away, unflexing the muscles in his chest and upper abdomen. "I probably just need to strangle something. It has been too long. I suspect the wild pigs have been avoiding me."

Seeing Norei stand up to the assassin sent a thrill through my entire form. If only she and I might have a moment alone, I was sure I could drive all thoughts of Lalala from my memory.

"But what about my routine?" Hubert demanded. "All my material is geared towards a two-creature act. You know, I say 'Pardon my flame!' and she says 'That burns me up!' I say 'You look a little tired.' She says 'At least I'm not dragon!'"

"We remember your act," Snarks remarked quickly, "as much as we might like to forget . . ."

The dragon fluttered his wings a bit at that. "Well, it was distinctive, wasn't it?" He stared down at the packed earth beneath his feet. "Distinctive, and totally designed for two!"

Maybe I could help the dragon get past his panic. "Indeed, weren't there parts of your act that didn't require two?"

Hubert looked up, a small spark of hope in his reptile eyes. "Ah, the one-liners! The very cornerstone of vaudeville! Surely, there are a few of them I might be able to rescue." He paused in contemplation. "Ah!" He looked expectantly at his audience.

"Take my damsel, please!"

His request was met by silence.

"Wow!" The dragon waggled his scales. "I'd sure like to add that blonde hair to my golden horde!"

Some of the audience began to shuffle their feet, as though they might have business elsewhere.

"It's no use!" Hubert glumly surveyed his audience. "It doesn't work if you don't have a damsel in the first place!"

The reptile let out a low moan. "I never realized how central she was to my success. Without her, I'm a dragon without a treasure, an overgrown fire-breathing lizard without a life!"

"I couldn't have said it better myself," Snarks agreed quietly.

Hubert stared at the demon. "What was that? You're right, you know." He lumbered in Snarks' direction.

"I am?" Snarks asked as he retreated from the advancing lizard.

"I may be nothing without a partner. But who says I have to team up with that damsel?" The dragon's nostrils began to smoke. "If she can change her act, so can I! She's got a giant, has she? Well, maybe it's time for me to get a demon!"

Snarks turned a very pale green. "What have I done?"

"Dragon and demon! It still has that snappy sound! Tell me—how's your singing voice?"

Snarks seemed genuinely undone by this suggestion. "As annoying as my speaking voice, I'm afraid. And I have pledged never to use it again! I came to the surface world and joined a monastic order to get away from the bright lights of the Netherhells."

"Oh dear. I would never want to interfere with somebody's vows." Hubert surveyed the rest of the assemblage. "But my new idea has merit. And look at all the raw talent before me!"

The rest of the assemblage redoubled their foot shuffling, as though they were sure they had business elsewhere.

Hubert waved at the black-clad assassin. "Dragon and Dealer—I could sing a song, you could kill something—" The reptile paused with a frown. "—No, not enough variety." He turned to look at me. "Dragon and Apprentice—I could sing a song, you could mispronounce a spell that would go horribly wrong!" He paused again, shaking his scaly head. "That would only fly in those sophisticated big-city markets." His gaze turned closer to the ground. "Dragon and Brownie—" He shook his head as soon as the words had come forth. "—only good for shoe conventions."

"But the elves do have really nice shoes!" Tap insisted.

Hubert blinked. "Elves? I forgot the most talented among us all." He stomped his tail enthusiastically. "Lalala! She would be a natural!"

"Lalala? How dare—" The Dealer flexed his brow and scalp muscles as he advanced upon the dragon. He stepped quickly back again after a single warning glance from Norei. "I really need to find a wild pig."

"She would be in her glory!" Hubert announced to the sky. "A real class act—I'd gladly give her top billing—the Princess and Her Dragon. Think of it! Her whole life is a song. Our act would be simplicity itself. She could just pronounce her name. The crowd would go wild."

He sighed happily. "Every eye would be on her!"

"Every eye is already on her, but only mine truly belong." The Dealer's hands clutched at the empty air as he stalked the reptile. "I have not yet strangled a dragon."

Hubert took a quick hop away. Norei stepped between the two.

"An elf princess?" Hubert's voice was rather higher than before as he tried to laugh. "With a scruffy old dragon? What was I thinking?"

"Wild pig," the Dealer said from between clenched teeth as he again strode away. "Wild pig."

"But I have not yet exhausted my options," Hubert announced. "What I really need is something new." The dragon looked directly at the dark rider.

The rider tried to retreat further beneath its hood. The dragon continued to stare.

"I WAS FINE JUST SITTING HERE," the rider finally replied. "IT'S RATHER A NICE CHANGE OF PACE. NOT HAVING TO THREATEN OR ANYTHING."

Norei looked surprised at that. "So you're not looking to escape?"

"WELL, IT WASN'T HIGH ON MY LIST. DO YOU KNOW HOW LONG IT HAS BEEN SINCE I'VE HAD A VACATION?

THAT'S ONE OF THE PROBLEMS WITH WORKING FOR THE ULTIMATE EVIL. THE JOB BENEFITS ARE TERRIBLE."

"See?" the dragon enthused. "So you'll need something to do with your time!"

The dark rider shrugged its hooded shoulders. **"WELL, SOONER OR LATER OTHERS OF MY KIND WILL COME SEARCHING FOR ME. THAT'S THE WAY ULTIMATE EVIL THINKS, YOU KNOW. IT WON'T BE VERY PLEASANT, EITHER. MY SORT THREATEN EVEN MORE EFFECTIVELY IN GROUPS."**

"Perhaps we can get some of them to join as well." Hubert shot a short burst of fire overhead. "I can be very persuasive."

The rider cowered ever so slightly. **"I REMEMBER."**

It was good to finally see the return of Hubert's enthusiasm. After all, in my time as apprentice to the greatest wizard in the Western Kingdoms, I had learned that former enemies could become allies. The dark rider already seemed more accepting of our company. It wouldn't hurt to have made him comfortable enough to pass along a little information.

"Indeed," I therefore said to the newcomer, "maybe it's time to change careers? What do they call you?"

"I HAVE NO NAME. I DON'T HAVE ENOUGH SENIORITY. THOSE OF OUR KIND MUST TRIUMPH OVER A KINGDOM OF OUR ENEMIES, LEAVING THE GROUND DRENCHED IN BLOOD AND THE SKY SCOURED BY FLAME. ONLY THEN DO THEY GRANT YOU A NAME. SOMETHING EVIL-SOUNDING, FULL OF 'X'S AND 'Z'S!"

"How about Fritz?" Hubert suggested.

"WELL. IT HAS ONE Z."

The dragon's wings were twitching with excitement. "This is a whole new beginning. It'll be sensational!"

"I DON'T KNOW." The dark rider seemed to lack enthusiasm.

"Doom," Hendrek added helpfully. "You got a round of applause only a short time ago."

"We'll call it 'Capture the dark rider!'" Hubert enthused. "We barely have to rehearse! We'll simply reproduce what happened before."

The rider cringed. "MUST WE?"

Hubert didn't seem to hear. "Of course, we'd go more for drama. I'll do more than simply grab the rider. I could toss him in the air, maybe juggle him between two fiery logs."

"DO I HAVE A CHOICE?"

"I think not," the dragon replied happily. "But we'll have to find a way to incorporate the snappy patter. And music! Dragon and Dark Rider will definitely need music!" He looked back at the newly named Fritz.

"Let's hear your singing voice."

"MY SINGING VOICE?"

"Surely you folks have singing."

The dark rider considered a moment before he replied. "WE DO HAVE A FEW TRADITIONAL SONGS, ABOUT DRENCHING THE GROUND IN BLOOD AND SCOURING THE SKY WITH FLAME."

Hubert beat his tail with enthusiasm. "Exactly what I'm looking for! Why not give us a sample?"

"IT WON'T BE GOOD."

"Give it a try."

The rider took a deep breath.

The cloaked fellow made a noise rather like a rusty saw cutting deep into very hard wood. I made a valiant effort not to cover my ears.

Hubert nodded. "There's a certain power there."

"I STILL DON'T KNOW."

The dragon frowned. "Well, hurry and decide. This opportunity won't last forever!"

"Opportunity?" asked a wonderfully melodious voice. "Did I hear of something we could add to our party?"

I knew those magical tones. I spun around to see that Lalala had returned. My heart rose within my throat.

And then abruptly fell back to its proper place.

Lalala was not alone.

5

"And how might you rescue a wizard's reputation, say in a hypothetical situation that might involve an innkeeper's daughter, two or three tax collectors, and a large flock of chickens? For cases such as this, it is always helpful to remember the occasional spell of forgetfulness."

—From *The Teachings of Ebenezum Famous Saying Set*, Card 43. (Be the first on your block to collect them all.)

"WHAT'S going on here?" Norei demanded.

That was exactly what I wanted to know.

The others in our party were no more happy than I. I heard muttered words from many nearby, including such words as "Doom," "Wild Pig," and "Nice Shoes!"

Lalala was back among us. But she had returned with a male elf by her side! And not simply any male elf, and especially not some small-statured, subservient fellow like the assistant that followed Dame Shamalama. Oh no. This fellow was as tall as Hendrek, as well-muscled as the Dealer of Death, with a blue-eyed gaze more penetrating than my master at his most intense. And handsome? I feared he was as fine-looking in his way as Lalala was in hers. These elves were all too magnificent for their own good.

"And who might you . . ." Norei's voice trailed away as she caught sight of the newest elf.

"How wonderful it is to see you all again!" Lalala exclaimed. She found us wonderful? I smiled. So what if she came accompanied by astonishingly handsome elves? I would forgive her.

Lalala waved to the elf at her side, her every movement a thing of beauty.

"I thought I would bring along the prince, since he will be co-hosting the party by my side. His name is—"

She made the sound of champions who might defeat all comers with but a single glance; a sound that combined the blare of trumpets, the pounding of drums, and the cheers of a grateful nation; a sound so wondrous and overwhelming it simply made you want to sit down and surrender.

Lalala smiled winningly when the unpronounceable name was done. "But you may call him—Dadooronron."

I noticed then that Norei was staring much too fixedly at the prince. "Da—da—" was the only noise that came from her startled mouth. I looked away. It was unseemly to watch my beloved drool.

The elves had cast a spell that even affected my beloved young witch. I realized she had been right to be concerned.

As difficult as it was, 1 turned away from the lovely Lalala. I could no longer afford to be captivated by her beauty. I glanced sadly at my cohorts as they all gazed in awe at our Elvin newcomers. It fell to me to somehow bring them all back to their senses.

"But you—the young apprentice?" Lalala called.

She wanted to talk to me? Unthinking, I spun about to look at her again. She smiled just for me. Who needed that thinking stuff anyways?

"Yes, I know who you are. You and your adventures are famous, even among the elves."

She knew me? She called me—famous? I stumbled backwards, overwhelmed, accidentally bumping into my beloved Norei.

"What?" Norei shook herself. She wiped her mouth, her wits about her once more. "Thank you, Wuntvor. Can't you see what she's trying to do?"

"Do?" I blinked. I was still quite captivated by Lalala's smile. "She called me—famous."

"You can't listen to her!" Norei insisted. "All of us here

are becoming besotted with their Elvin charm. Soon, we'll be doing anything they command."

Lalala laughed as though it was all in jest. "But all we want to do is have a party!"

Dadooronron happily agreed. "I think that lovely young woman is just taking this all too seriously. Have you ever been to an Elvin party?"

"Are you talking to—me?" Norei's frosty tone melted as she gazed into the prince's eyes.

He smiled winningly. "Of course. I noticed you from the very first moment we arrived."

Norei tried to look away. "But I wanted to—you did?"

"You are the very sort of person I want to see at our party," Dadooronron continued. "Trust me. No parties are more elegant. But the most important part of our parties are the guests."

Norei's face had developed an odd sort of smile. "Really?"

The prince turned to Lalala. "Look, my sister! Her hair! Her face!" He smiled back at Norei. "How lovely you would look in a gown of Elvin silk."

The other elf was her brother? I, and all of those around me, breathed a collective sigh.

"Silk?" Norei managed.

"I would assure only the finest for one such as you," Dadooronron replied.

"You will?" The young witch's gaze appeared to grow more wide-eyed with every passing word.

The elf prince bowed ever so slightly. "It would be my pleasure for one so lovely."

Norei blushed.

"Teeheehee."

I blinked. My beloved had giggled. I had never heard such a sound come from Norei before. An alarm gonged distantly, somewhere at the very back of my thoughts. Surely I should pay attention to it, right after I listened to whatever Lalala was saying.

"Well, if my brother can donate a dress," Lalala began, looking in my direction, "I can certainly find some gentleman's clothes for this handsome lad before me."

"Handsome?" She was speaking to me. I was not only famous, I was—handsome?

The elf princess laughed with delight. "I've always wanted to teach an apprentice a thing or two."

"La—La—" I replied.

"Teeheehee!" Norei tittered at my side.

"Ouch!" I jumped a foot as something sharp poked my back. I shook myself and looked behind me.

It was the unicorn. The magnificent beast motioned with its horn that I should step back into the crowd.

I blinked. "Indeed," I called to the elves as I spun about. "If you will excuse me?"

The crowd closed behind me as I stepped away. The Dealer of Death asked if the elves needed anything strangled for the celebration, while Hendrek asked if it might be proper to add a few festive decorations to his warclub. I realized the others would barely even know that I was gone.

"What did you do that for?" I whispered to the incredible animal as I rubbed at the sore spot by my spine.

"Someone had to bring you back to your senses!" the unicorn replied with a meaningful look in its flashing eyes. "I thought at first that you would have no problem with these elves. You distracted them completely. They didn't even notice me. There was no talk of festooning whatsoever. But now . . ." The beast shook its magnificent mane. "It was the least I could do in repayment."

It paused then, taking a single step in my direction. Its wondrous golden horn glinted in the sunlight.

"Besides." The unicorn looked scornfully at the princess. "I would never forgive myself if I lost your lap to the likes of her!"

I thanked the unicorn for its kindness.

"I would gladly do it again—and more," the beast replied wistfully. "If, when this is all over, we might find a few quiet moments . . ."

"We will have to talk about it then," I interrupted gently, for I realized that I would have to speak quickly to those behind me while I still retained my wits.

"Indeed. I have things I must say!" I stepped back to the front of the crowd. I looked to the elves before us, determined to speak in a loud, clear voice. "We have other concerns beyond planning the party. We need to talk to your leaders, and ours as well. There's danger lurking near."

"Do you mean that dark rider?" Lalala only now seemed to notice the creature. "We've never had one of those at our parties! What do you think, Dadooronron?"

"Those dark robes, that glowering aura of threat, that palpable rumble of evil; it makes quite a package. The rider will be a sensation!" the prince agreed. "But not so much a sensation as a certain young witch."

"Teeheehee," Norei giggled.

The princess nodded graciously at the cloaked newcomer. "We truly appreciate all our guests, even the ones who represent Ultimate Evil!"

"LALALA!" the rider chimed in.

So even the cloaked newcomer was happy. And who could argue with such enthusiasm for one as beautiful as— No! As wondrous as these elves might be, they still didn't seem to sense the seriousness of our situation. It took all my will to form a frown. Surely, there must be some better way to get my point across.

"Indeed!" I began.

"And such a voice!" the princess clapped her hands in

delight as the dark rider added a few unintelligible shrieks. "It just gets better and better! And we owe it all to our wonderful apprentice! Whoever imagined he was so clever!"

I was famous, and handsome and—clever? The princess obviously saw deep within my soul. Why should I need to point out anything?

"Indeed?" I sighed. "Lalala."

Hubert galumphed to the forefront of our group. "But princess! It's even better than you imagine! He's not just any dark rider! He's part of my act!"

Lalala smiled politely. "Your—act?"

"Dragon and Dark Rider!" Hubert replied with a flourish of his wings. "Two of the great marvels of the mythic world, together for the first time!"

The dragon performed an impromptu soft-shoe as the dark rider flung itself away from the dancer's path.

The princess applauded with redoubled enthusiasm. "Oh, this will be the best going-away party ever! Shamalama will never be able to question our judgment again!"

"I wouldn't say that quite so quickly!" an older, more critical voice snapped back.

I blinked again. Shamalama and my master were once more among us! I still couldn't get used to the manner in which the elves silently appeared in our midst. The way they seemed to be taking over was almost enough to forget the loveliness of Lalala.

But she had called me famous, and handsome, and clever.

I sighed. Norei giggled.

The wizard studied all of us gathered in the clearing. Besides the disapproving Shamalama, Ebenezum was the only other one who seemed capable of a frown.

"Wuntvor? Is something amiss?"

Yes! There was something I wanted to tell my master. I had been thinking about it, right before the handsome, clever, famous part. What could it be?

Maybe it was to share my observations on Lalala's loveliness. I almost frowned. Not that I could really hold onto a frown with the princess so near. I looked about at those gathered in the clearing. Everyone stared at the elves—the Dealer, Hendrek, Snarks, Tap, the dark rider—

That was it! Something about the dark rider—

Could it be how lovely Lalala looked talking about the newcomer? That seemed closer to my original thought. Perhaps if I studied Lalala in more intimate detail . . .

"Ouch!"

I spun around to see a magnificent beast with a golden horn glaring past me at the princess.

"Tell your master!" the unicorn whispered in my ear. "Get that elf away from your lap!"

"Oh look!" Dame Shamalama exclaimed. "You've brought a unicorn!"

"We have?" Dadooronron asked.

"Well, perhaps I was wrong, and you *have* thought of everything! A unicorn is the center of any party!" Dame Shamalama waved at the Dealer of Death. "I'm sure we have garlands around here somewhere. Would you be a good assassin and festoon the creature for me?"

"Festoon!" the unicorn moaned, but it made no attempt to escape. The magnificent beast knew when it was trapped.

"Wuntvor?" Ebenezum insisted.

"I'm sorry master," I replied as best I could. "I find it somewhat difficult to think."

"Indeed. It is as I suspected. The Elvin charm has been laid on a bit thickly about here."

"Do you speak critically of Lalala?" demanded the Dealer of Death.

"I would find nothing to criticize," Snarks remarked gently.

"Doom," Hendrek added in a particularly dreamy tone.

"Teeheehee!" Norei added.

"Must you?" Shamalama looked directly at Lalala.

"But Auntie!" The princess pouted very prettily. "It makes the party planning so much easier!"

"It is an unnecessary expenditure of Elvin magic," Shamalama chided. "And there can be unexpected side effects. This is not the sort of behavior I need to see from my elves! After all, we may need to come back here again someday."

"Indeed," the wizard replied with a shrug. "It is easy enough to remedy." He made three passes in the air, accompanied by a single word of power.

I seemed to be doing nothing but blinking of late. The whole world was suddenly brighter, if a tad less beautiful.

Some of those around me shook their heads. Others stretched and yawned, as if just awakening from a deep sleep. The dark rider—

"The dark rider!" I announced. "I wanted to warn you about the dark rider!"

The wizard tugged thoughtfully at his beard. "Indeed, Wuntvor. I see him. There must be some new Ultimate Evil out upon the land."

"More dark riders?" Dame Shamalama spoke with great disapproval. "It's no wonder we're leaving! Still, if you've seen one Ultimate Evil . . ."

Norei gasped, serious once more. "I meant to tell you about it too. I'd completely forgotten. That elf woman— that elf man—"

"Indeed, Norei." Ebenezum glanced critically at Shamalama. "Too much elf magic does produce serious consequences."

"She's gone and done it again, hasn't she?" the dame agreed with a sad shake of her head. "Little Lalala. She just turned 163, you know. She's barely a child. Full of Elvin mischief." She smiled at Ebenezum. "You remember another young, mischievous elf."

The wizard chuckled. "How well I do. I thought your charms had smitten me forever. Sometimes I still do."

"Ebbybooboo," Shamalama purred.

"Shammikins," the wizard replied throatily.

It seemed to me there still might be a bit too much Elvin charm floating in the air.

"But the dark rider!" I interjected.

The wizard nodded, not quite turning away from the elder elf. "We'll deal with the intruder in due time. Shamalama and I have combined magics that will get him to talk."

"I'd forgotten how much I'd missed our combined magics," Shamalama said with a coy smile.

"Indeed?" Ebenezum replied. "After being so long apart, perhaps we should practice—"

"Perhaps you should pay attention to what is going on right before you!" Norei insisted.

"Norei?" Ebenezum rumbled, turning away from Shamalama at last. "You may be feeling some negative after-effects of the elf's magic."

"I am quite myself, thank you," Norei replied in a tone that said she would never giggle again. She pointed to a nearby hillside. "We may not have to worry about that particular dark rider, but how about those three other ones over there?"

I turned to see three more mounted figures in the distance, who seemed to be studying us in the most threatening way imaginable.

"OH, DEAR," Fritz intoned. "MY VACATION IS OVER."

6

"You've got to have an audience,
You've got to have a crowd!
A friendly bunch to clap and cry
And sometimes laugh out loud!

You've got to have a cheering throng
To hang on your every line!
To make you think your dancing's tops,
And your singing voice just shines!
If we don't have an audience
It can get rather boring.
Alea sits and combs her hair
And Hubert starts in snoring!
Our dancing shoes are put away;
Our hats are on the shelves;
We're forced to laugh at our own jokes,
And listen to ourselves!"
    —An all-too-long excerpt from "A Dragon's Lament," a
            later song in the Damsel and Dragon repertory,
                                    thankfully never performed

THE three dark riders waited, and watched.

For the moment, we watched back.

"Doom," Hendrek said for all of us. "We might see how they fare against my cursed warclub Headbasher."

"I could strangle at least one of them," the Dealer of Death suggested.

"They may work for the Ultimate Evil," Tap remarked bravely, "but have they ever faced Brownie Magic?"

"They are no longer there!" Lalala pointed out. Her voice, while still musical, was not the symphony I had heard before.

I looked where she pointed. The hillside was empty.

"Buckles and laces!" Tap exclaimed. "Maybe we scared them away!"

"And maybe golden coins will fall from the sky," Snarks added, his sarcasm fully restored, "and we will never have to work another day in our lives!"

"No!" the assassin announced evenly, pointing to a hill opposite the last sighting. "There they are! They haven't gone. They've only moved."

Hendrek hefted his warclub, "Doom. So they might threaten us from any point upon the map?"

"THEY WON'T MAKE A MOVE AGAINST US," cautioned Fritz, our own personal dark rider. "NOT NOW. THIS IS JUST THE HARBINGER THING AGAIN."

"Indeed?" I asked, rather unsatisfied with that response. "So what happens when this harbinger thing is finally over?"

Fritz shook his skull-like head. "I DON'T HAVE ENOUGH SENIORITY TO POSSESS THAT INFORMATION. ALL I KNOW IS THAT WHATEVER HAPPENS WILL BE WORSE. MUCH WORSE."

"Doom," Snarks murmured.

"But enough about these intruders!" Dame Shamalama announced. "Our celebrations are always trouble-free. We'll have the party tonight, then worry about those 'riders' the next morning."

Even Ebenezum seemed surprised by that. "You still intend to have the party?"

"Well, there's certainly no rush," Dame Shamalama replied with a sigh. "You remember how this works. In the time it takes for the Ultimate Evil to actually show up, a bard could write a trilogy!"

"She has a point," the wizard conceded. "Very well. Party tonight, Ultimate Evil tomorrow."

She squeezed the wizard's cheek. "That's my little Ebby-booboo."

I once again made a conscious effort to close my mouth.

"I must go consult with Ding Dong," the stately elf continued. "We shall be seeing you all, oh, on about eightish?"

"We wouldn't miss it for anything," Ebenezum assured her.

"I hope so. We still have so much catching up to do." Dame Shamalama waved a final time before she disappeared.

Ebenezum tugged at his robes. "Indeed."

"Come children!" The Dame's final words hung in the air.

"I guess that means we need to leave as well." Lalala waved meaningfully in my direction. "But we can all do our own catching up tonight, can't we?" Both she and the prince laughed with delight as they, too, vanished from view.

I felt a palpable shimmer in the air as the world shifted about me, as though I was falling one moment, then standing on my head the next. And then that feeling, too, was gone.

"Doom," Tap the Brownie whispered just loud enough to hear.

The remaining crowd stared at the space where the elves had stood, as though the rest of them, like me, were still not quite sure exactly what had transpired.

"SO WHAT HAPPENS TO ME?" Fritz asked abruptly.

Hubert blew a smoke ring of surprise. "What do you mean, what happens? Why, you have to help me get ready for our act!"

The rider grabbed at its cloak in surprise. "WE'RE STILL DOING THAT?"

"Of course! If Vushta wasn't still in such a state of chaos, I would have had banners printed. 'Dragon and Dark Rider!' My name in fiery red, yours in deepest black. Just think of the drama!"

Hubert hesitated, studying his new partner.

"Unless you'd rather go back to your old life."

"YOU'D LET ME?"

Unfortunately, there was more than a vaudeville act at stake here. "Indeed. There would have to be some further discussion—" I began.

"NOT WITH ME," Fritz interjected. "DARK RIDERS ARE TERRIBLE CONVERSATIONALISTS. IT COMES FROM SITTING AROUND ALL DAY AND BEING THREATENING. THAT SORT OF THING JUST DOESN'T LEAD TO SMALL TALK."

The rider took a deep breath. "BUT I'VE DECIDED I WANT TO STAY. IT'S TIME FOR A CHANGE OF PACE. ALL THAT GLOWERING WAS GETTING A LITTLE OLD."

"Excellent!" Hubert cheered. "Then I suggest we get to work! If the rest of you would excuse us?" He waved for the rider to hop on his back. "You know, Fritz," the dragon continued as he launched himself into the air, "I was thinking of outfitting you with a flame-proof vest . . ."

Their conversation faded as I watched the unicorn stride up to the Dealer of Death. The beast proudly held up its golden horn.

"Go ahead," it said between gloriously clenched teeth. "Get it over with!"

"What are you talking about?" the Dealer replied, absently flexing his elbows.

The unicorn sighed. "You heard the elf woman. It's time I was festooned."

The Dealer studied the magnificently suffering beast for a long moment. "I think not," he said at last. "It doesn't matter what the elf woman said. The elves had us under some sort of enchantment. That makes our contract null and void. Besides, I can sense your feelings about festooning." He flexed his feet and lower calves. "Just because I'm an assassin doesn't mean I don't have a sensitive side."

"I don't have to be festooned?" the unicorn asked in glorious disbelief. "How will the elves react?"

"Indeed," Ebenezum interjected. "I believe I can take care of that."

The unicorn still appeared uncertain. "But won't the elves miss me? I mean, not that I want to be relentlessly admired—"

"I will simply say that your absence is part of a larger plan." The wizard smiled and nodded. "Indeed. You'll be part of our big surprise."

I couldn't help myself. "Big surprise?" I asked.

The wizard turned to me. "Wuntvor, we have much to talk about. Not only do you have to be properly prepared for the elves' party, but there are a few dark riders that need to be taken care of."

I frowned. "But I thought the dame said—"

Ebenezum shook his bearded head. "Simply because the dame and I are keeping company, do not assume we think alike on all things. Especially considering what will happen tonight. Elf parties—as peaceful and festive as our dame claims them to be—are full of temptations. Even for the Ultimate Evil."

The wizard paused to look over at my beloved. "Norei? You are staring at me very intently. Do you have something on your mind?"

"Oh, dear," Norei replied, a slight blush tingeing her cheeks. "It's just that we've seen a different side of you—"

"It is the first time we've ever seen you with an old flame," I added quickly.

"Indeed, Wuntvor. Norei." Ebenezum thoughtfully tugged at his beard. "There are some relationships for the ages. Then there are some best visited every hundred years." He paused for a second, then added, "I think you might guess from our conversations that Shamalama and I did not end our earlier acquaintance on the best of terms. Last time around, our relationship was destined to end. One way or another, it is destined to end again." He smiled, as if at some private joke. "So why not send it out with a few fireworks?"

He looked at all those still gathered in the clearing.

"Just wait until you see the extravagance of an Elvin party! It's the sort of thing that even the representatives of the Ultimate Evil can't resist. Now, of course, the notoriously private elves generally try to keep these things to themselves. But what if, through an errant spell or two, some of the magic were to leak out?" Ebenezum shook his head again. "How unfortunate! The forces of evil couldn't help but come investigate."

The wizard laughed again. "Usually, when you're talking about the Ultimate Evil, only the Evil is allowed to have a good time. This time, though, I think we shall turn the tables."

"Doom," Hendrek replied softly. "But isn't what you're proposing somewhat dangerous?"

"Well of course it's dangerous!" Ebenezum's laugh had turned to more of a cackle. "There could be dark sorcery, treacherous conjurations, fountains of blood and ichor! Otherwise magic wouldn't be any fun. That allergy to spells has kept me away from danger for far too long. Now it's time to roll back my sleeves and conjure!"

"Doom," Snarks agreed.

I looked to Norei. Norei frowned back at me. This did not seem like our usual wise and cautious wizard here. I wondered if the cure to his maladies might have some side effects as well.

The wizard smiled at all of us. "I expect to see every one of you in attendance tonight. All of you may have a chance to add to the fun."

"If you might excuse me?" said a gloriously polite voice from immediately behind us.

I whirled about. It was Ding Dong, Dame Shamalama's servant. And the small but remarkably handsome elf held a package in either hand.

"These are for both of you," he said to Norei and myself, his eyes turned towards the ground, his tone magnificently obsequious. He lifted his left hand towards me. "From Princess Lalala." His right hand raised closer to Norei. "From Prince Dadooronron. Within each package you will find fine garments appropriate for you to attend a party beyond your wildest dreams."

He bowed as we each somewhat hesitantly accepted our gifts.

"By all means," Ebenezum called from behind us, "get

dressed for the ball! With what's going to happen tonight, you'll want to look your best!"

"Certainly," Ding Dong replied. "Now, if you will excuse me, I must return to the Dame Shamalama."

"I'm counting on that!" Ebenezum called as the short elf disappeared.

Now what was that supposed to mean? Unless this new symptom that the wizard showed had now robbed his speech of all meaning? If Ebenezum were to lose his senses, how could he protect us with his spells—especially if he did something to attract the three new dark riders?

"Doom," I muttered softly.

"Wuntvor?" Norei asked. "Are you quite all right?"

I blinked, as if pulled away from some private thought now lost to me. "Indeed. Why do you ask?"

My beloved frowned and stamped her foot. "I mean, buckles and laces!" Norei looked very surprised. "Now why did I say that?"

But Ebenezum didn't seem to be listening. He was, instead, staring off into space with the strangest smile.

I thought then of the unexpected consequences of too much magic; something I had seen a few too many times during the past few months. Usually I was somehow involved in the spell gone wrong. But now, what with my master's long absence from active spell-casting, along with the heavy aftermath of major elf magic lingering in the air, could something still be going seriously awry?

The Dealer of Death frowned as he absently flexed his eyebrows. "Why do I have a sudden urge to put on a show?"

Snarks stared intently at me. "Don't take this the wrong way, but I never quite realized how attractive your lap could be."

The unicorn came up behind me. "Doesn't it just make you feel like strangling something?"

"Doom," Norei whispered.

Something was definitely amiss!

"Master!" I cried, trying to pull the wizard out of his deep conjecture. Why wouldn't he listen? I shouted in frustration:

"Buckles and laces!"

And the party was only hours away!

7

"Magic is tricky business."
—Quote from at least seven different tomes (usually found within Volume 3 of the longer works) authored by Ebenezum, greatest wizard in the Western Kingdoms, during his long and glorious career

"WHAT?" My master's head snapped up, as if he had been dozing.

"Indeed!" Tap the Brownie shouted. "I fear we're caught in some unforeseen consequence of all the magic hereabouts!"

Ebenezum looked at the brownie with new respect. "You mean my Shammikins—" The half smile fell from the wizard's face as he shook his head violently. "Elf magic! It sticks to you like leeches!" He paused, the corners of his mouth twitching upwards. "They are very attractive leeches, but still—" He made three more passes in the air, shouting two quick words of power. He paused, studying the air about him before he spoke again. "That should clear up any lingering effects."

"I have never before felt like putting on a show," the Dealer of Death said evenly. "Perhaps I should strangle an elf."

"It was a very strange sensation," Norei agreed. "It felt as though our personalities were like water, flowing freely from one of us to another."

The brownie stamped his tiny feet. "So that's why we spoke with the feelings of another? Buckles and laces!"

"So I wasn't actually responsible for certain things I might have said?" Snarks asked, a note of hope in his annoying voice.

"Doom," Hendrek rumbled. "For a moment there, I actually felt cheerful."

"Indeed. I admit that this Elvin magic is trickier than I remembered." My master thoughtfully tugged at his beard. "All the more reason, I suppose, to bring a surprise or two to their little party." His smile broadened. I never realized he had quite so many teeth. "It's a pity that the surprise might turn violent. Chaos! Destruction! Rivers of blood and ichor!" My master cackled once more.

"Indeed?"

"Wuntvor?" my master replied.

"Are you sure all is as it should be?" I asked politely.

"You've had to deal with a lot lately," Norei added. "I was wondering if before the festivities began, there might be time for a little nap."

But Ebenezum only laughed again. "Nonsense! I've never felt more full of life!" He thrust his hands high in the air. Sparks flew from the ends of his fingers.

I looked to Norei. "What should we do?"

Ebenezum whooped with glee. "You must get ready for the party! We should do nothing to keep my Shammikins waiting! Waiting for blood!"

I feared the wizard was totally out of control. I wondered if there might be any way I could get him to see reason.

"But master!" I called. "You said you wanted to talk?"

"That was before!" Ebenezum called back, as he looked dramatically about. "Before I knew what was really going on! You're a clever lad, Wuntvor! You'll know what to do at the party! I will say no more! Dame Shamalama wants peaceful, does she? Blood! Ichor! A totally new kind of celebration!"

With that, my master vanished in a large amount of blue smoke.

"I'll know what to do?" I asked the spot where my master had stood a moment before.

Norei leaned close and whispered in my ear. "We must be doubly ready. We should meet before the party, once we are properly attired."

I nodded. What else could I do? I would have to take the elves' parcel back to my room at the wizards' college.

The Dame Shamalama had made her intentions quite clear. As had the wizard Ebenezum. One way or another, there was going to be a party.

*

IT was purple.

I frowned at my reflection, and my reflection frowned back at me. I didn't know if I would ever get used to my new costume. It was a gift from Princess Lalala, of course. It would be an insult to the elves if I refused to wear it. I thought for an instant that I might make some excuse to avoid the party, but no, my beloved Norei needed me. And though he might not admit it, my master might have need of me as well, if only to save him from his recent strange behavior. I would have to attend, costume or no.

It was very purple, a bright and iridescent purple, a purple that appeared to glow from within.

It was made of the finest silk, felt and brocade—shirt, vest, breeches and cape, not to mention a matching hat—all of it was purple. It fit remarkably well, no doubt a result of Elvin magic. And the shoes, well, Tap would probably faint the instant that he saw them, as they were made of the finest purple leather, accented with violet buckles. I gazed at the mirror some more. All in all, I might indeed cut the figure of a dashing young gentleman. If I wasn't quite so purple.

I supposed I should be grateful. These were by far the finest clothes I had ever worn. I had nothing even vaguely similar to take their place. And I had to go to the party, for many reasons. So purple I would be.

The party would begin within the hour. And Norei and I were supposed to meet in mere minutes. Norei! If only the two of us might have time when we weren't in the midst of some crisis, especially a crisis that involved my master.

Purple or no, it was time to quit my room and go to face my destiny.

*

I left the college, looking for a sign. That was how we would find this celebration, or so Norei had explained, just before I had left to change my clothes. It seemed that Prince Dadooronron had passed this information along to the young witch. They were passing information? I decided I did not want her to explain.

Evidently, the elves would always provide their guests with directions. These magical invitations would only appear to those already invited, thus keeping out the riffraff. Though, from the way my master had spoken, some of the riffraff might be finding some other ways to see the elves.

I stepped from the front door of my lodging house into the early night air, wondering exactly what form an Elvin sign would take.

Three paces from the entry, and I was blinded by a flashing light.

Squinting at the new illumination, I realized it was a group of yellow letters, hanging in the air.

ELF PARTY THIS WAY.

Beneath the letters was a yellow arrow, pointing right.

I turned right, walking out of the campus and into the woods beyond. It would seem that finding the signs would be the least of my worries.

I walked down a moonlit path for some minutes. Apparently, the party was outside of Vushta proper. I saw no further signs, glowing or otherwise. I assumed the elves would let me know if I wandered off the path. I noticed the trail ahead was obscured by wisps of fog. What would happen if I couldn't find the trail?

"GIVE UP."

"What?" Someone had spoken from somewhere out of sight. Yet the voice sounded familiar.

"YOU HAVE NO HOPE."

"Fritz?" I called. The new voice sounded something like the rider's, only a bit deeper and somehow slightly more threatening.

"YOU DO NOT KNOW ME," the voice replied. "YOU DO NOT WISH TO KNOW ME."

I realized that the voice and I were in total agreement. I heard a rustling in the trees on the far side of the path from where the voice had come. I still could see nothing. I was quite certain I was surrounded by Fritz's more threatening cohorts. And, having dressed in this Elvin finery, I had thought it inappropriate to carry my stout oak staff! So I had only my wits, and those few spells I might somehow remember, to save me from the riders' attack.

Leaves shook from somewhere up ahead. Leaves moved by things unseen.

"IF YOU GIVE UP NOW, WE MAY LET YOU LIVE."

There was still no sign of those who threatened me. But then, how could you possibly see dark riders after dark? Unless you were close enough to see their glowing eyes.

The path turned before me. I saw a faint illumination around the bend. I cautiously approached the light.

TURN HERE FOR ELF PARTY, more yellow letters announced. So I hadn't lost my way! If I could find the others, we'd give these dark riders a real fight! I redoubled my pace down the forest path.

"SURRENDER," a voice said close by my right.

"DESPAIR," another added, not too far on my left.

"NO HOPE," a third joined in from somewhere overhead. I redoubled my pace again, breaking into a steady trot.

"DESTRUCTION," the right-hand voice said, perhaps a little behind me now.

"GIVE UP," said the one on the left, a bit more distant still.

"Doom." I blinked. That last word was spoken by a different voice entirely. Hendrek stepped from between the trees. "We were wondering when you would arrive."

"Arrive?" I asked, still a bit startled.

Hendrek pointed at an even larger sign than the two I had seen before. This time, the yellow letters announced: *ELF PARTY JUST UNDER THIS HILL.*

An arrow beneath the sign pointed straight down.

I let out a long breath. "I guess I have arrived." I noticed that the rest of my companions stood just beyond the yellow glare. They waved as I approached.

"Well, look at our apprentice!" Tap the Brownie saw me first. "And look at those shoes!"

"That costume is quite striking," the Dealer of Death rumbled.

"That's one word for it," Snarks agreed.

I felt my elbow nudged gently by a golden horn. I turned to see the unicorn, its eyes wide in wonder. "Don't listen to them," the magnificent beast murmured throatily. "Your lap has never looked better. Unicorns and purple just naturally go together."

The unicorn seemed gloriously subdued. "This changes everything. My reaction to the elves seems so petty. Somehow, I miss the garlands now. Never have I found purple so attractive!"

Oh yes. Purple. Running from the dark riders, I had completely forgotten the color of my attire. At least the others seemed truly back to normal. If we could keep our wits about us, we might still succeed!

"Wuntvor?" I head Norei's voice behind me. I turned and lost my heart for good.

While I was wearing purple, Norei was dressed in a

glowing gown of forest green, a color that contrasted wonderfully with her pale skin and auburn hair. I had never witnessed anything quite so lovely.

As wonderful as the elves appeared, there was something almost otherworldly about their beauty. Not necessarily a bad thing, until I saw this vision before me. Norei was beyond perfection. Norei was beautiful and real. If I had not been smitten with her before—well, now I was determined she would be the woman with whom I would share the rest of my life.

"You are—" The words choked in my throat. I couldn't breathe. I feared my face would soon match my clothes.

She smiled back at me. "I have to admit, I rather like this gown. Not the sort of thing a young witch usually wears. But come. We have to deal with the elves."

She held out her hand for me. I somehow managed to breathe.

"You look very handsome, in a purple sort of way." I knew she was teasing me, and I didn't mind. I could look at this woman forever.

"We need to plan for whatever happens—" She pointed to the hill beneath the sign. "—when we go in there."

"Perhaps we should stay together," I suggested. "We are always stronger as a team."

"I would like that very much. But I fear the elves will draw us apart. The one thing we do know is that all the magic hereabouts makes things very unpredictable. No doubt we can get help from the others, if our friends can keep their senses about them."

I thought about our last encounter with elf magic, and how I'd been repeatedly startled by the unicorn. "We need something to bring us back to our senses."

"Exactly." Norei nodded. "I may be able to enable a specific phrase to have a charge of power. If either of us feel ourselves slipping away, we can shout the words and startle our wits free of Elvin spells!"

"Mayhaps something we would not ordinarily say?" I realized then that I had not told anyone about my recent experience with the dark riders, nor the proximity of the three threatening creatures. Surely Norei should know about this, too.

"The dark riders——" I began.

"Are our friends!" Norei interrupted with a delighted smile. "That should be strange enough to shock us to our senses!"

"Um," I replied. I still hadn't told her about the dark riders. But she was smiling just for me! No, no matter how beautiful she was I had to focus on the danger. Hers was an excellent plan, except for one thing.

"But what if the Elvin magic is too fast for us?" I asked. "We could be trapped in this party—forever!"

Norei nodded, her smile intact. "I have a plan for that as well. If, after a few moments' time, we do not reemerge, I've asked the unicorn to come in after us. The beast seems the only one totally immune to the power of the elves."

I found myself smiling in return. "You have thought through every possibility. Truly, you are a wonder!" I sighed. How much more was Norei than simply beautiful!

She smiled ruefully. "Well, I may have certain abilities. But you do as well, not the least of which is that remarkable ability to survive. Just think of the adventures you've had, the foes you've faced, everything from the fiercest demons to Death himself! And still you triumph." She squeezed my hand. "Together, Wuntvor, we will survive this as well."

I frowned as I thought about what Norei had said. I did survive, didn't I? No matter that I had survived due largely to luck, the intervention of my friends, the spells of the wizard Ebenezum, and half a dozen nearly impossible accidents that even I couldn't explain. I was still standing here, looking straight into the eyes of my beloved. I could face any danger with Norei at my side!

Danger? I still hadn't told her!

"But, the dark riders——" I began.

I looked up at the distant sound of trumpets.

Ding Dong stood before us.

"The party begins! And you are our most special guests." He waved for the two of us to follow. "I will guide you past those magical devices set to destroy the unwelcome."

"But what of——" Norei began, waving in turn at the nearby cluster of companions.

Ding Dong peered at the others in some distress. "I suppose they can come as well! The creatures Lalala invites!"

Norei called for the rest of the party to hurry and follow us.

The Elvin servant smiled as he waved us all forward. The rest of our companions clustered close behind.

"Come and experience the wonder," Ding Dong announced, as the distant trumpets sounded once again. "It will be a party like no other."

Even he did not realize the truth of his words.

8

"You spin up on your toes;
You spit a bit of fire;
It's really such a romp.
You skip on down the street
With your big old dragon feet
And then you start to stomp! Stomp! Stomp!"
                    —The very beginning of "The Dragonetta,"
                    a Damsel and Dragon–created dance craze,
                        which fortunately has yet to catch on

THE hill opened before us, as if someone had flung aside a pair of fifty-foot-high earthen doors.

We were ushered into what I first thought was a vast hall,

with a hundred great torches illuminating the inside of the world. I saw Dame Shamalama before us in the distance, smiling, waving us forward, Princess Lalala on her one hand, Prince Dadooronron upon the other.

"Now we can truly begin!" she announced over the noise of the crowd.

I felt the same strange sensation as I had when the elves had left us earlier in the day. It was as though I was separate from the world around me, and was whirling about into a place that never was. I looked around me anew. What I thought were walls were gone, and the vistas about us now never seemed to end. It was like stepping into another world.

It might have been dark outside, but the inside of the hill was filled with the bright sun of noon. Once beyond the earthen doors, I saw no further sign of walls or support columns, only rolling hills covered by flowers.

I looked behind, and saw that Norei and I were still trailed by Snarks, Tap, Hendrek and the Dealer. The unicorn was no longer with us, no doubt due to Norei's plan. All four of the others, even the usually impassive assassin, gaped at their surroundings. The elves were making a good first impression.

A tall, authoritative elf stepped forward, intercepting Hendrek. He pointed to the doomed Headbasher. "I'm sorry, but you cannot bring your weapon here."

"Doom," Hendrek replied. "What do you suggest I do with it?"

"Just put it in the coat room." The elf clapped his hands, and a blue circle appeared before Hendrek that grew to the size of a window. Even from a distance, I could see the place beyond was crowded with hundreds of pikes, swords, bows, knives, whips, chains, maces, hooks and various other instruments of destruction—an awful lot of weapons, I thought, to bring to such a peaceful party.

"Sorry for the crowding," the elf said in a matter-of-fact tone. "Just fling the club anywhere. We'll make sure you get it back when the party's over."

Hendrek did as he was told. The window promptly snapped out of existence, and the tall elf disappeared in the crowd.

"Doom," Hendrek said again.

"We have other weapons that they cannot take," the Dealer of Death said evenly, flexing muscles randomly across his body.

"Not to mention Brownie Power!" Tap enthused.

"And the strength of unrestrained sarcasm," Snarks added. "I already think these elves need to be taken down a peg or two."

I looked back out to the festivities around us. It certainly was grand. There were long tables to either side of us, piled high with food and flowers, and beyond the victuals were what I took to be large barrels of ale and even larger vats of wine. Before us were a group of strolling Elvin musicians, playing softly but so sweetly that their tunes might break your heart. Beyond them were small groups, perhaps hundreds of them, standing and chatting here and there as far as I could see. While those around us were mostly elves, I noticed representatives of a couple dozen other species, from demon to dwarf, banshee to bog wombler, and even a couple of types that I had never seen before.

At the very center of the festivities was a raised platform, on which I had previously glimpsed the social director, prince and princess. After I had taken in the rest of my surroundings on my stroll into the party, I looked back again at the three. I was much closer than I had been before. I was immediately taken by the princess's smile.

"There you are!" Lalala said brightly.

"Wuntvor!" Norei whispered in my ear. "Remember, we must be vigilant!"

"Vigilant," I repeated as I smiled at Lalala.

"Ah, princess, how clever of you to find us!" Dadooronron joined in. "And that gown! Could it be? I have never
seen so enchanting a witch!"

Norei just barely suppressed a giggle.

"Vigilant!" she whispered instead.

Dame Shamalama floated down from the platform to
land a few paces before us. "But we must introduce you to
the others!"

A dizzying array of elves strode past us, all in bright and
varied costumes, each outfit more fantastic than the last,
and some of which, frankly, made my purple attire look
downright subdued. In short order, we were introduced to
Shalala, Doolangdoolang, Dowahdiddy, Shoopshoop, Mojo,
Beebopaloobop, Dingaling and more elf names than I could
possibly remember.

"But I mustn't forget our senior elves!" Shamalama continued. An elderly couple strode before us. "May I present
Shanananana-nanananana and Getajob."

But my attention was suddenly elsewhere.

My master, the wizard Ebenezum, had arrived as well,
appearing upon the dais as a stylish, deep blue cloud that
quickly dissipated to reveal the wizard within. He had also
dressed for the evening. Instead of his everyday wizard's
robes in basic black, tastefully inlaid with silver moons and
stars, he had opted for robes of royal blue, with the moons
and stars scattered about in threads of gold. In my opinion,
it made him look like quite the important mage-about-
town.

A number of tall and sturdy elves seemed to gather
around him, paying strict attention to his every word.

"Doom," Norei whispered by my side.

"Don't you mean 'vigilant'?" I whispered back. But I noticed I was growing upset as well, the kind of upset that
could only be calmed by strangling a wild pig.

"Buckles and laces!" the Dealer of Death exclaimed. "It's happening again."

"Too much magic!" Hendrek agreed. "It's washing over us again. If only I knew a spell that would help. Unless another spell would be too much?"

"This is already too much!" Snarks wailed. "I will not succumb—" He tripped over his own robes and almost fell to the floor. "Why am I so clumsy?"

But we all knew that I was usually the clumsy one. How could we do anything, individually or collectively, if our personalities were caught in this mystical whirlwind?

I tried to suppress my urge to strangle as I looked about at the others. Dame Shamalama had left us and was now approaching my master.

"A properly dramatic entrance, my dear Ebenezum," she called.

He waved at the score of tall, watchful elves that stood between him and the rest of the crowd. "And I am surrounded by members of the Elvin Guard?" Ebenezum shrugged. "I expected no less."

"Well, forgive me, my wizard, but there have been certain rumors about your strange behavior of late—"

"Rumors?" Ebenezum replied casually. "But that might mean you were spying on me?"

Dame Shamalama's tone grew much cooler. "Elves always need to know the moods of those who are coming to their parties. I don't know if I would call that spying—"

The wizard threw his hands up in disgust. "You spy but you do not listen! You don't even realize when you have danger in your midst!"

"Danger?" The dame laughed haughtily. "There's nothing any wizard can dish out that my elves can't handle!"

The wizard shook his head. "I wasn't talking about me."

"Then were you talking about your surprise?" Dame Shamalama insisted.

Ebenezum smiled ruefully, as though the dame's words did nothing but confirm his deepest suspicions.

"It's a surprise, yes. But it doesn't come from me."

A new voice boomed over the crowd, drowning their conversation:

"And now, ladies and gentle elves! Direct from command performances in Vushta and parts west, we present the newest sensation in all the nations! The creatures that you want to feature! The masters of flying fire and dread darkness, all in one fabulous package. Yes, give a hearty round of applause for 'Dragon and Dark Rider'!"

"This is your surprise?" Dame Shamalama asked in the stunned silence that followed.

"Thankfully, no," Ebenezum insisted. "As I said, the surprise isn't coming from me. And this definitely isn't it."

"No Auntie! This is the entertainment!" Lalala interjected brightly.

"It will be the best party ever!" Dadooronron agreed.

Whatever color was left drained from the dame's pale Elvin complexion. "I let them plan the party. What have I done?"

The sky was filled with fire.

The crowd gasped as a figure swooped down from far above. It was Hubert, and on his back was the dark rider.

They began to sing:

> "Things are spooky!
> Things are scary!
> Whether you're elf or dwarf or fairy;
> The Ultimate Evil is on its way!
> They'll kill you if they see you
> And then they'll fricassee you,
> But a dragon comes to save the day!"

Actually, Hubert did most of the singing. But the rider moaned to great effect.

The dragon landed and the dark rider jumped from his back. Both did a short but effective soft-shoe routine. The crowd stared in stunned silence.

The dance ended, and they began the second verse:

> "Oh they'll bake you into muffins,
> They'll be chewy, nasty tough ones!
> There'll be no way to get away!
> But as you're screaming no,
> Before they grind your bones to dough!
> A dragon comes to save the day!"

This was going to do for a while, wasn't it? At least in Damsel and Dragon songs one had the option of watching the lovely Alea. During this, one had no options at all.

"Buckles and laces!" Snarks covered his mouth in horror. "What did I say?"

"Doom," the brownie agreed.

"It would certainly be better if I had something to strangle," Norei concurred.

"Maybe we could all just strangle ourselves and get this over with," I muttered. Now where had that negative thought come from?

Lalala screamed and pointed beyond the performing pair.

The dark riders had appeared among us, waving their deadly looking scythes in the air as they cackled spectrally.

I realized the show could no longer go on.

Thankfully, we were under attack.

9

"All's well that ends."

— Fragment from *The Uncollected Notes, Sayings, and Gutter Sweepings of Ebenezum, Greatest Wizard in the Western Kingdom*, third edition

THE atmosphere of the place had changed yet again.

The merriment was gone. Instead, the arrival of the dark riders seemed to bring a wave of gloom, as if we were already defeated before the fight had begun. Despair. Destruction. No hope. Surrender.

"Doom," Norei cursed. "If only I could remember my spells!"

"I can remember some spells," Snarks volunteered. "After a fashion. If I can remember how to pronounce them."

Things were looking ever more dire.

"I will not allow this!" Dame Shamalama cried. "We elves are not defenseless. Lalala! Dadooronron! To my side! We must spread all our charm, now!"

The three elves huddled together. And I began to feel different yet again. I was no longer hopeless. Life was wonderful. Especially a life full of elves! I smiled. "Doom," I murmured, but I really didn't mean it.

The Elvin Guard had all somehow been armed with swords and lances, and were advancing on the riders. I realized they must all have gone to the coat room when I wasn't looking. Clever of them to bring all those weapons to a party that didn't allow them. But the company of elves could get nowhere near the dread trio. The dark riders swung their scythes through the air, causing a great whooshing sound, and a force that pushed the elves away. A pair of the noblest among the noble managed to edge their way close, but each was rewarded with a face full of hoarfrost, leaving both the elves frozen and blue.

This was terrible! I needed to help somehow. I used to be able to perform some magic, didn't I? But now I was having trouble remembering exactly who I was.

"Buckles and laces!" I screamed in frustration.

Another wave of good feeling swept over me. The dark trio seemed to slow their assault, but so did the elves surrounding them. And who could blame any of those before me? We all wanted to do nothing but bask in the glory that was Elfdom!

"It will not work, Shamalama!" cried my master, the wizard Ebenezum. "Their evil is too great!"

"You have always underestimated the elves!" the dame shot back. "Perhaps I cannot subdue them by myself, but Lalala and Dadooronron will join me!"

"Doesn't anyone want to hear the third verse?" Hubert wailed.

What was all this fighting, anyway? At the very least, it was in extremely bad taste. I just wanted to worship at the feet of Lalala.

The dark riders pressed forward. I was washed over with a wave of despair, followed by a new wave of love and happiness. The waves were coming faster now, overlapping, the emotions swirling together. Perhaps I felt suicidal love and happiness. Or perhaps I would be truly at peace if I flew into a murderous rage. Then again, perhaps it would be best if I just sat down and fell asleep for the next year or two.

"No!" the wizard insisted. "We need real magic to turn back this evil!"

He flung back his sleeves, ready to add his sorcery to the magic of the dark riders and the elves.

It was, I realized later, more magic than we had ever seen in one place and one time. So much magic that adding more might result in serious consequences.

Halfway through his second word of power, Ebenezum began to sneeze. It could have been the last vestiges of his allergy, or his body falling back on an all-too-familiar physical reaction.

Whatever was in that sneeze changed everything.

A great wind flattened us all. When the gale was past, and I could raise my head, I saw three separate groups of elves, each facing their own dark rider. The elves had skill and stamina, but the riders seemed to hold vast reserves of dark power. The elves darted forward individually, trying to break through the riders' guard, but the dark ones beat back every attack, sometimes through physical force, at others with their mystic might. Neither side seemed to have the advantage. I wondered why I should care.

"Ouch!"

I leapt up and spun about.

It was the unicorn!

"I got here as quickly as I could!" the magnificent beast cried over the sounds of battle. "I realized your lap was in mortal danger!"

My master sneezed again, the great nasal force propelling a pair of elves into one of the riders. The sinister fellow crumpled beneath the onslaught.

"Ouch!"

"Ouch!"

"Ouch!"

The unicorn quickly nudged our other companions, who rushed en masse towards another of the conflicts. The brownie leapt into the fray, trying to strangle the dark rider with his tiny hands, while Snarks had somehow gotten Headbasher and was doing his best to lift the cursed and heavy warclub.

"Wait!" I heard Hubert's voice above the cacophony. "He's part of my act!"

I looked about and saw a fourth group of armed elves advancing on Fritz, who was warily tap dancing the other way. In the meantime, I could hear the lovely Lalala scream as the two remaining riders rushed away from their attacking elves and straight for the podium, obviously attempting to take the most powerful elves as hostages.

All this was fascinating, I thought, but shouldn't I be more involved?

The dragon blew a pillar of fire above the elves surrounding Fritz. They ignored him.

"Don't you understand?" Hubert insisted. "This dark rider is our friend!"

I felt like I had been punched in the heart.

"Vigilant!" Norei screamed close by my side. "We have to defeat these creatures and save the day!"

"Of course!" This was clear to me as well. "Do you have any idea how to do this?"

The young witch frowned. "I would if I could remember magic! But all I can think of are clever quips!"

"Magic?" I replied. "I can remember magic!" All I had to do was concentrate.

Yes! I knew what to do exactly! I could feel the magic rushing towards me.

The two riders advancing on Lalala screamed as they were covered by an avalanche of shoes.

*

THINGS got back to normal in a remarkably short time.

"You wanted to prepare us for danger, didn't you?" Dame Shamalama asked ruefully after she had finally calmed down.

The wizard Ebenezum blew his nose and tugged his robes back into place. "Well, yes. I tried to tell you there was danger—"

"And I wouldn't listen."

"But you would believe what your spies told you."

"Of course! Knowing what we shouldn't is a cornerstone of the elf mystique! So you made us believe that you were the danger!"

"Your Elvin Guard was fully prepared," the wizard agreed.

Shamalama shook her head. "Ebbybooboo, I'm afraid you know elves a little too well. Perhaps that's why we only see each other every hundred years."

"Indeed," was Ebenezum's only reply.

"But it was the rest of you who saved the day!" Dame Shamalama smiled upon those gathered before her. "Thanks to you, we will deal with the captured dark riders, and perhaps learn the true plans of the Ultimate Evil!"

The Elvin Guard cheered.

"There you are, apprentice!"

I turned to see Lalala by my side. Even without the aid of elf magic, she was quite striking.

"I never really got a chance to get to know you," she said softly, "and now that you've saved us—"

"Yes?" asked Norei, suddenly at my other side. "What do you plan to do?"

"We have to go," Lalala said sadly. "Once you have a goodbye party, you have to say goodbye. But I couldn't leave without a thank you."

I felt a tiny shock as her lips brushed against my forehead. And then she was gone.

"I'm glad to see her go," Norei said simply.

"You're not the only one," the unicorn called from somewhere nearby. "One big visit from the elves, and I'm still garland free!"

"Norei," a deep voice spoke from nearby. "We also did not have the chances I had hoped for."

"Vigilant!" Norei replied. "Dadooronron. I think it's best if you go, too."

"If you truly think so," the elf prince said sadly, then he, too, was gone.

Norei squeezed my hand. "It's for the best. They were a beautiful dream, but we're looking for reality."

"And there's nothing more real than Brownie Power!" Tap popped into the space between Norei and myself. "What a rain of shoes! I couldn't have done it better myself!"

"And we are back to ourselves!" the Dealer of Death stepped near, idly flexing everything. "It is good to know your fellows, but perhaps not quite that well."

"Doom," Hendrek agreed.

"I may have to go somewhere until the nightmare of thinking like a brownie goes away!" Snarks added.

"We may all need to take a day or two to recuperate," Ebenezum said as he approached. "I certainly know I've had too much magic lately."

"We'll be going then!" Dame Shamalama called. "See you in a century, Ebbybooboo!"

Then she and all the elves were gone.

"A day or two to practice?" Hubert enthused. "We can really hone the act!"

"**DO I REALLY HAVE TO LEARN TO TANGO?**" Fritz moaned.

"A day or two off?" Norei looked at me. "Whatever shall we do?"

I knew we'd think of something.

Except the Queen

by Jane Yolen and Midori Snyder

What worse fate can be suffered by an immortal than to be stripped of magic and banished to our world to grow old and die? This is the punishment visited upon the fairy sisters Serana and Meteora for playing a trick on their queen. But when evil omens begin to accumulate, even without their powers the siblings know the queen has more convoluted plans for them. "Except the Queen" is a winning mixture of dark magic, mysterious schemes, threatened lovers, unexpected laughter, and a few good-old homegrown witches with a civilized taste for single malt scotch.

Jane Yolen has been called "the Hans Christian Andersen of America" and indeed may have written more genuine fairy tales and similar fantasies than any other contemporary writer. Most of her 250 books, which include The Princess Who Couldn't Sleep, The Witch Who Wasn't, The Wizard of Washington Square, *and my personal favorite,* Dove Isabeau, *are intended for children and young adults, but she has a number of short stories and novels for adults as well. A mother, grandmother, poet, storyteller, and editor, she writes, "I live part-time in Massachusetts and part of the year in Faerie, otherwise known as Scotland."*

Her collaborator, Midori Snyder, was raised with so many multicultural influences that her writing reflects her considerable knowledge of international myth, as evidenced in fairy tales and fantasy novels that include Beldan's Fire, The Flight of Michael McBride, The Innamorati *(which won the Mythopoeic Award for Novel of the Year),* New Moon, Sadar's Keep, *and* Soulstring. *She lives with her husband, Stephen, and children, Carl and Taiko, in Milwaukee. When she is not writing, she studies karate, plays the mandolin, and makes theatre masks.*

My dearest Meteora,

The view from my window is nothing like the deep woods: a few spindly trees sending out fervent prayers for a spring that never quite comes. The pigeons crowd my windowsill hoping for a blessing of crumbs. How I wish they could understand that with this enforced middle age has come a loss of magic, something I have never quite understood but feel full well. In my head I am more powerful than ever, making swift connections, understanding life as never before. But evidently the body is the source of fey energies.

Except for the Queen.

Always except for the Queen.

Who knew that bitch would go on forever?

My fondest wishes (oh that I could
really grant them still),
Serana

My dear Serana,

It took a while to receive your letter. The child in the postman's costume who comes once a day can scarcely read well enough to deliver mail. Today a neighbor's bills were cluttering my box and when I went to redeliver them at the flat downstairs, I discovered that the tenant had received all of my precious mail. A scruffy boy with an indolent face and dirty fingers handed me the lovely lavender envelope of your letter. Remember how we used to amuse ourselves by turning that kind into runaway dogs? Oh, how my body twitched to do the same again.

I shall tell you of my living situation only if you promise not to feel any more sorry for me than I do for myself. After they banned us—and in full summer no less—I found shelter in this city in an attic apartment of an old building not too far from a lake. Except for the crows residing in the elms outside my window, my first month was quiet. Alas, in the fall the house erupted with college students and now my head aches from the constant din. Were we ever that noisy? That loud in our passion? Our play or mischief-making? Do they never study, these students? I light candles, mutter the old words, thump around the house and, when all else fails, as well you know it does, I bang my broom against the wooden floor and wonder how I could have become so powerless. At least Baba Yaga has her iron teeth.

As to the Queen, I can guess why she still rules. Who knew the threads of power would become unknotted and leave us as we are now? As pretty seedlings we gave away our wishes like kisses, squandering our power, giving it to lovers, to children, to friends, never thinking for a moment we might be emptied like an upturned basket of seed corn left to scatter.

Except for the Queen.

She was always more clever than us. She clamped her wishes tight between her thighs and made those boys cough up their treasures before bestowing one small brush of her lips. Even old men like Merlin made fools of themselves, and she took him for everything he had. She has made a fey's life of stealing and hoarding power for the purpose of her own glamour. And now as we grow old, she exists, an unseemly youth masking an old nag.

There's a girl crying in the flat below. Remember when our hearts used to break like that? I shall go down there. I may not be able to give the brute who has hurt her so a face full of warts, but I can still make tea and offer a comfortable shoulder.

My loving best to you as always,
Meteora

My dear Meteora:

How your letter, the script as perfect as new ferns uncurling, made me recall those wonderful times. Wonderful except for the Queen, of course. My small finger itches where the magic used to reside. Your new place of residence sounds edenic compared to mine, but then you were always luckier. I live on a side street in N—a city that could delight the senses if it just learned to pick up its trash. The collectors have gone on strike again today. That is three days in a row, a not-so-magical number when it comes to garbage. And to think I used to love turning over a farmer's midden heap if he forgot to leave me milk. Well, multiply that midden by a million and you have what assaults my nostrils today. I have had to keep the window closed tight, which gives me the screaming megreems. These city folk do not understand that fairies—even middle-aged ones—need air.

Humans really are the dregs. Forget that child weeping downstairs, or turn her heart to stone. It is better that way.

Ever thine,
Serana

Dear Serana,

You're right. I never should have gone downstairs to that weeping girl. What was I thinking? I offered solace and the surly child snapped at me, clutching the door as though she might slam it in my gentle face. *Who did I think I was? Her fucking mother?* she screeched. Dreadful-looking creature she is, too. Woeful offspring of misery. Cropped hair, sticky as thistle and a green that even Puck would find offensive. Only a troll could love the silver rings that pierce her brows. Her eyes, which beneath all the black running tears might well have been a pretty blue, were red and baleful with weeping. And no wonder she was a crying and wretched thing. Some dark Unseelie trickster has tattooed her neck with the twisted sign for trouble and its oily aura swirls around her. Take care, my gentle sister, we are not alone in this world and we do not have the protection of our court.

I let her slam the door and made my way upstairs without so much as uttering a word. I do not want to help her, or call the Unseelie to my side. But Serana, dearest Serana, these mortal children aren't all dregs. Just hopelessly misguided and dangerously ignorant. And haven't we in our own past made much sport of their innocence? We were scarcely older in our time than that girl down there and yet we had so much power. Capricious, we bestowed our love on some and our scorn on others. We imagined our power, like our lives, to be immortal. If only we had known this age would creep like a canker in the bud.

I'm tired tonight, sitting at my candle, writing these lines to you as outside early spring storms weep against the window. The changes have come slowly, but now that they are here, accumulated into unfamiliar shapes, I am surprised by this foreign body, these veined hands that can write letters but no longer shape the destiny of others.

Forgive my melancholy. It comes more often these days. I wait for your letters, Serana, your anger and your sharp tongue. It will be a knife to cleave me from these dreary thoughts!

Always yours,
Meteora

My dear Meteora:
I sit here in the dismal dark which had once been such a friend. No candlelight to pierce the gloom. Only the memory of your last letter to warm me. I am cold, cold, Meteora, who was once so warm. Fire shot through my veins and I remember so often dancing till dawn. The partners we had then. The daft little fauns with their capering legs and high

trilling giggles. The village men, half-drunk on our wine, half-drunk on our beauty. Or at least on the glamour we cast over ourselves.

What I miss is not the glamours, nor the dances, nor the glowworms caught in the trees for lanterns. I miss most the friendships, for you are but a piece of paper and ink to me now. Human friendships seem as gossamer as their lives.

And yet. And yet.

And yet I think I am missing something. That *we* are missing something, dearest Meteora.

Let me try to explain. Everything the Fey do has meaning. This we know from our acorn cots. And yet, sundering us from companionship, the friendships of touch and taste and the intertwine of limbs? All this seems to have none. So I have been asking myself these past gloomy days, what meaning have we not understood, so deep in the gloom of these new lives?

Here, I have lighted a candle. See how it pushes back the dark. Where it touches the edges of the room, there is a soft glow, like those living lanterns in our trees. What if, old friend, we are meant to be glowworms in these, our last years? Shall we try to hang upon humanity's top limbs and give them light? Is that the meaning? In other words—that green-haired downstairs child of yours. Can she be helped?

I have a similar child who sleeps on my doorstep upon occasion. He is thin as a scare-bird, his hair a toss of straw. He shivers and moans in his sleep. I touched him once and his dreams spoke of monsters that would fright even you, Meteora. His blood runs with something the colour of bile. His anger is as bitter as vetch. He has been vomited into the world by something even he does not dare name. What if I tried to help him as I would a wandering, love-lost fey?

Oh I know what you will answer even before you say it, for it is what a moment ago I would have said myself. That we should be finding ways to return to Faerie, not meddling in humanity's running sores. Well, our own threw us out, Meteora. For some reason. (And not just because of that silly trick.) All we have left are these children and our glowworm dreams. Even if we cannot help them—you with your tattooed girl, me with my straw-haired boy—we shall at least be back in the game.

Your old dear,
Serana

Dearest Serana,
Indulge me, sister. There is much to tell you. Sit in your favourite chair—that one with the lion feet that you complain about having to trim the talons. I know how safe you feel there and its rumbling purr soothes you. Fill your crystal thimble from the whiskey bottle you hide under the bed. Oh my dear, forgive me when I tell you that fiddler has long forgotten you and will not be back for it. It is his loss, of course.

So much has happened since last I wrote, and your letter has coincided with my news in wondrous ways. This is what comes of being sprouted from the same pod. They tried so hard to separate us, knowing that one alone was trouble enough but two together was an invitation to chaos. Well, we've had our fun, it's true. We have always have been irrepressible, even in our gloom, but especially in our righteous indignation. It's no doubt why we are out here, in this mortal place. The trick was harmless, hardly worth the notice of the council, and yet I believe now that the Queen used it as a ruse, gladly willing to sacrifice a moment's modesty in exchange for something craftier. How else could she have so easily fallen for our sport? And yet, there she was, head thrown back, twined like mistletoe with that common mason who was laying his mortar in a new trough. If only I could have kept from laughing, she might never have been able to catch us. I flame to think she made us confess our part before everyone and then had us sent away. Punished as though we were children! And crossing the border to this world, how our bodies aged in so brief a moment.

But the events of the last weeks have convinced me that she wanted us gone for other reasons. Gone, my sister, from all that we knew, from all our joinings, our friends. Gone for reasons I cannot put my weathered thumb upon. But mine nose does itch and my eyes tear. We have always been too clever for our own good.

Now you are sitting up. I know you. Pour another dram and take it quick, even though it burns the throat. I need you to see the game that has no rules, and here in this place, so many more players, perhaps even my muddled green-haired child.

There is a pattern emerging like silk from the spider, spinning in all direction threads that tremble with possibilities. Had we remained in our world, the Queen might well have feared our curious natures. But out here, separated from each other, bereft of the greater portion of our power, and seeming weak with new-found age, we present no threat. The Queen no doubt assumes we will stumble into nothing but our own misery. How little she knows our true gifts, those that have nothing to do with magic. We sense the spider's thread, feel it come over us even here like a troubling sadness because unlike the Queen, it is our nature to push back the dark. We have been miserable, weeping into our candles, melancholy and dour. But it is not for ourselves that we feel this, but the others who cannot know they are being played.

But what do I *really* know? Only a little, but it is a rough-coated seed.

I have a garden now behind the house. Something I acquired when the last of the nestlings moved away from downstairs. A hardscrabble bit of soil that I have tended back in the semblance of health. A few days ago I found a man, bare feet the colour of mud, wandering the spiral path through my recently planted flowers. He looked wild, like one of those that sleep in the parks at night, dark shuffling men who will not meet your gaze. Here he was, grey-headed as the hare, bearded and unkempt, dressed in faded trousers and torn shirt. I rattled the stones in my pocket as he bent to touch the blossoms of fairy spuds. He straightened when he saw me, brushed the dirt from his hands and smiled. There was nothing of the haunted men in his face. Those eyes were blue and smooth as robin's eggs, but the smile, crooked to one side, made me wary all the same.

"Name's Jack," he said and gave me his hand.

Jack. Who could ever trust a mortal with such a name? The hand was big, rough callused and dry, the fingernails ivory ovals. I gave him my hand, fool that I am, and he received it with surprising gentleness. He waited, until I remembered that here we are expected to give our names at the slightest touch.

"Sophia," I answered. Wisdom, yes, I needed the call of wisdom as I watched the smile widen like a snare, the eyes sparkling a little too bright. I took my hand back.

"Pretty garden. Unusual," he nodded.

I merely nodded and went to work.

"Could you use a scarecrow?" he asked.

"Whatever for?" I scoffed.

He nodded toward the oak and ash trees that line our earth. And there, amid the green leaves I saw them, black and glossy, and too many to count. The crows were silent, except for the nervous rustle of their wings as they waited, cloaked together on the boughs.

"Well?" Jack asked again.

"Yes," I said.

He shambled away, boldly whistling a tune stolen from our fairy rounds.

He returned later, lugging something large and rattling.

"I saw this design in a dream," he said, struggling under the awkward weight of his configuration. "Seems right that it should go here." He planted it just off center of the garden. He balanced it, so that the small charms depending from the length of the outstretched arms jangled nicely in the wind.

Despite my disapproval at having this Jack in my garden, I stared in wonderment. He had made it from the King's copper, and bright and green together it was. Not a thing to frighten the crows, I knew, for even they had leaned forward of their perch to catch sight of the gleaming figure. The charms clinked together and the crows called to it. Lifting from their branches, they took turns settling on the arms which swayed up and down with the shifting weight and caused the charms to sing out even more. The crows cawed their pleasure. No. It would not scare the crows, but it might keep off darker creatures.

Jack gave me his crooked smile. "Well, that's not much help, is it?" Charming and charmed. Even at my age, I flushed.

I let him stay awhile, help me even. The scent of a man in my garden was not unpleasant. Though it was soon joined by the prickled stench of smoke. The girl appeared beside the garden path, a bag in one hand, cigarette in the other, and stared. Just stared, pulling on that cigarette as if it were a breast, poor dear. I had not seen her since she insulted me and turned me away from her door.

"Sorry," she said.

"Not to worry," I answered, still digging.

"Here." She handed me a bag.

Curious (oh ever so), I took the bag from her and felt the hard roots rattling in the bottom. Iris, I thought. Blue Flag perhaps. But when I looked inside, I paled. Two mandrake roots, male and female, withered and intertwined. I shut the bag, trying to hide my disgust and—I'll admit—my fear.

"How charming. Thank you."

The girl cocked her head, her gaze keen. She frowned. "Guy at the market said I should plant 'em. Said I'd like them. But you don't, do you? So what's wrong with them?"

Serana, how could I tell her that these roots bled when cut? That they inflicted suffering, they twisted a true lover's knot into the hangman's noose? That whoever she loved she might ruin? Whoever loved her might strangle her in love's embrace?

"They're wonderful," I lied. "I should like to meet this man and see what else he has."

"Every Wednesday and Saturday at the Farmer's Market over by River Park. Just the other side of the university," she answered. She tossed her cigarette down and stubbed it out, then skulked away, her shoulders folded like a rain-soaked thrush.

I have gone twice to the Farmer's Market and not found the man who would sell mandrake roots to a young woman marked with trouble. But when I do, I mean to know the reason of it. Even as I burned the mandrake at midnight I felt the spindled threads of a sticky web vibrate.

And what of your unhappy young man? Who dreams such dark thoughts without having first been poisoned? And who would do such a thing? Glowworms, yes! We must be the light for these two who would otherwise be lost to darkness. Someone is stirring the cauldron, someone is poisoning them. Keep your wits about you fierce, Serana.

Always yours,
Meteora

My dearest Acorn Sister, Meteora:
To touch the hands with the Jack? What were you thinking? He is a trickster and a guyser, a breaker not a maker. What good will he offers you, I cannot imagine. You think your hair-changer is a problem, then my fern, you do not

know the half. Listen to what I have been up to, for I have taken my own advice and stepped into a story already half told.

Yes, I brought the doorstep waif to my rooms, my little straw man, my bird-scare. I dropped him, fully clothed, into a bath of warm water. It hardly roused him, for the poison I noted in his dreams runs deep in his veins. While he soaked, I got out my stones, the aquamarine for cleansing, and the salt. The very colour of the stone seems to soak up the hot blood. I stuck it beneath his knees, and sprinkled him with the salt and said the words. No, my dear, I may be stuck here in a body like a mouldering toadstool—but I did not forget the words!

The spell worked slowly. There is too much iron in the bones of this building, too much space between me and the Woods. But it worked, Meteora, in the end it worked, though it took hours and all of my hot water to make it so. The boy opened his eyes. Would you believe me when I say those were fey eyes? Deep bronze, shot through with haze, the lozenge-shape of cat's eye. For a moment. And then they were human again.

I do not know what this means. I doubt anyone except the Queen knows. But there is something going on here, Meteora, more than an exile for a small trick. I believe we have been dropped into this cesspit for a reason. Your change-hair girl, my bile-blood boy, the Jack—and the two of us.

Surely we are not meant to bring the girl and boy together. Surely not. For that would be too simple. And the Queen has never been simple, whatever else she may be.

I send a kiss for courage,
Serana

Dearest Serana,
As always we are of one mind; even distance cannot change the concordance of our thoughts. But I fear treading a

muddy path. These children may well be in our way as wounded birds. They may have been sent to us or drawn to us as we to them. I cannot tell. Is it possible that we are being tested? Watched even? The crows outside my windows are restless, cawing loudly in the early morning. But two days ago, I woke to silence and peering from my window saw a hawk, pale as rose quartz in the dawn's light, perched on the fire escape of the building opposite mine. Our gaze met, and as her beak opened, one of those awful car alarms sounded with frightening urgency (worse than the horns of the Wild Hunt), startling her. Unused to the worthless cacophony as I have become, she took flight and hasn't returned. Who knows who sent her? And for what reason?

As to the girl, whose hair is now black as soot, since handing me the bag with mandrake roots and seeing my displeasure, she has been reluctant to approach again. Oh, would that I had been able to dissemble a false expression of gratitude. Once I might have used a glamour, but not any more. You know I am cursed with an honest face, scrubbed clean of deception as a milkmaid on Sunday morning. Though she will not approach me, still she hovers. When I work in the garden I can see her, a slender shadow leaning against the railing of her balcony. I catch the sharp reek of her tobacco—and something more. Fear perhaps, animal musk, the residue of burnt wax. Perhaps all she knows of the game is a pricking in her thumb, a tapping in her dream that causes her to wake and feel a presence lying in the bed at her side. Perhaps she wonders who to trust? And how can she think clearly with that mark on her neck?

It was raining yesterday, so under the shelter of a blue umbrella I ventured out to the street where these children gather in shops drinking bitter brews. (Have you fathomed yet all the strange concoctions they drink? I am as paralyzed of speech as when I was a seedling garbling the words of a spell—do I want "mocha," "skimmed," "decaffeinated"—I stammer and every time receive a cup of something unrecognizable—oh for a decent cup of tea!) Tucked between the shops are "parlours" where these children change themselves into walking spells. Their ignorance astounds me, how little they realize the spells of undoing and confusion they allow stamped upon their arms, their shoulders, their legs. I saw a boy with wings etched on his back—did he know that he has damned himself seven years to be tormented as a bird lost in the wood? I saw a few with blessed spirals, may their lives be always turning toward the mysteries, but most were dull and stupid, a heart that will always be broken, a butterfly for a short and meaningless life, a snake that devours the will, and barbed wire, proclaiming a life of pinpricked sorrow.

And then, from across the street, I saw him, turning a closed sign on the door just before he slammed it and locked it. I swear to you, my sister, I shivered to the hollow of my fey bones. The hand that clutched the sign was a bundle of five twigs, spiked with thorns. He sniffed and I pressed in the doorway of a coffee shop, suddenly very afraid of his gnarled face. There was a glamour, of course, a mask that hid the rotted wood of his flesh, the lichen on his cheeks dotted with blood-red fruit. But I saw him clearly where others did not.

Who summons Redcap to the game out here? None of us alone has that strength to call him. Except the Queen.

I thought I had courage and yet now I tremble. The crows are frightened, the hawk startled. The girl hovers at my back and even I cannot say for certain whether she rides the dark horse or flees it.

What say you, Serana? Are we two strong enough to push back this darkness? We could, and mayhap we should, run screaming. How fares your child? Is he also part of this dark web? And have you any sense of what is afoot?

More precious now to me you are than ever before.

Your sister,
Meteora

Dearest Meteora:

Redcap? I shiver at the name alone. When I read it on your page, I blurted it out. The smell of blood, so like that of iron, slammed through my nostrils.

I will not say it aloud again lest it become a summons. Redcap. (I write it, which carries a different calling.) I hate that you have seen him, but it explains so much. And so little.

The last one I saw was in a Lowland peel tower, where he waited for unwary travelers, his cap so stained with their blood it was a deep, pulsating, malignant crimson. I remember his teeth were green and he bent over with the weight of all his sins. No eater could have ever cleansed that hide. I left immediately I spotted him, and reported him to the Queen. As I had to.

The Queen. It all comes back to her, doesn't it? But what game does she play with the Unseelie folk, the dark court, the unholies? Or do they, somehow, have her in thrall?

No more. My head reels with it and soon I will be as useless as my bile-filled boy. Have I told you the latest? He refused to eat for three days and then, *eglande nate*, as the priests liked to call us, the evening of the third day he sat up on the pallet I had made for him, waved his hand in the air like some overbearing princeling, and said, "Goddess, but I'm starved."

Well, that "Goddess" settled it. He *had* to stay. I rattled around my little cupboard of a kitchen and came up with three eggs, which I coddled in their shells. Just in case he was really a wicked spirit, a changeling who would be forced to speak out in wonder. But he just gobbled them down and demanded three more. Three more! That was all

I had. Had the child no understanding of the difficulties I incurred getting those six eggs? No chickens for miles, and the doors of the groceries and bodegas—as they call the shoppes here around—well bound between iron staves. And for me, making fool's gold causes my hands to swell and hives to break out on my back and under my breasts.

But I gave him the last of the eggs and went without supper myself, all so I could question him.

He fell asleep before I could ask more than his name. He gave that so freely, I cannot believe it to be his True Name. "Vanilla Blue," he said. Yet he neither smells like the fresh, sharp vanilla nor has the longing that blue conjures. I suspect he knows the power of names.

I told him to call me Auntie Em, borrowing the first initial of your name. Forgive me. Somehow that made him giggle and I cannot figure out why.

Tell me, sister dear, if you ever see that Redcap again. And I will let you know should I see any myself. If the Unseelie folk are moving to this world, well—there goes the neighbourhood. (That is a joke I heard in front of the local bodega, though it seemed unfunny at the time. Now I am no longer certain.)

> Your loving
> Serana

Dearest Sister,

I too learned the hard way about fairy's gold in this place. The first time I thought to touch it I pulled back a hand of blue warts, bristling like cauliflower buds. You know how vain I am about my pretty hands that even in age still can boast of some delicacy. I wept, shocked, for the gold had made the crossing intact into this world and so I thought it no harm.

And then I realized why it had happened thus: our mother's petticoat, that last scrap of fairy silk, her magic

the first seven days. Without an original receipt, a store credit will be issued at the lowest selling price. With a receipt, returns of new and unread books and unopened music from bn.com can be made for store credit. Textbooks after 14 days or without a receipt are not returnable. Used books are not returnable.

Valid photo ID required for all returns, (except for credit card purchases) exchanges and to receive and redeem store credit. With a receipt, a full refund in the original form of payment will be issued for new and unread books and unopened music within 30 days from any Barnes & Noble store. For merchandise purchased with a check, a store credit will be issued within the first seven days. Without an original receipt, a store credit will be issued at the lowest selling price. With a receipt, returns of new and unread books and unopened music from bn.com can be made for store credit. Textbooks after 14 days or without a receipt are not returnable. Used books are not returnable.

Valid photo ID required for all returns, (except for credit card purchases) exchanges and to receive and redeem store credit. With a receipt, a full refund in the original form of payment will be issued for new and unread books and unopened music within 30 days from any Barnes & Noble store. For merchandise purchased with a check, a store credit will be issued within the first seven days. Without an original receipt, a store credit will be issued at the lowest selling price. With a receipt, returns of new and unread books and unopened music from bn.com can be made for store credit.

lingering with the scent of rosemary. I stole it from her trunk before they exiled us, wanting a memory of her to carry with me to this strange world. To hide it from the Queen's prying eyes, I stitched a length of it into a purse and filled it with a cache of finely wrought fairy gold. I realize now she let me bring it—no doubt knowing that I would be unable to touch the gold. The bitch—she must have laughed, peering into her cat's eye and seeing me wandering the city's parks in search of moth and toad to take the warts away. But I have outfoxed her. I had rolled the remaining length of the fabric around my middle when I left—just thinking to make a pillow on which to lay my head—for I miss these familiar scents of home that remind me of our mother and our once-loving circle.

After the warts were gone, I took my silver scissors and cut out a pair of gloves such as women of a certain age here do wear on festive days. They work—for the gold touches nothing but the honourable power of our mother, even now beyond the reach of the Queen's corruption. I have made a pair for you and happily, Awxes, the crow, has agreed to carry them to you, along with a share of the remaining gold. I hate to think of you suffering in that iron city with no eggs, no milk and no sweets with which to lighten your day.

And to aid you in the task of caring for a child clearly born to the velvet. Who else but a highborn thinks nothing of being served by a woman, demanding food as though it was conjured from air? Unless of course, he is not a highborn, but a throwaway—a stolen mortal suckled at birth by a fairy and then returned to this world? He carries the milk of our kind, the distant memories of our song, but is lost to that world forever. Remember how the Queen once favoured such, raising boys like pups at her knee, wrapped in ribbons, petted and kissed until they grew older and the melody of their voices changed to that of men.

Sister, my dearest, can you imagine how we should feel if

we had been cast away as children, banished to this dark world knowing only the bright? What poison might we have swallowed if it promised to return us even to the gates of that far-off place?

Press your scare-bird gently, read his dreams. I think he comes to you following the fading scent of your magic—clinging to it as do I our mother's petticoat. We are never so old that we do not seek the comfort of our sweetest child-hood memories. But have a care—for perhaps if he does come from the Queen, perhaps he serves her still, seduced by promises we know she will not keep. And then he too may be like my child, haunted by something far darker than the Queen.

I must close this now, for the girl is coming up the stairs. I know the shuffling sound of her feet, hesitant, desperate as a hound-hunted vixen. I can smell her skin, a faint lavender nearly rubbed away by bitter rue. There is the knock, her breath heavy behind the thin layer of wood. She has been crying again.

These night weary eyes, how they miss you so!

Meteora

Oh adorable Sister, Loving Friend:
The gloves fit, the silk as soft as the inside of a lover's thigh. See, I remember lovers. One of the few nouns I can recall without work. And the gold. Like little fairy lights shimmering in the mist.

So with the gloves to hand, I went shopping for groceries.
Groceries.

Where once I would have searched out the petals of shade-loving trillium or the sweet sap that drips behind the bark of trees. Where once I would have beaten out butter-flies for the nectar in red flowers. Where once . . . Is that not the burden of my tune these days? Where once. Instead I bought groceries, spreading the gold around so that I did not beggar any of my local bodegas. Eggs and milk and the tiniest carrots stripped of their earthen coats, and a cheese veined with blue like marble, and a crisp hollow cracker that longs to be filled with something sweet. And chocolate. I think if there is one thing humans have that we do not, it is chocolate. Have you discovered it yet? Sweet and tart at once, it melts on the tongue like some dark honey from a hive of foreign bees. If the benighted bird-scare of a boy wants to eat, then I shall feed him. At least until I fathom out why he is here.

After that I went uptown, a long day's walk, and found a great store with a name that sounded like the wild north wind. Nordstrom. There I purchased a pair of green broad-waled trews and a green silken shirt to fit the boy child. You think him royalty? I am not so certain. He still smells. And it is a very human smell. If that is a spell, it is a very good one. I cannot see the joins.

But he was remarkably grateful for the food and the clothes. He said, "How can I thank you, Auntie Em?" So innocent-sounding. Too innocent methinks.

"Let me cut your hair," I told him.

And foolish child, he let me, sitting there still, only his fingers beating against the table, in a rhythm so wildly nervous, my right foot tapped along with him.

I cut his hair with a pair of plastic scissors I had found at the bodega, for I would not chance my silver shears so now he has a shaggy look, which well suits him.

I think I may call him Robin.

The hair I cut off is safe inside one of the gloves. I am not stupid, Meteora, just old. With the hair I may be able to do a small conjuration. Perhaps it will tell me why he has come here, or who sent him. Perhaps it will say if he is the hunter or the hunted, the haunt or the haunted, for without some direction, I cannot move forward with him. I do not believe—no, I dare not believe—that he is here for no reason.

Your loving
Serana

My dearest Serana,
Dressed in the green, and still not certain if he is royalty or not? Surely he gives himself away—a gesture, a look, the tilt of the chin. All those born to the silver have such airs that no amount of mud and twig can change them. Remember when the Queen sat at the midsummer feast refusing to eat because some downy-headed page set the dish too far from her elbow? We waited and waited, stomachs knotting—for if the Queen doesn't eat, no one does—until at last old Graeg humbled himself and his house to rise and serve the Queen. And how his dame turned shades of deep purple, the shame of it to see her Lord playing the servant to the Queen, who should have risen to serve the oldest first. The rules of hospitality apply to everyone except the Queen, it seems, who does as she pleases.

I would say *test* your Robin, but in truth, I think it's hard to be certain in this world where they are raised with no such rules. The young here are all possessed of that royal carelessness, even when they have no rank to speak of, no right to such privilege. Perhaps that is why I like them. They have nothing, are nothing, know nothing, and yet seem so perfectly content to behave as though the world were there to follow after them, bowing and scraping . . . and cleaning. I begin to sound like a foolish mortal midwife—both in love with and angered by my charges.

And so I should feel like one. It is a strange reversal indeed. I never wanted to come here, much less to soothe unhappy children. And yet here I am, unable to stop myself. Like the farmer's wife who could hear her cow mooing in that world beyond the knoll, but kept the fairy cradle rocking with one foot, I am sitting here, listening to the distant chime of fairy bells, while I make cups of tea and let them talk—endlessly it seems—about themselves until, exhausted, they toss their smokes (thoughtlessly into the garden I have laboured at) and return to their beds.

They are easy enough to figure out—all except the girl. She comes and goes muffled so deeply in her own thoughts I think it only by instinct that she finds her way to my small rooms and then seems to wake, startled to find herself in my kitchen or standing at my window. She has given me the use of a name, "Sparrow," though I have also heard her called "Ginny," "Nina," and "Bat Girl" by the children who trudge through the halls. Though she answers to all, there are some dark-lipped boys who murmur other names in her ear that make her flinch. These she will not answer, but shrugs them off the petal of her ear like the rain-soaked slugs.

Sparrow came to my room a week ago, just as I was finishing my last letter to you, tears marring her pale face.

"Can I come in?"

"Yes, come in, come in," I answered and opened wide the door. But she hung back, uncertain for a moment as Awxes bid her noisy farewell and lifted away from the window ledge.

"Weird," she said. And then she crept in, her eyes nervously sweeping the room. I have hung my crystals against the pane, for though I may do no more magic with them, the pull of their power is irresistible. Sparrow went to them and stood in their pretty light. Her arms hugged her body, one hand cupped around her elbow, while the other hand reached across her chest and pressed against the trouble-tattoo on her neck as though to hide a bruise.

"I'll make tea," I said to fill the silence, for you know how I hate silence.

In my tiny kitchen, I topped-up the kettle and while it

waited to boil, I plucked the dried leaves; a tea to loosen the tongue; heartsease and sage, chamomile and strife-not. It was oh so fragrant, strong enough that even I would have spilled my secrets if prodded. As I poured the tea, I heard her sigh, a sound so pitiable and lonely I almost wept. Even the crystals chimed unhappily in echo. I turned, mugs in hand, to find her in the kitchen, seated at the table, where in the evenings I write to you. She never asked my leave to be in here, which rankled, for at this private table I have my few precious things to remind me of you; the single candle-stick, its sister which lights your room, black beetle shells and carved acorns, the tiny silver dove and the beads of royal amber. Sparrow thumbed drops of wax that spilled on the cloth and then rattled the amber beads in their dish.

"Tea?" I said to catch her attention and slid the mug over to her.

She looked up, astonished, I think, to find me so close—though it is the room that makes us close, for everything I feel, the echo of magic, my long life compared with hers, the presence of you, is in this room. There is no space for lying or deception, only truth. And I saw it. Beneath the black smeared makeup her eyes were green, gold threads twinning the dark, troubled yolks. She looked away, duck-ing her head to sip the tea. Then she grimaced.

"Got any sugar?"

I roused myself from the table, my thoughts distracted by those eyes, perplexed that they seemed to peer out from behind a mask of black makeup, pale powder and cruel tat-toos. I rattled the canisters looking for the sugar, and when I found it, turned back to the table.

Sparrow was gone. Her mug of tea steaming on the table. And as I stood there holding out a canister of sugar, I saw too that my silver dove was also gone. It is in her pocket no doubt, being stroked between those hungry fingers. How could I have been so stupid? How could anyone love such a desperate and thieving child? And yet, I saw those eyes, green and gold, trapped, like the sparrow she calls herself, in a cave. If it gives her solace then she must have it, I suppose, though already I miss it.

I, who have stolen more silver spoons than most in my youth, cannot now complain too bitterly. In any case there is no one to complain to. I'm going to the garden to dig. That is the only cure for frustrated rage when one can no longer give warts, or boils, or curdle milk, or tangle the weft. Though I remember now where I saw a sheltered patch of poison oak. Maybe I shall leave a bit of the sap on the door-knobs.

Never turn your back on your scare-bird, Serana—no matter how prettily he speaks. Whatever they are, like the Queen, these two do not play by the rules of hospitality.

Muckle-mad and grumping,
Meteora

My dearest Muckle-Mad,
Your warning came too late. I had already turned my back on my scare-bird, my Robin, going out to search the stands outside the bodega for berries and a red onion—red, not gold, seems to hold the most power. When I returned, I found the willow basket with your letters an inch to the left of where I had left it, no longer between two of the nails holding the mantle over the fire, but directly on one.

I did not say a word, did not show that I guessed he had taken the basket down. Had probably riffled through the letters. Had possibly read what you had written. Not Vanilla Blue at all but definitely Robin, that rapscallion of the green. To let him know I guessed would lose me my one bit of an edge.

"Join me for tea," I said, and he got up from the divan— the couch as they say here—rubbing his eyes as if he was just up from sleep.

We had Miracle Mint, strong enough to disguise what else I put in. I used the berries, a single blue at the bottom of his cup, twice broken, twice blessed. And without prodding, he said—not even reluctantly—that he'd dreamed he was a crow, flying over a landscape that looked more like a chessboard than a meadow.

"A chessboard?" I asked.

"Squares of black and red, and . . ." His hand described a draughts-board.

"How . . . odd," I remarked, though I thought it all of a piece.

He shook his head, his cornsilk hair covering one eye. "That's not the odd part. I was hunting for something."

I asked carefully, "What?" Drew a quiet breath. Waited.

"Some . . . some girl," he said, "with purple hair. Or maybe black. Hard to tell from that height. And a tattoo on her neck like a bruise. Isn't that weird?"

I smiled at him as if fondly. "Definitely . . . weird." But all the while I wondered if he were testing me or I him. And I could scarcely wait until he was gone back into dreams so I could do something about my suspicions.

*

WELL, I had to wait until nighttime, of course. What fool would cast during the day? Eyes as wide as daisies could see, ears as sharp as holly spines would hear. Besides, the night promised a full moon that breeds better spells than any. And the fact that we have so little magic left, I knew I needed all the help I could get.

I double-locked the door, difficult to do with that iron bolt and key, but I managed. Soft towels are better for this than potholders. It has something to do with the weft, I think. And I closed the curtains on all the windows but one, and that looking out on the trees where the full moon shone down with rigour. Those spindly trees are nothing like our forests, but they were all I had.

Then I took out the glove with the hair stuffed inside like some sort of daft mattress. I made a circle of Robin's hair with a candle at the center, a red candle, beeswax and berry-stained. Luckily there was no wind to puzzle through the hair and destroy my symmetries. Luckily there were no passers-by to call out drunkenly and disturb the line of my chant. The streets were still of sirens and motor horns, and I judged I had arrived at the moment for my spell.

I pricked my finger and let a drop of blood bead there, then put the finger—blood first—onto the flame to put it out.

Yes, I know, blood castings are dangerous. But any way I looked at the tea leaves, the picture was muddled. We live in a dangerous place now, Meteora, and something had to be done. My scare-bird may be a good boy brought low by dreams. He may be the Queen's tool. Or he may be a spy from the Unseelie Court, with Redcap his master. I had to know for sure, or at least as sure as my feeble spells might tell me.

So danger or no, I went the way of blood. The spiral of smoke began to twist upward and I held my breath. Slowly it formed a picture. I was relieved, of course, that such a casting still worked here, in this rough, magic-lorn city. But though you will have guessed what I was going to do with the hair, you will *not* have guessed what the picture showed. You will be as startled as I, as unbelieving, and as frightened.

There was my Robin and your tattooed girl doing what we have done, you and I, in our prime. Their mouths were devouring one another, breast to breast, cock and cunt, so entwined nothing could part them. And all about them were dancing stars.

It is those stars I do not understand, sister. What have we all, unwitting, stumbled into? Meteora, blood of my blood, brood of my brood, take care. This is a deeper, darker stranger knot than we can pick apart by ourselves, more mixed and messed. Come thicket, come thorn. We have already touched what we should not have. And now we must go on. The road back is worse than the road forward.

I have given Robin another meal and he is now bound to me by rules of human conduct, if not enchantment. He has said nothing I think applicable to the dire situation we are in, though I pried as carefully as I might. But I have done something else as well, something which might be dangerous to you as well as to me and for that I ask forgiveness. It is, of course, the only logical next step I could have taken. I have given Robin a ticket for the bus and paper dollars for food and drink, as well as this letter to take to you, across so many miles. He is the child standing before you now, hand out, waiting for a reply. There are rowan shavings in his trouser waistband as proof against witches and a sprig of thistle sewn into the lining of his jacket to protect him from the worst.

Think carefully before introducing him to your Sparrow. If you do not believe it to be the right thing to do, send him back to me at once. He will have his return in his pocket.

But if my vision is true, they must meet anyway, so why not now, under our guidance?

With hope, that pale sister of belief,
Serana

Sister,

Why me? Why in the name of the Goddess, in the name of our beloved Greenwood, have you sent this boy to me? It is so like you to cast trouble behind your back and I, only because I am but a few seasons younger, am forced to take the responsibility. It has ever been so. Remember the miller's baby? How you wanted the little thing while it slept, pretty as a rosebud? And then it woke up, wailed and shit itself and you were less charmed. Do you remember who returned that mewling creature to its rightful mother? I still carry the scar on my thumb from the silver blade. And what about that harper? You gave him the power to play a tune that might honour you. But he forgot all the other tunes in his head, drunk on you, and the fairy rounds were forced to dance over and over to that one wretched tune. Even you held your hands to your ears but could not bring yourself to unbind his love. It was me they sent to cut the strings and it was me who had to console him when he woke from his dream, his ears still itching with the memory but his hands unable to find the notes.

I am furious because, regardless of the vision that gave you your reason, I know now the *real* reason why you have sent this boy to me. You have your habits, your little twigs set just so on the branch and this child is nothing short of a rampant summer storm. How often when we were little did you forbid me to touch your things, the polished mirror, the ivory combs, the silver hairpins arranged in their pretty patterns in your bower. "Paddle foot" you taunted me, slapping my hand away. "Magpie" was all I could offer in hurt reply and when you weren't looking, steal a pin or turn the mirror upside down and then hide, giggling into my palms while you shouted and bullied the little sprites that attended you. You have no sprites to attend you now and so you send this child, this pad-footed hound, all gullet and wet fur, to me to curry and comb and feed.

Yes. He arrived on a day of thunder and sheets of rain. He was as sodden as driftwood, his shirt and trousers weighted down by water and mud. He said nothing, but thrust your letter in my hand. I took it and almost closed the door on him, believing him to be one of those children downstairs who periodically bring me my mail that seems forever to go astray in this house.

"Hey," he shouted. "Auntie Em said I was supposed to stay here."

"I don't know any Auntie Em." And then I remembered that was supposed to be your name. "Wait, are you Robin?"

He smiled at me, through the tangled wet curls, the skin pale from the chill, but the eyes dark and gleaming and sister, oh my sister, I groaned knowing too well what you had done. Pretty thing he is. Enticing, long limbed and soft lipped. He came into my house, trailing water, set down his bags and asked, "Do you have anything to eat? I'm pretty hungry. Is that the kitchen?" And pointing out the way for himself, entered my kitchen and opened the cupboards. I stood there speechless, your letter in my hand, as he rummaged and found my bread, my butter, the thin sliver of roasted meat, the two ripe tomatoes, and the cheese. And he talked the whole time about nothing, his mouth working around my food.

"Show me the return ticket," I demanded after reading your letter.

He grabbed a pear and took a bite. "I don't have one."

"Yes, you do. My sister bought you one."

"I exchanged it."

"For what?"

He inclined his head toward the door—still opened wide to the hall—and I saw it. A black and battered fiddle case. A fiddler! My face grew hot and every hair on my head was scorched.

You knew, didn't you? He didn't even have an instrument when he was with you, but something in you knew! Was it the tune hummed softly under his breath when he slept? Or the toe keeping time to the reel in his head, or the fingers tapping a pattern of notes on the arm of your lion's foot chair? You knew you couldn't resist him—just as you couldn't resist one like him oh those many years ago. Your pride suffered then and never again wanting to be bound to such a man you have sent this muckle-gyp, this pair of grinding jaws, this honeyed-face boy with the long fingers, to me, your sister in exile.

I refused to cook for him but it scarcely mattered for he

helped himself to whatever he could lay his hands on, which turned out to be plenty. Sated at last, he rose from the table and dragged himself to the soft chair where I like to sit and read. I waited. But not a finger did the boy lift to tidy the mess he had made of my kitchen. Dishes, rinds, peelings and sticky knives all lay on the counters. The cheese sweated in the heat. But from this Queen's pet or Redcap's hammer not so much as a word. He took off his shoes, unrolled the wet and filthy socks, and set them without a thought on my side table—my side table!—and promptly drifted to sleep. I looked at his naked feet—long and slender boned—they are aristocratic feet, the second toe reaching above the big one, the arch high and delicate.

He slept and I went to bed, only to be awoken much later in the wee hours of the night by the sound of his fiddle. It is coarse and husky, the wood poor quality. But he played it well and I knew that it could seduce me, too.

"Stop that!" I demanded. "I'm trying to sleep."

"Sorry," he muttered and the house grew quiet again.

But I can tell you I slept uneasily, hearing him sigh and pace.

At last I shouted from covers, "Play the rude thing then if it brings you peace. But make it soft."

And then I heard it. The reason you saw fit to send him to me. Sad was the aire he played, a man lost and grieving in the throat of a tune. No demon born, no Unseelie knows how to keen so quietly into a set of strings.

He can stay, but he will not eat unless he works. I sent him to the garden, shutting my ears to the complaining. He was to clear a new patch, dig up the hard pan of packed soil and the crabbed grass that I knew would mock his efforts. He has been at it all morning and every time he leans on the shovel to take his ease, I am there at the window urging him on. But he has paid me back for this injury—as only a clever child can. Even as I finish this letter at my recently cleaned kitchen table, he is standing in my living quarters, playing his fiddle. I can smell the earth and wet leaves. He has tracked the mud into my house, is standing on my red wool rug—that rug that carried Caliphs across the gold desert—and is playing a naughty reel to mock me. The strings sing like an old farmer and I am filled with nostalgia for a time that will never come again.

Oh, I am angry with you. He will be a handful. And yet listening to him play, I know it will be impossible to stay angry—with you, my blood-sister, and with the scare-bird boy. Sparrow hovers at her window—a mistrustful shadow as always, watching him bend and work in the garden. If these two are meant to be together it will be up to them to find a way. I will not force the pattern. No doubt his fiddle calls to her. The boy I will keep working in the garden and let the living earth return to him some sense and humility along with love and diligence.

Fractious, but still your loving sister,
Meteora

Oh dear Paddle Foot:

I knew you would do the right thing. You always do the right thing. It is annoying, but true. Only you never know when to shut up. There. I have said it at last. And I say it with love and a certain amount of trepidation for I treasure your letters, all I have now of our old life. But really, Meteora, you are so like your name, flashing across any universe you happen to inhabit.

Shut up.

You are best when you are fixing things, mending broken boxes or heads or hearts. When you cut the strings that are binders, when you uncurdle the brownie's milk, when you set aright a spell that has gone so miserably wrong, then— oh then—you are what you are meant to be.

Only for Mab's sake, shut up about it.

The memories you curse me with are so one-sided. Have you never understood that? The miller's babe was a mistake, granted. But I recognized it immediately and had not the wherewithal to take it home. Only you could do it—as you did. The harper was not there for dancing nor bound by love, but to twit the queen and oh! I can still see her face, a rowanberry red, as he went on his seventy-dozenth round of the song. And I did not need to hold my ears, dear sister, having stuck lamb's wool in them ahead of time, knowing what cost my trick would account. Remember, I am the far-seer, the visioner.

As for touching my things—do you not remember that as a little one, you burned yourself badly that way. Look at the puckered skin on your ringman finger. The reminder is still there. You never seemed to recall that on your own, much as I iterated. A meddler you were then and still are. A meddler and a mender.

So I send you the boy that you can meddle and mend to your heart's content. I have seen that you need to fix this broken thing, whatever it is.

> Your loving older (and therefore wiser) sister,
> Serana

Dearest Sister,

Older indeed and yes, I answer grudgingly, a wee bit wiser. The scar of my burned finger reminds me, and the twist of white hair, not from age, but the spell gone awry. I know these truths in my calmer moods—but oh how those moods escape me now. I dash from leaf to stone, a mouse beneath the outstretched shadow of the owl's wings. It makes me breathless, angry and weary. And in my frustration I want not so much to be victorious and happy in my meddling, but quietly content in my modest misery and loneliness.

Jack has joined himself to my garden and daily I find small sculptures left as offerings amidst the plants. I watched

Robin leaning on his shovel, shoulders gleaming with sweat like a lathered pony, talking with Jack. Like his sculptures, there is balance in Jack, in the way he stands, feet apart, hands opened, compact and a little heavy in the middle. I can almost feel his shoulders take the weight of the boy's grief and transform it into something both lighter and yet more dense with purpose. But of Sparrow I see little. I hear her shuffling on her porch and when I turn, she ducks inside, almost as if afraid of me. Or perhaps Robin. He knows she is there. I am certain of it. The heat rises from his heart and I can hear the song that wants to burst forth. Perhaps I shall take him with me to the Market and let him choose among the plants the one that most becomes him. King's Crown? Heartsease? Butter-and-cheese? Or Mother's Pride? And in that choosing I may yet be able to read his destiny.

Your sister,
Meteora

Dearest Meteora,

There now, my darling sister, we are in accord. If fearing something together makes a pact.

As I was alone at last, I did what I could to cleanse my little houselet of Robin Scare-bird's presence, hoping that would help. I have burned the lint he left behind, thrown out any food he has touched, scrubbed the rooms on my hands and knees, with a soap I made of rowan and bleach. My hands are the worse for it and my right leg aches from buttock to bone, but it is done.

Except for a bit more of his hair which I found in my good brush. So I have done another blood casting. The picture that spiraled out of the smoke was as clear as the first. There is something to come of this coupling, should they ever get down to it. But this time there is a strange blurring around the edges of the vision, a single crow's feather in the left corner, and a bit of ginger root in the right. I do not know what this means. You know the old charm, "One crow for sadness, two for mirth . . ." So now I fear it. And I send this warning to you.

If they see one another, this boy, this girl, they will be swept into each other's arms. But whether that is for sadness or mirth, whether it is for good or ill, I no longer know. However, I do know this: whatever you give Robin to plant, do not let it be Arum. Never Arum.

So this time I am afraid I have been the meddler and you must use all that is left of your magic to mend if you must, or bend if you will, else we will be broken on this wheel forever.

Your frightened sister,
Serana

Dearest Serana,
The hawk carries this letter to you for I am troubled. The last lines of your letter were torn away when my letter was roughly shoved into the narrow slot of my box. Whatever your final words were I don't know them. All that was left was your proclamation "I do know this." If I could spell as I once did, I might know the truth of these wayward words. But now I can only stare at the ruffled edge of the paper and wonder whether there is another who has advantage of your knowledge. Please, dearest sister, write me soon—the hawk will wait for you, though not for long.

*

I am edgy. And your Robin even more so. He chose the Arum—I thought at first as a joke—and I wondered even whether it were sensible to give so potent a plant into the hands of a young man. Stranger still to watch it arrogantly thrusting itself up in my garden. I'd half a mind to pull it out, stalk and root. But no sooner did I touch it than the Jack's own laughter stopped me and I blushed furious, my hands wrapped around it as though to throttle youth and sex. I have left it, but, oh, what misgivings. Even the crows call in the trees as if to reassure one another that they are safe.

I saw Sparrow today. She leaned out on her porch, hands clenched on the railing like a fledgling balanced for a first flight. Robin upturned his face and saw her. And that damn plant, it bloomed, spreading pollen everywhere in the sudden gusting of the wind.

Worried as a tree knot,
Meteora

Meteora, sister, oh fool, fool, why did you not immediately ask about those lines? Why did you not find a way to reconstruct them? Why move forward when your heart warned against the Arum anyway? Surely you could have guessed that if you found Arum—the Wake Robin plant—that you should root it out, burn it, bury it, cut it into a million pieces and scatter those pieces into dry sea sand. You were bright enough to know what the mandrake root meant, but not this? Sister, I weep. It is not only Robin the Arum will awake. Someone else is waking, too. Not just your Redcap. He is dangerous, true. But we know what the true danger is.

The crows know it. The stars know it.

The sleeper wakened is someone more twisty, more devious, more cunning than we can guess. And how did I discover this? I read all this in the tea leaves—spearmint for settling my already unsettled stomach—upon receiving your latest letter. The leaves formed a kind of crown, though when I turned the cup around, I saw that it was not a crown but a fence, a hedge, a knot of vines.

A knot of vines as knotted as my stomach.

I am afraid, Meteora, so horribly afraid. We have meddled in something larger here than we are ready for. It is a Matter of Kings, of this I am sure. What such homey tricksters as ourselves are doing in this hedge I do not know. But we will not come out of it whole.

Fool you, but more foolish I not to warn in the letter both top and bottom.

*

WAIT! The above was written but an hour ago. An hour. Sixty small minutes. A tick of the human clock.

Outside the wind has ceased its moan. The stars are looking coldly down, except for Red Mars, as the humans call it. It alone shines like an ember in a long-banked fire. I cannot get warm looking up.

I have been watching out of my window and feel rather than see something below, coming through the spindly trees. Time is stilled, my sister. The clock that came with this apartment stands with its hands clasped at midnight and does not move.

I hear the bells on her horses' bridle nearing. So I do the only thing I can. I am sending this message stuffed into a wooden locket, tied with twine to a pigeon's neck. In a moment I shall whisper your name and your city and your street in the bird's ear. The Queen will be expecting me to send my mail by fierce hawk, by fiercer eagle, by reluctant crow. She will not expect a pigeon, homely and unadorned, to be my messenger.

If you do not hear from me again, or if I write and do not say the name of your favourites, consider me dead. You can guess as well as I who comes through the trees as if down a straight road. She has already crossed the river of blood, and her coming has stopped all the clocks of Christendom. Even the recorded muezzin on the mosque down the block no longer calls out.

It is a moment of reckoning. I shall not give her your name.

Sister, sister, speak of me with love. It is something the Queen will never do. I send a kiss for eternity. I will not mind the pain as long as you are safe.

Serana

Dearest Sister,

I send this to you, praying to the Goddess, that you are still here—knowing you are still with me, gentle sister, for we cannot be, cannot exist without the knowledge of the other. And so I need to know how have you fared? What have you learned? I need your help now more than ever.

Your sight was true as ever and your letter finds me shaking, for I've seen battle. It came like a chained dragon released unexpectedly from my breast. I, who was last to anger, soonest soothed, who could have known such fury lay waiting? So prodigious it was that now I wonder is such rage an unlooked-for power of our strange-come middle age? As we lose the finer touch of magic and little spells that now seem so domestic—our candles, butter churns, even the simple pleasure of man and maid—does an older power offer recompense for our loss? Do we become closer to the rough-hewn rocks, the well of fire at the earth's heart, the tempest in the starred night, all these things eternal from which we were seeded? I wept with you when we lost those powers we had called our blood. Yet now I believe true power flows deeper beneath the skin, beneath the bone, buried in the heart, raw and unpredictable.

Were I a mortal woman, how frightening such an awakening might be, how fearful I would be of the dragon beneath my breast and how quick, as they are here, would I be tempted to lull such a beast into submission with draughts. I see them on the street, these mortal women, and we appear of an age, our bodies mature, our faces lined with tales. In some the dragon light flickers bright in their eyes like garnets, but most, as faded as their youth, peer out from eyes dulled as scoured agates.

Perhaps the Arum woke this dragon in me. But I was not the only one, as you predicted. Walking out at night, Jack and I stumbled on Sparrow and Robin in the gardens twined as in your vision. The child rose from the soil, drew her clothes around her in dark shame and fled before I could stop her. Robin lay there erect, miserable and moaning in the moon. If only Sparrow could have trusted me. If only she could have believed that such a sight is as old as earth to me, and one as welcome as man and maid in the furrows of newly plowed soil. But she did not trust, running away. And now I am full of doubt. Did she read my letter? Did she tear away the lines of warning? Both of these children seem to dig into our hearts for news of themselves.

Two hot and sultry days passed without sight of her. It was late in the afternoon. Robin sulked beneath the withered shade of the trees, the fiddle listless in his hands. Jack struggled to balance a sculpture in the center of the garden, something with a spiral to soothe the brooding of these unhappy children.

As I worked the garden, my ears pricked to the soft murmur of the crows, the scrape of beak against the bark. The air stilled into afternoon and I sat back on my haunches, worried. Beetles hid beneath the leaves, the little brown sparrows scattered into the shrubs, the stones shrugged into the earth. I plunged my hand into a patch of dried leaves and shuddered as I brought forth a twisted mandrake root. I looked over the garden and saw now where the blooms were withering, or stalks grew pale. I went to each and found dark tokens of unbinding, nightshade blossom, manglewort and even the red spotted caps of kills-quick.

Sparrow. It had to be. She knew a man in the market. She laid her hands to these dark roots and set them here to hurt me. The coils of fury shifted and angry scales slid against bone. I pulled the brutish offerings out, braided the roots to keep them from bleeding malice and rolled them in a bit of our mother's silk I carry in my pocket. The white silk was stained crimson and I could have wept at the profanity were it not for the heat in my breast, the steam rising in my throat.

I rose from the ground, the air swirling around me. At the edge of the garden Jack swore as the sculpture crashed to the ground and crushed my flowers. But it was not his trickery that made the sculpture fall. I promise you that. Though at the moment I did not know it.

Rage at all of them boiled and I opened my mouth, prepared to shout curses. But Awxes appeared suddenly, her shadow long over the garden and her caw a harsh alarm. One for sorrow. She flew to the house, crashing her body against the glass of a second story bedroom. She fell away from the ledge and then returned, her beak striking the panes. The flock lifted and followed her, laying siege to the windows.

I saw smoke coiling in a scorched pattern around the window. I felt it, a groan, a shift as a pawn was toppled. Robin staggered to his feet, and staring wildly at the window began to run toward the back stairs. I followed him, from the garden to the house, up the stairway to the second floor. Behind me Jack lunged up the stairs, calling, "Sophia, Sophia!" On the landing, Robin pounded his fits on the door, shouting Sparrow's name. But I could see already no mortal strength could unbind such a door.

"Away," I shouted and pushed him aside. I placed my hands on the door and shuddered at the skin of treachery.

And then it happened. Amid the harsh battle cries of the crows, Robin's desperate shouts, even Jack calling out the name that wasn't mine, I descended into a prescient calm. It was silent and through the door, I heard Sparrow's muffled sob, the soft thump of her body, the harsh rasp of breathing. The dragon in my breast unfurled the blistering heat of its rage and I shoved with fiery hands against the door. The wood smoked beneath my palms and I pushed hard until it groaned and cracked against the hinges. Wind and smoke howled around me as I entered the room, blind with rage and still not knowing why. Only instinct, the throb of the earth's heart.

Sparrow was there, lying on the floor, the pale ribbon of her naked body mottled with shifting shadows of crow wings beating against the window. The air was moist with the rotten stench of wormwood punks burning on the floor. Hovered over her was a man, a quill poised over the soft mound of her belly, ink dripping from the sharpened point. He laid the pen against her flesh and she sighed. Dark spells cast in ink and blood marked the white skin of her torso. The inside of her thighs were scorpions that she should take no pleasure in either touch or cock, a brindled hound snapped the curve of her breast as though to tear away the flesh. Black adders slithered into knots over her shoulders holding her in bondage, and between the thin stands of her ribs a stake wreathed in mistletoe stabbed to the heart. I knew what he meant to place on the mound of her belly. The spell of undoing, of the monster birth and the ravaged womb.

I should have been afraid when he looked up at me and snarled. Those high cheekbones, that skin of polished wood, eyes like bloodstones. Highborn of Unseelie Court. Sister, I shudder to write the name of Long Lankin, blood drinker, soul swallower and servant to none but Redcap.

"Go," he ordered and waved his hand to brush me away like an autumn leaf, thinking me an old woman of no consequence.

Power surged in my breast. Retrieving stones from my pocket, I hurled them hard, not at the highborn blood, but at the glass. They shattered the windows and the crows flooded in a rushing river of black water into the small room. The highborn threw up his arms as Awxes attacked his face, the quill skittered across the floor, the pots of poisoned ink toppling and spreading stains into the wood. He ran for the door, but I was there. I should have stepped aside. But I couldn't, my rage would not let me. I struck him, struck hard across that cruel but perfect face and spun him around. He recoiled and struck me back, howling as the skin of his hand burned the moment it touched my furrowed cheek. It hurt, blinding horrible hurt, but rage held me upright on my staggering feet. I struck again, blindly this time but felt the skin of his cheek split, and blood scalded my palm. Robin shouldered Lankin aside and dashed to Sparrow. He pulled her into his arms, growling and baring his teeth like a mastiff. Then Jack was there, and he grabbed Long Lankin by the scruff, threw him against the wall, and pressed his arm across the royal throat to hold him prisoner. He could not know the power of the highborn he treated so rudely.

"Do not," I cried, my hand held out, though useless to offer a spell of protection.

Thick smoke and the crack of lightning sizzled in the room. I heard Jack cry out as the first blast knocked him into the walls. I, too, was hurled back, but stood again and threw myself forward, over Robin and Sparrow, shielding her from the second blast so that the flying splintered wood would not pierce her naked skin. Crows shrieked and cawed, stabbed with daggers of wood. They fell to the floor, wings beating frantically, blood mingling with the spilled poisoned ink. The girl sheltered between Robin and me never moved.

When the smoke had cleared, I raised myself and counted the damage. Four crows were dead. Jack was rolled into a ball, his shirt covered with splintered wood like the quills of a porcupine, dots of blood where they entered. Two jagged darts of wood pierced Robin's hand where it lay over Sparrow's face protecting her.

"Jack," I called to the slumped figure and he raised his head, then his hand, and answered.

"I'm all right. And you?"

"I survive," I answered.

"And the girl?"

I sat back on my haunches and Robin gathered Sparrow onto his knees, his terrified eyes searching her face. Her arms were limp, her head rolled back lifeless. But her eyes watched me, moved to follow mine. I plucked a tiny arrow from her black hair. Elf-shot to keep her still and unmoving yet aware of the pain while he marked her. I broke it, and tucked the feathered shaft in my pocket.

"She will be. Robin, help me get her to bed."

We rose and carried ourselves away from there.

*

AND so here I am. There are the three whose true names I do not know staying in my tiny rooms. I washed their wounds and gave them all tea. No one spoke much. The tea was brewed strongly to make them sleep so I could think.

Jack sleeps sitting up in my old chair; on my bed, Robin curls watchful as a hound at Sparrow's feet. Your messenger has come to my window with your letter—too late, too late! The Arum has woken the Dark Lord, Long Lankin as well, and now he haunts my Sparrow. But why her?

She is nothing but a mortal girl. Unless, of course, she is more.

There is something else of Sparrow I must tell you. As she lay naked, I saw the true colour of her hair. In that tri-angle, the hair blazed like spun gold against her cream-coloured belly. She hides her hair beneath the garish dyes, I can see that now. I have seen no woman, mortal or fairy, with hair such colour. Except the Queen.

I am tired, the soft breath of sleeping mortals has made me too weary to think. My dearest sister, I miss you more than I can say. I would you were here, across the table from me, your capable hands around a mug of tea. And in the steam spirals together we could read the pattern. For all my great dragon rage, there comes now tears such as I have not

shed since a child. These storms are more than I can bear
alone.

Eternal power comes with a price, it seems.

Weary and weeping,
Meteora

Darling Sister Meteora:
Your letter arrived and, as I finished reading it, burst into
flames. As did my heart.

I am enclosing some aloe cream for your burns, the best
the local store had. It does not smell like aloe, I am afraid,
but like machinery. Still, the pharmacaria assures me that it
will "work magic" which—if she but knew magic—she
would not promise so rashly.

That Long Lankin should have entered your house, without warning, without permission, without . . . but I forget,
we have no ability to ward as once we did. We can keep out
unwitting humans and a pigeon or two. But the Highborn—
hard enough to ward against when once we had our own
powers—are surely unstoppable now.

And while you were engaged in that battle, I had a smaller
one of my own. Or rather I ran from it. For remember, I heard
the jangle of the Queen's bridle bells. I heard the clop-clop of
horse's hooves. Not the full rade on the move, but a single
horse.

The Queen was coming alone.

And that so frightened me, I ran from the house, into the
darkling streets, turning widdershins each time, certain I
could hear the horse with its rider behind me.

At last I came to an alley where bits of old news magazines whirled in eddies and where two ancient crones hovered over a fire. Their skin was stretched like black paper
over fine bones and they were spreading some sort of ointment along the inside of their scrawny arms.

They must have heard me, I was breathing so loudly. Looking up, they stared at me with hard eyes like walnuts, then signaled me in to them with cupped hands.

Where else could I go? I was winded and afraid, but they seemed so insistent that I joined them, warming my hands over the fire while it snapped and snarled at me from its garbage can grate. But the rest of me I could not warm. Fear made me shake as if with an ague.

Then the two put a cape around my shoulders made of some strange yarn, and lucky it was that I was wearing Mother's shawl or the iron strands in the thing would have burned me clear to the bone. They called me "Sister," and offered me protection, and while I scoffed at such, they spoke strange words of binding.

"Hi-di, hi-di, hi-di ho," they sang.

I did not know the spell, but clearly it worked, for the Queen never came near, though I could hear the bells on her bridle walking back and forth, back and forth all along the midnight streets.

"Thank you," I said, "I am beholden . . ."

"You ain't beholden nuthin'," said one.

The other added, "Till we earns it."

I nodded and stopped shaking. Though we all knew it was already past payment.

We stood for what seemed like hours over that fire, the crones humming and chanting—I cannot call it singing exactly, as the words were odd and unrhymed. Syllables of power, I suppose. I was quiet at the first, but by the end I was chanting along with them: "Hi-di, hi-di ho . . ." And I could feel something, more than warmth, creep into my fingers. A tingling, a touch of magic.

When dawn began to sneak down the stone corridors of the city, the Queen and the horse fled backwards.

"Sisters," I said to the old women, "come to my house.

I have fresh-bought bread and spearmint tea." If they would not take thanks, then I could at least give them hospitality. And what greater than bread and tea.

The one looked at me and laughed. "Tea?"

The other said, "Nuthin' stronger?"

"Wine," I whispered, "but it is morning."

So I brought them home and nothing was there to greet us but the wine and bread and a bit of sunshine lying thick as butter on the window.

Dearest Meteora, there *is* magic in the city, though not what we are used to. I do not think I have seen the last of these crones. The taller one is called Shawnique, the older one Blanche. They throb with an odd power I cannot name. They think me strange, laugh at my gloves, at the cloves in all the corners of my room, but their laughter is not harsh. Not at all. Almost, I think, it is conspiratorial. Their power is built on something other than leaf and thorn. It has iron at its base, and paving. It has strong bones.

Now I have done a last blood casting, this time with my own hair. And the surprise of it is so great, I must come and tell you mouth to ear, for I dare not commit it to paper lest the wrong hands touch it, the wrong eyes see it. I know the Queen has forbidden our meeting, but we must chance it. I will bring the two crones if I can. Get out a bottle of wine, bake some dark bread—they like it crusty—and we will find our way to you. I send this by pigeon. Keep the crows away. I will try to find other bird messengers, for I do not know how soon we will get there.

In haste,
Serana

Sister—

You travel with the crones? And you thought to chide me about my Jack? So we have found strange-enough bedfellows in this world. Yes, I know what you are thinking, the arch of your brow rising in question. But in these times, I am in need of comfort. And it happened as it must. The Arum no doubt is to blame. Or else my loneliness.

I have sent the crows away as you bid. Though Awxes hardly needed my bidding. That night, I gathered the corpses of the valiant crows and, wrapping each one in green silk, placed them in a straw basket and walked into the wooded park near the lake. Night was descending and, frightened as I never once was before in the comforting dark, I dug beneath the decaying leaves and laid those bundles out in a trough of softened earth. Awxes found me there, weeping as I covered those fallen warriors. She strutted over the mounds, head thrown back and black-beaded eyes glistening in the rising moon. I was not to weep, but to work, not to coil fitfully, but to fight, she warned. There was no time to waste. And then she left and I heard the clap of their wings as the murder flocked above the trees and was gone.

I returned home to find Jack awake and in my kitchen, cooking—an extravagant dish of eggs folded over herbs, mushrooms and daubs of cheese. There was toast and a mug of tea, hot and steaming, new potatoes frying in a pan, blackened with my butter. He had set the little table for two, the good silver laid out just so, framing the porcelain plates, the linen folded into cloth lilies. A new taper was in the candlestick and it burned with a cheering flame. All my precious things had been carefully set aside on the window ledge. I was astonished into speechlessness—an impossible state for you to imagine of me, I'm sure. I was wet, cold, my fingers chafed and stained with dirt. I sank into the chair and chin in hand, studied the mortal man in my kitchen.

His forearms were muscled where the sleeves of his shirt were rolled back. He moved with grace, long, dexterous fingers cracking eggs, rapidly beating them in the blue bowl, and swiftly, elegantly turning the pan so that the mixture might cook quickly and evenly. He said nothing, but cast his glance my way, questions lying there, but good manners holding them in check. Never speak first when dealing with the fey—that old interdiction. Well, it seems he's learned a thing or two from someone with common sense.

I let him put the food in front of me. I took a bite, and it was delicious. We ate in silence. And you, who tells me to shut up, would have been amazed. When it was done I asked but one thing of him: "Will you help me hide Sparrow and Robin? Others will come."

"Yeah, you should all stay with me. Just across the court-yard." He pointed out the window to an old five-story building across from mine. "Up there. I have the loft on the top floor."

"Are you sure you want to do this thing?"

"If you're asking do I know what I'm in for, the answer is yes. Sort of," and then he smiled. He brushed back the thick gray hair, those eyes too bright a blue.

"How? How do you know this?"

"When I was ten years old my mother left us and my father, bitter about it, deposited me into the reluctant arms of my mother's sisters. Three of them, each older and stranger than the other. They were neither gruff nor kind, but drank small glasses of whiskey and told stories."

"Stories?" I asked, sipping my tea, watching him over the rim of my cup.

"Yeah, the kind that make the hair on the back of your neck stand up and send you either running for the shrink's couch or into art."

"And since you are of normal size, I am assuming you went into art," I replied, trying to conceal my ignorance. I have no idea what conjurer he imagined would turn him small.

He laughed and it was a pleasant sound in my kitchen that drove away the dampness of my joints. I must have guessed correctly.

After we finished eating, he wrapped the sleeping Sparrow in a blanket and picked her up in his arms like a child. Robin grew possessive and so Jack surrendered her into the boy's arms. Walking close together, we crossed the courtyard, past the ruin of my garden to his building. An old rickety lift pulled us to the roof and I have not been so frightened of a cage since that time we tried to trap a Roc and nearly got our fingers nipped off. And being surrounded by so much iron made me wheeze. But when we entered Jack's abode—oh my sweetest sister—even you would have been wild with happiness.

It is a garden of sculptures, wood and leather, twigs and fur, our people plucked from his dreams and rendered into the solid flesh of the greenwood. Stones with holes, shells with coiled secrets, a tortoise carapace, dried fronds of bracken, bones that greeted me in the low, contented hum of our ancestors. The whole place smells of linseed, cedar shavings and charcoal. There are slender stalks of rowan and blackthorn woven into the frames of the beds and chairs. Safeguards against the Unseelie Court, though I wonder if he knows that. There those children sleep together, like chicks storm-fallen from their nest and once more returned. I share a small room with Jack in the back of the studio. Small and cozy as the cot where you and I once told our youthful secrets. It is more a place for rest than passion. I laugh to see myself there now—though I value it for its tenderness.

The poisonous ink gave Sparrow a fever and my healing skills have been sorely tested in this place. I've melted beeswax into a paste, adding a bit of my blood, the sweat of a city mouse caught behind the pantry, cobwebs in the corner of Jack's bookshelf and the squeezings of rowan berries. It works but slowly. Most of the frightful tattoos are disappearing now—though the one for trouble seems deeply etched. An old one, perhaps the first to mark her.

Jack has made her soup but Robin suffers no one but

himself to feed her, raising her head to the spoon and managing to get her to take but one sip, or two. She is a ribbon of white flesh, but she is tough for all that—sturdy like her namesake.

Robin knows something, but he is silent. I hear him whispering to her in the dark, hear her feathered answers. He tells me nothing, as though he means to protect her even from me. A greenwood child to be sure. I am now minded of how little we cared for those mortal children scrabbling underfoot in the Queen's court. Did they learn our secrets? Do they conspire against us? All of us? Can they not know the difference between us of the courts? Until the Sparrow speaks, I shall know very little.

I am waiting. I am waiting. I who would meddle the locks, cat-curious worrying the knot on a package full of secrets, must now wait. I watch at the windows, hidden behind a spray of maidenhair ferns and watch for your coming. Look for the scarecrow and follow the upward tilt of his right hand. It points to our window.

Your loving sister,
Meteora

Meteora, we are coming, Sister, riding the winds.

The old women have a green ointment they call unguenta. I recognize toad essence, almond oil, sweet flag, and water plantain. Maybe a touch of belladonna. We have plastered the unguenta on our hands and wrists, armpits and forearms, and it made me tingle all over. We touched a jay's feather to the ointment and anointed our foreheads.

"What is this?" I cried, but before I could say more, we began to rise from the ground and fly.

Oh, sister, to be able to fly again, across this vast city so spectacularly hung with imprisoned stars. To dip and soar. To lift my sagging body above the gravity of the situation. That last is a joke; the crones taught it to me.

We are not as fast as the white-capped sparrow who brings you this note, for we must make frequent stops. The crones have small bladders and our arms go frequently numb. We have to avoid phone lines and the telescopes of city dwellers checking out their neighbors. "The jeeper-peepers," the crones call them.

But we come. Watch the skies.

Your loving sister in haste,
Serana

Dear Auntie Em,

You and your sister Sophia sure have a wacked sense of humor. I know your true names but I'm not so stupid as to use them here. You can't believe how many weirdos are out there looking for these letters. Honestly, you guys have no idea about secrecy. None. Good thing you know nothing about e-mail, otherwise the whole fucking mess of my life and Robin's would probably be all over cyberspace right now and that skull's head wouldn't have needed to attack Sophia. And then I'd be dead. Or worse, bound by blood.

Don't panic. I guess I should have said that first. Sophia is all right. Jack and Robin made it to her in time. But that's why I am writing to you—to warn you about what's coming and to tell you my story. Sophia didn't think she had the strength to write all this down—you know her. She can't shut up. She made me promise to tell you my whole story. There's not that much to it.

I never knew my mother. My old man just sort of dragged me around as if I was an afterthought, feeding me when he remembered to eat after a binge. I didn't mind the drinking so much. He'd leave me alone then. Maybe it was the DT's, or maybe it was just being sober that made him crazy. I'd wake at night hearing him beating at the walls, demanding to be let in. Then he'd weep, really howl. In the morning he'd pull me outta bed and beat me as though somehow it was all my fault. And I grew to believe it. I was shit, I was there to be savaged for some reason I couldn't know. He made me cut my hair, shaved it close like a boy's. The only peace I had was at school—but of course, bruises make a bad impression and before long some teacher would be calling social services and we'd be out the back door and on the run.

All this lasted until I hit puberty. We were in a motel— one of those dirt-cheap places up North near the woods. He woke in one of those moods and like always, belt in one hand, he grabbed at my shirt and yanked it—to lay the strap on my back. And there they were. Boobs. Mine. I hadn't told him that my periods had started. But my boobs did a pretty good job of convincing him that I wasn't a kid any more. He put away the belt—and somehow that silence was worse than the noise of his beating. He got on his knees and pleaded with me. Pleaded.

"You're like your mom, baby, I miss her. I need her. Help me baby. Help make me happy again."

He touched my hair, which was longer than usual. Touched my face. And when he tried to touch my breasts, I freaked. The beating I could take because deep down I knew the problem wasn't me. I was paying the bill for someone else. But if I let him touch me like that, it would be about me and I would never, never be free again. I grabbed a chair, swung it at his head and bolted. No shoes, no money, no coat. It was a good thing I slept in my clothes.

I may be young, Auntie Em, but I know the road you travel right now. I never met Shawnique and Blanche, but I met others in the weeks I traveled alone in the woods. Crows, ravens, jays. Sometimes flying, showing me the way, sometimes appearing as strange women in my dreams. And when I'd wake, there beside me I'd find food, a pair of shoes, a man's hat, a packet of matches from some roadside tavern. I probably should have stayed away from the town but I got lonely for the sound of voices. I went there and idiot that I was, I got picked up for begging and then dumped into a home for runaways, which was okay for a while. The food was good—hot for a change. The sheets were clean. But the dreams just kept coming. Dreams of places I'd never seen before, weird folks tripping through them. I made friends—guys who like me had the same weird dreams. We swapped stories—until the first one was killed by some muggers. Then another friend was drowned in a culvert, and a third was pushed under a train. It scared me. I could feel something closing in on me. Even my dreams made that clear. It was my fault. My fault, my fault. So I ran. Again.

I followed the crows here. Hooked up with the students living below Sophia and just tried to get my shit together. I wasn't very good at it. I drank a lot. I smoked a lot. Dyed my hair. Thought about cutting, but when someone suggested I get a tattoo—to change my "aura"—I figured it was as good a way as any to punish with pain. Nothing went right after that. Just shit after shit. I was so depressed and the dreams just got worse and worse. I never slept.

One day I just couldn't help it. I started howling like my old man, crying for something that wasn't there. And that's when Sophia showed up. I knew the moment I opened the door and saw her standing there. Not as harsh-looking as my dream crow women, but full of herself in the same way. You know the rest (of course I've read your letters. But don't blame Sophia. Robin read them, after all. We swapped notes at Jack's house).

But I couldn't just give in like that. Too many people I'd cared about wound up dead or tried to hurt me in some way. How was I supposed to trust? That day I came to tea, I saw the letters in the cedar box on her table. I saw where you had written my name. So the next day when Sophia was down in the garden, I snuck in and read them. Redcap—I guessed he was the tattooist who marked me. Playing me, just fucking with my head like a cat messing with a mouse.

When Robin showed up it got weird. I couldn't help it. I wanted him. Maybe I was jealous, too, that Sophia was suddenly paying so much attention to him. I wanted to know who he was, why did he matter to her? Why didn't I matter as much any more? I snitched your letter—about the Arum—tore the page and went to the market and found it. They were hippies, tripped out organic types that sold it to me, but the chick who wrapped it up for me gave me pretty much the same warning. I didn't care. I wanted it to wake Robin. Of course it woke everything else. Even me. It was my first time—honest, though guys have been after me since I ran away from my dad—and there's Sophia and Jack tripping over us in the garden. God, I felt so stupid. Stupid and really gross. I just wanted to hide from them all.

My roommates told me I was being a drag and I needed to get wasted. So they took me to this bar and there was this beautiful, really beautiful guy. Two minutes later he was next to me and I was drunk without even taking a sip. I was relieved that he found me attractive when I thought I was ugly. That he wanted me when I didn't want myself. So I invited him back. I can't write about the rest. You know it already. The crows were there. Again. But so was Sophia and Jack and Robin.

Robin and I have been talking. Sharing really. I begin to understand that I am something more. I who always considered myself less. I know why the Queen is looking for you. It's because of me. I know her dreams—they are my dreams, the ones that have haunted and carried me along. I'll tell you more about it when you get here.

But be careful. The shit is hitting the fan here and it's really dangerous. Last night one of the guys in the apartment below us got attacked by someone or something in his apartment. Sophia figured they were looking for her. So after the cops came and went, she headed over to her place to get the letters. Two seconds after we saw the lights go on in her apartment window, Jack started cursing. I looked out the window and saw these two guys—well, not guys, because they looked more walking dead—heading up after her. Jack grabbed a rusty pole and Robin took a kitchen knife—I wanted to come but they yelled at me to stay put. I don't know what happened exactly. I saw Sophia in the window turn and then it went dark as the lamp was knocked over. Jack and Robin must have got there pretty quick because a second later I see those thugs crashing out the window trying to make a quick getaway. One's got Jack's pole in its belly. Only they don't fall—they fly, huge raggety wings, snake-necked like vultures. They don't have bird heads—just those skull human heads.

Sophia wasn't hurt bad. A nasty gash across her left arm—but Jack's been treating it. You're wrong about him, by the way. He's a handy guy to have around. He won't let her get up until he's sure there's no infection.

So here's the thing. You better get here as quick as you can. Tell the crones Jack's got a bottle under the bed reserved just for them. It seems he knows their type only too well.

See ya (soon I hope),
Sparrow

PS. Forgive me, dearest Sister. I have let Sparrow write my letter. I am in too much pain right now to sit and give it the thought it needs. She does run on, though, and I know how you hate that. I dare not let the others know how much the Bannachs hurt me. I have so precious little magic in me and they too much. Jack's cures are working—but they will not work for long. I need you. I have folded and folded this letter until it is small enough to tuck beneath the wren's left wing. I can only hope that she finds you.

Blessed is the mother who bore us and the sister who dwells in my heart,

Meteora

Sent back by the same wren: Sister, the bird is tired. My arms are tired. Only the crones keep us going. But we will be there anon. We are half a state and two counties away now. So Blanche tells me. We have to fly at night or be shot for terror. I ask why and that is the only answer they give me.

Shawnique says she hopes the Jack's bottle holds a good single malt. She suggests an Islay. Her great-grandfather was a Scots trader. I do not know what she means. But I trust them. By bine and by briar, I trust them.

Serana

Post Scriptum: How does shit hit a fan? It sounds awkward at best, and messy at worst. I do not yet understand these children, though I try.

Dearest Serana,

Take care of the mourning dove who brings you this. She will be your guide to us. We have fled because it was too dangerous here. As Jack was the only one among us who might safely venture outside, I anointed his left eye with oil that he might have partial sight into Faerie. Perhaps it was a rash act—I feel certain he may yet come to regret it. For even I, lying abed sickened with poison, saw that when he returned with victuals, his face was somber, his blue eyes dulled.

"What's happen?" I asked.

"I was walking and a man in a red baseball cap nearly slammed into me. I thought it was just a guy so I side-stepped to avoid him. He hissed and when I looked at him a second time, he whipped off the red cap and I saw him more clearly. Pointed teeth, the long ears and the green cast to his pale skin. I didn't look away quick enough. My face showed that I recognized him."

"We gotta run," Robin said.

"Sophia's too sick," Jack disagreed.

"They've marked you," Robin argued. "Look out the window, see for yourself."

Jack peeked around the edge of the curtain and we all heard the sharp intake of his breath. "Damn it."

"If we don't get the hell out of here there's not much we can do to stop them on our own," Robin said.

"I know a place," Jack said. "We'll take the truck."

I told Jack that I could not travel by one of those creatures of metal and noise. That it would kill me far faster than the poison. Sparrow agreed. Robin again had the answer. He instructed Jack to wrap me in sheepskins and then quilts. Robin gave Sparrow gloves and a heavy green jacket. He borrowed Jack's leather jacket, with its painting of a skull and roses on the back. I wondered watching these children dress to protect themselves from the burning iron. I think them changelings but now I wonder, uncertain. Steaming and sweating in fever and summer's heat, I was carried to the truck and placed in that infernal machine. Sparrow clutched rowan branches in her gloved hands and Robin cradled his fiddle. Jack did the driving. We sped away from there, the look of outrage and shock on the face of the Boggle and Bloody Bones left to watch. But even they could not follow the iron trail of the machine.

The journey was worse than the poison. Once Jack pulled over that I might hang my head out the window to vomit. What a sight I must have been. I could not hold a thought together, raddled between my misery and fear of the machine, Redcap's host, grief at mayhap never seeing again your face and anguish at looking so ravaged in front of the children, in front of Jack. Even this disgraceful middle-age gave me some small measure of dignity. Wretched and retching old hag.

We arrived at a small shabby house, in a desolate neighborhood of the city. Not far away were the massive girders of a huge bridge that appeared to span a river, separating this ill-tide collection of houses with the brighter lights of the city on the other side. As Jack carried me into the house, I noticed things painted on walls and fences in riotous colours. Most were meaningless, but here and there amid the outsized letters and curled symbols I saw the words of warding spells.

Now dear Sister, I am being cared for by one of Jack's old aunts, Vinnie. And like your crones and our strange children, what a mystery she is. Ancient, hump-backed and bucked-tooth—through which her speech whistles. She wears men's trousers and shirts of old white linen. The house is full of cats and the smells of piss, the dusty perfume of dried lavender and sweet incense. But she knows her spells and cures. A goodywife, maybe one who has long ago herself suckled the brood of Faerie and returned. I am healing. The poison ebbs and I can think again. I have washed and put myself aright.

Robin plays his fiddle and now I can see that like the words painted in brilliant hues it too has the power to shield us. The Jack, the Sparrow, the Robin and the Goodywife. I sit down at the table to eat again brown bread and butter, lamb stew flavoured with mint. A cat warms my lap, gently kneading my thighs, and Vinnie, whistling between her teeth, pours neat glasses of Scotch. Sparrow's cheeks grow rosy in the pale skin, her magenta-dyed hair gold as the rising sun at the roots. Is this how it should be? Changelings and Highborn, young and old, man and maid sitting together thus at the table? I miss you, yes. I fear what is to come, but for once I do not feel alone or betrayed.

Your meddling, mending sister,
Meteora

Meteora, dear Sister,

Shawnique knows the bridge. She says, and I quote, "Major mojo there," which I take to be good news.

We will be there by midnight, "give or take a few." That's Blanche.

Do not, I beg you, though, ever eat at a place called MickyD's. The crones love it but there is nothing of substance or freshness there. Only grease, which they assure me is a food group, though what this means is a puzzlement.

Be sure to save some whiskey for them. And some spearmint to settle my poor belly.

I have not read the leaves in days. But I do not need to do so to know that we have come to the final battle. The skies are alight with it. Red Mars growls down. The Seven Perfect Sisters send out shooting stars. And two more signs: My fingers tingle and Blanche complains that her water stings. Have you ever known such that did not presage war?

We make our stand between the girders, for good or aye. Give this poor owl who brings you this letter a mouse as reward, or at least a bit of meat, should you have it. I have sent the poor thing in haste and without supper to your bridge.

Serana.

Beloved sister—I scribble this last note and hide it here beneath the salt where I know you think to look for it. Redcap and his clan pursue us in the hunt. It is a blood pact they want, blood to bind their power, blood to pay the tithe and rule both houses. There is more to say but no time.

Dearest Serana,

So it has come to me this day to lay quill to paper and recount the end of the story. I do this for the Council—for Sparrow and Robin—to make certain that what has happened will carry the weight of the tale to make the law true. It is a tale for all to read, yet I seem only able to find my voice in this comforting habit of letters. So I will write of that night as though to you, my sister, even though you have no need, for you saw much of it with your own eyes. Except, of course, the very end.

Here I smile, hearing the old proverb, "He lies like a witness," and I am certain that we, though cot-sharers, peas in the pod, will recall so many things about that night differently. No doubt the crones too have their version, trapping it into a song of clapping and stomping feet, giving it shape in rhyme.

No sooner had I given your half-starved owl a mouse—produced by one of Vinnie's cats as an unasked-for offering—and read your letter than I heard the wind worrying the windowpanes, tapping, insistent, like the fingers of a child rattling a locked cupboard. Four cats, fur lifting on their spines, perched on the ledge, their dangling tails twitching and their eyes glowing bright.

"What is it, boys?" Vinnie asked, quickly knocking back another dram of whiskey. "Are the rats playing beneath the sill again?"

The cats' ears flickered, agitated, but they refused to turn. An old marmalade tom with one chewed ear arrowed his head low, and nose against the pane, growled softly. From where I sat, I could only see the pale reflection of our candle's flame and Sparrow's face leaning over it, wreathed in the darkness of the night beyond. The wind gusted more fitfully, and the panes hammered loose in their wooden frames. The startled cats hissed, backs arched high and away as little windlings slipped their spindly fingers beneath the sill and pressed their filmy bodies through the narrow cracks. Once inside, trailing torn wings, they flung themselves wildly around the room with the frenzy of mayflies. They hid, darning themselves into Vinnie's braid, ducking down behind Sparrow's ear, nestling in Robin's fiddle, their voices trilling out from its wooden belly. One with wings folded wriggled into the breast pocket of Jack's shirt. I held my hands up to them, beckoned them not to fear and four of the poor wee things landed on my palm, their silken touch a cold puff of air.

"They come, they come. The Seelie and the Unseelie, the shriven and the cursed, the newly made and soon to be dead. Flee, flee for here will they meet and here will they decide it once and for all. We cannot know the outcome and those who would stand in the middle must flee. Their dispute will destroy us like the summer lightning that sweeps the grass into flames and kills the crickets."

Sister, I prayed for you at that moment—riding in the night sky, in the arms of crones, who surely, like those at my table, were caught in the middle, in the crossroad between fairy and mortal. You were out there, riding toward a storm, the quickening eddies of old hostilities drawing you to me and to this battle. But of those at my table only Vinnie had wits enough to know the worst of it.

"We're outta here," she barked, clapping her black hat on her head. She picked up a heavy walking stick, its handle stout and club-shaped, its point wrapped in metal. Iron by the smell of it.

"Where to?" Sparrow asked, threading her fingers through her hair, dislodging the windlings who clung like spider's web.

"The bridge. Here, you'll need this," she said and from a closet pulled out three more rounded sticks, the length of my arm. White ash they were, with animal spells inscribed in black, "Baltimore Orioles, Chicago Cubs, Detroit Tigers." Jack grabbed one with a strange smile and, gripping the wooden handle with both hands, swung it with obvious pleasure.

"You kept my bats," he said. "I thought Mom sold them all with my cards."

Bats, I thought, wondering. For these were not small, furry flying creatures, but clubs of some sort.

Vinnie grimaced. "She was crazy, not stupid. Those are

ash—you never give away ash. It comes in handy when the rats prove too much for the cats. Like now."

"I'll take my fiddle," Robin said, refusing the wooden bats, and tucking his fiddle under his arm.

"Bit risky, isn't it?" Vinnie asked.

"It can do things." Robin lifted the fiddle to his chin and scraped the bow against the strings. The fiddle howled and the windlings wailed, ducking into cups and bowls. The cats scattered out the room as though their tails had caught fire. The planked floor boards rumbled and lifted from the frame, nails screeching and popping from their ancient grooves. Puffs of magnificent brown spores chuffed up from the twisting floorboards, and I caught the scent of burial dirt, spiced with bones and blood. I choked on it, and the others coughed hard, gasping in the thickened air.

"Stop! Stop!" I shouted hoarsely.

And he did, returning the fiddle underneath his arm. His skin was white, the hooded eyelids a bruised lavender. His mouth turned cruel, and the chill throbbed in my recent wound as I beheld his gaze. His eyes were black mirrors, smooth as polished stone, and when he tossed his head, the coiled strands of hair parted and revealed the long shape of his ears. Not quite, but almost. Then he shuddered and the pale skin flamed a rosy colour once more.

"What are you?" I whispered.

"Don't be afraid of me, Sophia," he answered softly. He held out one hand toward Jack, who gripped his bat more tightly, ready to swing. Vinnie clucked her tongue softly against the roof of her mouth. Only Sparrow waited, hands in her pocket, an understanding sadness like a shadow on her face. "I am like Sparrow. A mistake, something that shouldn't have happened. I am the darkness to the light, the Unseelie bound to the Seelie. Born too low and sent away to the world of man as a changeling. And so too did my nature change, here in the world of men." As he spoke, his mouth was a bruise in his face.

"Do you serve them?" I asked. "Or are you free?"

"Free. I was recalled to Elfland when it was thought that my time here would make me a clever servant, the one best to serve the deed. They hadn't counted on my refusal. They want me dead, Sophia, because I would not bind Sparrow as blood slave to Redcap. It was my fault they sent Long Lankin to do the task that I refused. Prick her with the silver needles, draw the spells of binding on her skin. I ran from them, tried to find a city large enough to disappear in, but they found me anyway. They could not murder me outright. Fallen though I was from favour, the honour of blood did not permit it. Instead, I was poisoned, left to die slowly over days, tortured by nightmares. Auntie Em found me on the doorstep. She was right, you know. You are glowworms pushing back the darkness."

"You read the letters." I was appalled, but not surprised.

"All of them. I knew I had to come here. I knew I had to warn Sparrow. Explain it to her. She had a right to know."

"So the warning was given. What are we doing here now?" I asked him, confused and yet watching all the little threads braid slowly together in a single strand of story.

"Robin and I, we're here to make a stand for ourselves," Sparrow answered, reaching out her fingers to twine in his. It was a statement that was both brave and magical.

"We'll be making a stand in the boneyard if we don't hightail it outta here right now," Vinnie snapped. "Talk about this later." She nudged Sparrow toward a low door in the kitchen and behind her Robin followed close, then Jack, still gripping the bat uncertainly. I hesitated until I saw the grey slag-heap faces of the boggles pressed against the windowpanes.

I darted after the others, descending into the musty, dark

cellar. In the dim light of a single bulb the floor appeared like an ocean of shifting fur. Cats, dozens of them, swirled in agitated circles around our ankles, hissed and spat. Kittens mewled from baskets stacked around the edges of the room. Above the front door splintered and the cats flowed up the stairs behind us in a wave of caterwauls, and flashing teeth, their claws scrabbling on the wooden stairs.

"C'mon, quick. There's a tunnel here that leads out to the bridge. The cats will hold them for a while." Vinnie bent low and scurried into a small narrow passage.

There was no light in the tunnel, we felt our way by running our hands against the smooth, ribbed walls. I could smell the river's water and it carried the fresh tang of the Greenwood. The smell grew stronger and abruptly the way led upward again, rising to gentle slope. Ahead, Vinnie called to us to stop. Moonlight slivered into the tunnel, as grunting softly, she pushed against a matted wall of twigs and branches, forcing an opening. Within moments we were out on the banks of a river directly below the bridge. The wrench of iron made me ill and I stumbled, doubled over by the rank taste of it. Vinnie grabbed me and hustled me toward a narrow set of concrete stairs. Looking back, I noted the children fared better than I, but Sparrow leaned heavily on Jack nonetheless.

"It won't be so bad on top," Vinnie encouraged. "They won't follow us so easily this way."

"Where are we going?" I asked.

"Not the briared path of righteousness, nor the lily path of wickedness, but the green path to—"

"Elfland! The road to Elfland, atop this monstrosity?" I shouted, heaving with the stench of iron.

Redcap's horns sounded in the distance, a call that curdled the mist and drove the stink of sweated hounds and boggleman on the winds.

Vinnie cackled as she bullied me up the stairs. "Gotta

find a way wherever you can. The old paths don't disappear so easily. They lurk. You may choose not to use them. But some do. That's why I'm here. To watch what comes over the bridge."

We were standing suddenly on the bridge, a wide-open expanse stretched like a road between the banks. Though I could feel the threaded bones of iron buried in the concrete flesh, I could stand and the worst of the pain and illness subsided. On the far banks gold pricks of light wavered as though seen beneath the shimmering surface of a green pond.

Oh my sister, it was the way home. In the click of a beetle's wing I saw myself abandoning these children and returning home. So strong was the pull, I would have gladly hid myself in an acorn husk, just to be living again in my woods. Behind me, I heard Sparrow sob. I turned, suddenly realizing that I was not the only one entranced by this familiar sight.

Robin had his arm around her, consoling, pulling her toward the middle of the bridge. On his face I saw the look of longing. Even Jack had lowered his cudgel to stare in wonder at the distant lights of Elfland.

Vinnie stood beside me, her ancient face softened until I saw the echo of youth. "Every time I come up here I can almost touch it," then she shook her head. "I can't cross no more, only get close to it. Get close and remember oh those years ago, a woman in labor and the infant put to my breast. I was paid and sent home across this bridge." She tapped her cheek with a gnarled finger. "Still got the one good eye." She seized my shoulder, her grip strong. "Will you open it for us?"

"Open it?"

"Yeah. Only you can open the way. You're one of them."

And then I tasted bitter gall. I was here, but by the decree of my own banishment the way would not open to me.

Vinnie had made a mistake. She had thought I could save them all and so she had brought us here, to this open bridge before a door that would never open no matter how hard we flung ourselves against it.

"I cannot," I stammered.

She gripped my shoulder harder, more insistent. The cold street lights glared in her eyes.

"Or won't. Haven't I done enough? Don't I deserve this? Don't they?" and her chin jutted toward Robin and Sparrow.

Miserable, I looked away from her and whispered, "I am banished. I can no longer return. There is nothing I can do," I answered miserably.

Vinnie's glare darted over my shoulder and she spun me angrily. "Yeah, there is. You're gonna hafta fight, then. You're one of us now."

She spun me around and there was the hunt riding towards us. The Highborn, their ranks established in the silver tines of horns that rose high above the carved faces of the masks. They flowed through the city street, the silver shoes of their mounts leaving trails of sparks. The hounds bayed, bogans and knucklebones padding behind them, their rock-hard knuckles striking the surface of the road. They snarled and snapped their jaws. The fiery flanks of the mounts hissed and steamed as they scorched the houses of the narrow streets. Overhead the Bannachs rode, their great tattered wings blocking all sight of the stars. We were alone on the bridge, the door to Elfland close at our back and the full Unseelie Court riding to snare us.

And it was my fault. My fault for ever meddling.

"Get behind me," I cried out and thrust myself in front of them. "I may be banished, but the law still applies. They dare not harm me, lest I have done them harm."

"You still need us at your side," Jack argued and stood to the left of my shoulder, his ash cudgel over his shoulder.

Vinnie flanked me on the right. Behind me, I felt the children and imagined their backs pressed against the invisible wall.

The hunt approached us, and the huntsman blew his horn, calling the slavering hounds to heel. Through the front line, the leader pushed his mount to come alone onto the bridge. His mask of silver was shaped like a halfskull, the human side beautiful, the other twisted in pain. Redcap.

"Stay," I said. "I must meet him alone."

"No," Jack argued.

"It is the only way." And I walked away from them toward the center of the bridge. Oh sister, my sister, was I ever in such fear for my immortal life? For well I knew his swords could do what mortal weapons could not. That only the law which binds us both held it in check. Perhaps now I think he must have been amused, curious as a cat to draw this drama out, thinking himself with all the time in the world and no one to interfere. I wasn't bold so much as foolish in believing in the law—a law that had changed while I was banished.

"You have no right to hunt those under my protection," I called out.

The gathered broke into raucous laughter, slapping at their thighs and rattling their spears and sheaves of quivered arrows.

Redcap removed his mask and a bogan page scurried up on clawed feet to take it from his master's hands.

"You have no power to fight me, Meteora. There is nothing you can do to stop me."

That he knew my true name and spoke it aloud so all would know it was frightening enough. But I did not dare show my fear.

"Ask your servant, and see where I marked him," I answered, pointing to the highborn in a wraith's mask. Long Lankin removed his mask with an angry jerk, revealing the red gash marring the plane of his cheek. It had festered into a ragged furrow as all ill-gotten wounds must.

Redcap scowled, puzzled. Obviously he'd not been told. His anger burned and his eyes slitted. "And who gave you such power?"

"The same that awarded it unto you." I could feel the words gathering in my mouth, like some sort of spellcasting. "Before we existed there was power from this body of earth, these veins of fiery blood. We are but children before its grace. And I have learned that even in this age, in this body I still can find it without the leave of Elfland." Serana, I knew as I was speaking these brave words, words meant to push back Redcap's certainty, that they were in part true. Though I was aged and weakened, I was not without magic. I held it in my mouth. And the mortals here had power, too, though we knew it not. Nor called it so. Yet surely Vinnie's milk had once had the power to suckle and sustain a child of Elfland. Did not the gifts flow both ways then? When would we honour that truth?

"What gives you the right to claim these mortals as your own?" Lankin asked.

"The law," I answered.

And then he laughed and the hunt followed suit. The sound of it echoed over the water of the river below us.

"The law was broken when the tithe was not paid in blood."

A cold wind went up my back and lingered there. I shivered, but not entirely with the cold. "What blood tithe?"

"The one the Queen owes me. For stealing a child that was marked for me."

I whirled about and looked behind me, at Sparrow, at Robin, looking small and lost under the bridge's wide-open arms. Then slowly I turned back. "Those here are mine now," I said, but my voice lacked conviction.

"There is no one with the power to grant such rights to you who is of the Seelie Court.

"The Queen—"

"Especially the Queen!" Redcap shouted. "She has played her games and lost. She has no cause to tread these roads, no claim to the blood I had marked as my own sacrifice. The tithe will be mine and I shall see you threshed as barley beneath my sword unless you bend your knee and vow to serve me."

In that moment of silence I could only wonder where you were, Serana, what had I accomplished in my meddling, and how had I not seen this pattern of betrayal? I could not stop thinking of your early warning—leave these dregs, these children alone. Hadn't we always lived separate from the Unseelie folk? Hadn't we always left politics alone? And yet I could see it now, how we have changed as our world has changed, succumbed to this human hand which cuts swift as any faerie sword at the breast of our lands. All of us are changed.

Except the Queen.

And then it occurred to me. The Queen. Searching the streets of that iron city where you lived. Mandrake roots twisted like strangled lovers. A girl marked with the sign of trouble. And us, sisters of the greenwood sent forth precisely to meddle.

"What mark?" I shouted back defiantly. I searched the skies for you, praying on the Goddess that you would appear. "What mark on the child proves your claim?"

"Bring the girl here," Redcap demanded.

Two of his ogre pets lumbered toward us but before they could reach us, Sparrow shoved past Jack and Vinnie and came to stand beside me.

"Fuck you," she shouted. "You don't own me, asshole." She tore off her shirt, and in the pale light of the moon her torso gleamed, silver gilding the bare and flawless skin of her shoulders. She pushed back her brambled hair and showed her neck, curved like the white arch of the swan. The twisted knot of trouble was gone.

Only then did I see Redcap frown, and the mount beneath stumbled, quivering with the heat of its rider's rage. "How is this possible?"

Even I wondered at this. I knew the spells of unbinding. I had worked them a little. Goodywife spells. And all but this last one, the one on her neck had faded. But how had this one been so completely removed that the Redcap's glare had not raised it up again, like yeast to dough?

"I come to claim what is mine," Sparrow called. "I woke Robin and his blood is bound to me as mine is to him."

Robin came quietly to stand beside Sparrow. He was changed, too. His eyes gleamed green and gold. Horns budded on his high forehead and along his neck scrolled a tattoo of briar and rose together.

"Cast off whelp, spittle of a banshee's lips," Redcap hissed.

"But yours none the less," Robin cried out, "and so I have made a pact already. The tithe is paid, father. You cannot amend it."

Father! And then I saw what I had not seen before, how like they were around the jawline, around the eyes, though there was no meanness and no cruelty in Robin's face.

"Then you own her," Redcap roared, "what good it will do you." His mouth was a thin line. Then he smiled and opened his arms, though even I could read those arms as the bars of a gaol. "Come and be welcomed into our house again. Rule with me."

Robin shook his head. "You've mistook my meaning, father. For there is human blood in me, no matter how hard you tried to erase it. And I have surrendered unto Sparrow the gift of that blood. See here where the prick of my finger still heals. And on her the same."

"No! No!" The Redcap's voice was a shriek now, like the wind in a storm. Only dogs could hear it and come to its call. "It will not happen thus. This bitch, this knot of grass will not rule in my place. I have no fear of her or you. For there is no law without the Faerie courts, and here on this bridge I alone will decide the outcome."

And I saw the sword leave its scabbard, so swiftly and like lightning it flashed toward Sparrow. I gave no thought but flung myself between her and its flame. Sparrow fell beneath me, screaming. I find it hard even now to recall the searing of my flesh. The blade bit deep, scraping the bone of my arm. Hot blood cascaded across my chest, coiled my neck like a snake. I wanted to rise, dazed, but could not. Could only watch what happened next.

Robin, Jack and Vinnie stood over me, and Sparrow huddled between the protective cage of their legs. Jack swung and the crack of the ash struck away Redcap's sword. Elf darts flew like swift birds through the air. Resin puffed in the air as the sound of Robin's fiddle buckled the concrete, exposing the staves of iron and hurling chunks of broken rock. Yet I despaired, for no matter how valiant, I knew these would not be enough.

And then I heard you, Serana—or perhaps it was the crones—singing in that deep calling voice. I looked up and saw you overhead, depending from their arms, pale as milk-weed caught in the sturdy boughs of ebon branches. Your voice called to me, and I felt your pulse as though it were my own.

"Sister," I cried, and fainted, who had never fainted in her life.

When I came to, I thought it was you, laying a hand on my shattered arm, stopping the flow of blood. But it was Sparrow, crying, holding my arm, her palms clamped over the wound to staunch it as the fight roared over our heads. And it was then I knew for certain why the Queen searched for her.

Blood calls to blood.

Sparrow gave me her strength, what little of it she had left. And had I not stopped her, she would have unknowingly emptied herself of the gift to see me healed. This I could not let her do, and so I sat up and held her face between my hands. "Enough," I said. "Look!" and I pointed to Redcap.

She turned and saw what I saw, you, my sister, crouched as a tiger on Redcap's back, a fat aging tiger but one whose claws still could make a mark. You raked at his face and he flailed on the back of his horse, angry, astonished, caught short. Meanwhile, your black crones slid beneath the bellies of the horses, calling back and forth to each other, and the faerie horses, their eyes rolling with terror, buckled before the calls of these crones.

Almost, I thought, *perhaps,* I thought. Faint hope, like a caged bird, beat in my breast.

But then you fell from Redcap's back and he turned, his second sword in hand, searching for you.

That was the moment of my greatest despair. I could think of no greater loss, no greater horror, than to lose you, sister. I shudder even now, even writing these words, for they bring back that terror worse even than the stench of blood, the pain in my arm, the torment of the iron beneath my body.

There on the bridge, that span between the mortal world and that of our realm, I thought to die with you, my sister, the crones, Vinnie, the children of our blood and my Jack, still fighting to protect me. I tried to struggle to my feet to meet this death with honour. And wavering as I stood, I heard a sound I thought never to hear again.

The horns of Elfland.

And suddenly there was the Queen's court riding out onto the bridge. They came swiftly, the bells of their horses' bridles ringing madly, their arrows nocked in the great ash bows. And as they came, the Unseelie withdrew from us in haste, scrambling up onto their addled mounts and dragging with them their wounded to the far side of the bridge. And as suddenly you were next to me, your arms around me, my sister, and how we smiled and touched each other with wonder to see our faces so changed. For we had not yet known how aged we were until we saw the other, how mortal we looked, how little difference now between me and the crones, between you and Vinnie.

When the Queen arrived there grew a space all around us and strange it was to be here in this most midway point across the bridge.

The Queen sat on her snowy steed, holding a torch high in her white hand. In its light her eyes blazed with fury. She called out to Redcap, "You are forbidden to hunt a child of the royal blood."

"A changeling has no rights," he shouted back. "And neither do you here."

"Not a changeling," the Queen said, and I remember now the sound of my own gasp. "My child. Born of my body, my blood."

"I can smell the stink of human. Your glamour cannot hide that."

"Because she is both."

"And yet you are immortal? How is that possible?" he demanded.

"So long have I carried the weight of Elfland on my shoulders and this secret in my heart. I am ready to let it rest now in the hands of others. Come, and bring your people with us before the Council. There you will learn what you must." She put her hand out to Sparrow to take her up behind on the white steed. But Sparrow turned her back on her mother and put her own hand in Robin's.

All these revelations, and what I heard and marveled most at was that the Queen had a heart!

*

THE Queen's court brought us horses and Jack helped me on one and then climbed up behind to hold me steady on the beast's back. I smiled wearily, for I knew well this beast and he would have carried me as though I was no more than a feather. Yet it did Jack some good to feel he was protecting me.

Sparrow rode with Robin, and well did I mark how he carried himself in the saddle. I was surprised again when the Queen stretched out a hand to Vinnie and Vinnie took it without hesitation, hoisting herself behind the Queen.

I saw the joy in your face when they brought your grey and I laughed—though not so as you should see me—as you struggled to pull yourself up into the saddle until a page came forward and boosted you like a farmer's wife, his hands firm on your bottom. I know your pride and it rankled, I'm sure.

And there at bridge-end, the gates of Elfland opened for us and we, Seelie and Unseelie, mortal and Elvin, and those children a bridge between our races, marched into the world I had thought barred to me forever. We all went through but you, dear sister, for the door closed in your face, and there I last saw you, tears streaming down your cheeks, while above you, the crones hovered in the air, their feet paddling like swimmers.

*

IT all came out at the Council meeting, the High Court gathering to hear the Queen speak and watch with what dignity and humility this once arrogant creature revealed the truth about Sparrow.

Dear sister, it seems that our beautiful world of oak and thorn has been dying. Too much has been lost, too many haunts gone beneath the iron of cities. And so too has fey power diminished. Like the two of us in the city, the faerie world had become aged and broken. That which nourished our power thinned.

What was more, the Queen had discovered she had become pregnant in a dalliance with a mortal. Such a thing should not have been possible without the renouncing of blood. And yet it had happened. At first she thought to lose the child, drink it down in bitter brews of pennyroyal. But the child turned in her womb and it gave her pause. While she carried it, she found her power oddly strengthened, renewed. Spells that had been broken were suddenly reforged.

So she wove a glamour that none might see the change in her. But she heard the discontented murmurs of the Unseelie Court and knew they had felt the change, too, though they did not know what it betide, and sought their own solutions in blood of a different fashion.

The Queen feared for the life of her child.

It was Vinnie she called to assist at the birth in secret, for the Queen trusted few and Vinnie remained only long enough to suckle the child. Long enough to set her longing for Faerie. It was put out that the babe was a changeling child of a favoured serving woman. Only in private did the Queen bring the infant girl to her breast that she might know her true mother.

But Redcap came to know of the Queen's favour to the child through the serving woman, her mind broken by Lankin on a spring eve. Lankin never got the whole truth of it, though, for the woman died rather than revealing all. So Redcap believed the child to be that changeling, a babe who had captivated the Queen, and he conspired to have her be the tithe when the time came for it, thus giving insult to the Queen.

But finding her serving woman dead, the Queen guessed Redcap's intent and sent Sparrow to her father when the child was four years old. She believed that once the child was out in the human world, Redcap might lose interest in her and leave her alone. She did not count on cruelty having such a long memory. When word had come that Redcap had cast out his youngest offspring across the borderlands into the human cities, the Queen grew worried that he'd been sent to find her own child. And so she banished us, each to the place she knew Sparrow and Robin had last been seen, hoping that we should find them and keep them apart.

Apart! When I think, sister, how we conspired rather to bring them to one another! Meddlers and menders that we were, we knit the only strands that could hold the Faerie world together.

But then what did we know? Only our own aches and pains, only our own disgrace. And how could the Queen have guessed that Robin would disown his own clan and the cruelty of his father's court. How could she know that Sparrow and Robin, being raised among humans, would learn to love?

*

SPARROW and Robin are joined now, and the Court has decreed a new house, a new clan with rights afforded unto it in the world of Elfland. Alone each world will destroy itself, but twined together we can rebuild the strands that once wove our histories. It gives me an odd sense of accomplishment, of strength. Power shared is power restored. Even Redcap has agreed to a limited truce.

I am to remain here in Elfland. I am still recovering from my wounds and Jack, my beloved Jack, tends me. The courts have allowed him to stay as my consort, though there is nothing of that unequal nature in our friendship. I watch him at his work, the sprites hovering around him, singing their surprised joy as he creates his sculptures. He whistles, barefoot and grey-headed, but utterly at peace in this world.

Strange, too, but when I had again power enough to use a glamour and return to my youthful self I chose not to. I rather like who I am now. I have the density of stones, the girth of silent trees, and there is nothing so beautiful to me as a face that wears its tales well in the lines around the eyes. Even the Queen now slips off the mask of youth and in quiet moments sits with me, two old women, our hair greying, watching the children as they come at last into their own between this world and the other.

Vinnie comes and goes as she pleases, for the doors of Elfland are now open for those who can see them. Though she never stays here long. Her cats, she says, need her. Though cats, I have noticed, do not seem to need anything except food. She promises to remain the carrier of all our letters.

But you, Serana, my beloved sister, how fare you in exile? I sorely miss you. You must tell me all.

And so our letters begin again.

Your loving sister,
Meteora

My darling Sister,
Vinnie is better than any bird, for she can tell me that the letters have gotten to you and how you look.

I miss you terribly, my sister, but that you are alive and in Faerie with your Jack comforts me. That the Queen's child is returned to her with a consort of her own kind and choice delights me. That our battle has been won—at least for this turning—nurtures me.

And now I can tell you what I could not, as we lay between the iron girders, too wounded and too frightened to talk. What I came to tell you, braving the Queen's anger and the end of the world.

It is this: I had known all along that one of us would return to Faerie and one would not. The Queen had said as much to me before we were sent into the human world. She took me aside, and spoke a curse into my ear so that I alone carried the burden as she alone had carried hers. Her voice was soft but her words hard.

Two go out and one alone
Will be allowed to come back home.

Two go out, but one will stay
Who breach the power of the Fey.

At the time, I was so shocked that we were leaving, that we were to be severed from the green filtered world of Faerie, I did not comprehend that we sisters might be severed, too. And then, when I had time to think, I was so overwhelmed by my aches and pains and my loss of the great magics, I had no wish to far-see which of us would stay and which go back. To be honest, when at last I gave it thought, we were so far into our troubles, I could only see one footfall in front of the other.

And to be even more honest, sister, I hoped, I wished, I prayed the one returning would be me. And oh, how the guilt of that prayer troubled me. As I am sure the Queen meant me to feel. For I am certain she felt that pain and hardship would keep us to our tasks.

As you now know, she sent us to the outside world because only we could possibly save her child who had been secreted away all those years ago to keep her safe from the Unseelie folk. Secreted by a human the Queen trusted, the child's true father, and who betrayed her trust.

But all's well that ends, dear sister. And do not worry. I am content to stay here, in the human world, not only because you are safe, but because I have years yet to explore this city magic, full of electricity and power. Where our Elvin world has the dark woods and secret valleys, the city has alleys that twist and underground systems that run miles deep. This is the new Faerie. The Crones are my guides.

So, though we never meet again face-to-face, breath-to-breath, Meteora, we can still be in touch. When Vinnie cannot cross the border, due to illness or crankiness or cats, there will still be the little birds to sustain us. Write to me daily and I will write back.

Do I envy you the skylark mornings, the late-night dances, the easy magics? Do I long for sweet couplings under a bank of ferns? I have instead the flickering lights of humanity's cities, the blare of bebop, the new steely magics. And the man down at the bodega is sweet and has touched my hand twice so I have some hope there as well. He has a lovely face the colour of new bark and eyes as dark as cinnamon. And I am thinking that my bed, with its new number mattress, is ever so much more comfortable than a bank of ferns.

I suppose I envy you, but really only a little. I suppose I envy all in Faerie a little.

Except, of course, the Queen. Never the Queen.

AFTERWORD

Some Facts(?) About Fairies

THE landscape of Faerie, together with its inhabitants, is altogether so vast a canvas that this anthology, however impressive I believe its contents, cannot begin to encompass the breadth and scope of The Middle Kingdom. A list of its mortal practitioners alone would be formidable and would include, of course, Hans Christian Andersen, James M. Barrie, L. Frank Baum, Algernon Blackwood, Fredric Brown, John Collier, L. Sprague de Camp and Fletcher Pratt, Charles Dickens, Dianne Duane, Lord Dunsany, John Gardner, Parke Godwin, the Brothers Grimm, W. S. Gilbert, P. C. Hodgell, H. T. Kavanagh (for the Darby O'Gill stories), Andrew Lang, George MacDonald, Arthur Machen, J. K. Rowling, William Shakespeare, Edmund Spenser, James Thurber, J. R. R. Tolkien, Mervyn Wall, Oscar Wilde, and the contributors to this book, as well as many of their contemporaries—and that list does not take into account the representations and examples of Faerie in art, dance and music (Felix Mendelssohn and Arthur S. Sullivan immediately come to mind).

The diversity of elfin myth reflects the cultures and countries from which it originates, and the words "elf " and "fairy" are limiting, for there are many kinds of sprites in Fairyland, each with her, his—or its—distinct characteristics. Here is a modest catalog of some of these beings, together with their powers, and a few superstitions associated with some of them.

BANSHEES—Of Celtic origin, they are also called *benshi*, literally "women of the fairies." They make themselves known to mortals just before someone dies, when the banshee sings or croons to warn the family, though I have heard that they are not always accurate. When I first started collecting books as a hobby, I found a copy of *Ripley's Believe It or Not*, which included several bars of music said to be the "actual" notes of a banshee's wail, but Ripley did not reveal the source of the claim. There is an amusing tale of a banshee in H. T. Kavanagh's *Darby O'Gill and the Good People*, though in the 1959 film adaptation, *Darby O'Gill and the Little People*, there is nothing funny about the banshee; she constitutes one of the only times I ever shut my eyes while watching a movie.

BROWNIES—One of the few wholly helpful elves, brownies delight in doing housework, though they do have a penchant for privacy and independence, as witness the elves in the old tale of "The Elves and the Shoemaker," and the temperamental brownie in Megan Lindholm's "Grace Notes."

DRYADS—In Greek myth, dryads live in oak trees and speak not only their own language, but also can communicate with elves and pixies, as well as growing things. Dryads, though gentle, prefer to be left alone; if approached, they will seek seclusion within their trees, or if they are not near them, they travel through other dimensions to reach them.

ELVES—Folklore and fiction depict a variety of elves. Some are diminutive, some are full-size. According to one set of myths, they are wanderers, pitching the tents of Fairyland in different places, only to move on after a time. But others make their homes in forests, especially preferring alders, ash, birch, blackthorns, elders, hazel, oak and thorn trees. A mortal who approaches a stand of ash, oak and thorn risks being pinched by invisible fingers, but elfin hostility may be warded off if one carries a bundle of twigs from the three trees bound together with red twine. Birch trees are especially dangerous; its elves have white hands capable of inflicting insanity or death. (Tolkien's evil sorcerer Saruman brands his army with the mark of a white hand.) The wisest and most reclusive citizens of Faerie are the grey elves; they are said to be powerful magicians.

FAIRIES—Although etymologically linked to elves, fairies tend to have a better attitude toward the human race, though their smallness understandably makes them wary of great galumphing mortals, especially if they lumber into a fairy ring: a place in the forest delineated by a circlet of mushrooms where the fey folk like to dance. The mortal who is determined to traffic with fairies must possess a knowledge of woodlore. Eating primrose enables one to see them when they are invisible; four-leaf clovers cancel their spells, and Saint-John's-wort, besides its traditional use in herbal healing, is supposed to be a mighty protection against fairy magic.

GNOMES—Though generally regarded as a distinct race of mythical creatures who, like Tolkien's dwarves, live underground and mine precious metal and jewels, gnomes are sometimes regarded as a subspecies of fairy. See *Kobolds*, on the next page.

GOBLINS—Elves who have succumbed to "the dark side of the Force" are called goblins and sometimes hobgoblins. At best they are household mischief-makers, but fairy tales generally depict them as treacherous and thoroughly evil. Perhaps this is why, in the world of Harry Potter, they are the bankers?

KELPIES—A water spirit that often takes the shape of a horse and, as in Patricia A. McKillip's "The Kelpie," attempts to drown mortals. Yet some kelpies try to protect humans from drowning, so if you meet one, be sure which kind it is before mounting!

KOBOLDS—German folklore differs on the nature of kobolds. Some are mine-dwelling gnomes, but others are regarded as helpful household brownies.

LEPRECHAUNS—Irish fairies generally described as old men who, if caught, will procure their release by rendering up gold or other treasure (which sometimes disappears at daybreak). They have also been known to grant three wishes. When not captured, it is best to leave a saucer of milk outside the cottage door for them, lest they work mischief during the night on one's house or barn.

NEREIDS—In Greek myth, the oceanic equivalent of nymphs (q.v.). There are fifty nereids, all of them the daughters of Nereus, the sea god.

NIXS AND NIXIES—In German myth, male and female water spirits armed with javelins and other sharp weaponry. Said to lure mortals into slavery, they bring to mind the underwater folk who live in the lake at Hogwarts in *Harry Potter and the Goblet of Fire.*

NYADS—In Greek and Roman myth, these are freshwater nymphs who, unlike the sea-dwelling nereids, inhabit lakes and streams.

NYMPHS—The Greeks and Romans regarded nymphs as minor nature goddesses, living in streams, lakes and underwater caverns. They are beautiful and reclusive, but basically are well disposed to humans, provided that the latter are virtuous.

PIXIES—Southwestern British dialect (*pisky, pixey*) for elves/fairies. Among their other magical powers, they are said to possess ESP. Their penchant for leading mortals away from paths through the forest, or other natural places, gave rise to the words *pixy-led* and *pixilated* (according to *Webster's*, a portmanteau of "pixy" and "titillated") and brings to mind the situation of the doomed trio in the haunted woods in *The Blair Witch Project*.

POOKAHS—Small nature spirits (some say demons) who inflict mischief or worse on humans. They are well-known in the British Isles, and their name is the inspiration for Shakespeare's Robin Goodfellow, or Puck, in *A Midsummer Night's Dream*.

SPRITES—An all-inclusive word for elves, fairies, goblins, pixies, etc., derived from the French *esprit*: spirit.

SYLPHS—Similar to nymphs, except that sylphs are spirits of the air, but unlike nymphs, whose origin is rooted in antiquity, sylphs were postulated into being by the sixteenth-century Swiss physician Paracelsus.

UNDINES—From the Latin *unda*: a wave. An undine, or ondine, is a water fairy without a soul. She can gain one only if she marries a mortal and gives birth to his child, but should her husband prove untrue, she must return to the sea. This myth has been effectively employed in a nineteenth-century novel by Friedrich de la Motte, Baron Fouqué and in a twentieth-century drama by the French playwright Jean Giraudoux.

—Marvin Kaye